KU-545-839

Ali-A Adventures

GAME ON!

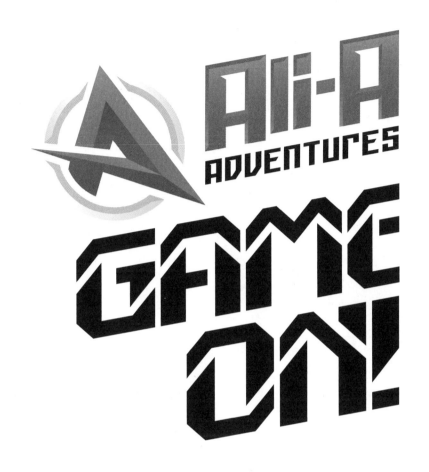

PRESS START

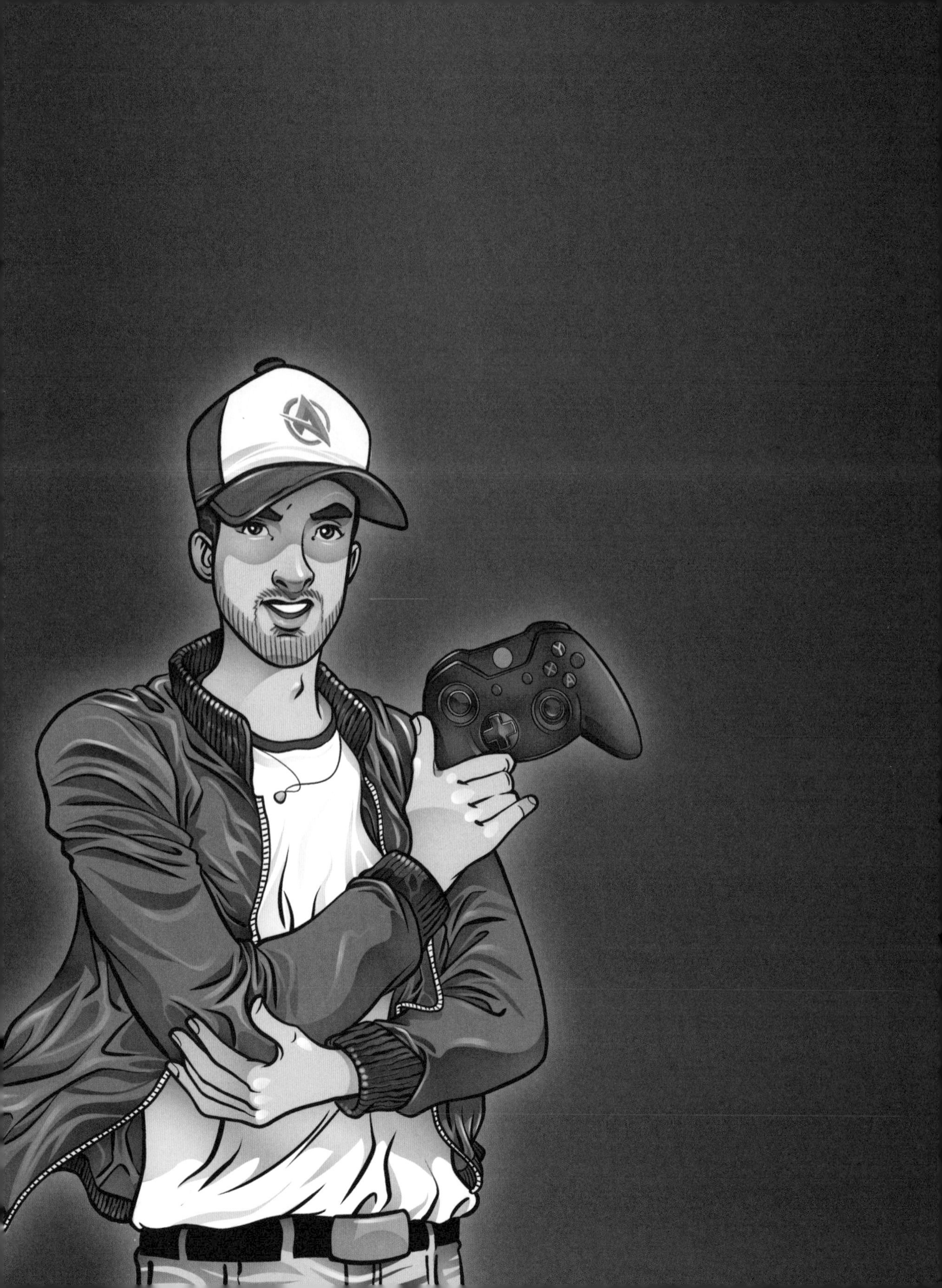

THANK YOU FOR PICKING UP MY VERY FIRST BOOK--
ALI-A ADVENTURES: GAME ON!

JOIN ME AND CLARE (AND EEVEE, OF COURSE!)
AS WE GO ON OUR FIRST BIG ADVENTURE TO SAVE
THE WORLD.

I REALLY HOPE YOU ENJOY THE BOOK AS MUCH
AS I ENJOYED WORKING ON IT!

ALI-A

PUFFIN BOOKS

UK | USA | Canada | Ireland | Australia
India | New Zealand | South Africa

Puffin Books is part of the Penguin Random House group of companies
whose addresses can be found at global.penguinrandomhouse.com.

www.penguin.co.uk
www.puffin.co.uk
www.ladybird.co.uk

 Penguin
Random House
UK

First published 2017
001

Written by Alastair Aiken and Cavan Scott
Lead artist: Aleksandar Sotirovski

Printed in Italy

A CIP catalogue record for this book is available from the British Library

ISBN: 978–0–141–38816–8

All correspondence to:
Puffin Books
Penguin Random House Children's
80 Strand, London WC2R 0RL

Ali-A Adventures

GAME ON!

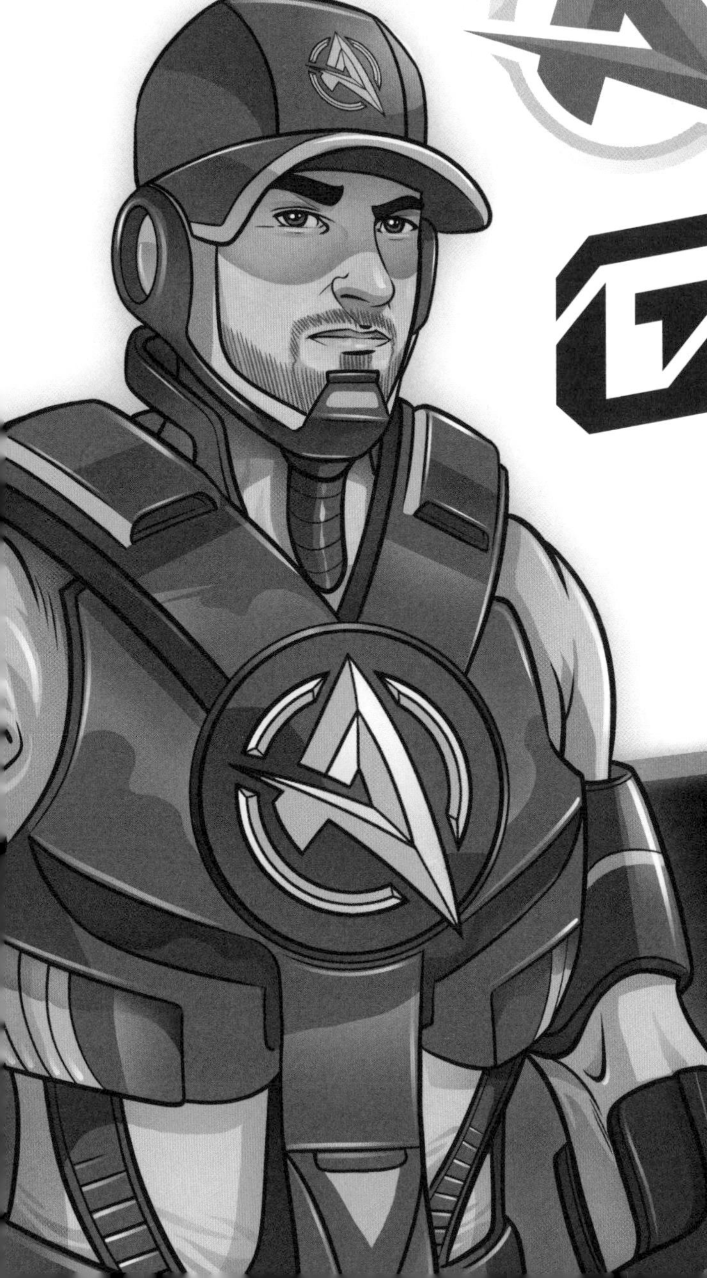

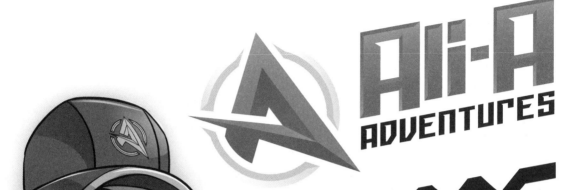

PUFFIN

MEET THE HEROES

EEVEE
ALI AND CLARE'S
FOUR-LEGGED FRIEND
IS NO ORDINARY PUP!

ALI-A
HE'S CONQUERED THE
GAMING WORLD--NOW
HE'S HERE TO SAVE THE
REST OF IT.

CLARE
SHE'S AN ACE GAMER
AND AN AWESOME
ADVENTURER.

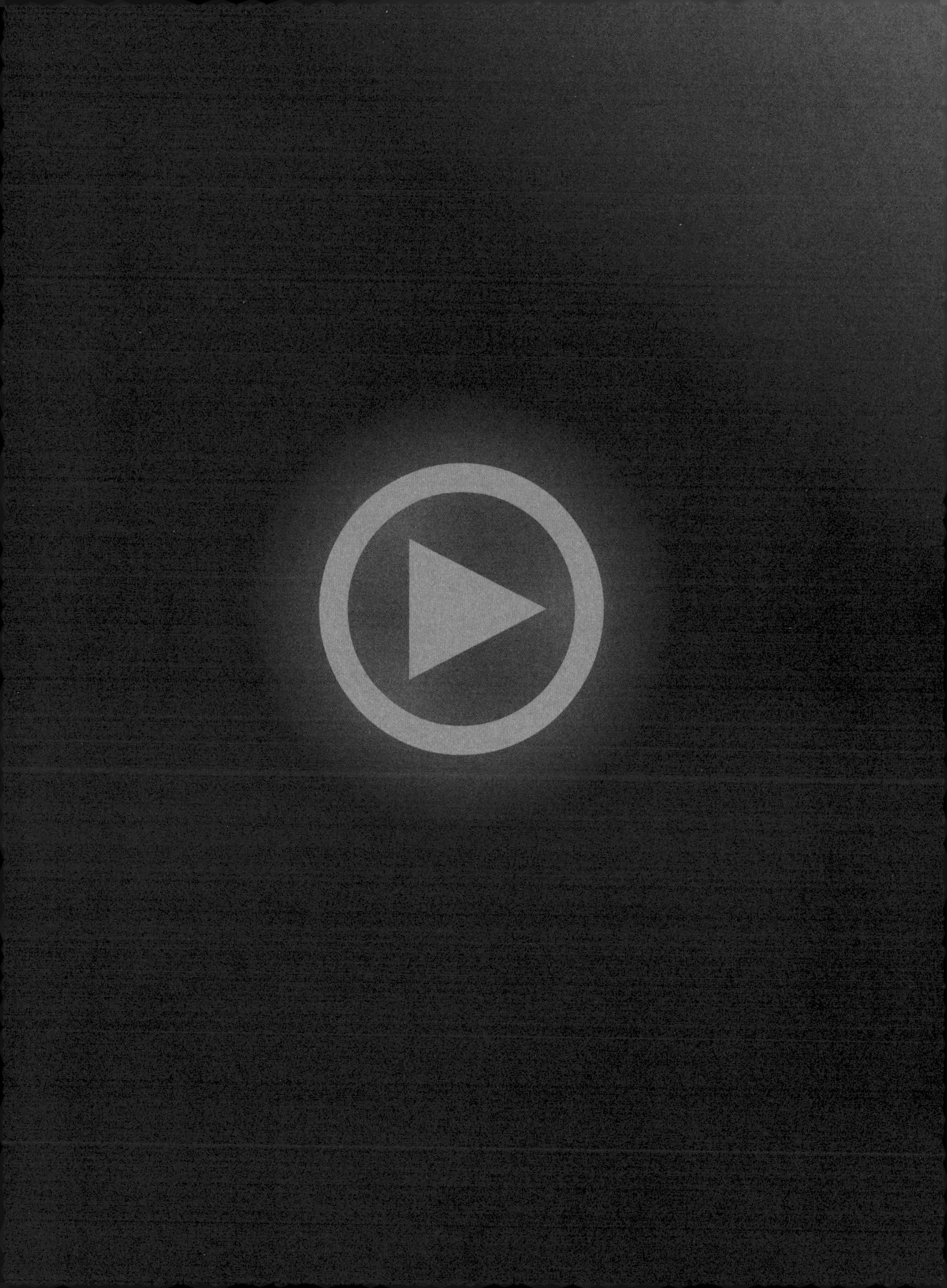

LEVEL ONE

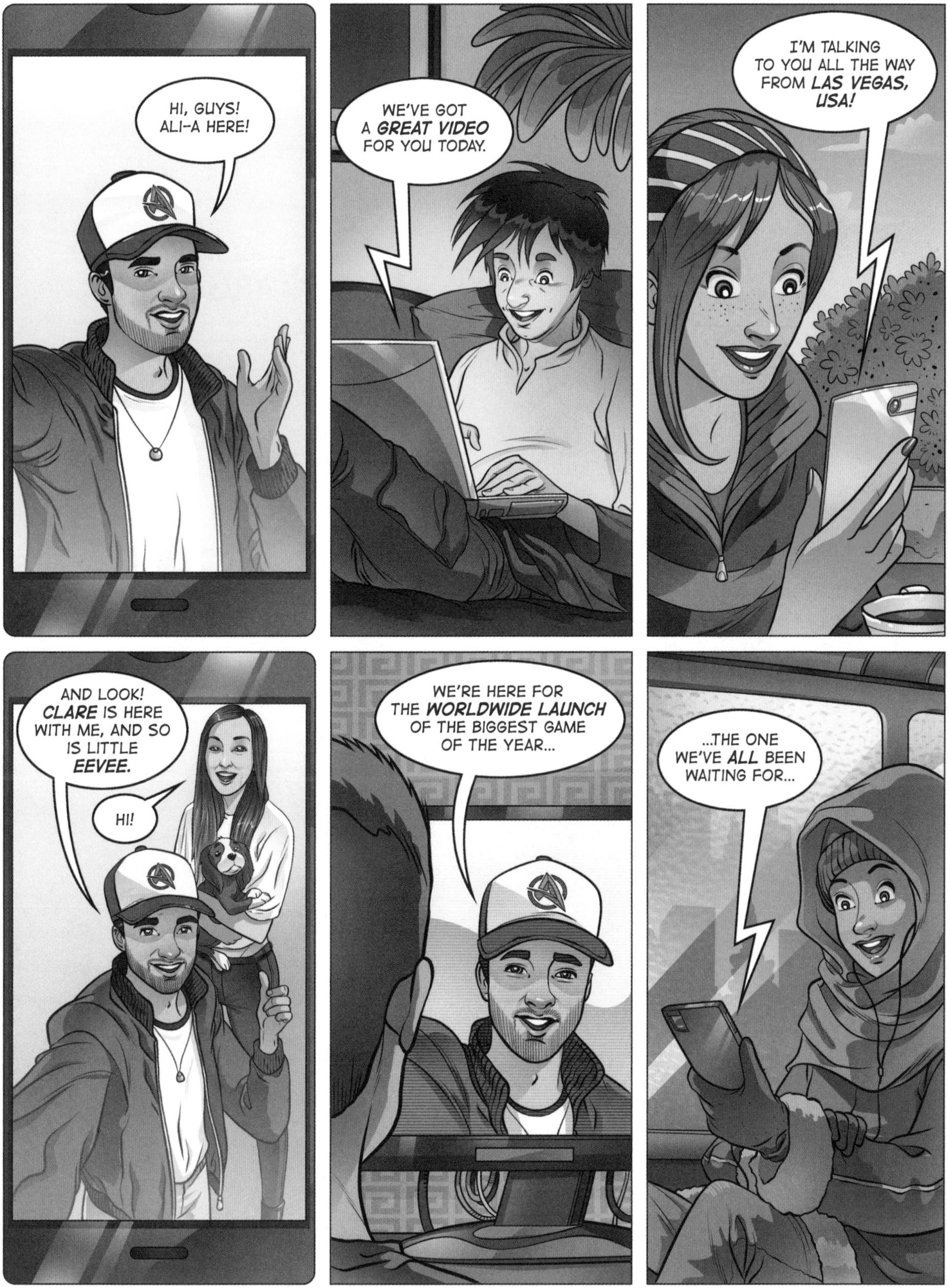
HI, GUYS! ALI-A HERE!
WE'VE GOT A **GREAT VIDEO** FOR YOU TODAY.
I'M TALKING TO YOU ALL THE WAY FROM **LAS VEGAS, USA!**
AND LOOK! **CLARE** IS HERE WITH ME, AND SO IS LITTLE **EEVEE.**
HI!
WE'RE HERE FOR THE **WORLDWIDE LAUNCH** OF THE BIGGEST GAME OF THE YEAR...
...THE ONE WE'VE **ALL** BEEN WAITING FOR...

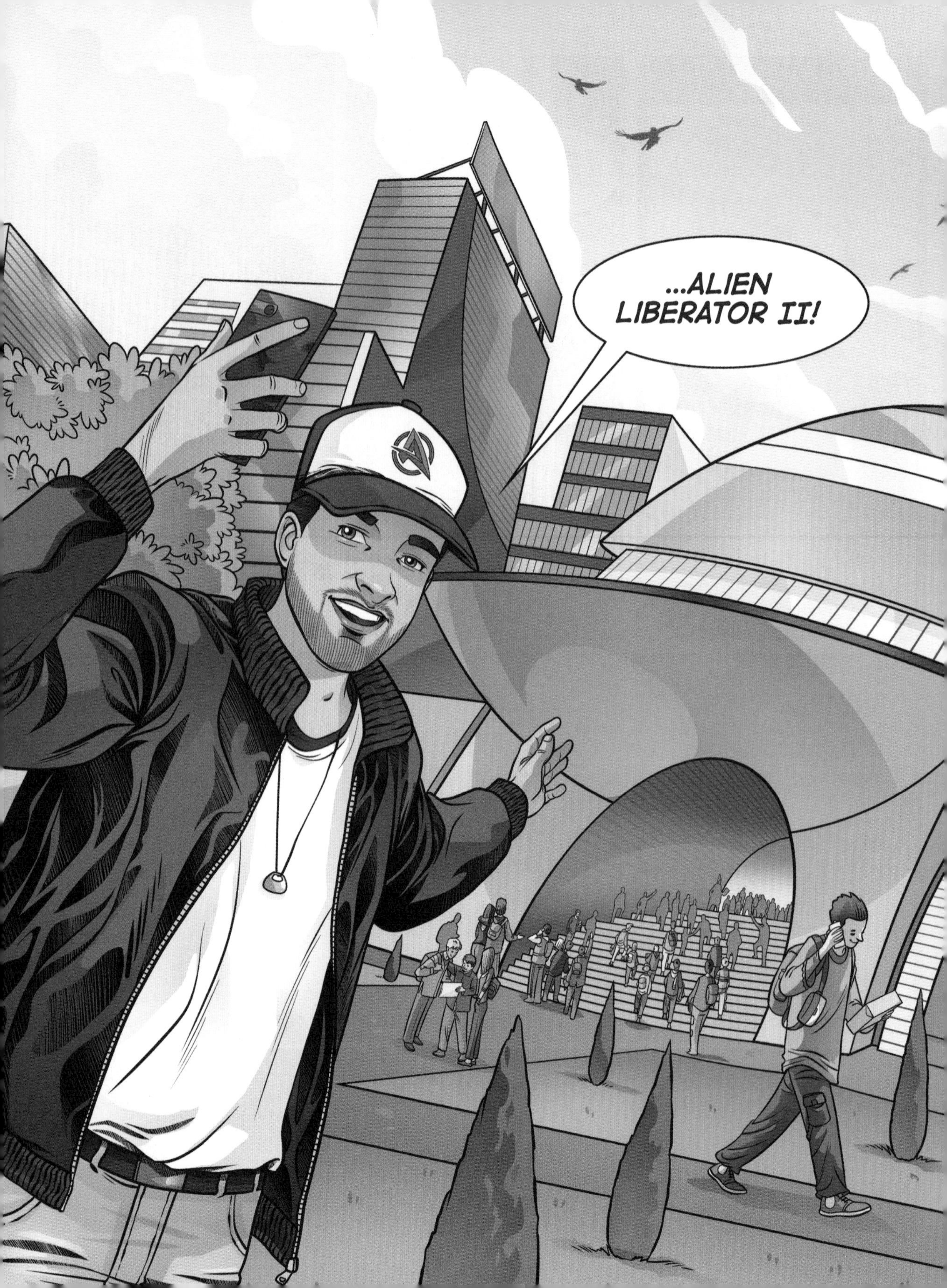
...ALIEN
LIBERATOR II!

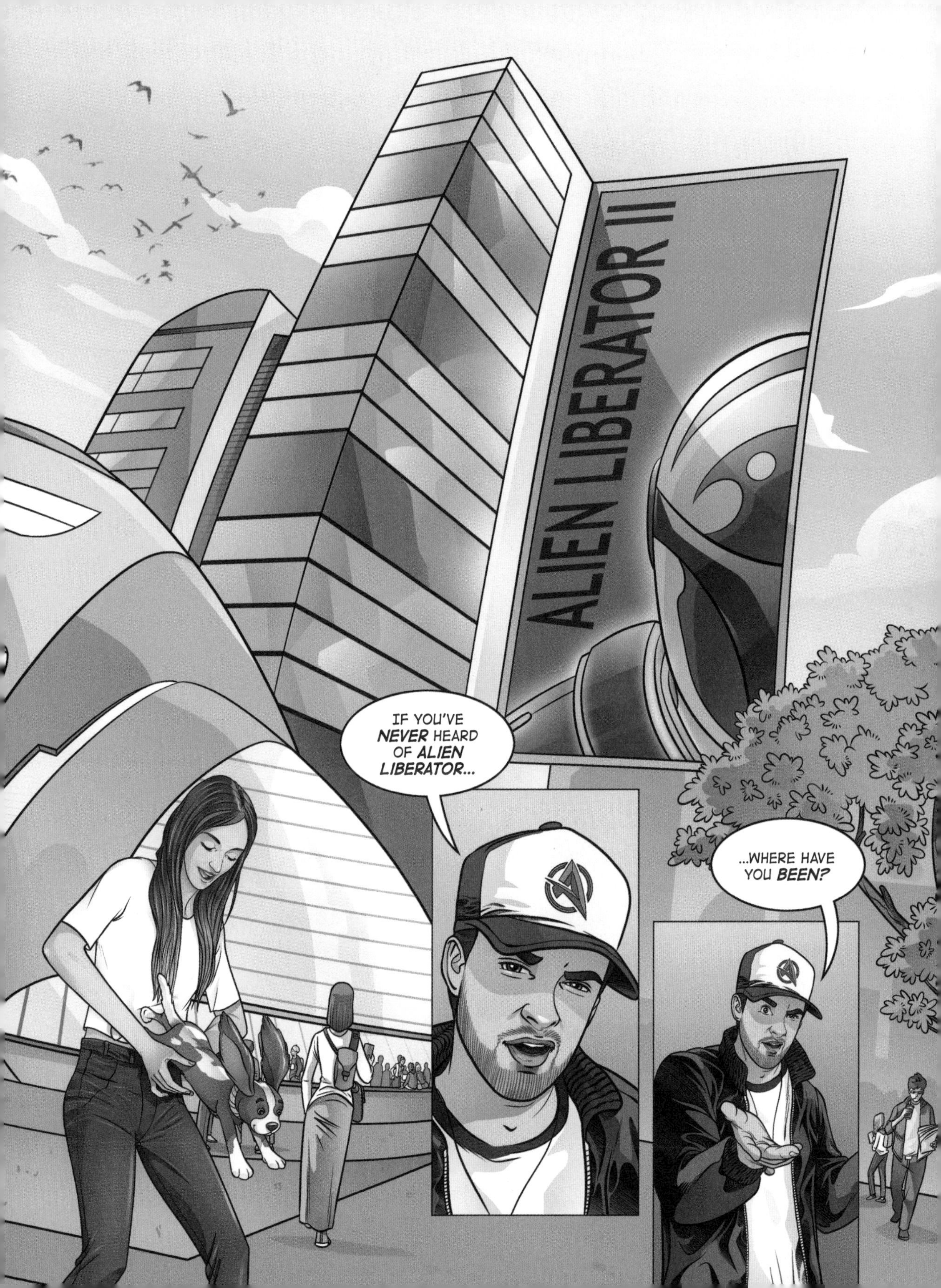
ALIEN LIBERATOR II
IF YOU'VE **NEVER** HEARD OF **ALIEN LIBERATOR**...
...WHERE HAVE YOU **BEEN?**

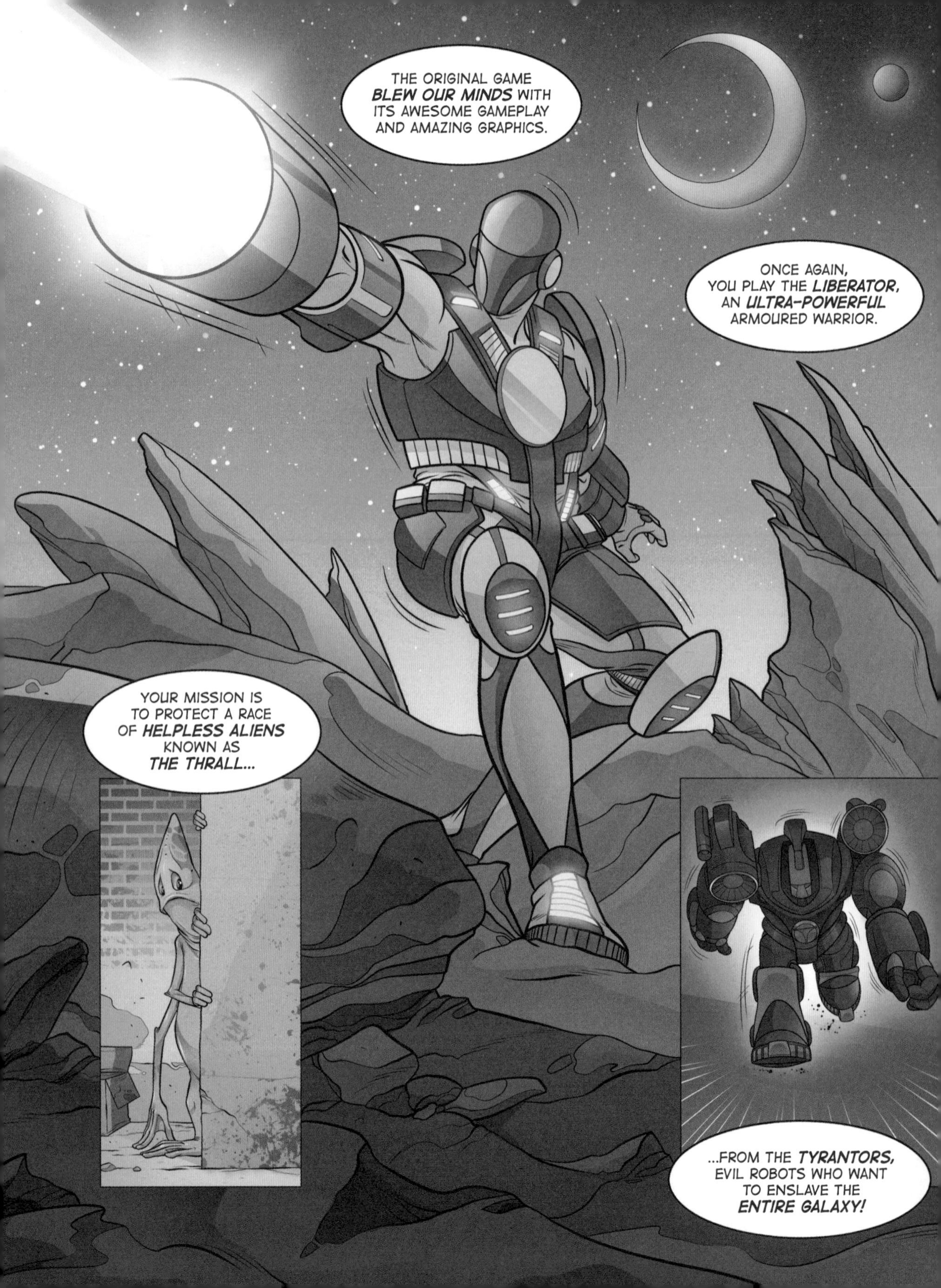
THE ORIGINAL GAME BLEW OUR MINDS WITH ITS AWESOME GAMEPLAY AND AMAZING GRAPHICS.
ONCE AGAIN, YOU PLAY THE LIBERATOR, AN ULTRA-POWERFUL ARMOURED WARRIOR.
YOUR MISSION IS TO PROTECT A RACE OF HELPLESS ALIENS KNOWN AS THE THRALL...
...FROM THE TYRANTORS, EVIL ROBOTS WHO WANT TO ENSLAVE THE ENTIRE GALAXY!

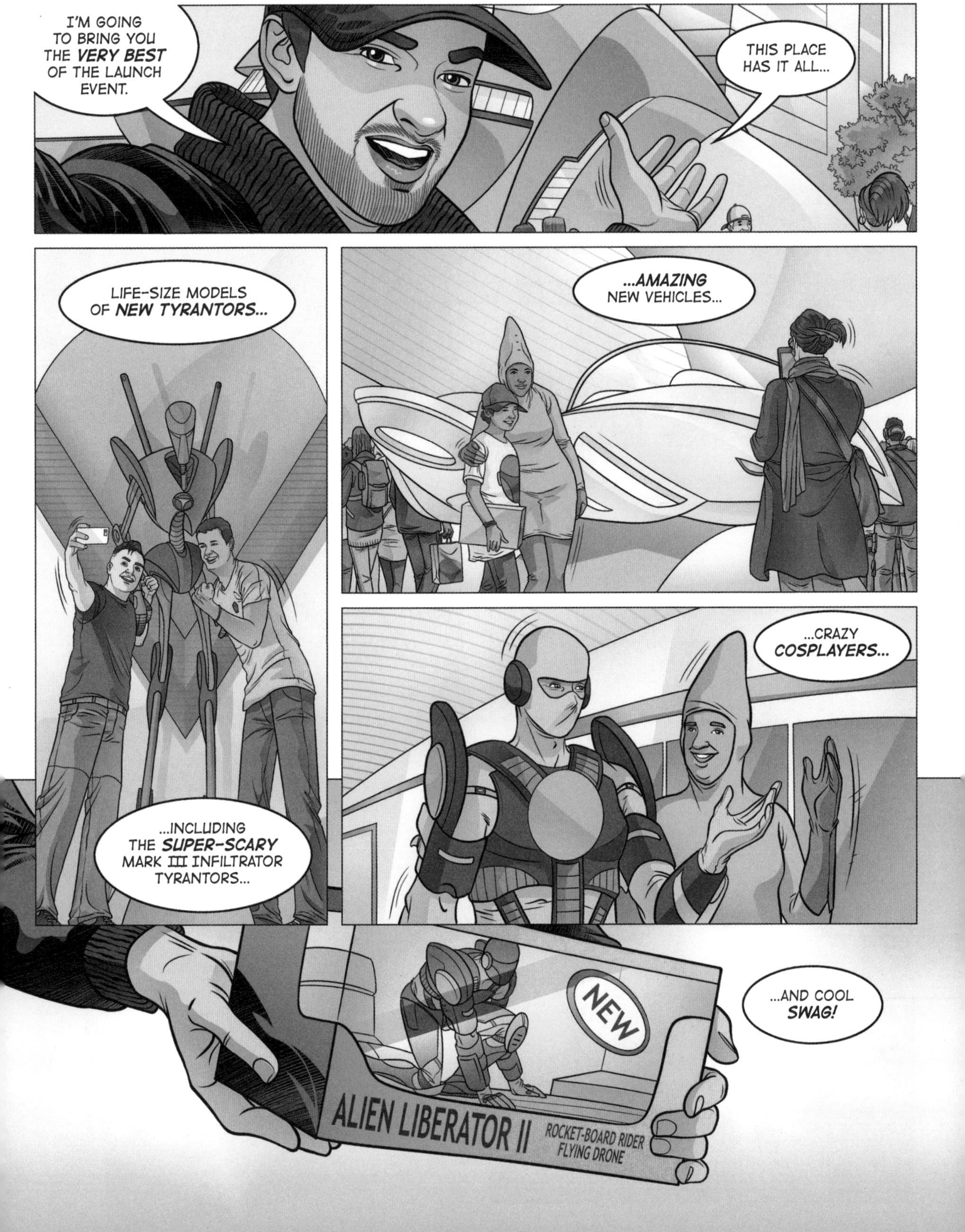
I'M GOING TO BRING YOU THE VERY BEST OF THE LAUNCH EVENT.
THIS PLACE HAS IT ALL...
LIFE-SIZE MODELS OF NEW TYRANTORS...
...INCLUDING THE SUPER-SCARY MARK III INFILTRATOR TYRANTORS...
...AMAZING NEW VEHICLES...
...CRAZY COSPLAYERS...
NEW
ALIEN LIBERATOR II
ROCKET-BOARD RIDER
FLYING DRONE
...AND COOL SWAG!

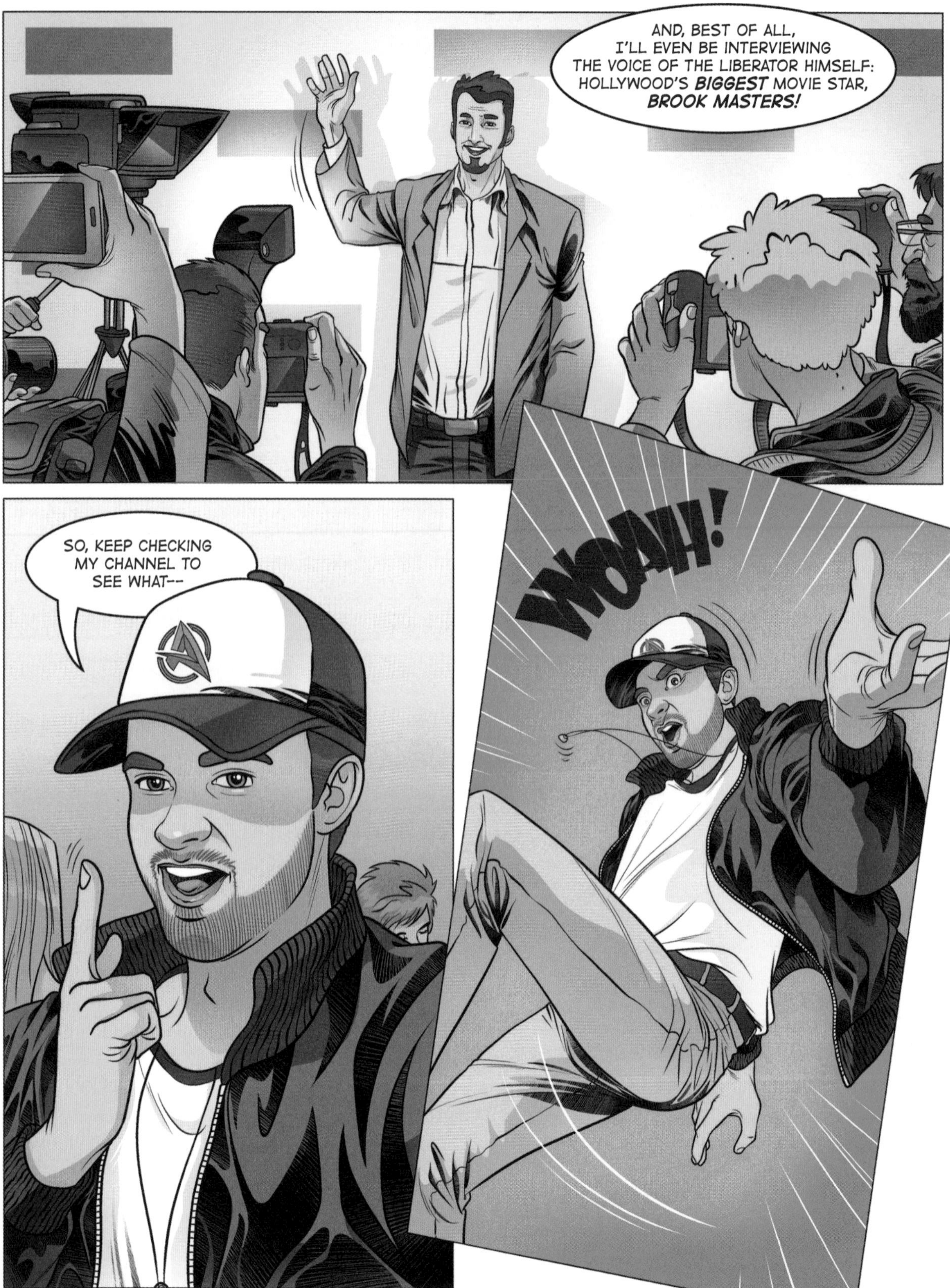
AND, BEST OF ALL, I'LL EVEN BE INTERVIEWING THE VOICE OF THE LIBERATOR HIMSELF: HOLLYWOOD'S ***BIGGEST*** MOVIE STAR, ***BROOK MASTERS!***
SO, KEEP CHECKING MY CHANNEL TO SEE WHAT--
WOAH!

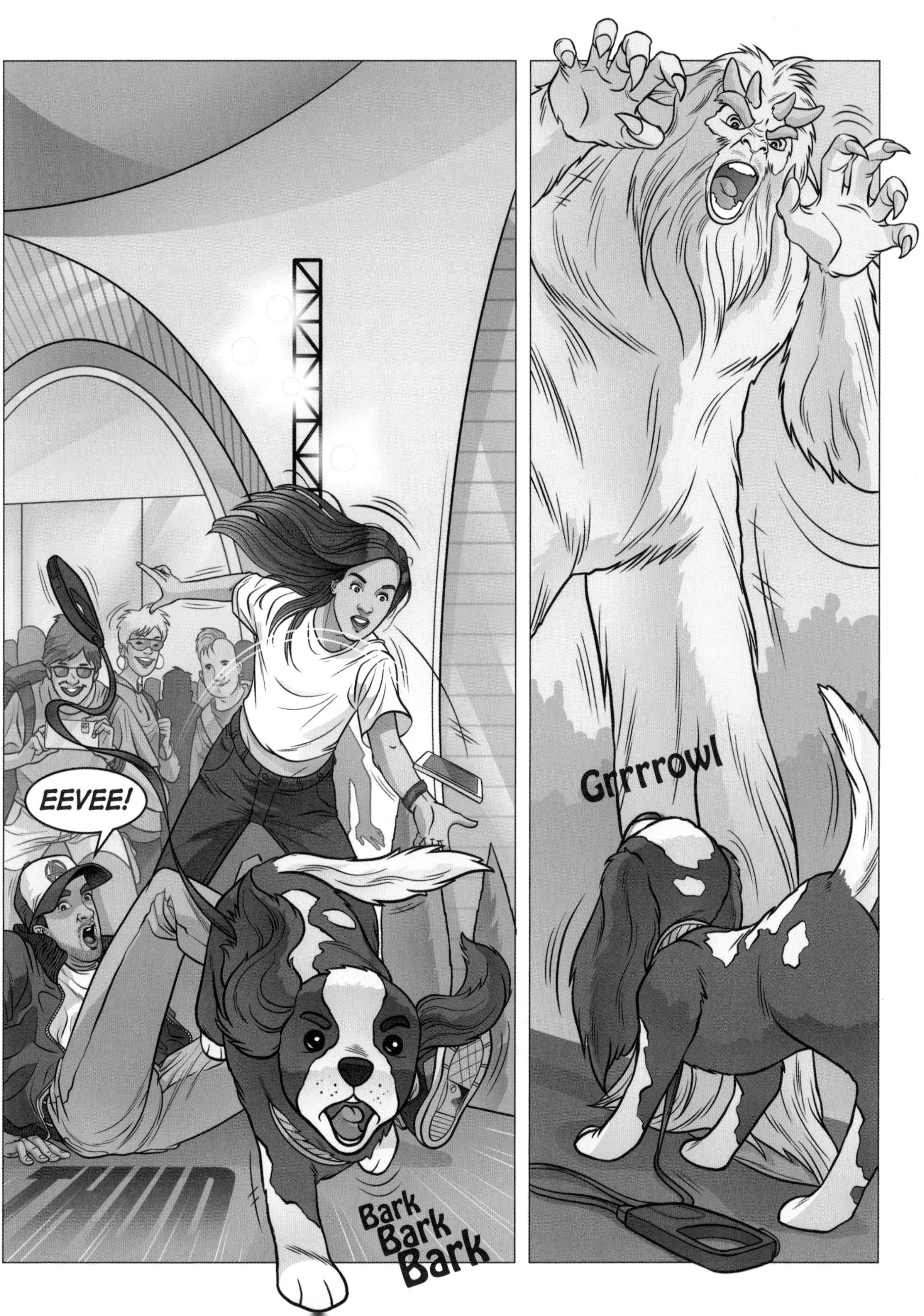
EEVEE!
THUD
Bark
Bark
Bark
Grrrrowl

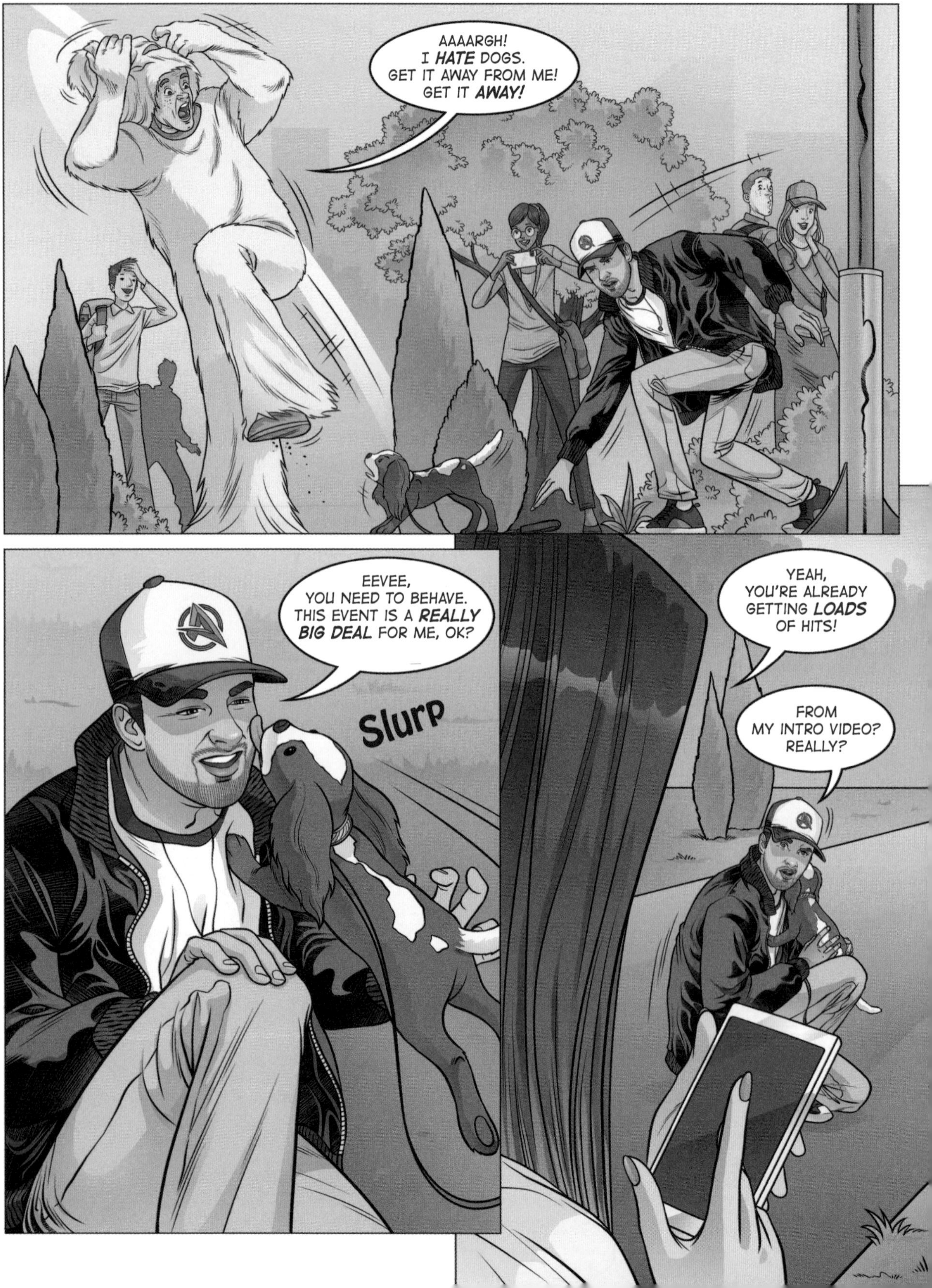
AAAARGH! I HATE DOGS. GET IT AWAY FROM ME! GET IT AWAY!
EEVEE, YOU NEED TO BEHAVE. THIS EVENT IS A REALLY BIG DEAL FOR ME, OK?
Slurp
YEAH, YOU'RE ALREADY GETTING LOADS OF HITS!
FROM MY INTRO VIDEO? REALLY?

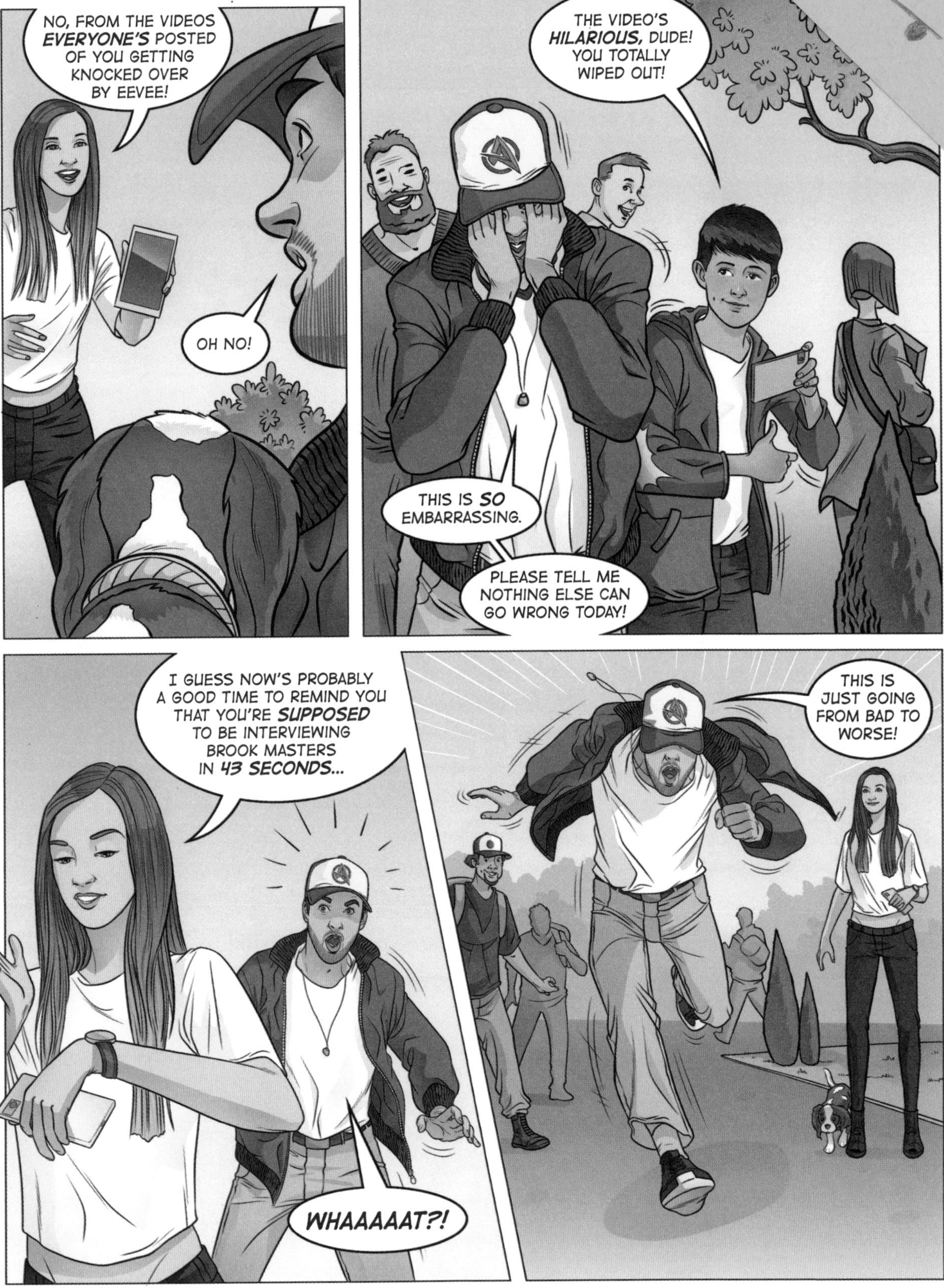
NO, FROM THE VIDEOS EVERYONE'S POSTED OF YOU GETTING KNOCKED OVER BY EEVEE!
OH NO!
THE VIDEO'S HILARIOUS, DUDE! YOU TOTALLY WIPED OUT!
THIS IS SO EMBARRASSING.
PLEASE TELL ME NOTHING ELSE CAN GO WRONG TODAY!
I GUESS NOW'S PROBABLY A GOOD TIME TO REMIND YOU THAT YOU'RE SUPPOSED TO BE INTERVIEWING BROOK MASTERS IN 43 SECONDS...
WHAAAAAT?!
THIS IS JUST GOING FROM BAD TO WORSE!

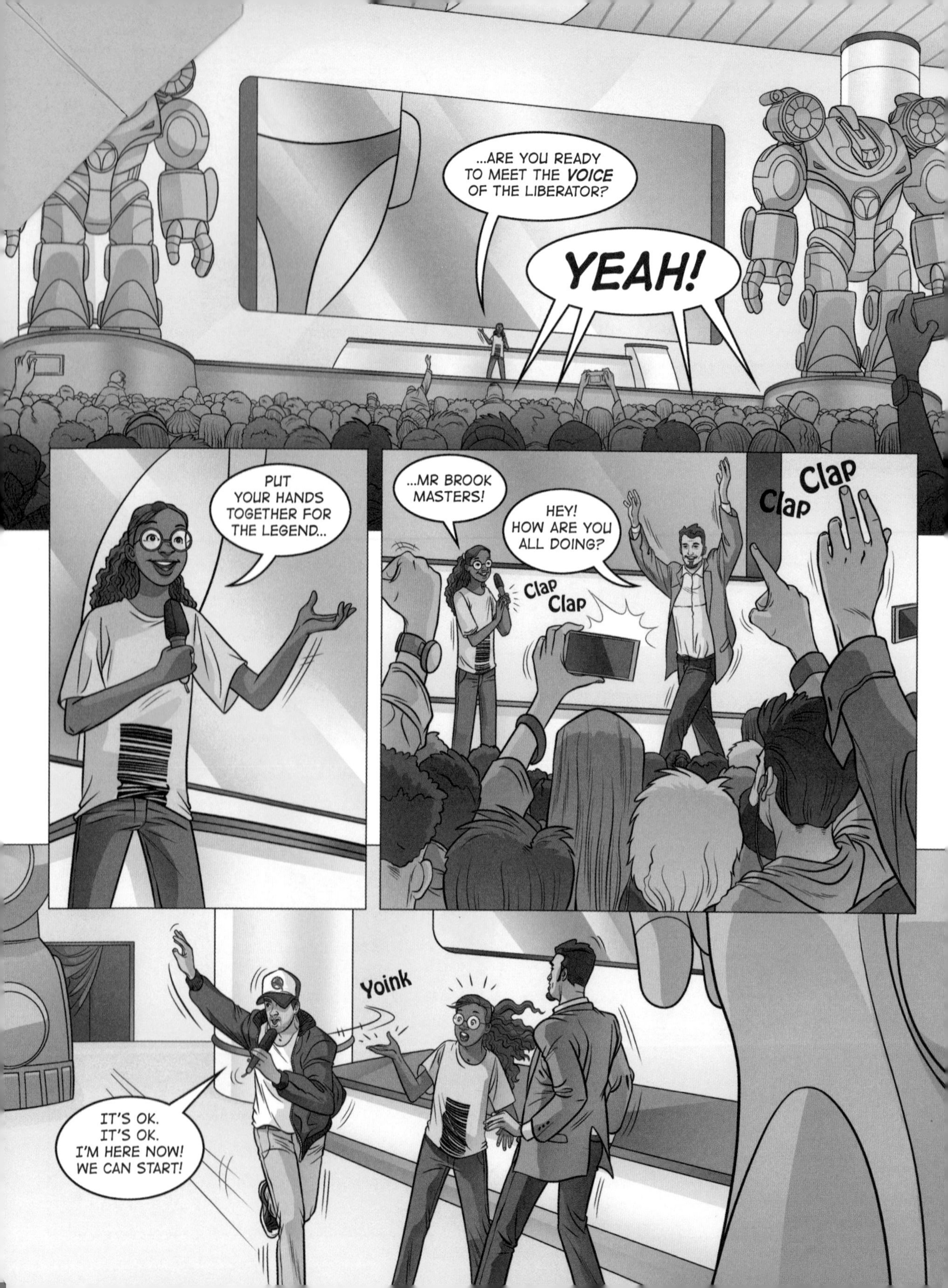
...ARE YOU READY TO MEET THE VOICE OF THE LIBERATOR?
YEAH!
PUT YOUR HANDS TOGETHER FOR THE LEGEND...
...MR BROOK MASTERS!
HEY! HOW ARE YOU ALL DOING?
Clap Clap
Clap Clap
Yoink
IT'S OK. IT'S OK. I'M HERE NOW! WE CAN START!

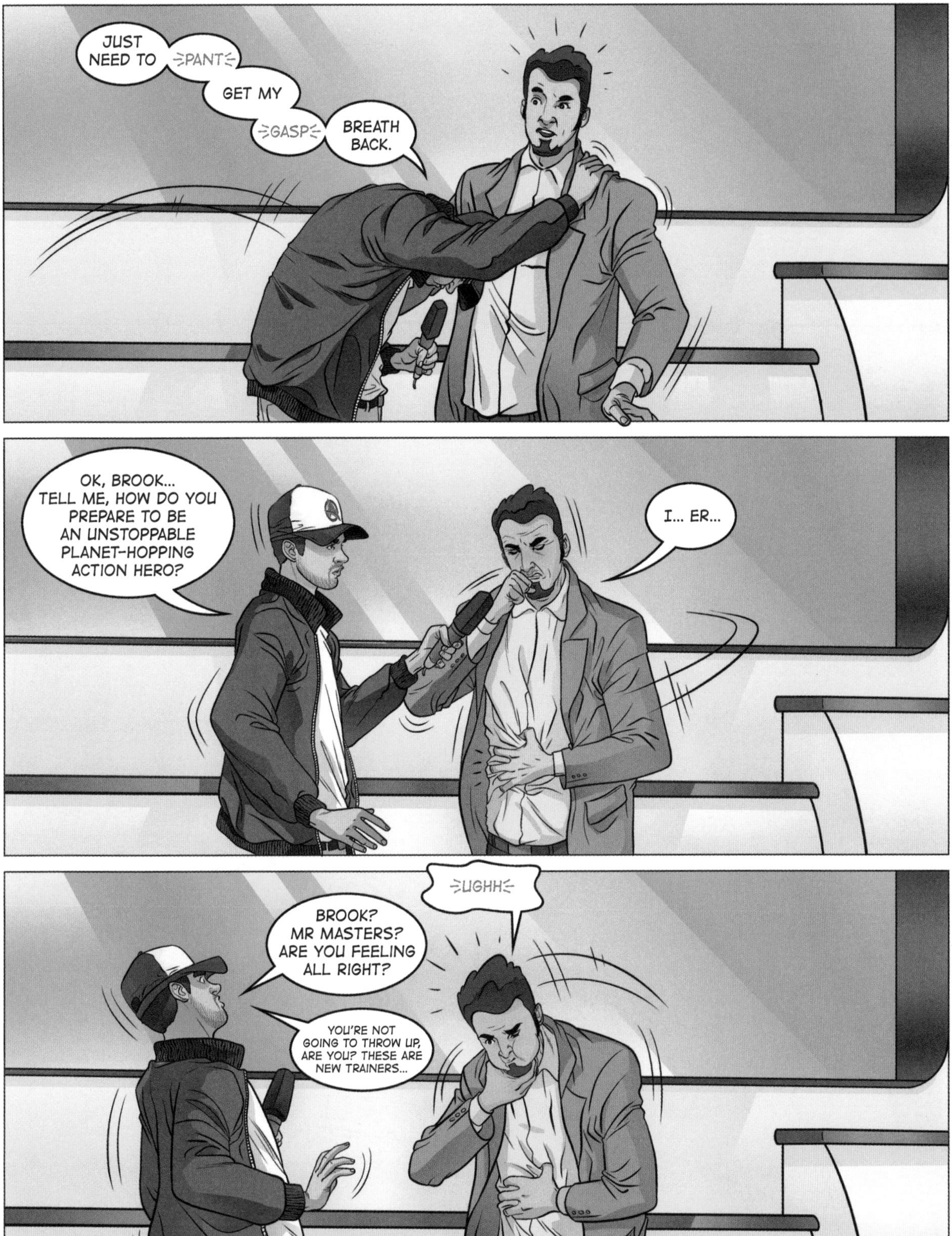
JUST NEED TO
=PANT=
GET MY
=GASP=
BREATH BACK.
OK, BROOK... TELL ME, HOW DO YOU PREPARE TO BE AN UNSTOPPABLE PLANET-HOPPING ACTION HERO?
I... ER...
=UGHH=
BROOK? MR MASTERS? ARE YOU FEELING ALL RIGHT?
YOU'RE NOT GOING TO THROW UP, ARE YOU? THESE ARE NEW TRAINERS...

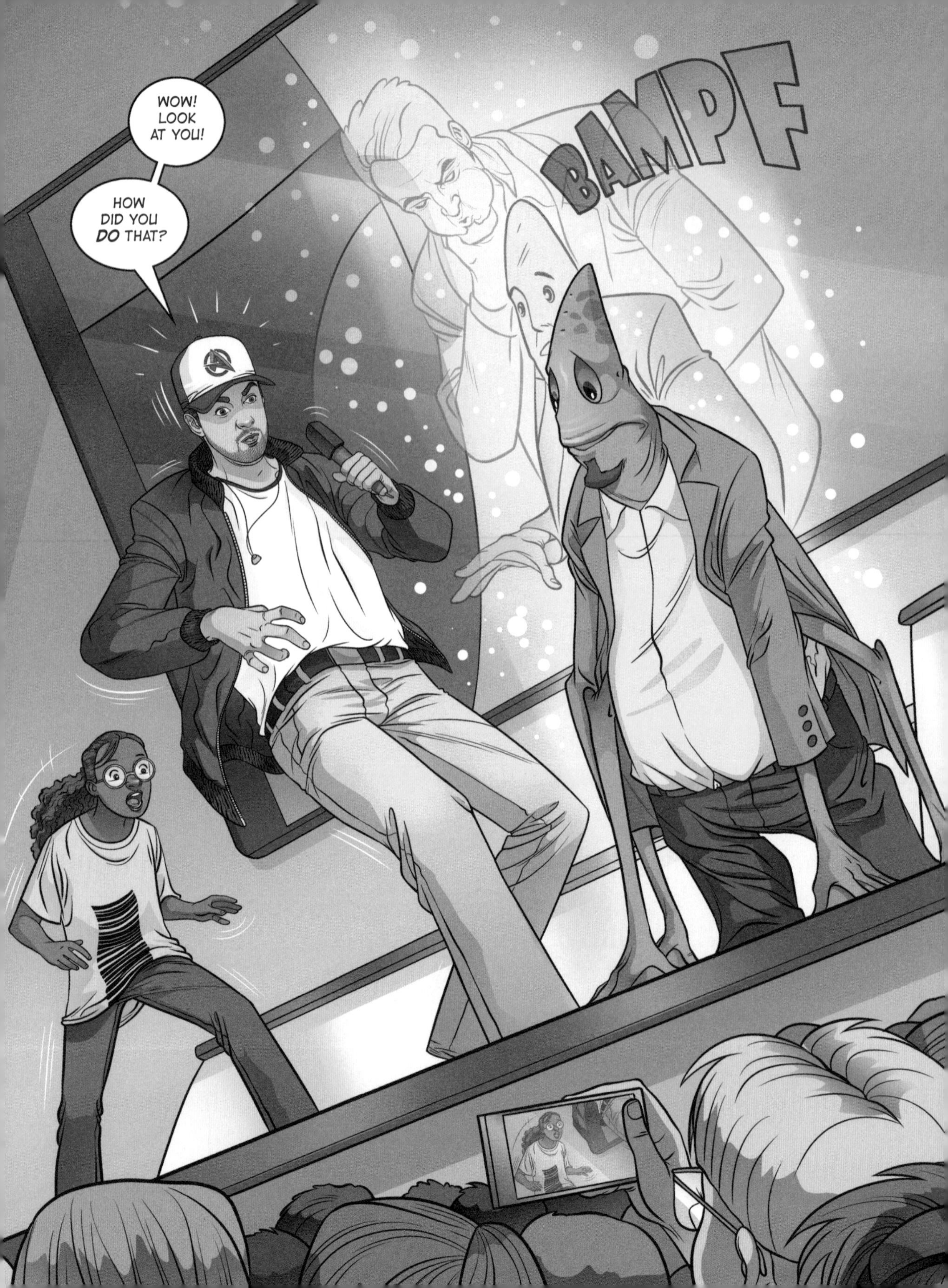
WOW! LOOK AT YOU!
HOW DID YOU *DO* THAT?
BAMPF

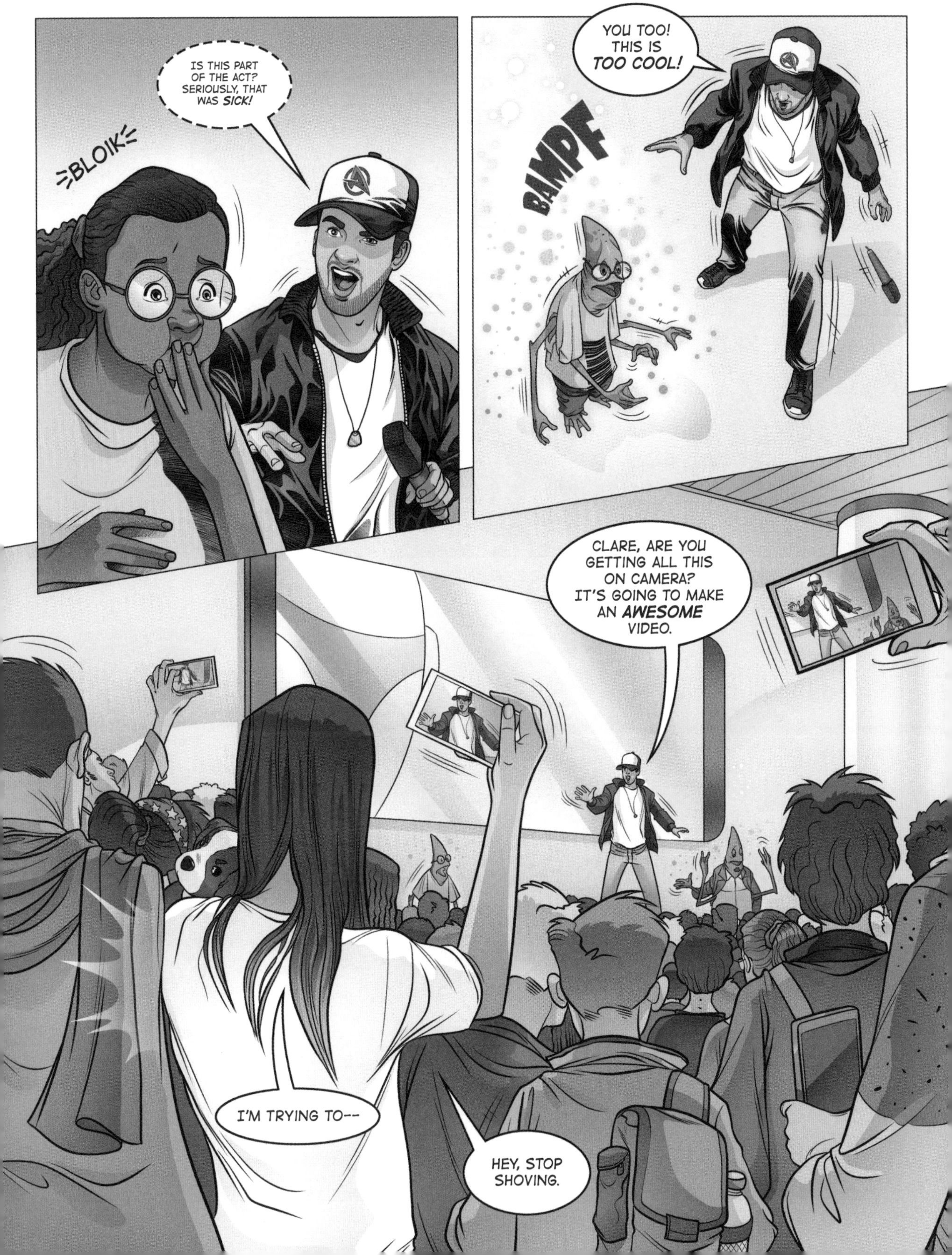
IS THIS PART OF THE ACT? SERIOUSLY, THAT WAS SICK!
BLOIK
YOU TOO! THIS IS TOO COOL!
BAMPF
CLARE, ARE YOU GETTING ALL THIS ON CAMERA? IT'S GOING TO MAKE AN AWESOME VIDEO.
I'M TRYING TO--
HEY, STOP SHOVING.

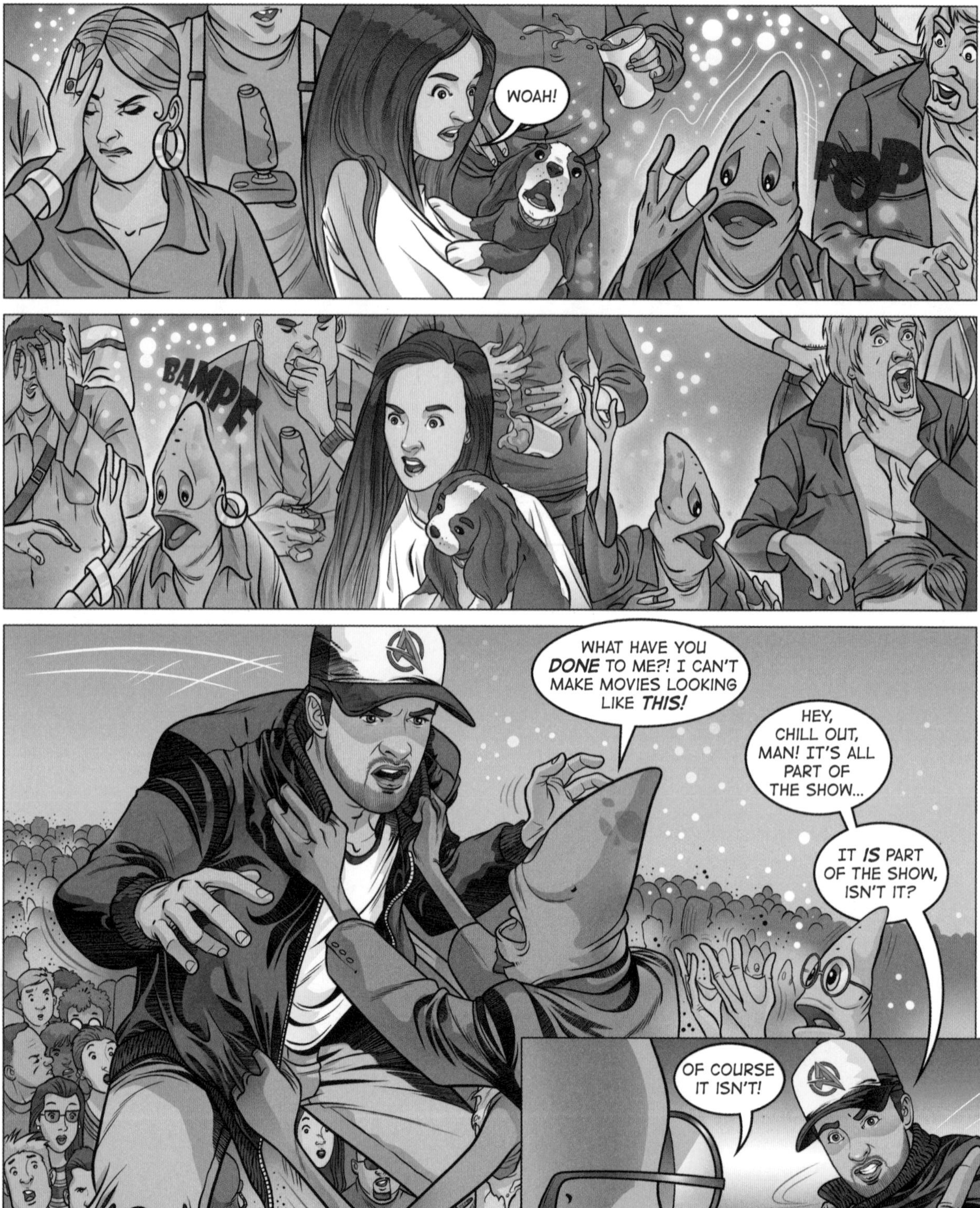
WOAH!
POP
BAMPF
WHAT HAVE YOU DONE TO ME?! I CAN'T MAKE MOVIES LOOKING LIKE THIS!
HEY, CHILL OUT, MAN! IT'S ALL PART OF THE SHOW...
IT IS PART OF THE SHOW, ISN'T IT?
OF COURSE IT ISN'T!
SOB

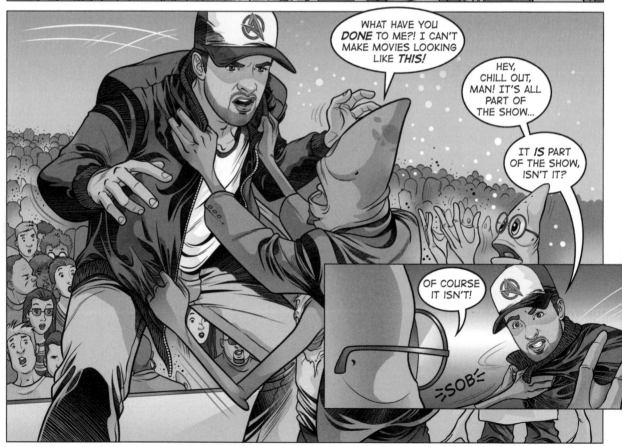

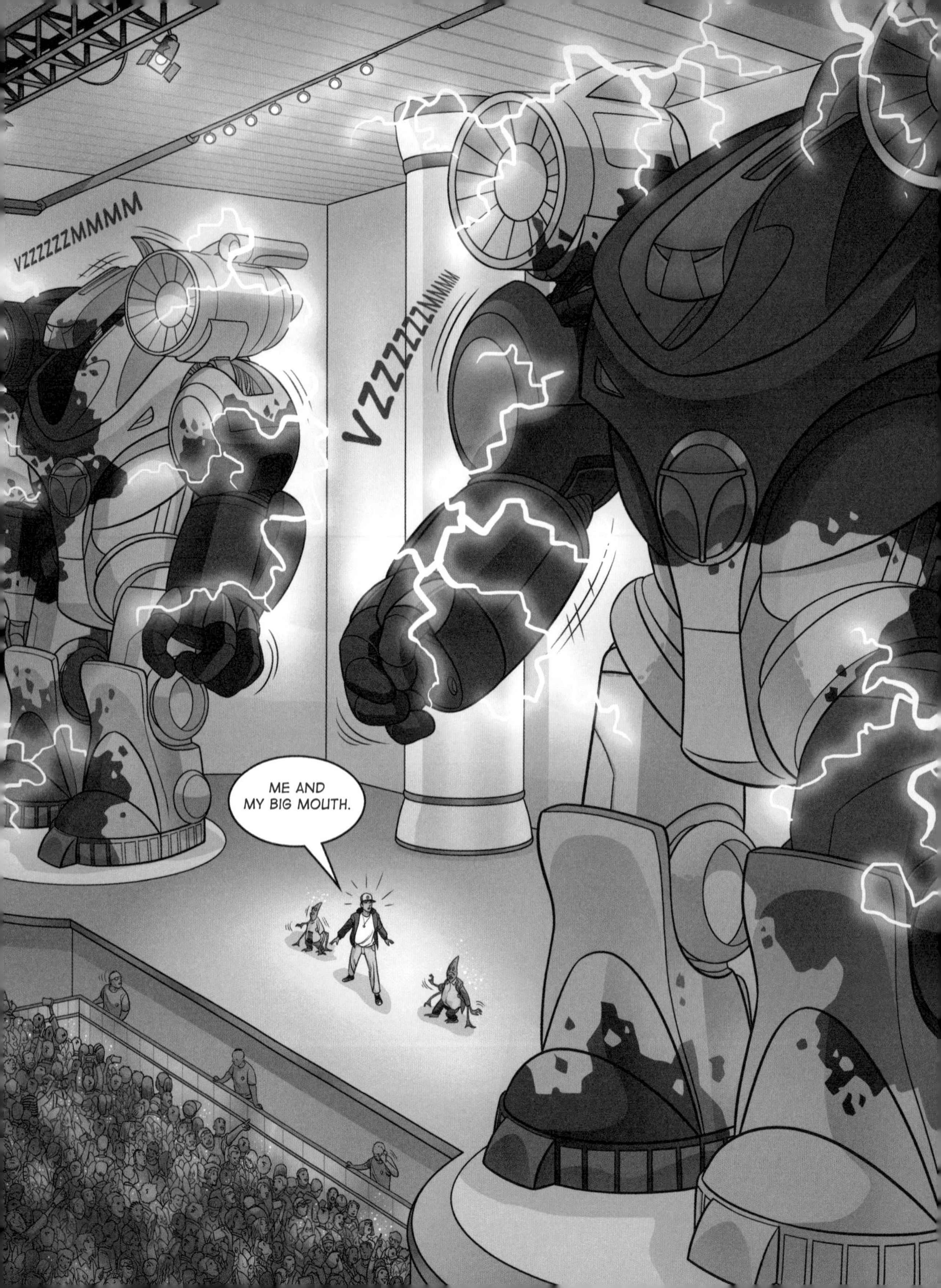
VZZZZZZMMMMM
VZZZZZZMMMMM
ME AND MY BIG MOUTH.

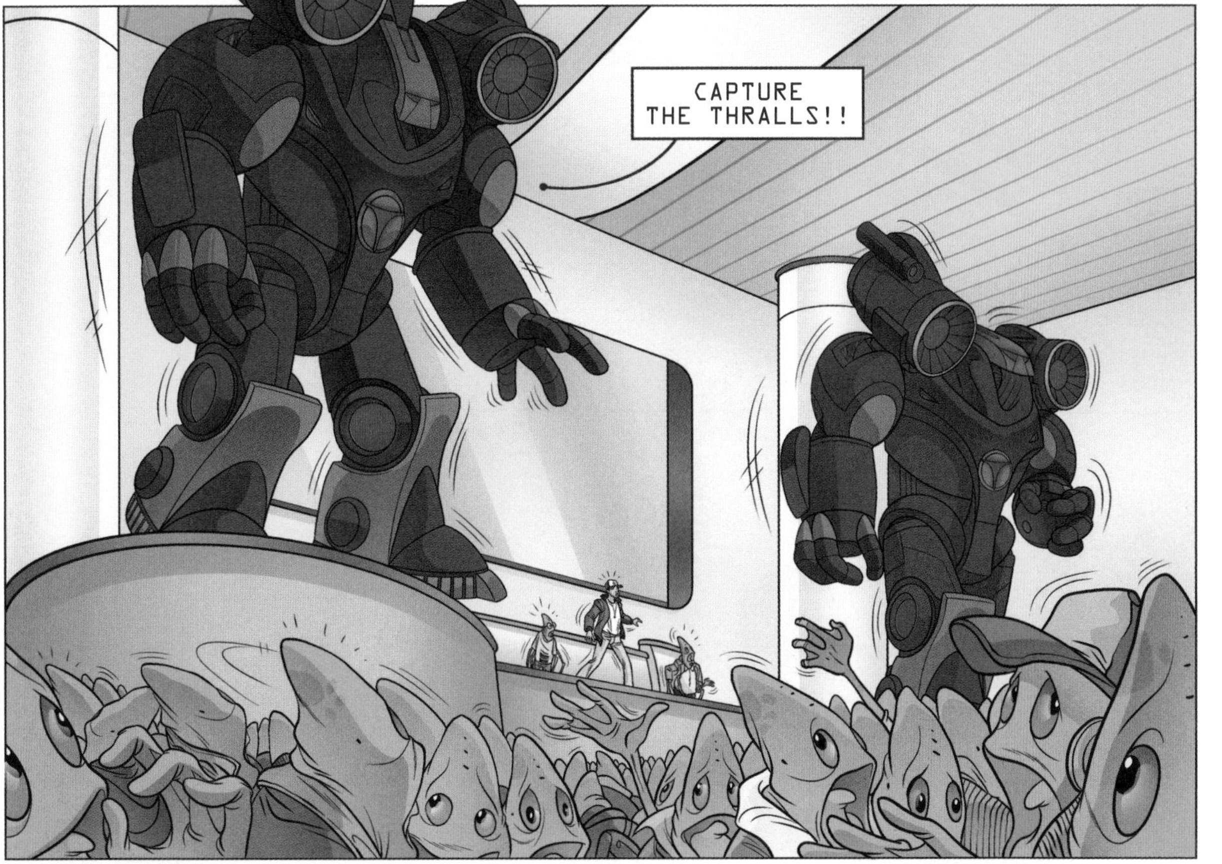
CAPTURE THE THRALLS!!

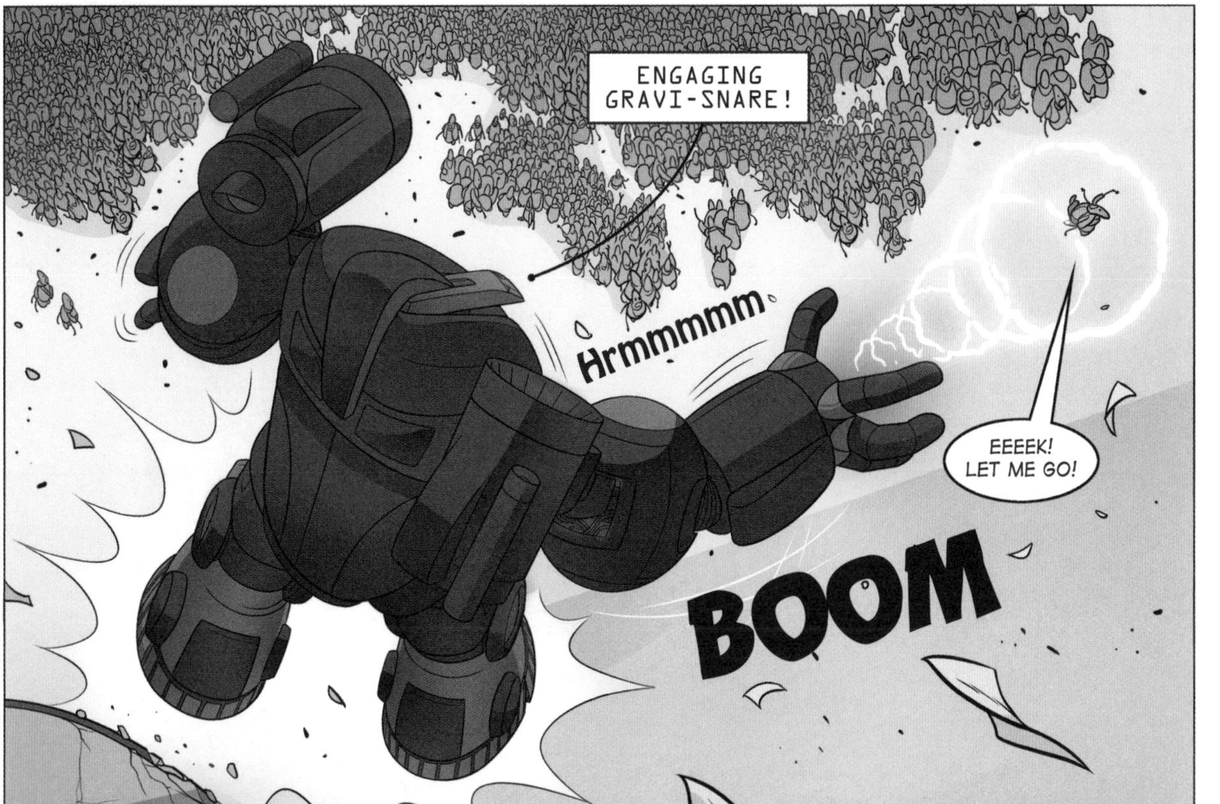
ENGAGING GRAVI-SNARE!
Hrmmmmm
EEEEK! LET ME GO!
BOOM

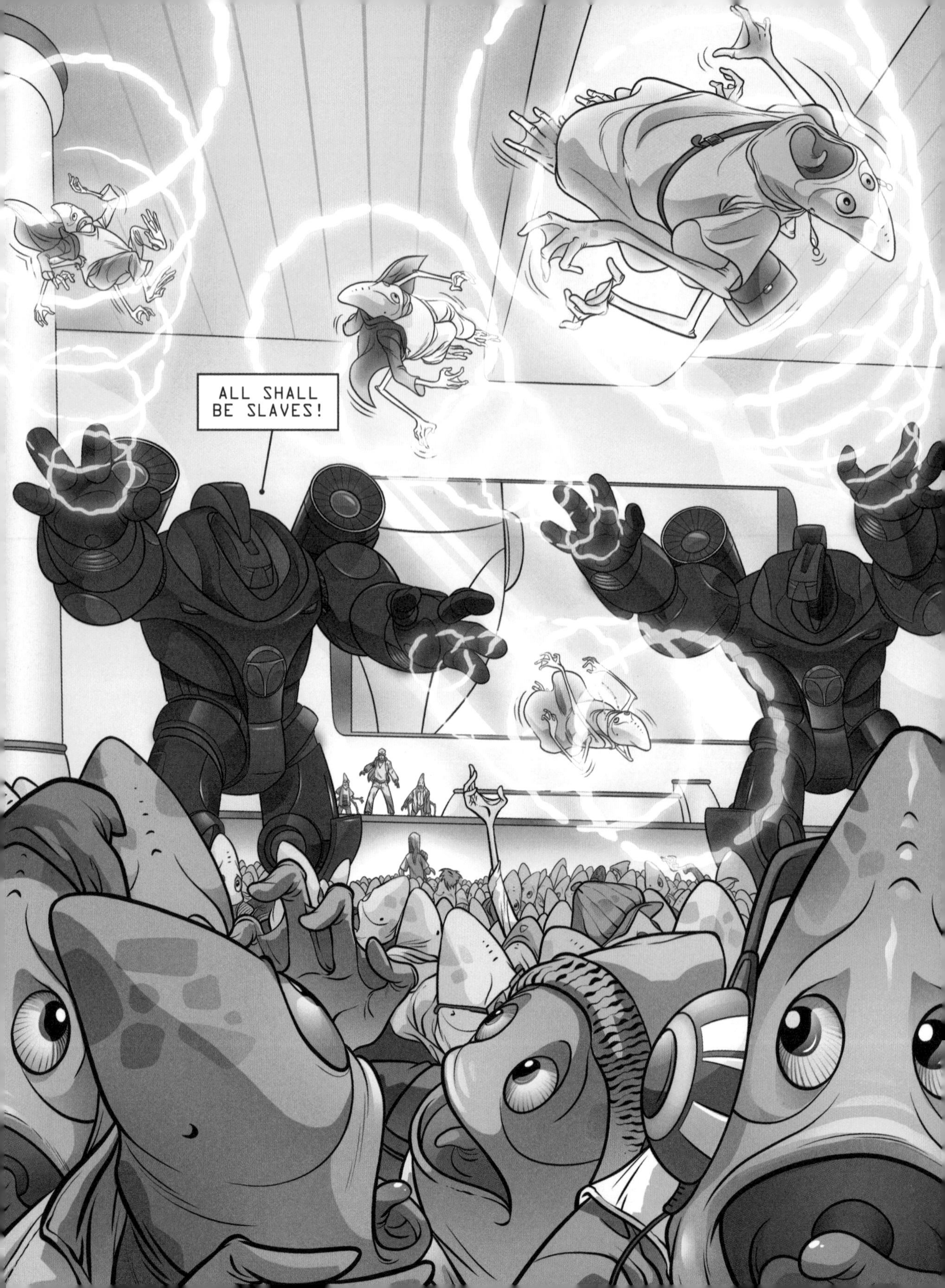
ALL SHALL BE SLAVES!

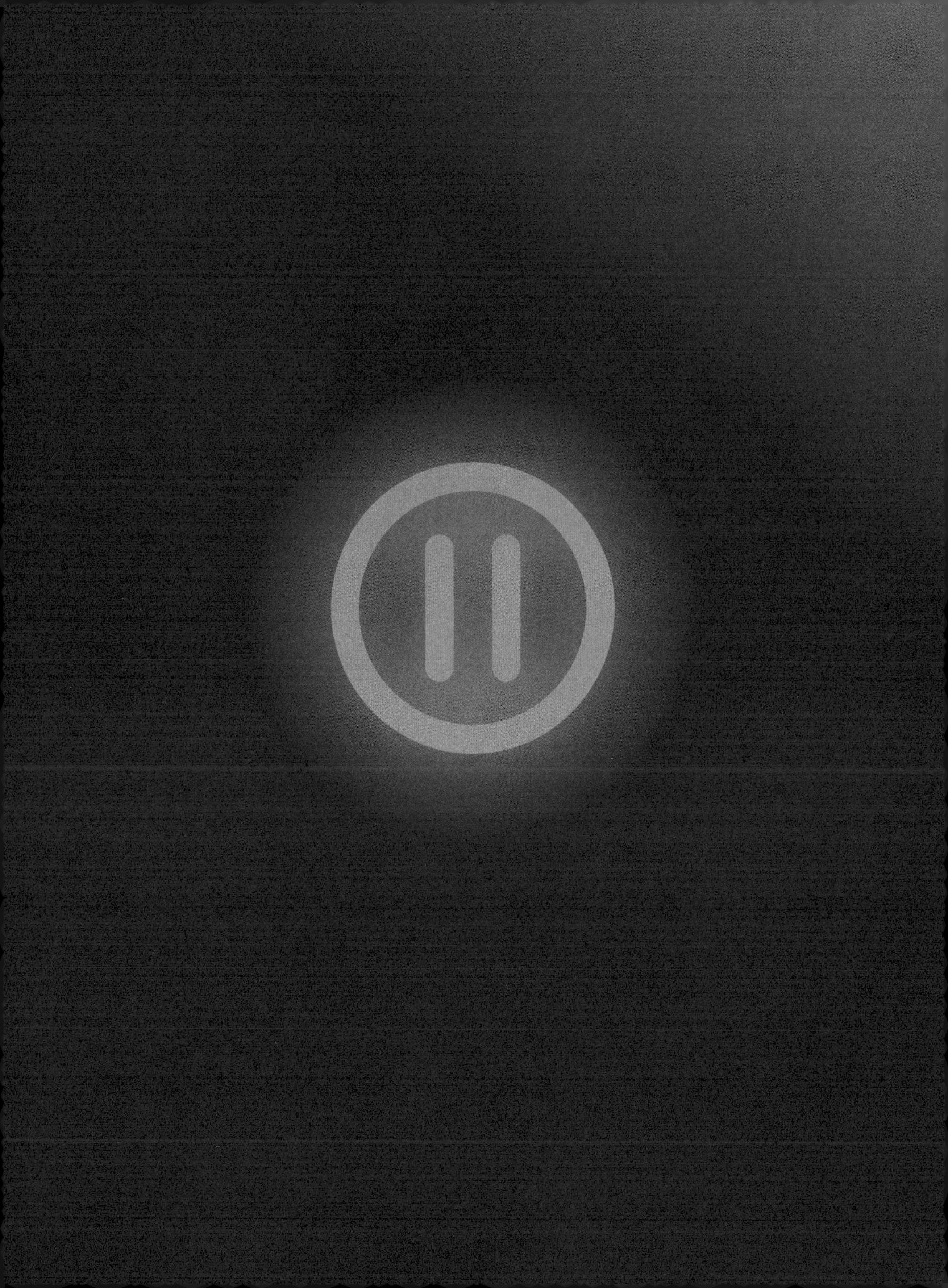

LEVEL
TWO

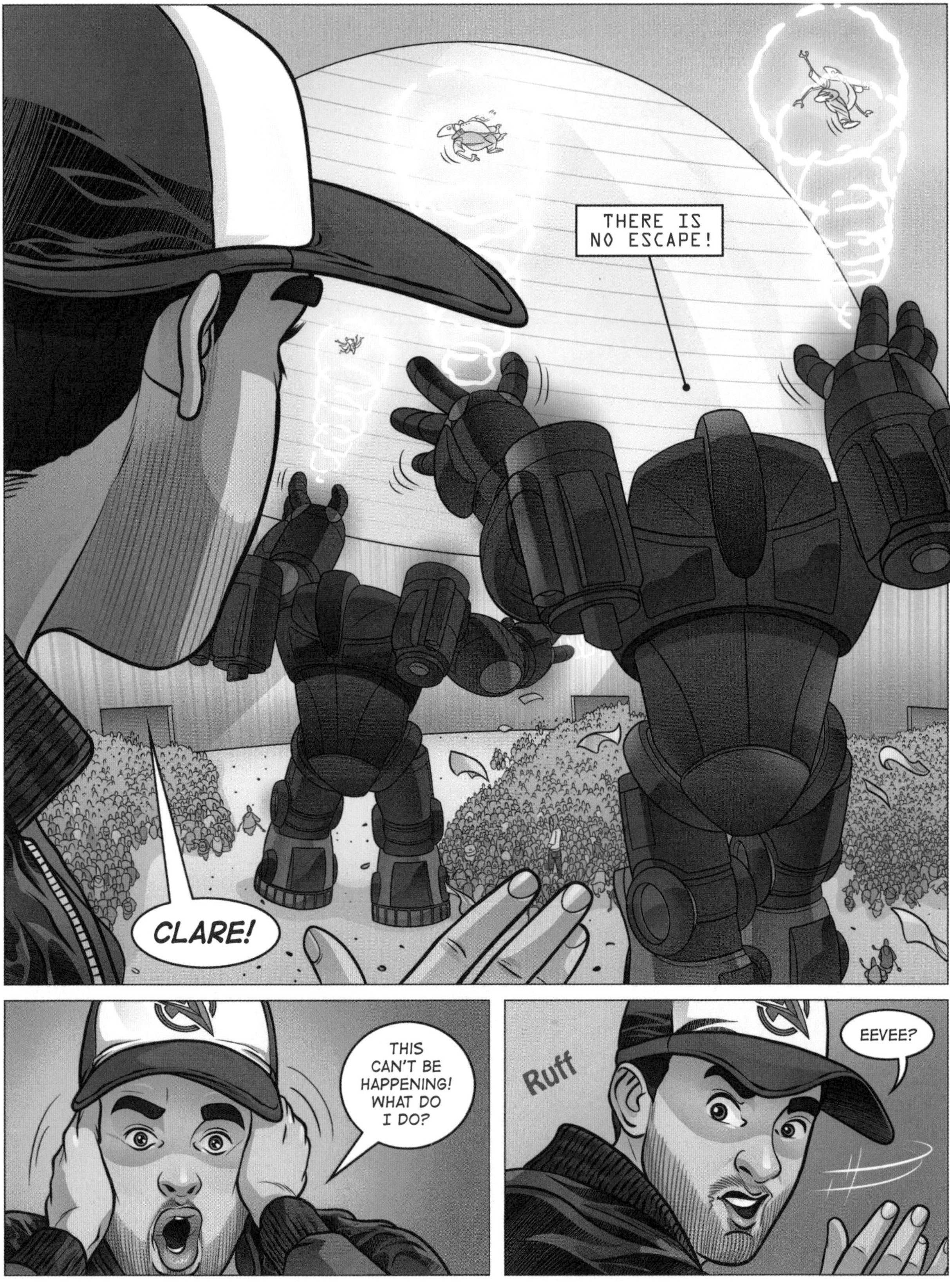
THERE IS NO ESCAPE!
CLARE!
THIS CAN'T BE HAPPENING! WHAT DO I DO?
Ruff
EEVEE?

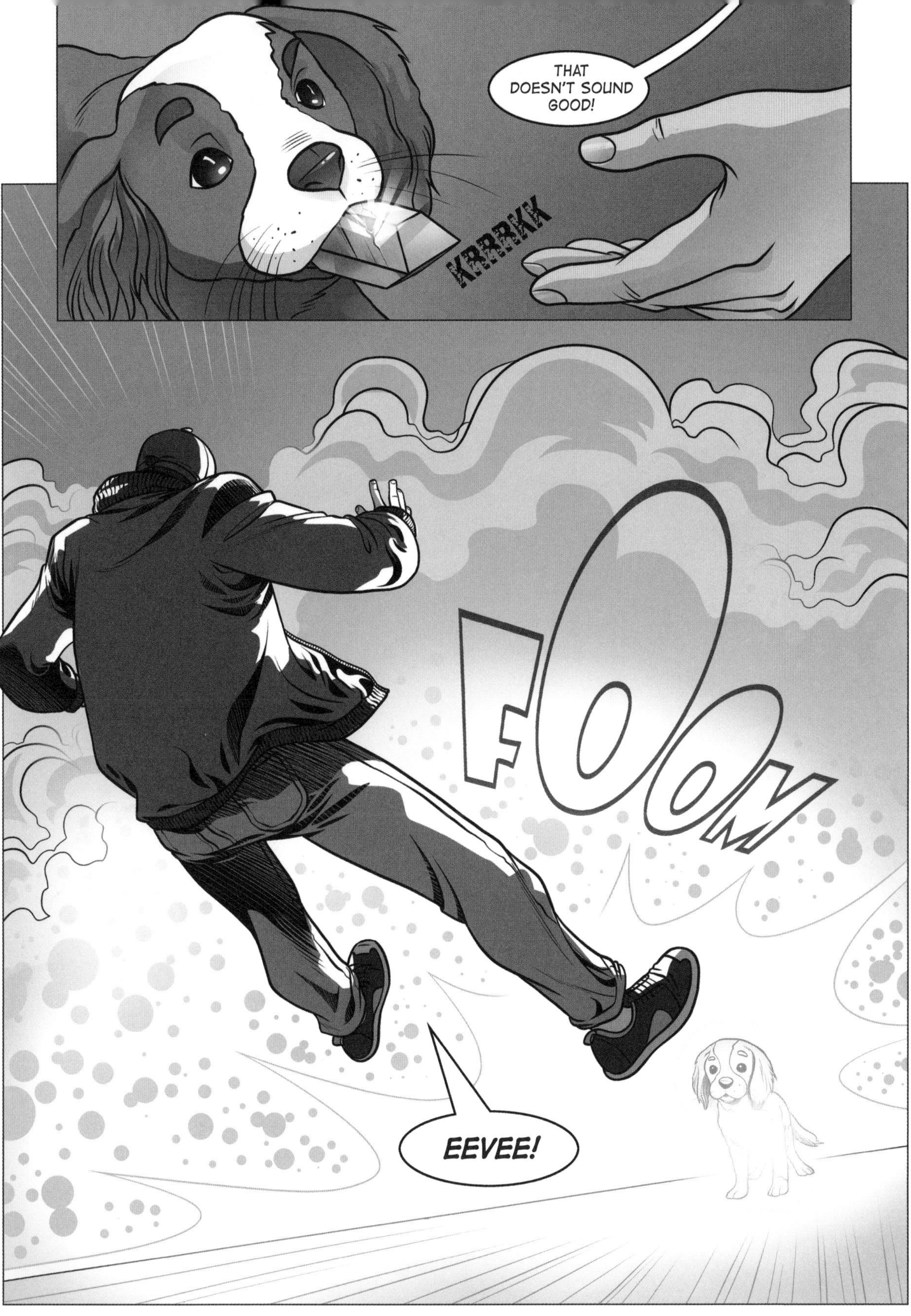
THAT DOESN'T SOUND GOOD!
KRRRKK
FOOOM
EEVEE!

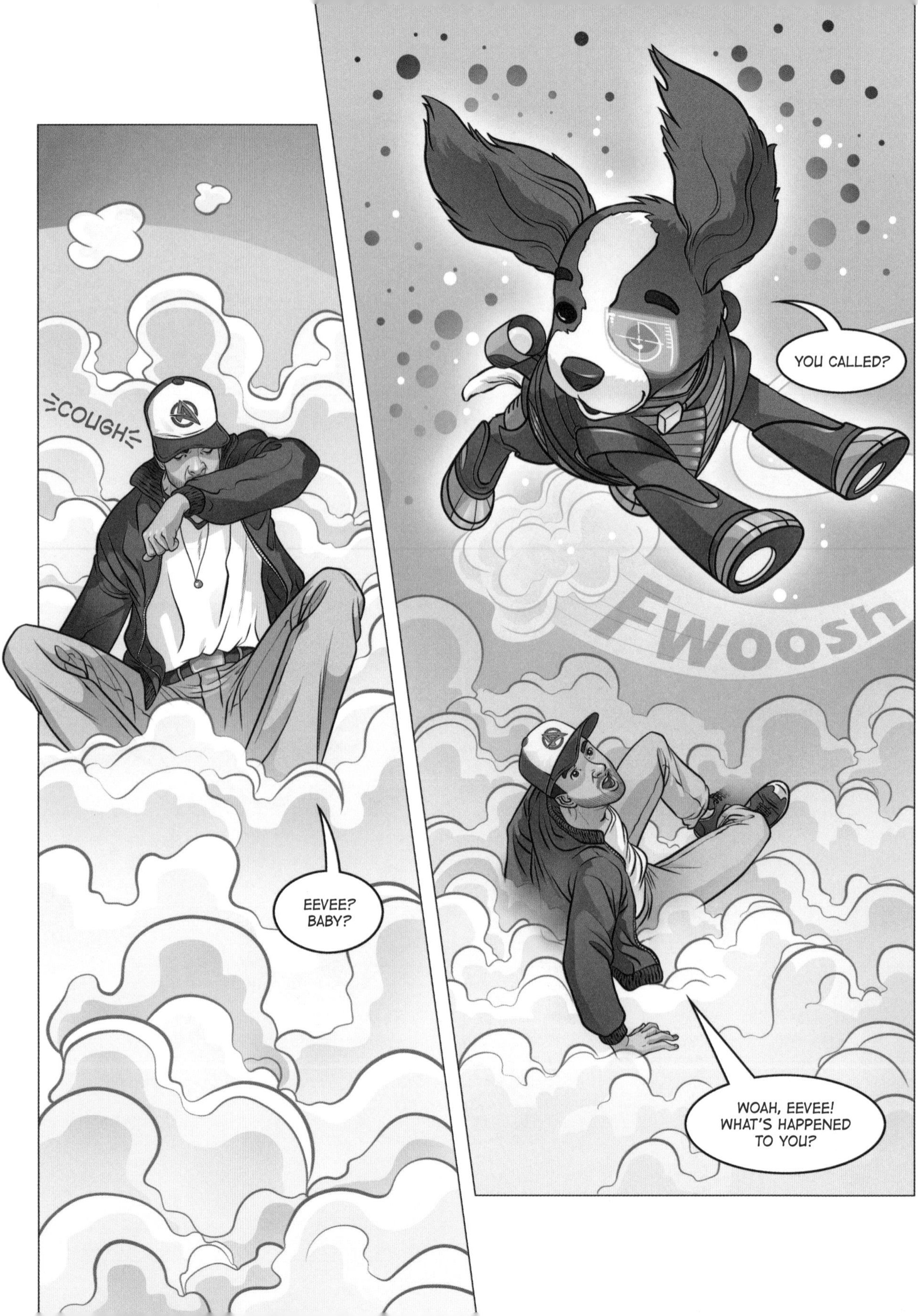
COUGH
EEVEE? BABY?
YOU CALLED?
FWOOSH
WOAH, EEVEE! WHAT'S HAPPENED TO YOU?

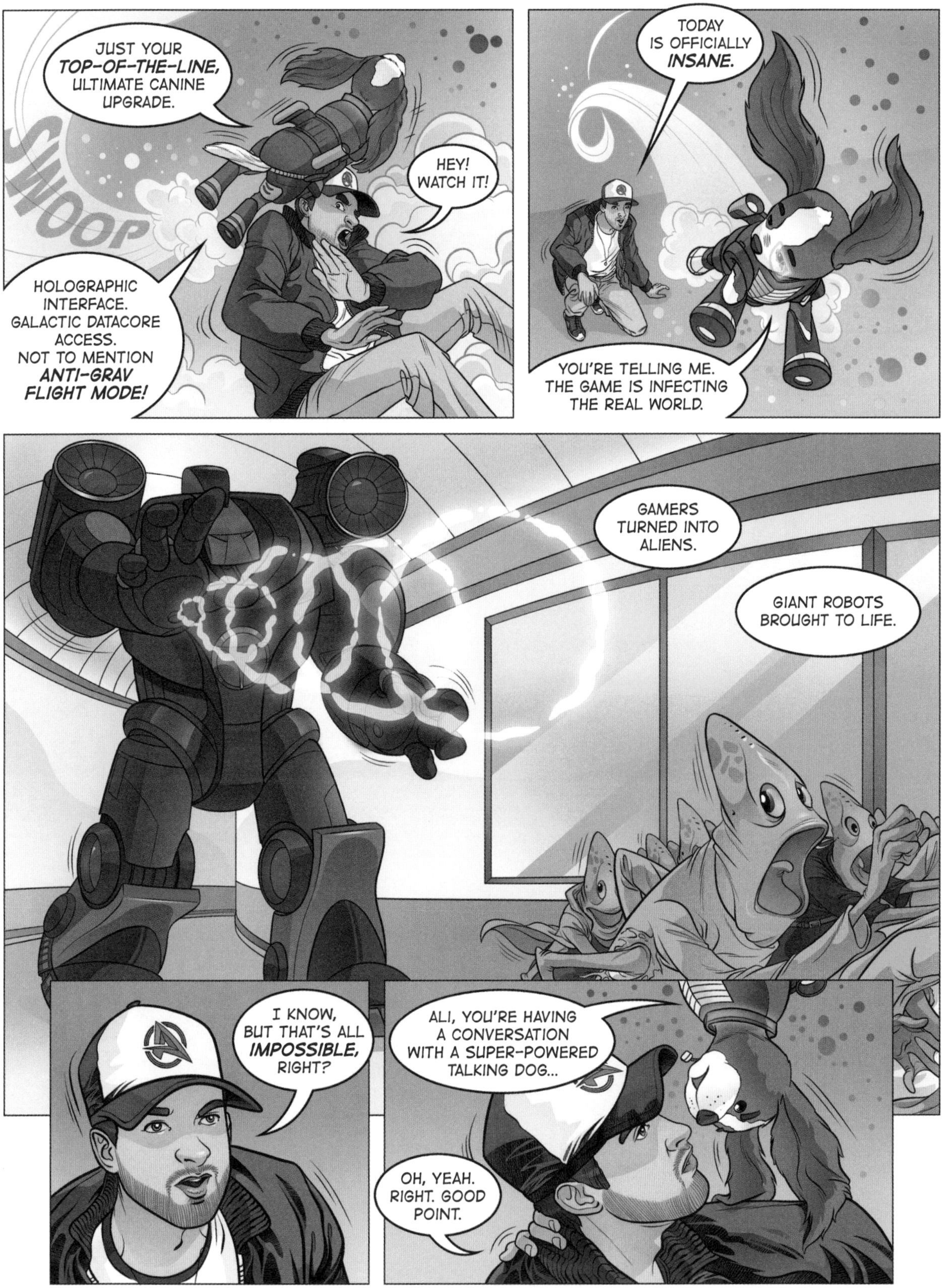
JUST YOUR *TOP-OF-THE-LINE,* ULTIMATE CANINE UPGRADE.
SWOOP
HEY! WATCH IT!
HOLOGRAPHIC INTERFACE. GALACTIC DATACORE ACCESS. NOT TO MENTION *ANTI-GRAV FLIGHT MODE!*
TODAY IS OFFICIALLY *INSANE.*
YOU'RE TELLING ME. THE GAME IS INFECTING THE REAL WORLD.
GAMERS TURNED INTO ALIENS.
GIANT ROBOTS BROUGHT TO LIFE.
I KNOW, BUT THAT'S ALL *IMPOSSIBLE,* RIGHT?
ALI, YOU'RE HAVING A CONVERSATION WITH A SUPER-POWERED TALKING DOG...
OH, YEAH. RIGHT. GOOD POINT.

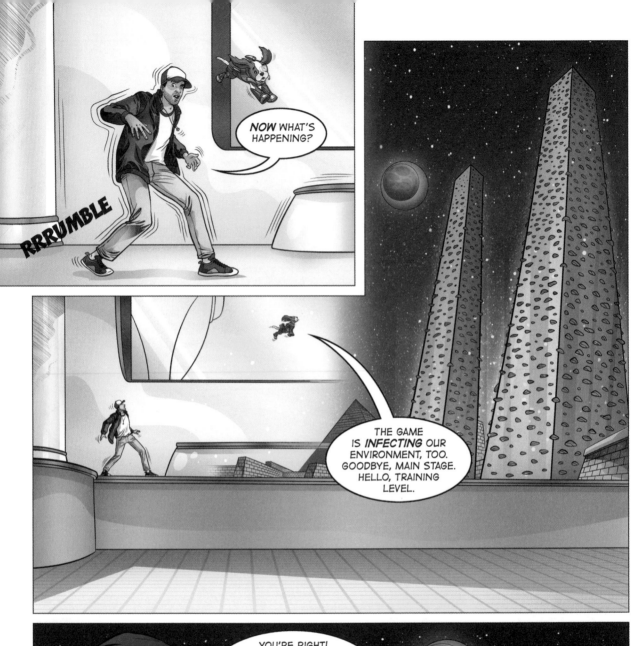

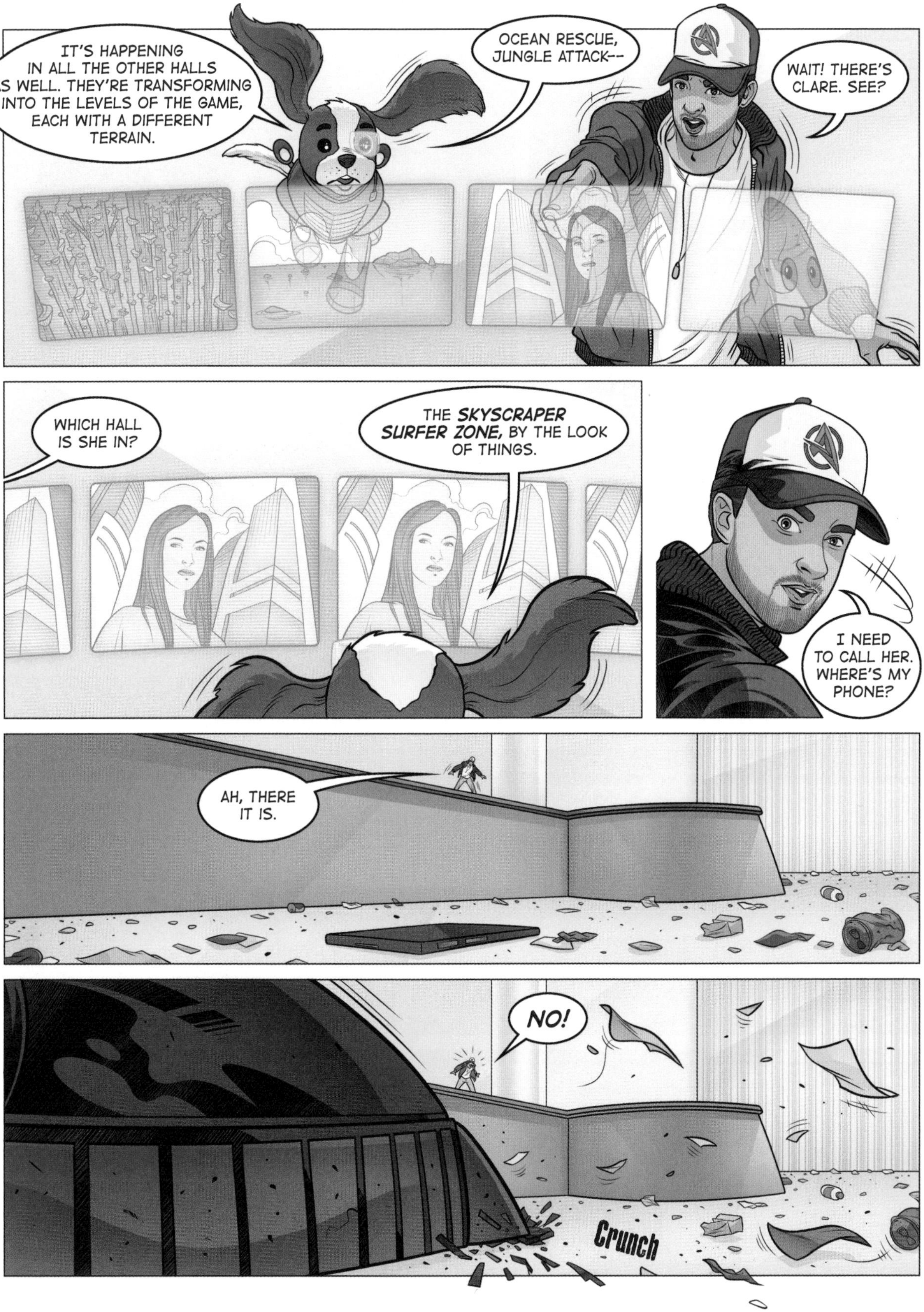
IT'S HAPPENING IN ALL THE OTHER HALLS AS WELL. THEY'RE TRANSFORMING INTO THE LEVELS OF THE GAME, EACH WITH A DIFFERENT TERRAIN.
OCEAN RESCUE, JUNGLE ATTACK--
WAIT! THERE'S CLARE. SEE?
WHICH HALL IS SHE IN?
THE SKYSCRAPER SURFER ZONE, BY THE LOOK OF THINGS.
I NEED TO CALL HER. WHERE'S MY PHONE?
AH, THERE IT IS.
NO!
Crunch

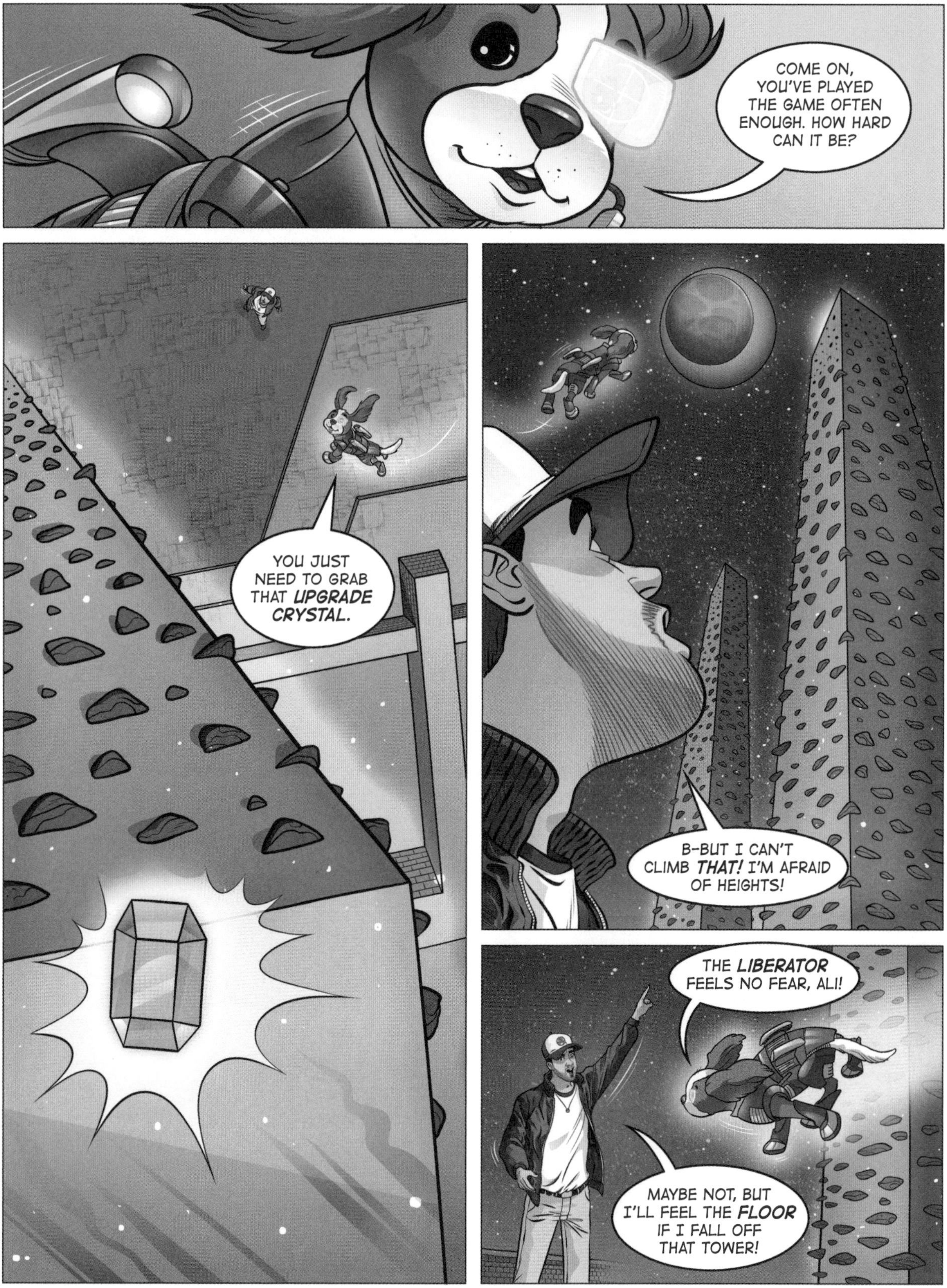

COME ON, YOU'VE PLAYED THE GAME OFTEN ENOUGH. HOW HARD CAN IT BE?
YOU JUST NEED TO GRAB THAT UPGRADE CRYSTAL.
B-BUT I CAN'T CLIMB THAT! I'M AFRAID OF HEIGHTS!
THE LIBERATOR FEELS NO FEAR, ALI!
MAYBE NOT, BUT I'LL FEEL THE FLOOR IF I FALL OFF THAT TOWER!

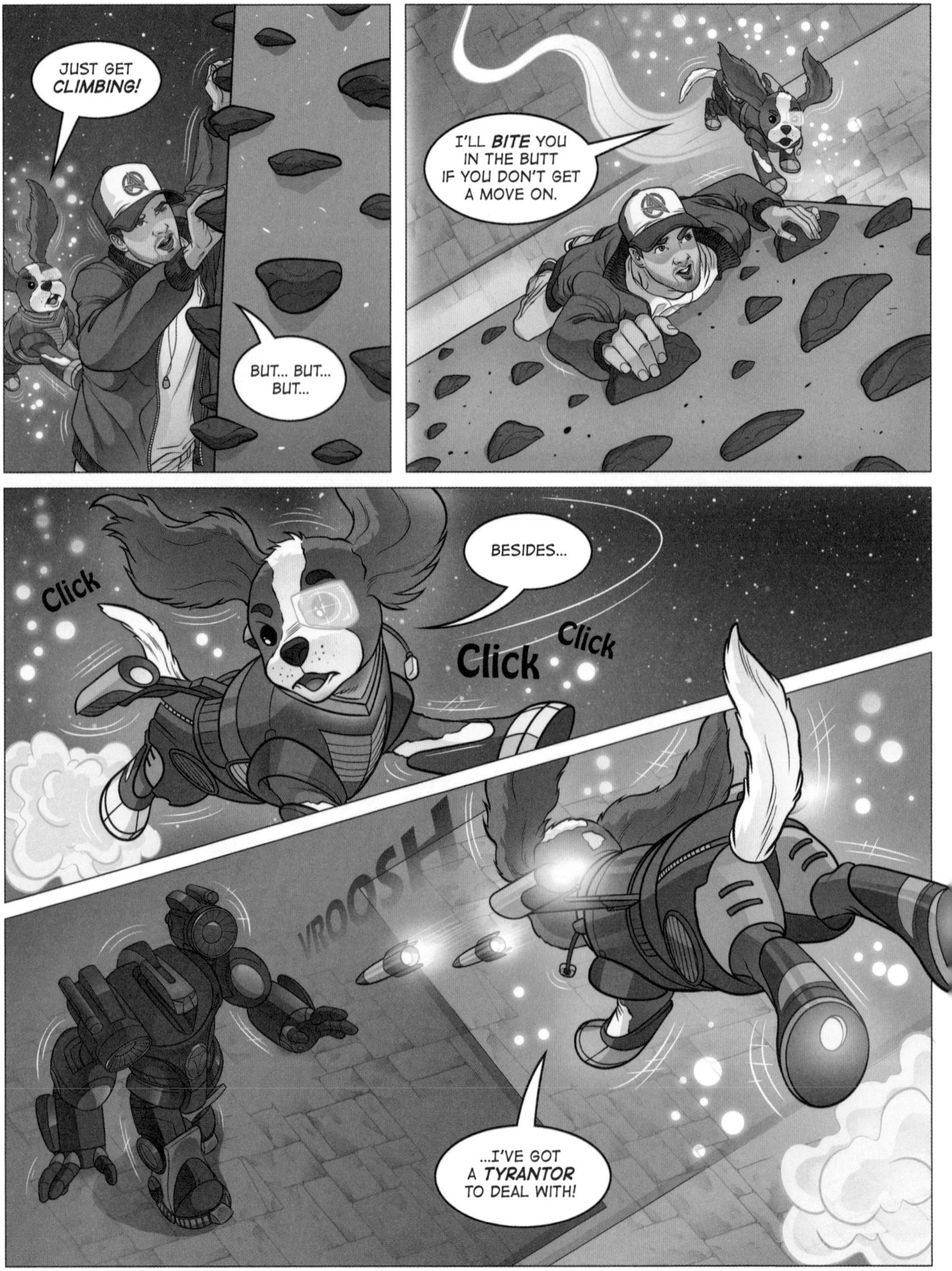
JUST GET *CLIMBING!*
BUT... BUT... BUT...
I'LL *BITE* YOU IN THE BUTT IF YOU DON'T GET A MOVE ON.
BESIDES...
Click
Click
Click
VROOSH
...I'VE GOT A *TYRANTOR* TO DEAL WITH!

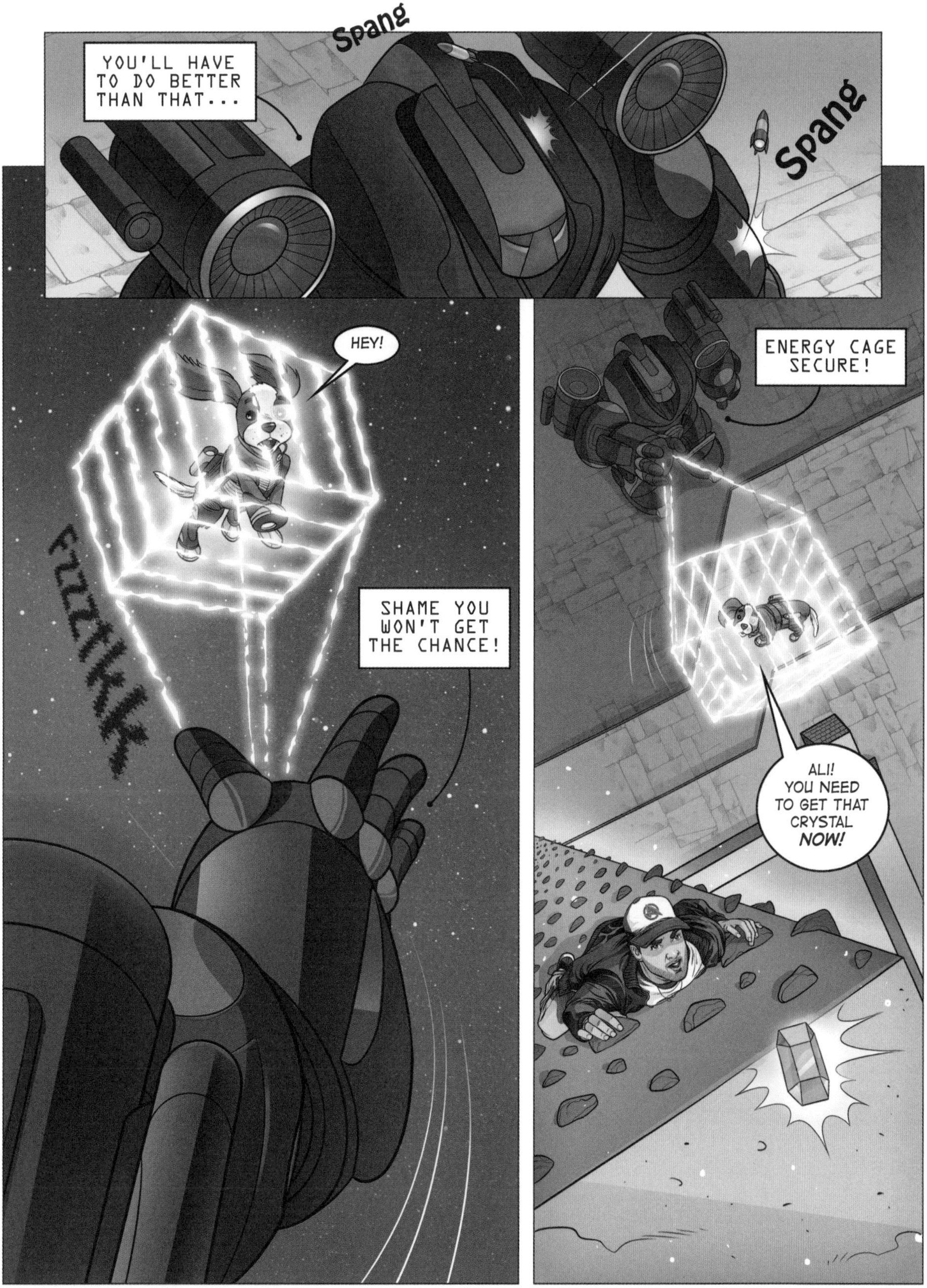
Spang
YOU'LL HAVE TO DO BETTER THAN THAT...
Spang
HEY!
FZZZTKKK
SHAME YOU WON'T GET THE CHANCE!
ENERGY CAGE SECURE!
ALI! YOU NEED TO GET THAT CRYSTAL NOW!

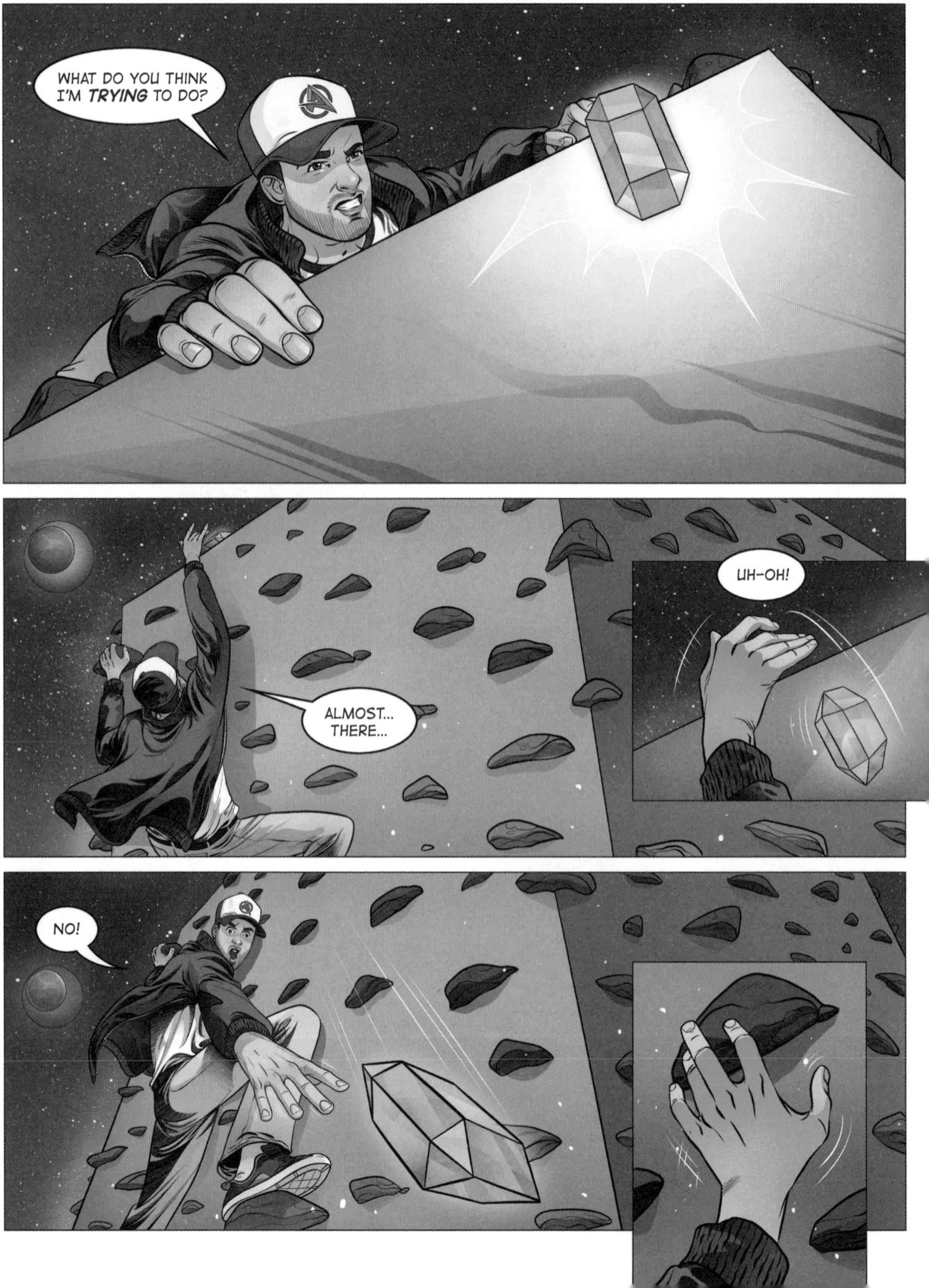
WHAT DO YOU THINK I'M *TRYING* TO DO?
ALMOST... THERE...
UH-OH!
NO!

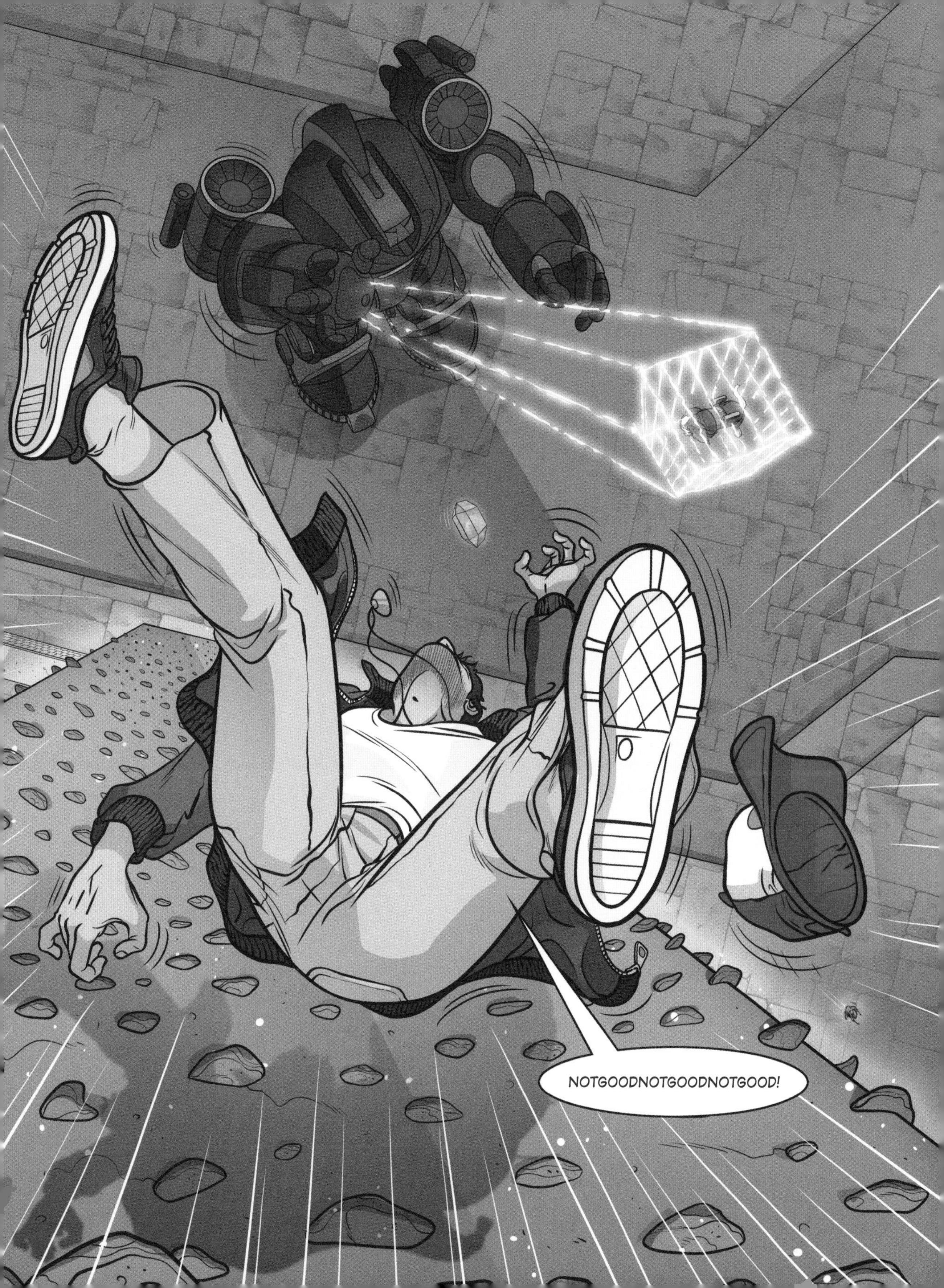
NOTGOODNOTGOODNOTGOOD!

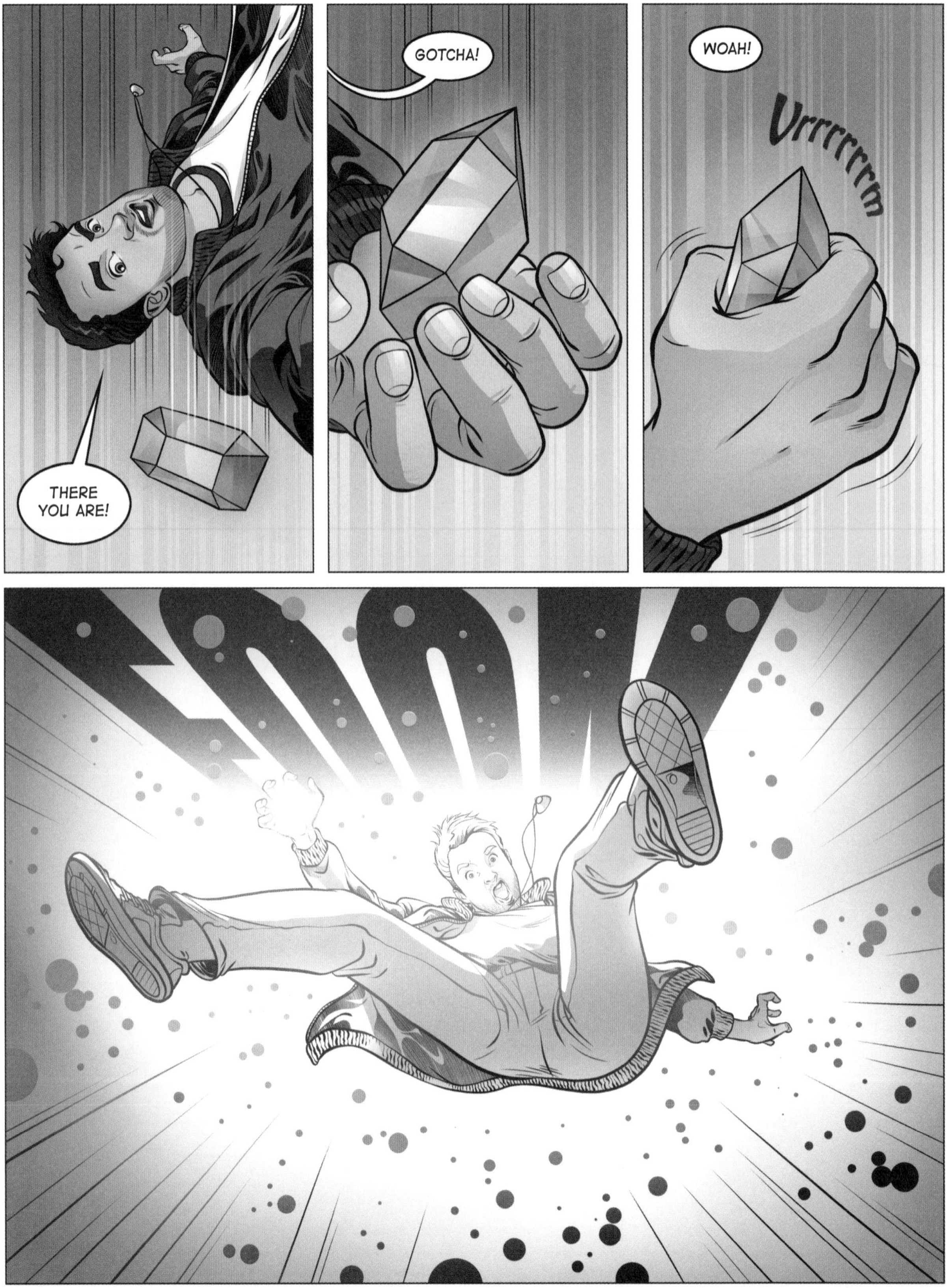
THERE YOU ARE!
GOTCHA!
WOAH!
Urrrrrrm

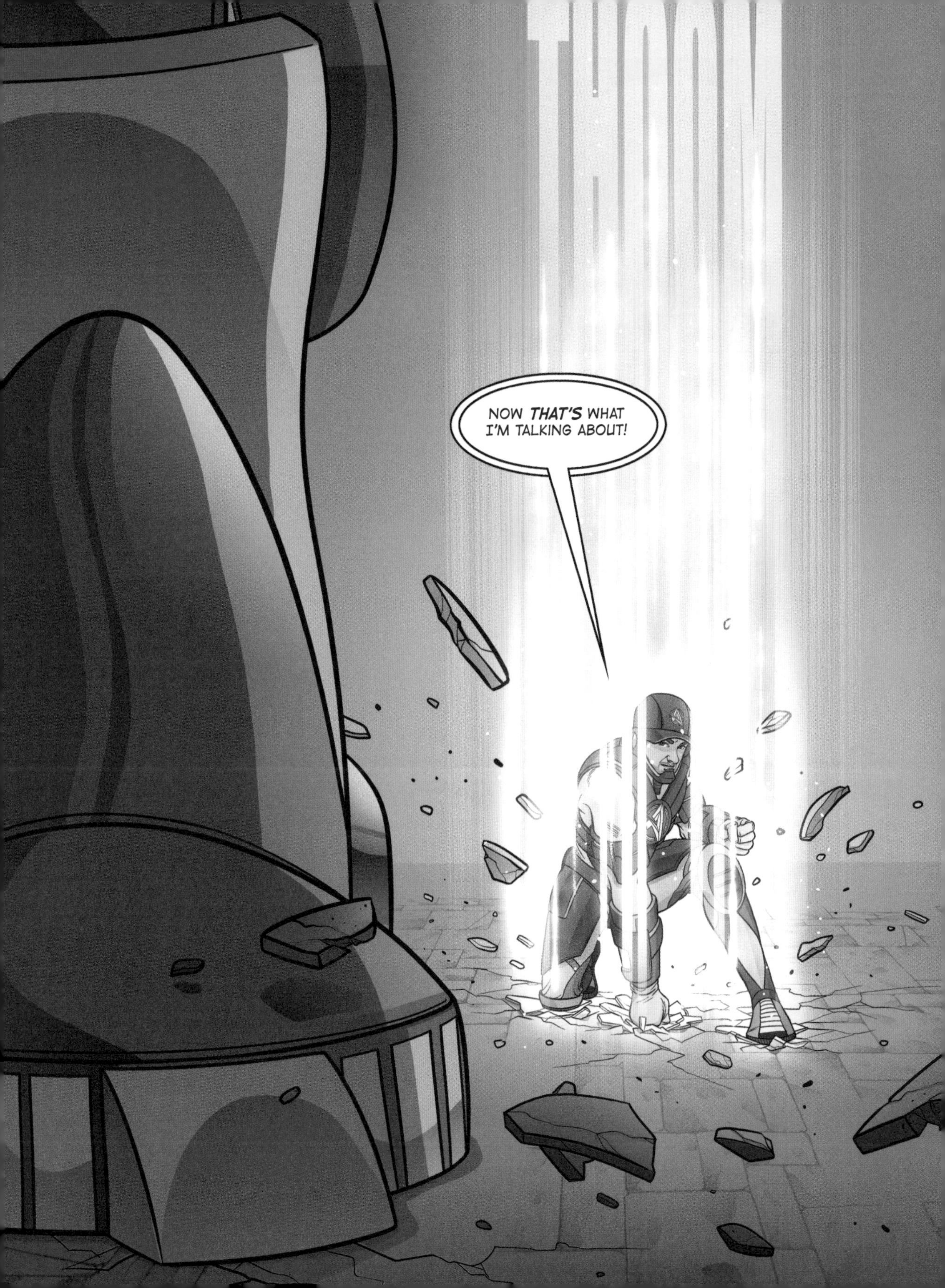
THOOM
NOW THAT'S WHAT I'M TALKING ABOUT!

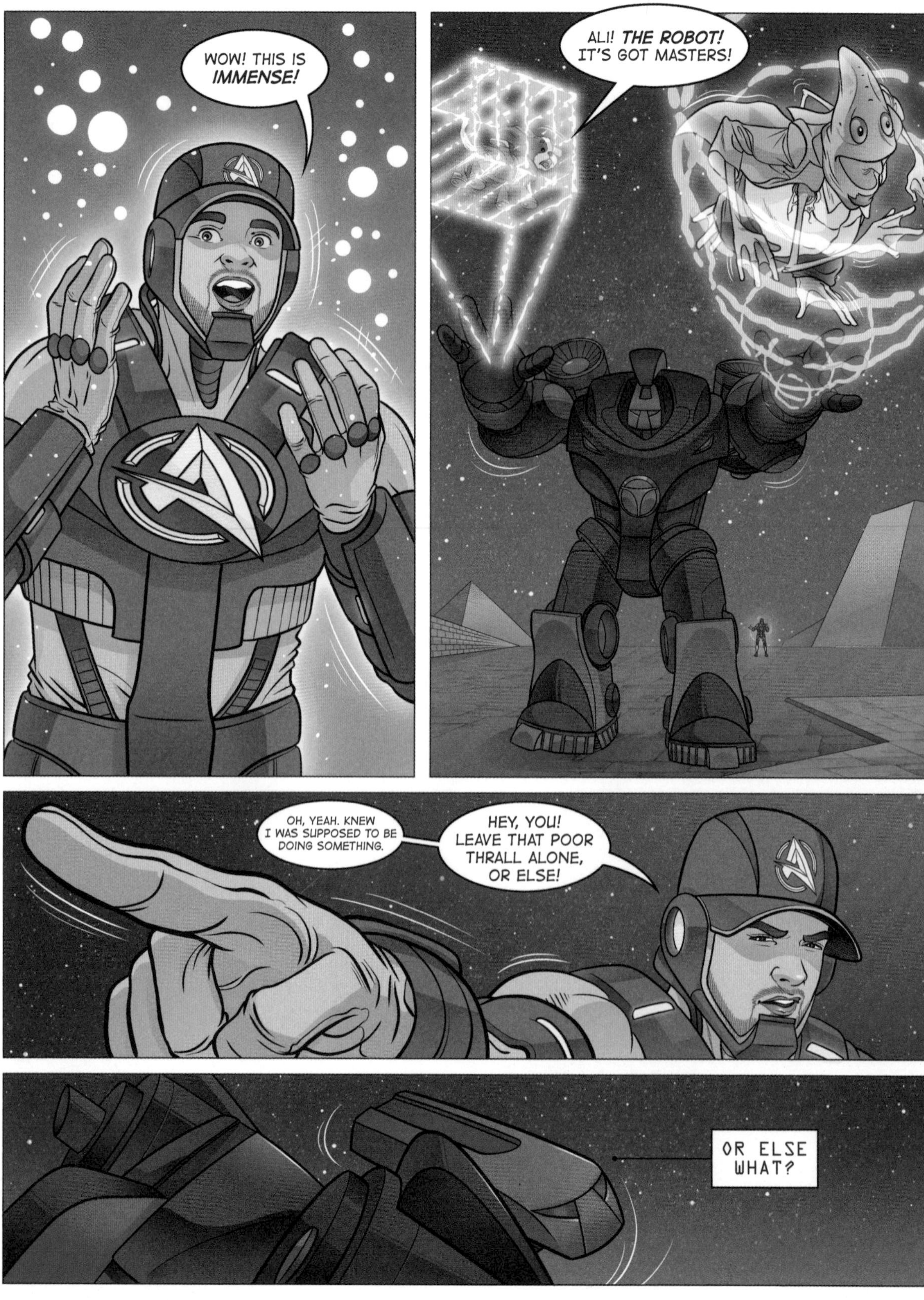
WOW! THIS IS *IMMENSE!*
ALI! *THE ROBOT!* IT'S GOT MASTERS!
OH, YEAH. KNEW I WAS SUPPOSED TO BE DOING SOMETHING.
HEY, YOU! LEAVE THAT POOR THRALL ALONE, OR ELSE!
OR ELSE WHAT?

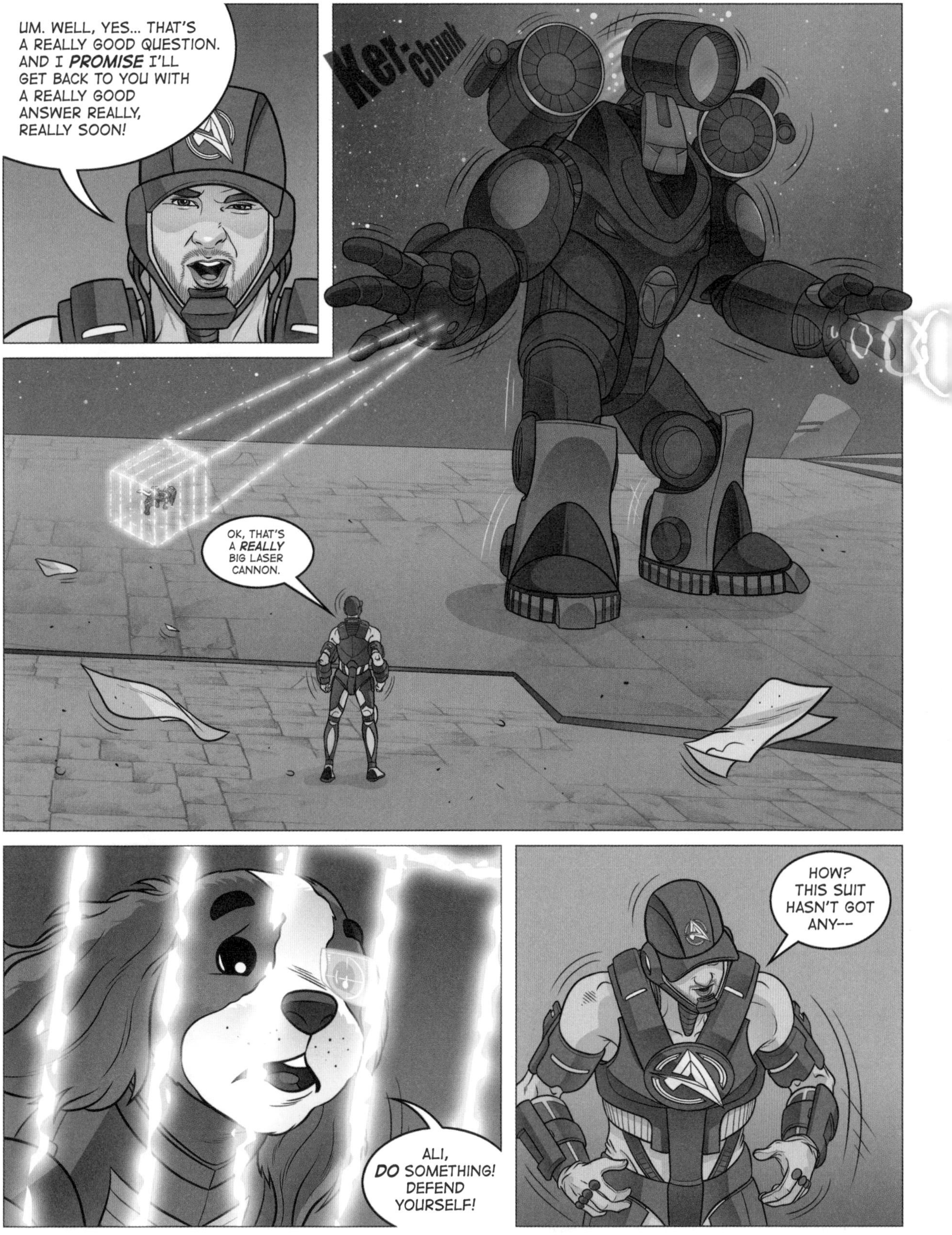
UM. WELL, YES... THAT'S A REALLY GOOD QUESTION. AND I **PROMISE** I'LL GET BACK TO YOU WITH A REALLY GOOD ANSWER REALLY, REALLY SOON!
Ker-chunk
OK, THAT'S A ***REALLY*** BIG LASER CANNON.
ALI, **DO** SOMETHING! DEFEND YOURSELF!
HOW? THIS SUIT HASN'T GOT ANY--

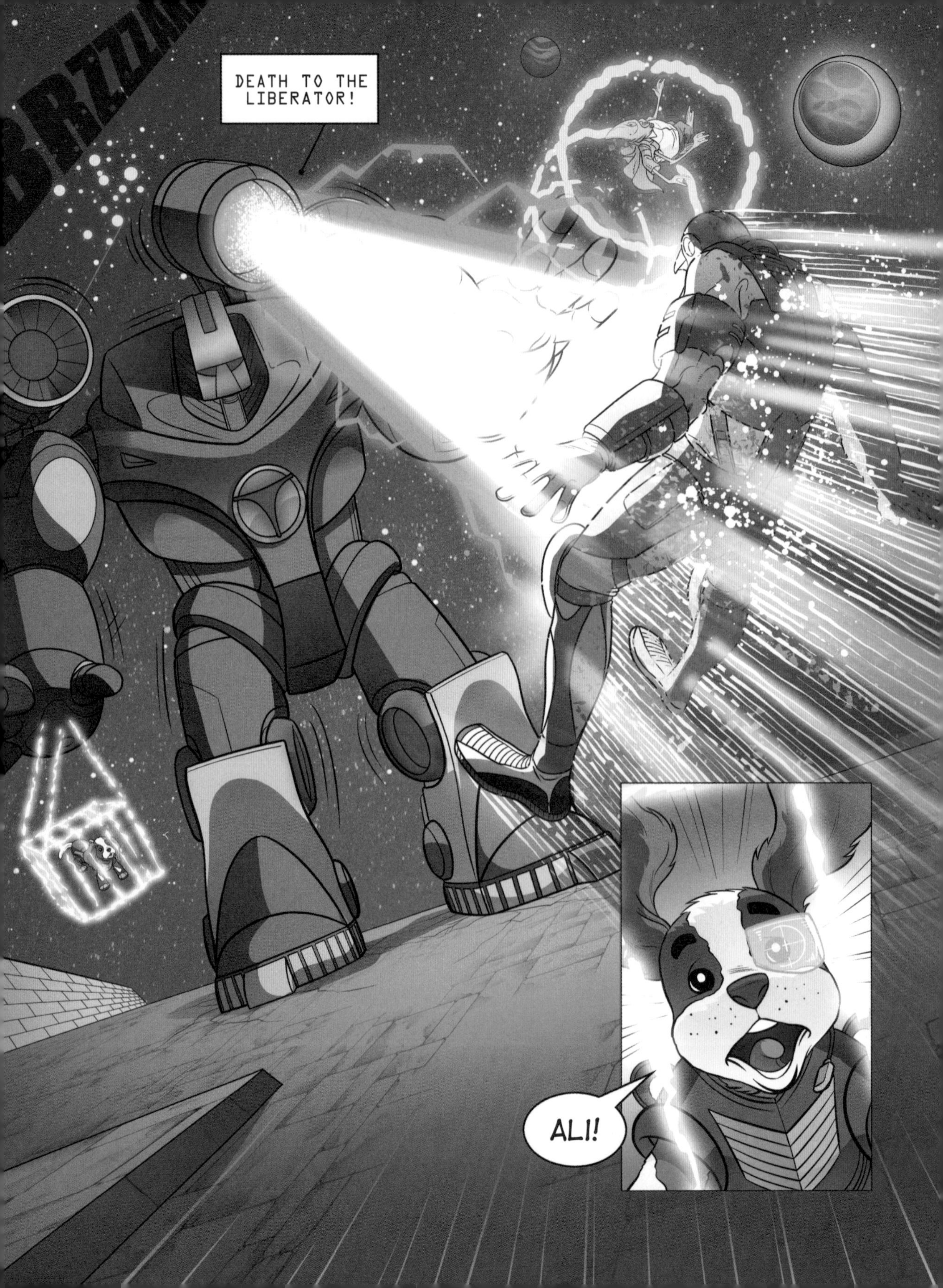
DEATH TO THE LIBERATOR!
ALI!

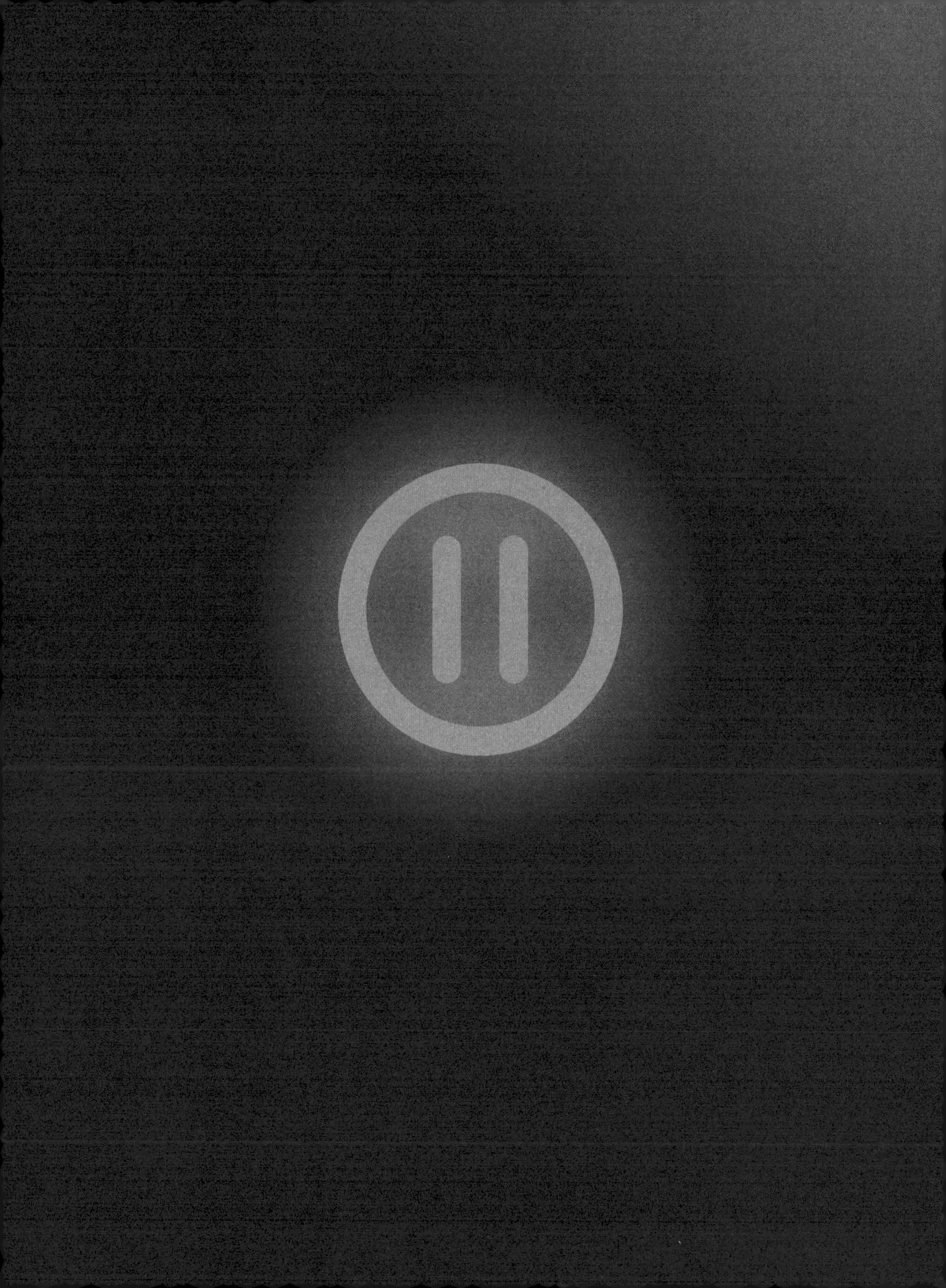

LEVEL THREE

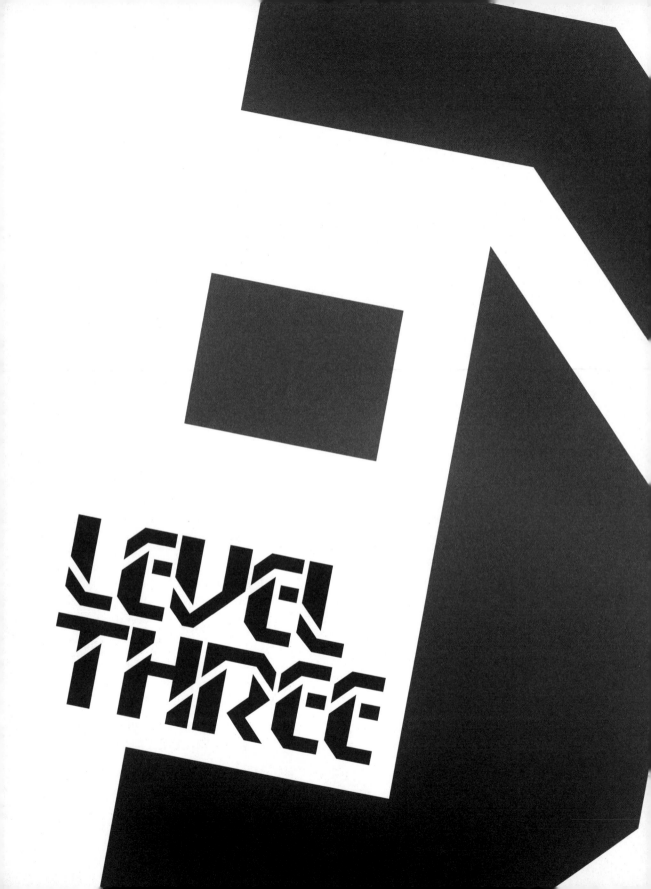

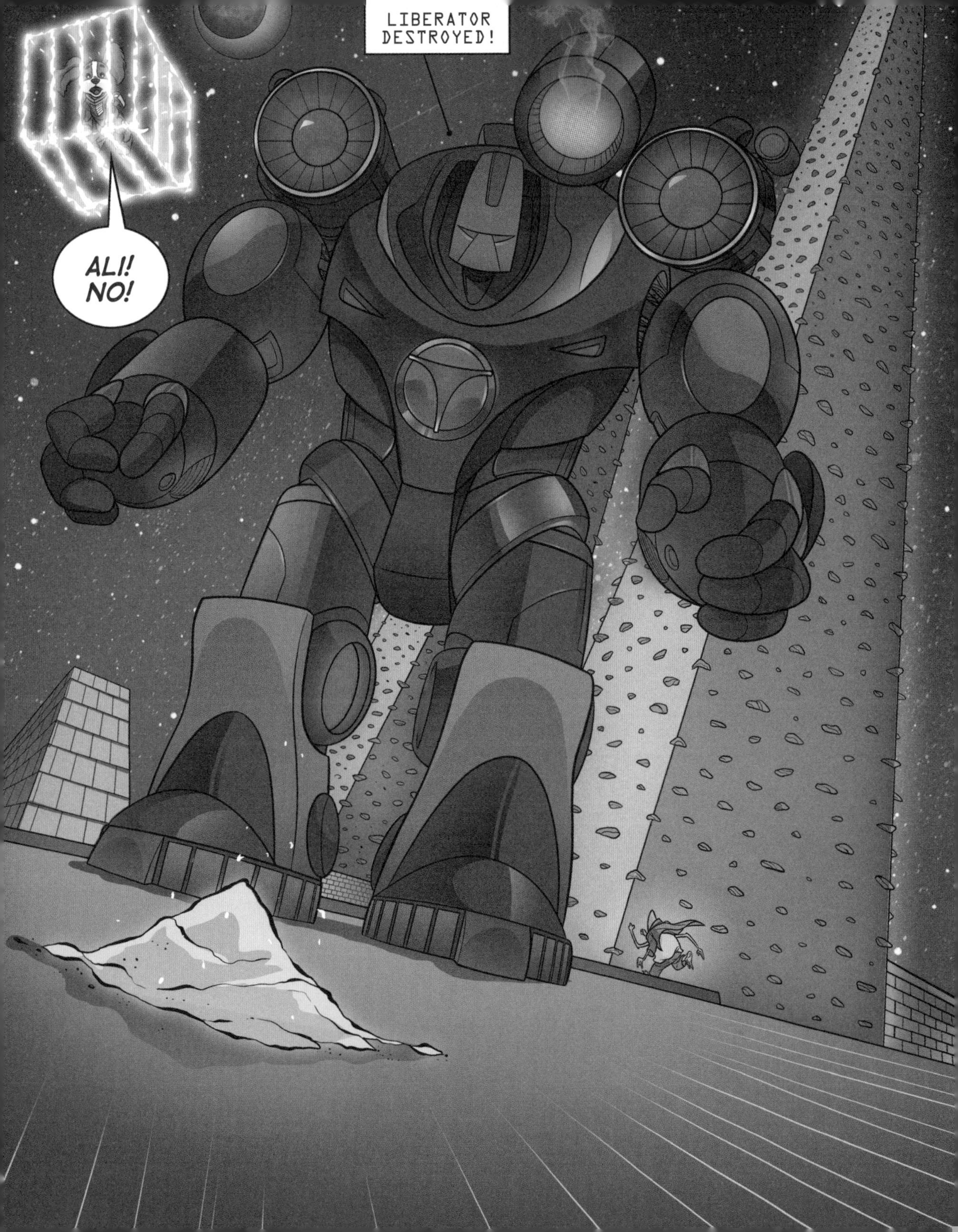
LIBERATOR DESTROYED!
ALI! NO!

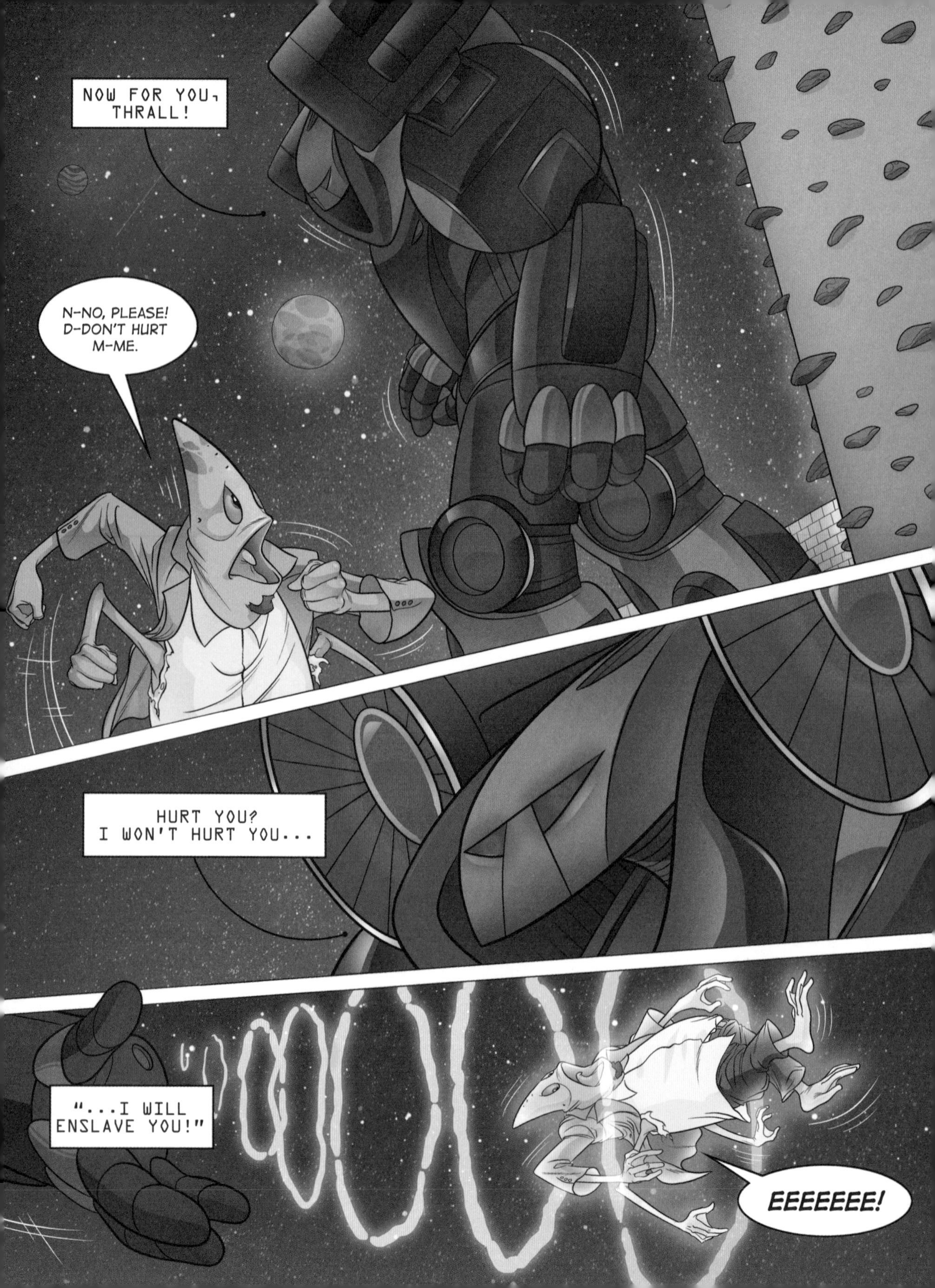
NOW FOR YOU, THRALL!
N-NO, PLEASE! D-DON'T HURT M-ME.
HURT YOU? I WON'T HURT YOU...
"...I WILL ENSLAVE YOU!"
EEEEEEE!

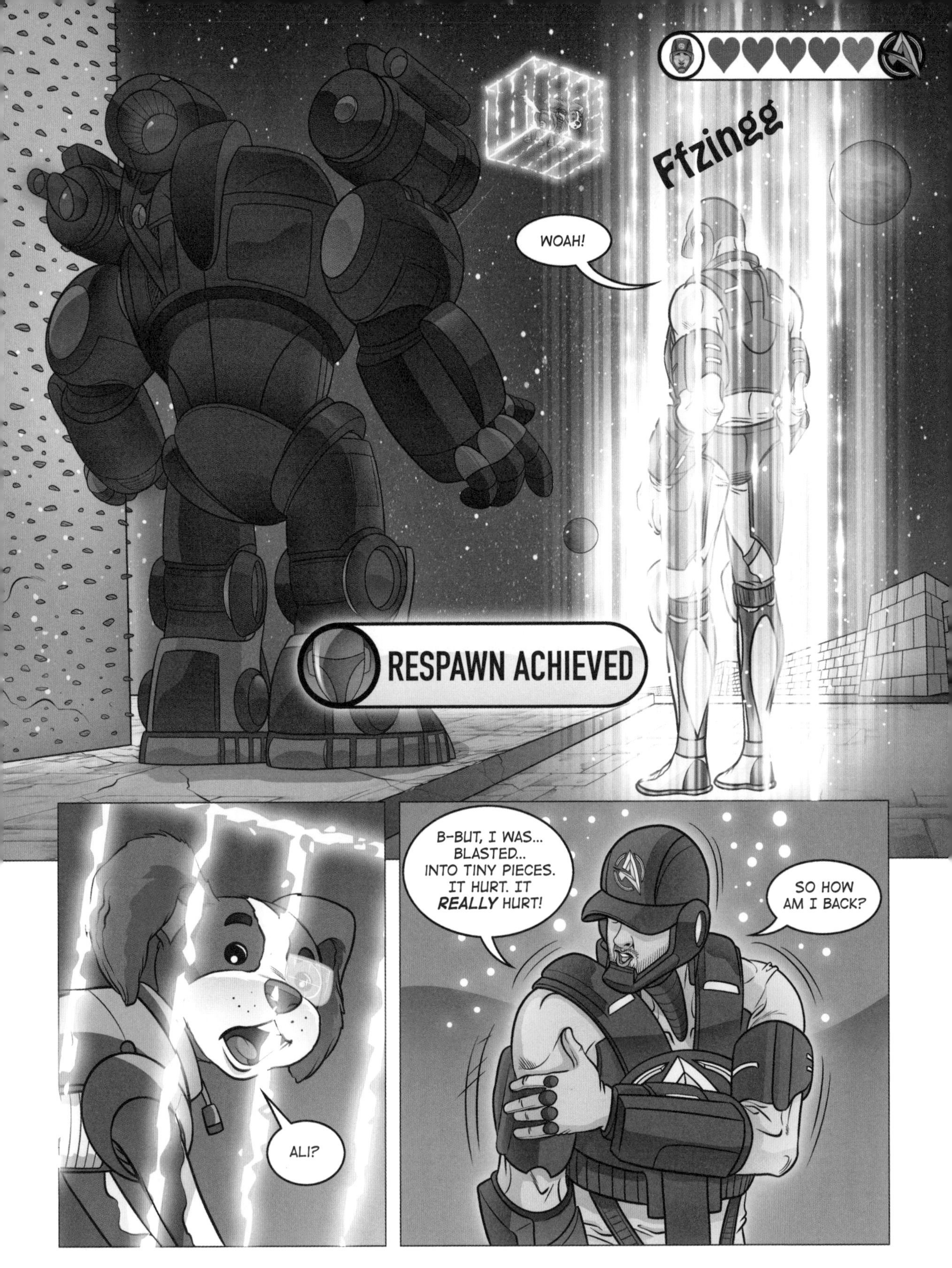
Ffzingg
WOAH!
RESPAWN ACHIEVED
ALI?
B-BUT, I WAS... BLASTED... INTO TINY PIECES. IT HURT. IT *REALLY* HURT!
SO HOW AM I BACK?

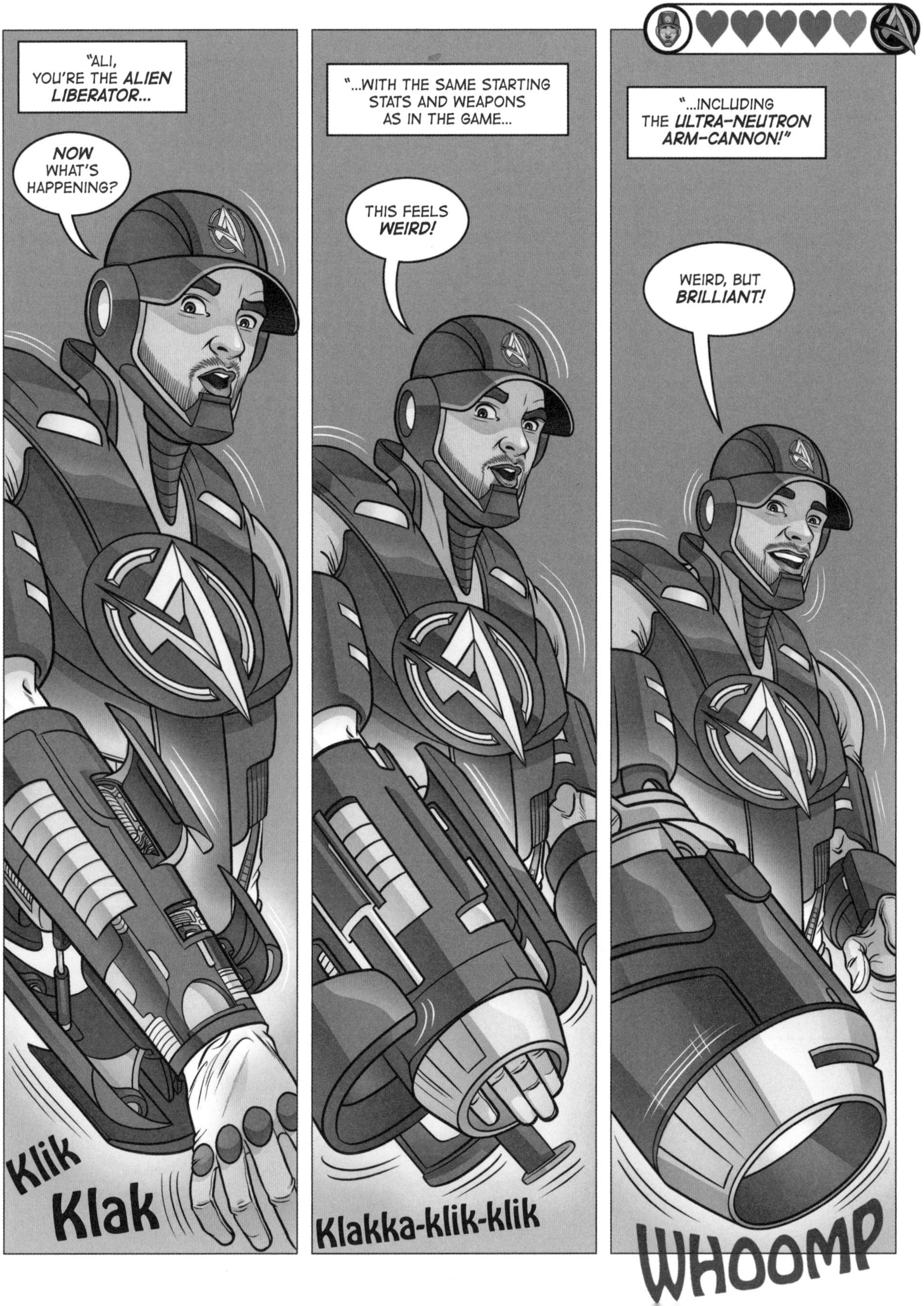
"ALI, YOU'RE THE *ALIEN LIBERATOR*...
NOW WHAT'S HAPPENING?
Klik
Klak
"...WITH THE SAME STARTING STATS AND WEAPONS AS IN THE GAME...
THIS FEELS *WEIRD!*
Klakka-klik-klik
"...INCLUDING THE *ULTRA-NEUTRON ARM-CANNON!*"
WEIRD, BUT *BRILLIANT!*
WHOOMP

HEY! TIN MAN! I'VE GOT SOMETHING FOR YOU!
YOU HAVE?

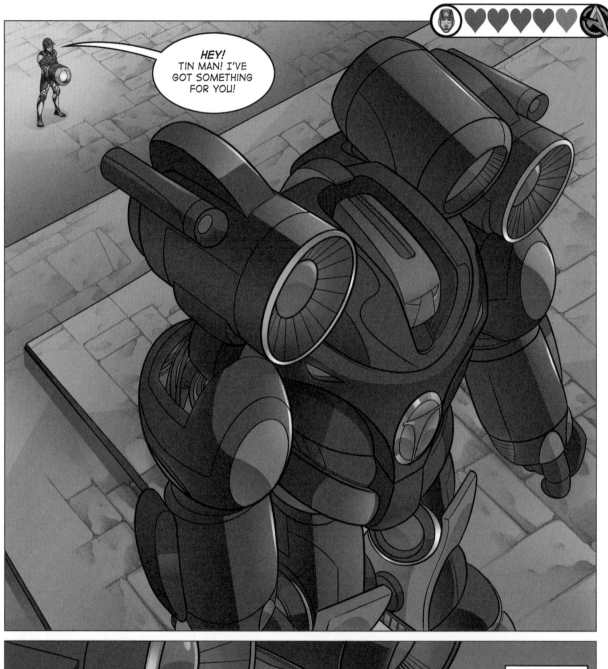

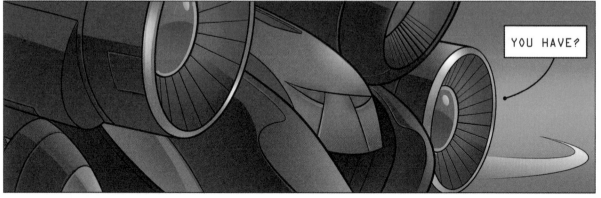

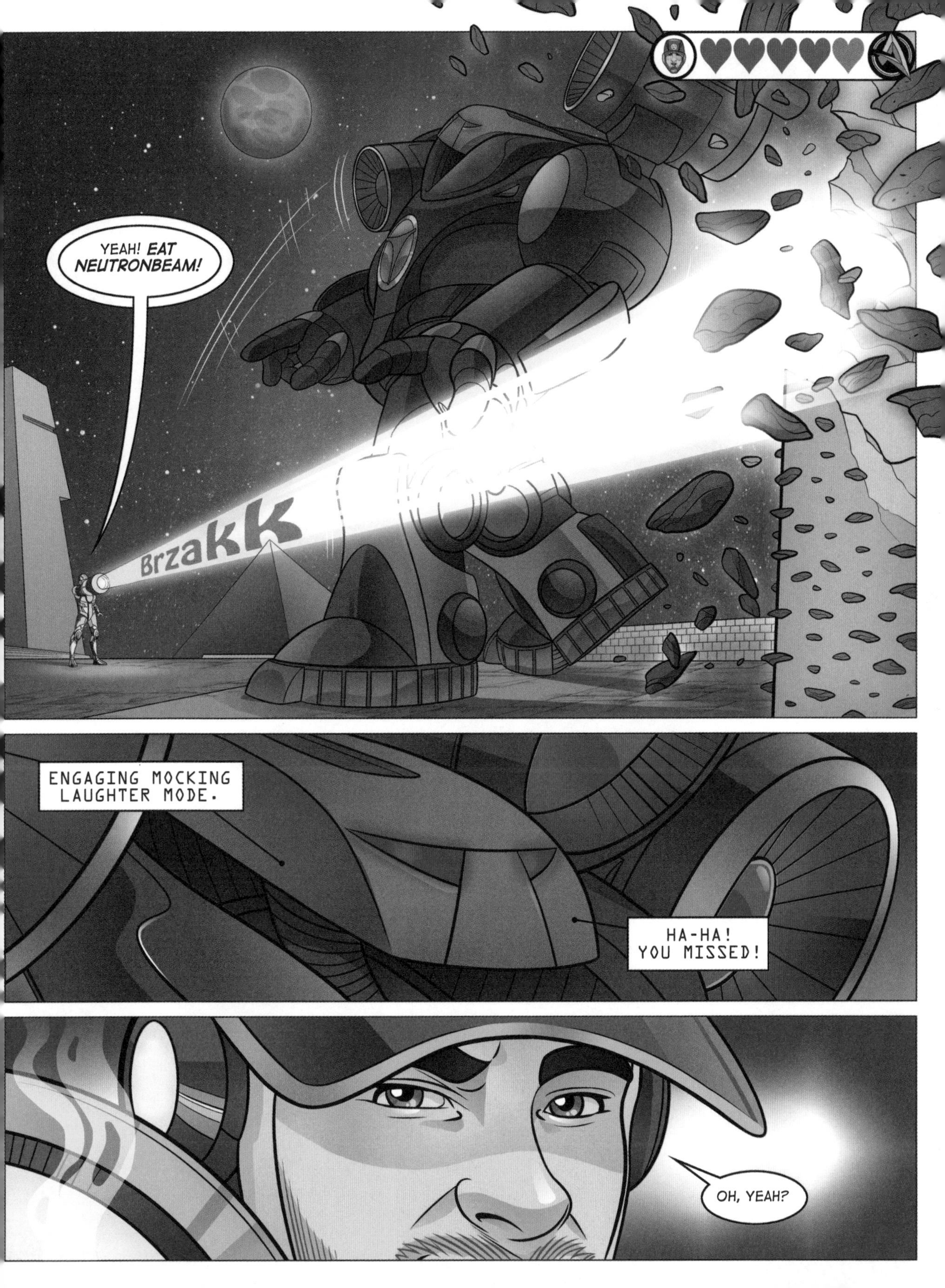
YEAH! EAT NEUTRONBEAM!
Brzakk
ENGAGING MOCKING LAUGHTER MODE.
HA-HA! YOU MISSED!
OH, YEAH?

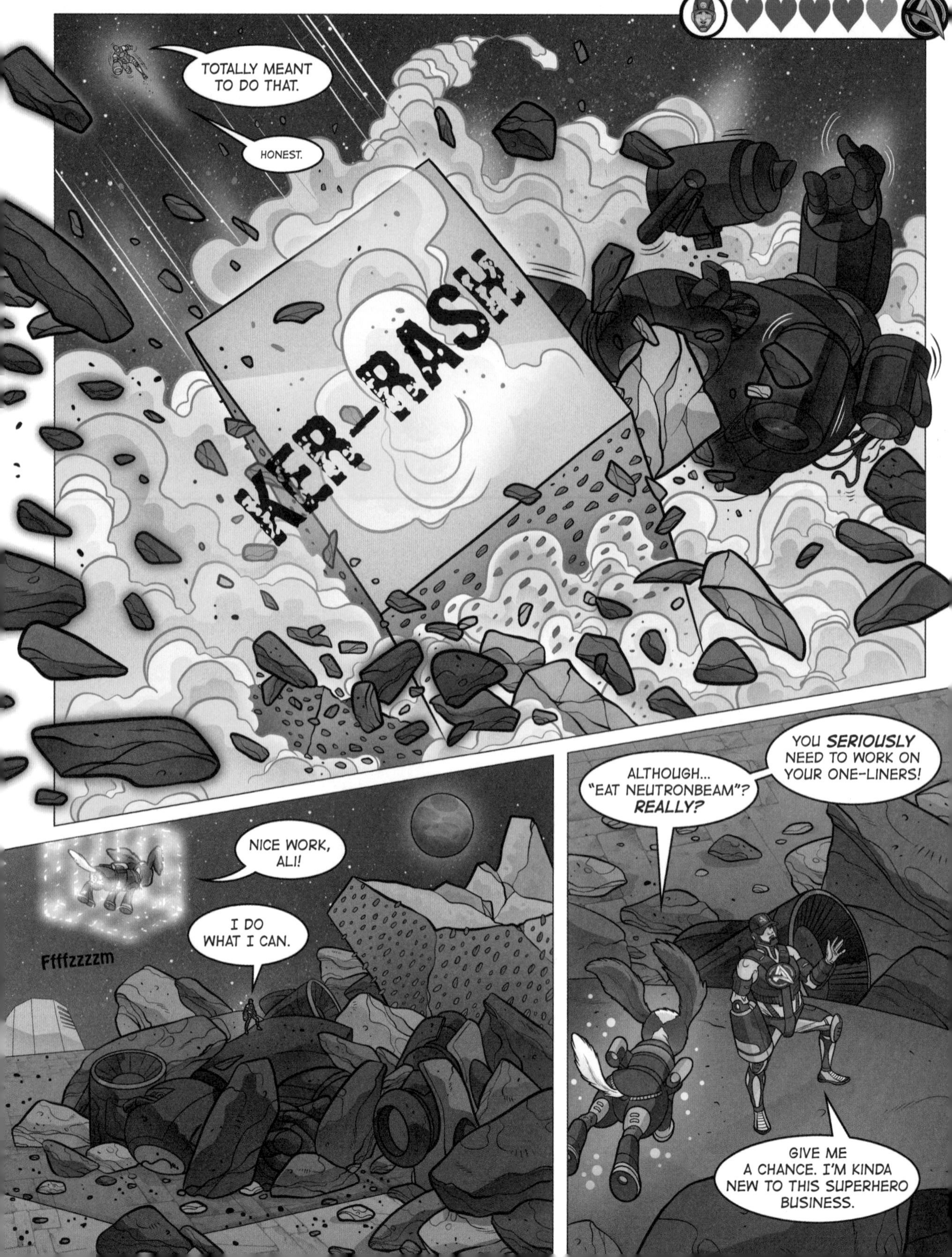
TOTALLY MEANT TO DO THAT.
HONEST.
KER-RASH
NICE WORK, ALI!
I DO WHAT I CAN.
Ffffzzzzm
ALTHOUGH... "EAT NEUTRONBEAM"? REALLY?
YOU SERIOUSLY NEED TO WORK ON YOUR ONE-LINERS!
GIVE ME A CHANCE. I'M KINDA NEW TO THIS SUPERHERO BUSINESS.

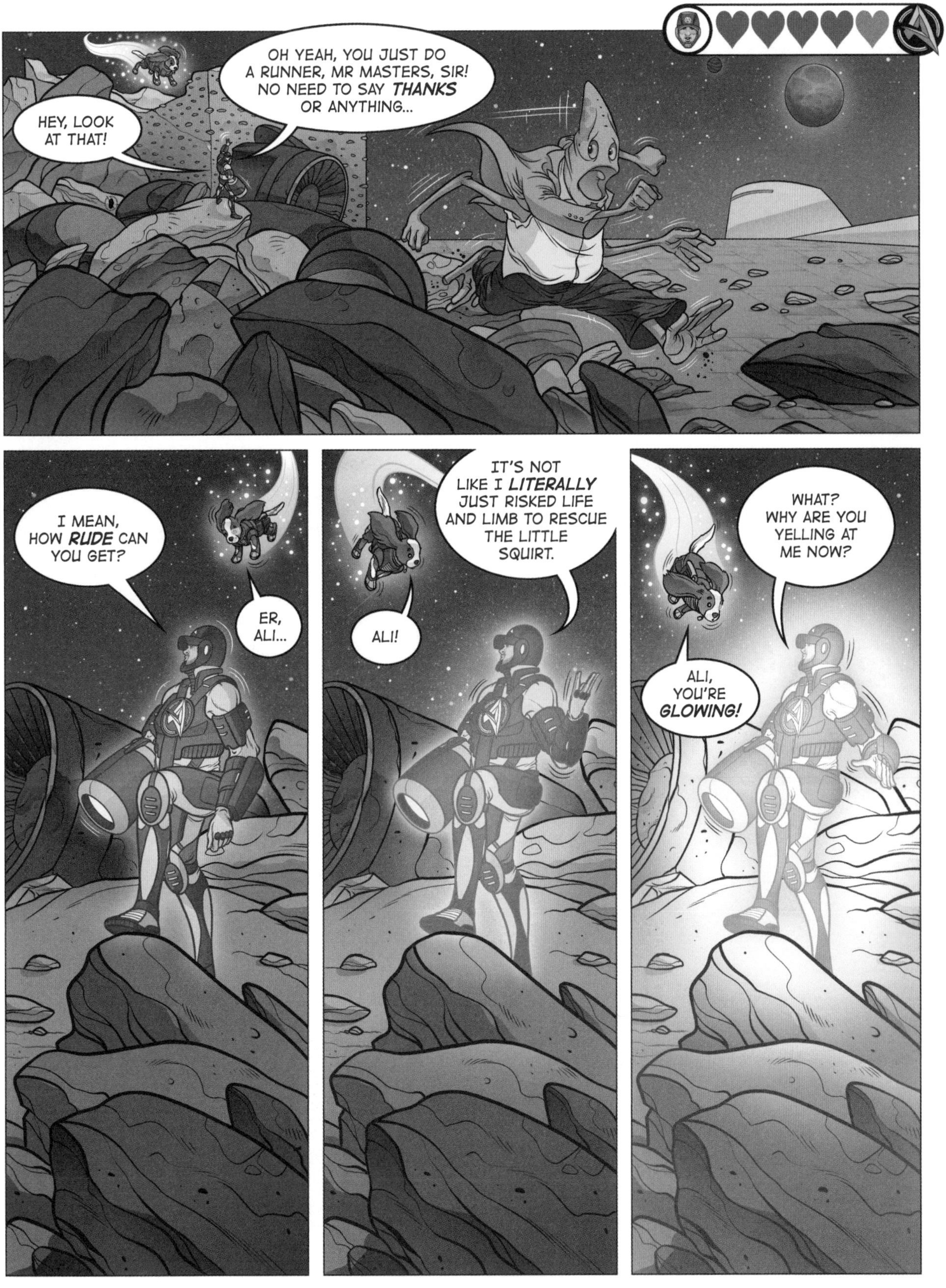
HEY, LOOK AT THAT!
OH YEAH, YOU JUST DO A RUNNER, MR MASTERS, SIR! NO NEED TO SAY THANKS OR ANYTHING...
I MEAN, HOW RUDE CAN YOU GET?
ER, ALI...
IT'S NOT LIKE I LITERALLY JUST RISKED LIFE AND LIMB TO RESCUE THE LITTLE SQUIRT.
ALI!
WHAT? WHY ARE YOU YELLING AT ME NOW?
ALI, YOU'RE GLOWING!

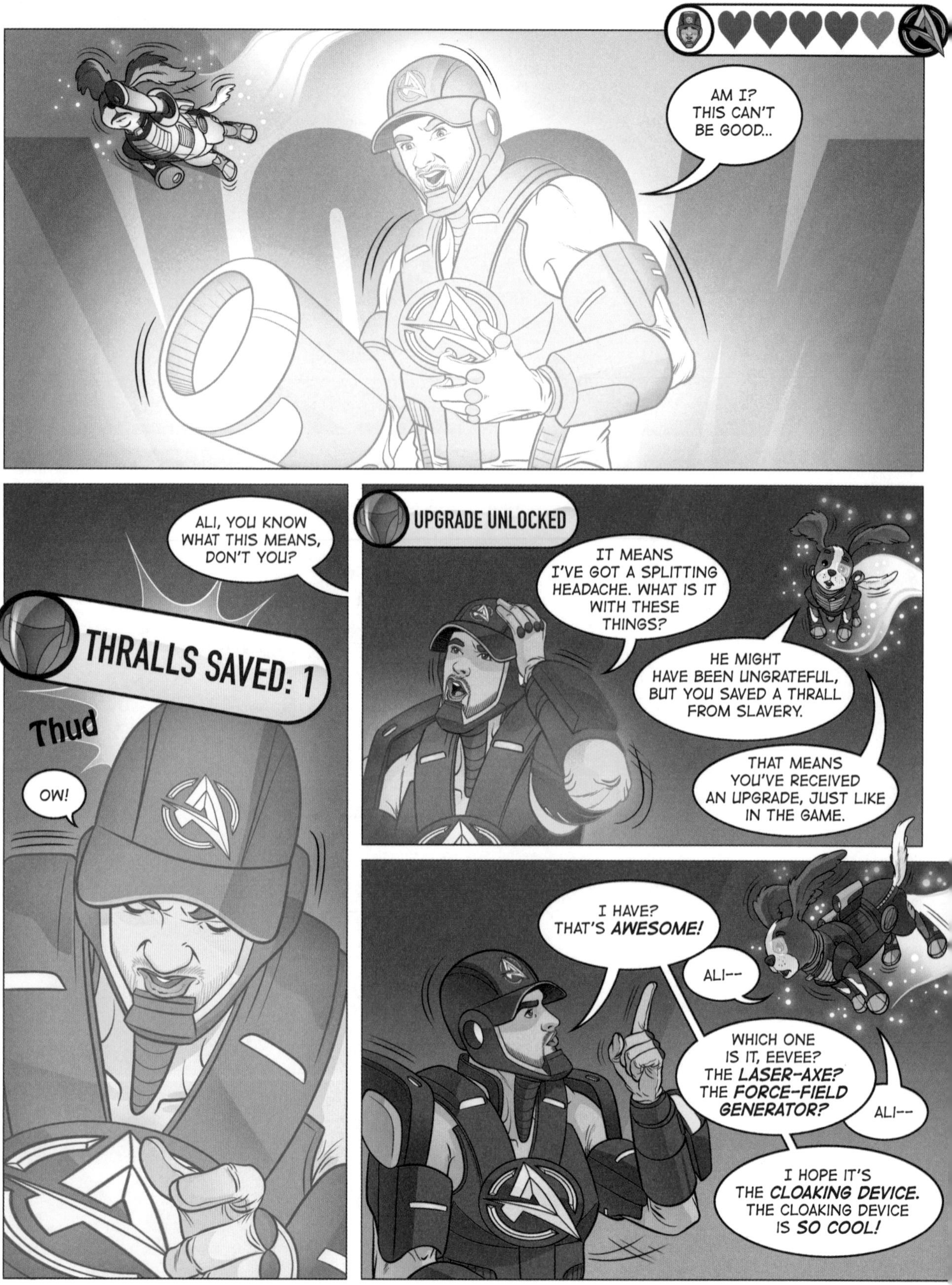

AM I? THIS CAN'T BE GOOD...
ALI, YOU KNOW WHAT THIS MEANS, DON'T YOU?
THRALLS SAVED: 1
Thud
OW!
UPGRADE UNLOCKED
IT MEANS I'VE GOT A SPLITTING HEADACHE. WHAT IS IT WITH THESE THINGS?
HE MIGHT HAVE BEEN UNGRATEFUL, BUT YOU SAVED A THRALL FROM SLAVERY.
THAT MEANS YOU'VE RECEIVED AN UPGRADE, JUST LIKE IN THE GAME.
I HAVE? THAT'S AWESOME!
ALI--
WHICH ONE IS IT, EEVEE? THE LASER-AXE? THE FORCE-FIELD GENERATOR?
ALI--
I HOPE IT'S THE CLOAKING DEVICE. THE CLOAKING DEVICE IS SO COOL!

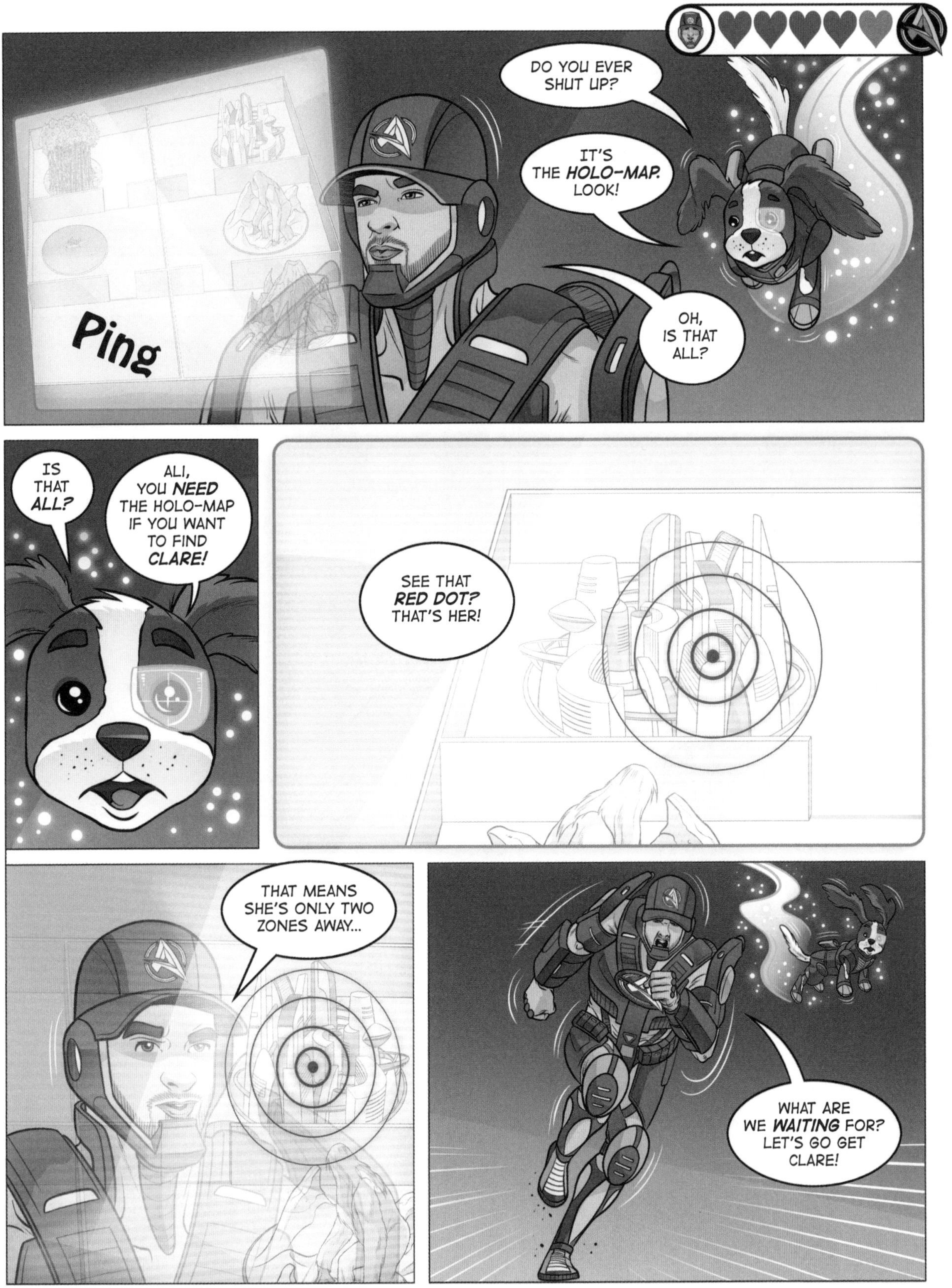
DO YOU EVER SHUT UP?
IT'S THE HOLO-MAP. LOOK!
Ping
OH, IS THAT ALL?
IS THAT ALL?
ALI, YOU NEED THE HOLO-MAP IF YOU WANT TO FIND CLARE!
SEE THAT RED DOT? THAT'S HER!
THAT MEANS SHE'S ONLY TWO ZONES AWAY...
WHAT ARE WE WAITING FOR? LET'S GO GET CLARE!

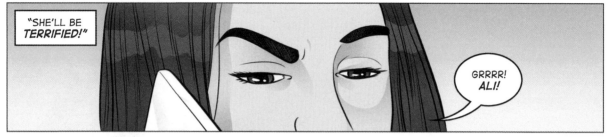

"SHE'LL BE *TERRIFIED!*"

GRRRR! *ALI!*

SKYSCRAPER SURFER ZONE

THIS IS JUST *TYPICAL!* WHY ISN'T HE ANSWERING HIS PHONE?

FORGET ABOUT YOUR PHONE...

"...THAT'S THE *LAST* OF YOUR WORRIES. THOSE TYRANTORS ARE GOING TO CATCH US ALL."

WE'LL SEE ABOUT THAT!

COME ON, EVERYONE! THIS WAY...

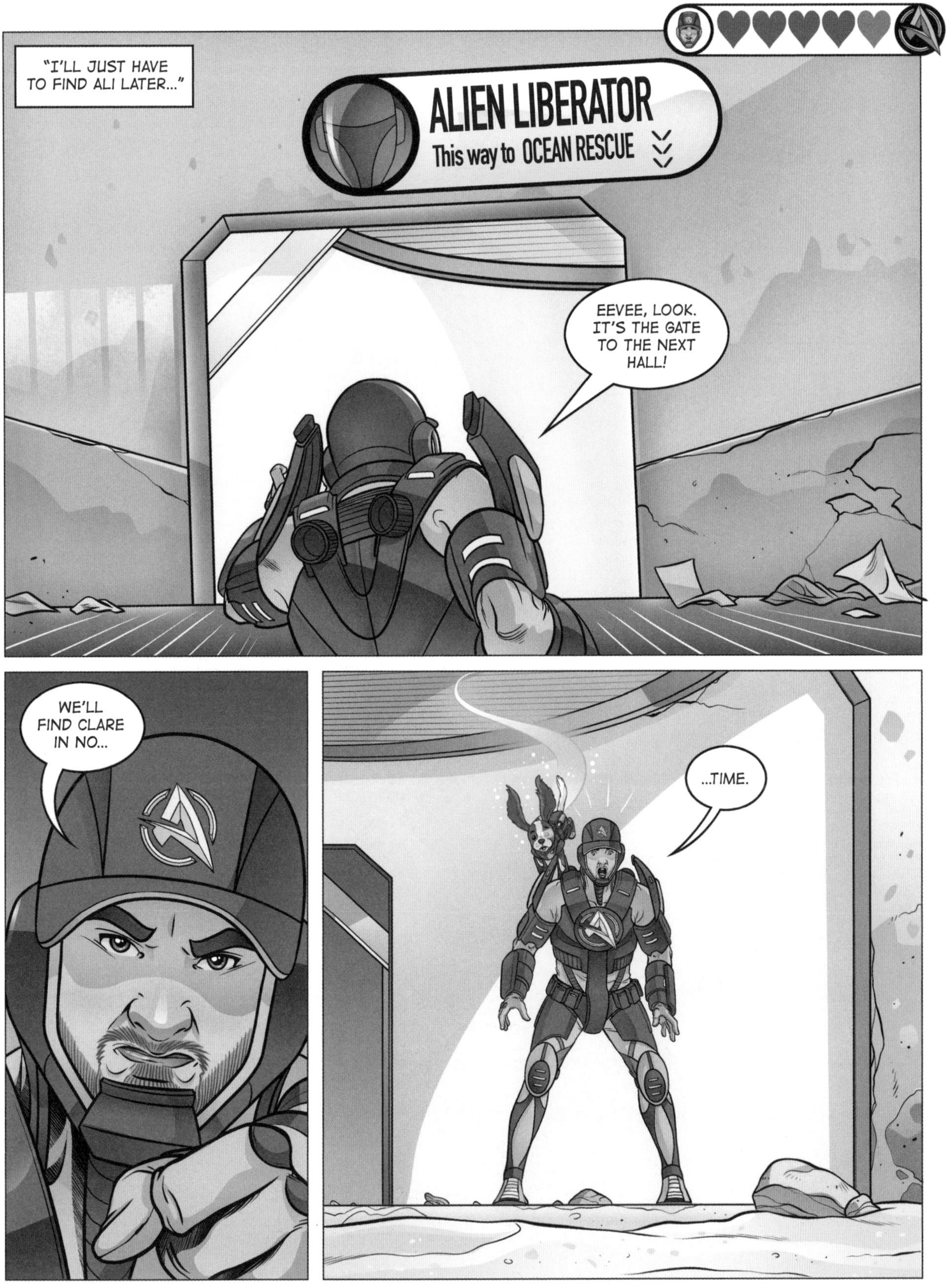
"I'LL JUST HAVE TO FIND ALI LATER..."
ALIEN LIBERATOR
This way to OCEAN RESCUE
EEVEE, LOOK. IT'S THE GATE TO THE NEXT HALL!
WE'LL FIND CLARE IN NO...
...TIME.

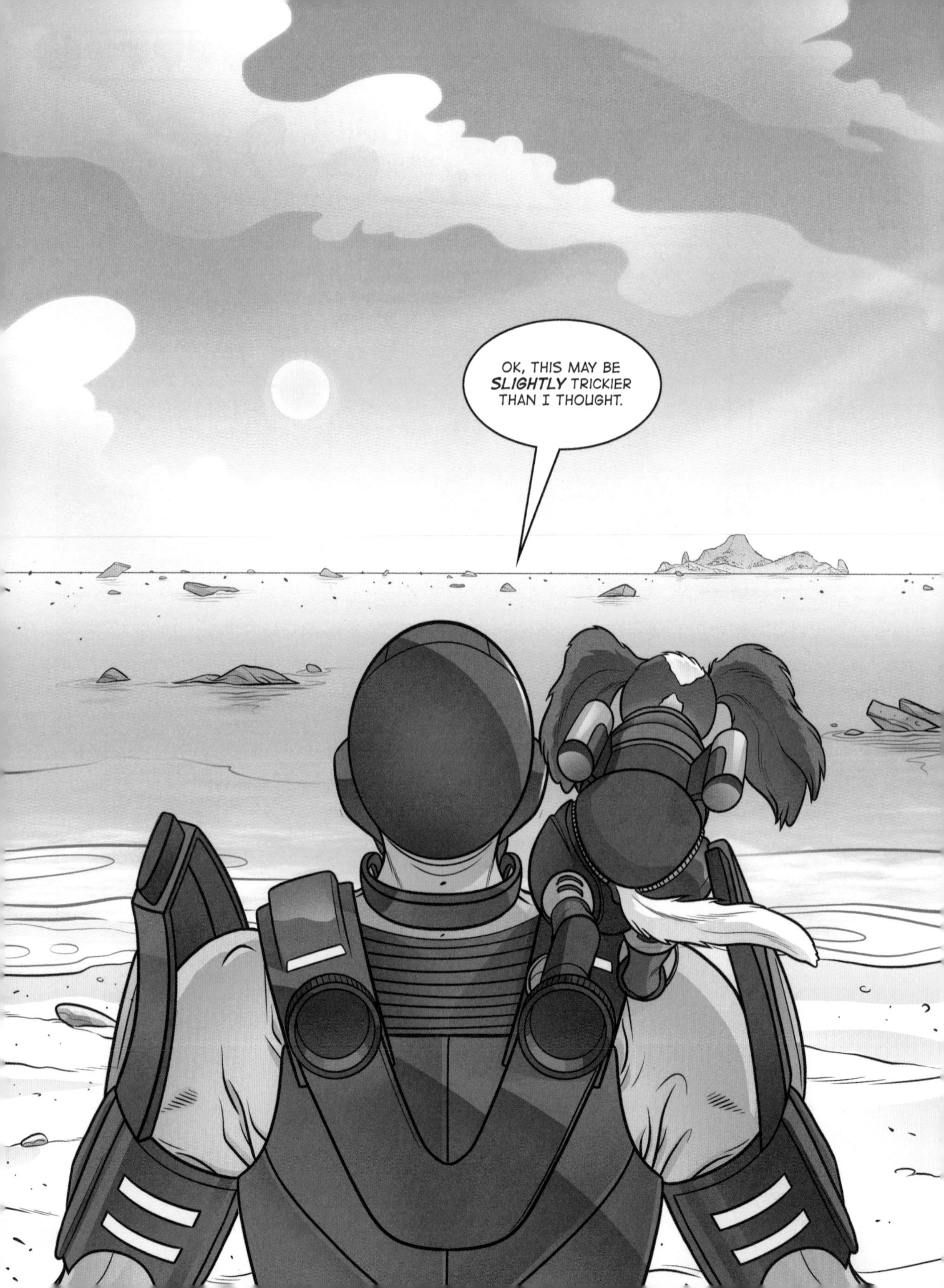
OK, THIS MAY BE SLIGHTLY TRICKIER THAN I THOUGHT.

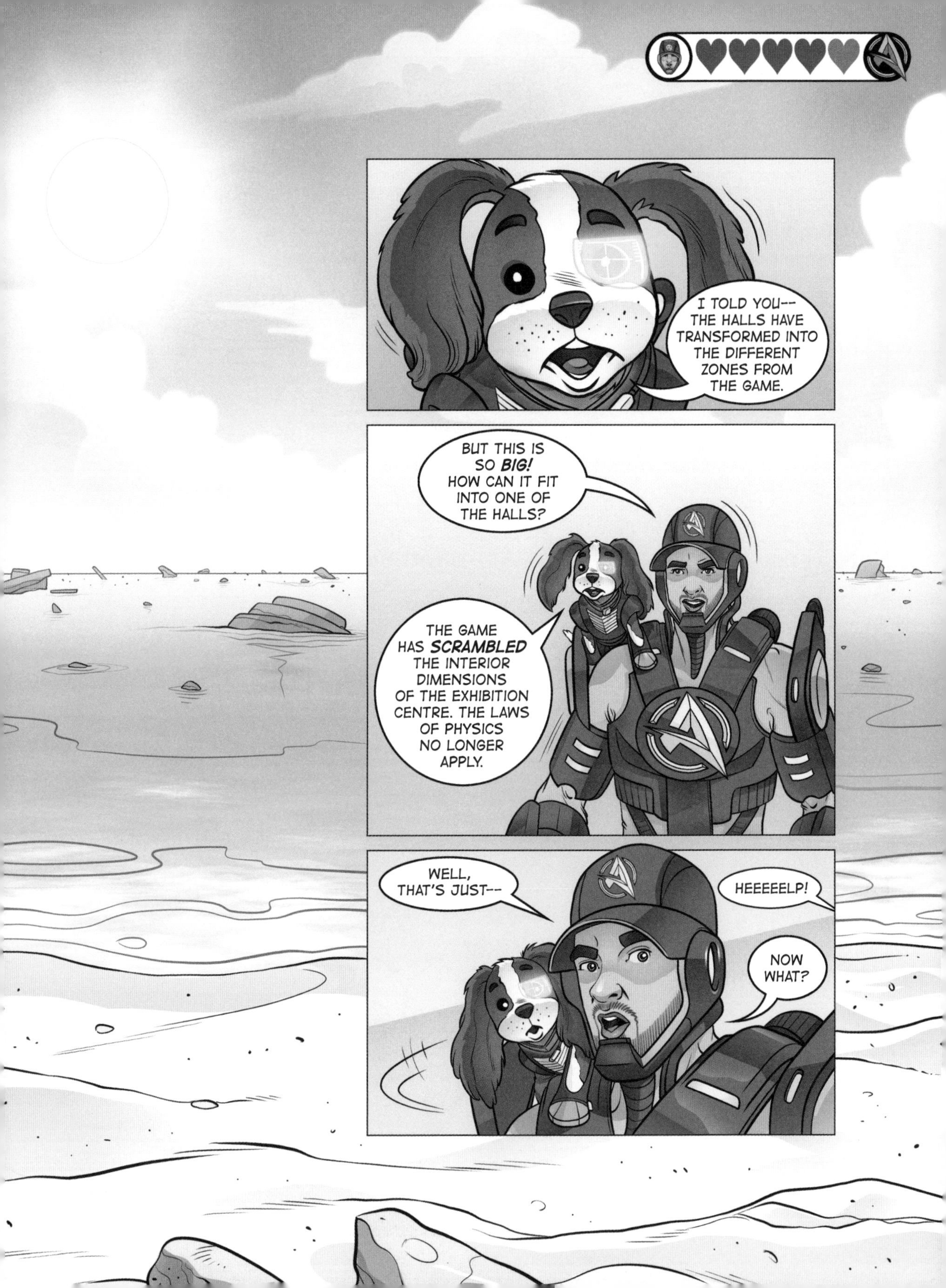
I TOLD YOU--
THE HALLS HAVE TRANSFORMED INTO THE DIFFERENT ZONES FROM THE GAME.
BUT THIS IS SO **BIG!** HOW CAN IT FIT INTO ONE OF THE HALLS?
THE GAME HAS **SCRAMBLED** THE INTERIOR DIMENSIONS OF THE EXHIBITION CENTRE. THE LAWS OF PHYSICS NO LONGER APPLY.
WELL, THAT'S JUST--
HEEEEELP!
NOW WHAT?

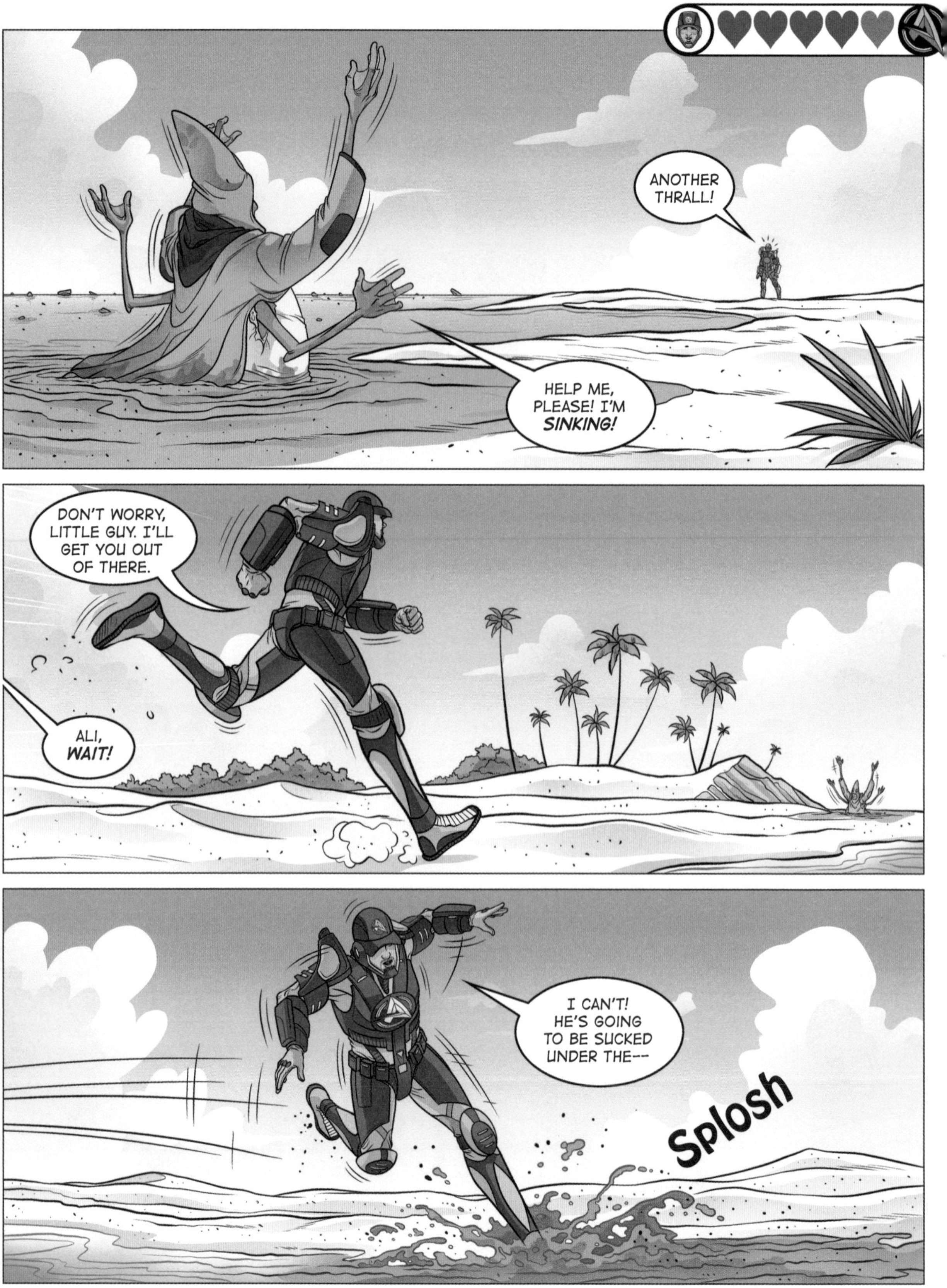
ANOTHER THRALL!
HELP ME, PLEASE! I'M *SINKING!*
DON'T WORRY, LITTLE GUY. I'LL GET YOU OUT OF THERE.
ALI, *WAIT!*
I CAN'T! HE'S GOING TO BE SUCKED UNDER THE--
Splosh

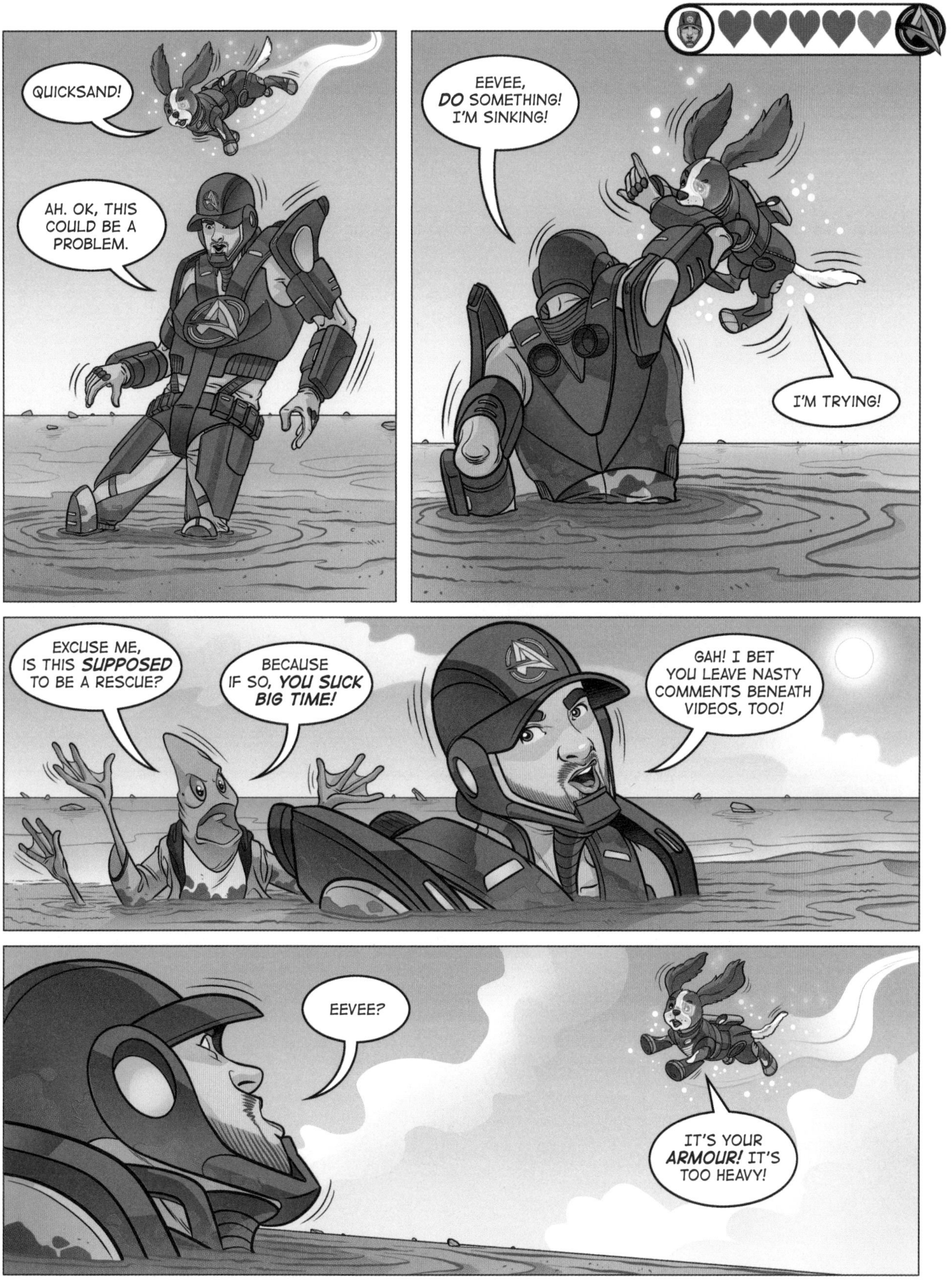
QUICKSAND!
AH. OK, THIS COULD BE A PROBLEM.
EEVEE, DO SOMETHING! I'M SINKING!
I'M TRYING!
EXCUSE ME, IS THIS SUPPOSED TO BE A RESCUE?
BECAUSE IF SO, YOU SUCK BIG TIME!
GAH! I BET YOU LEAVE NASTY COMMENTS BENEATH VIDEOS, TOO!
EEVEE?
IT'S YOUR ARMOUR! IT'S TOO HEAVY!

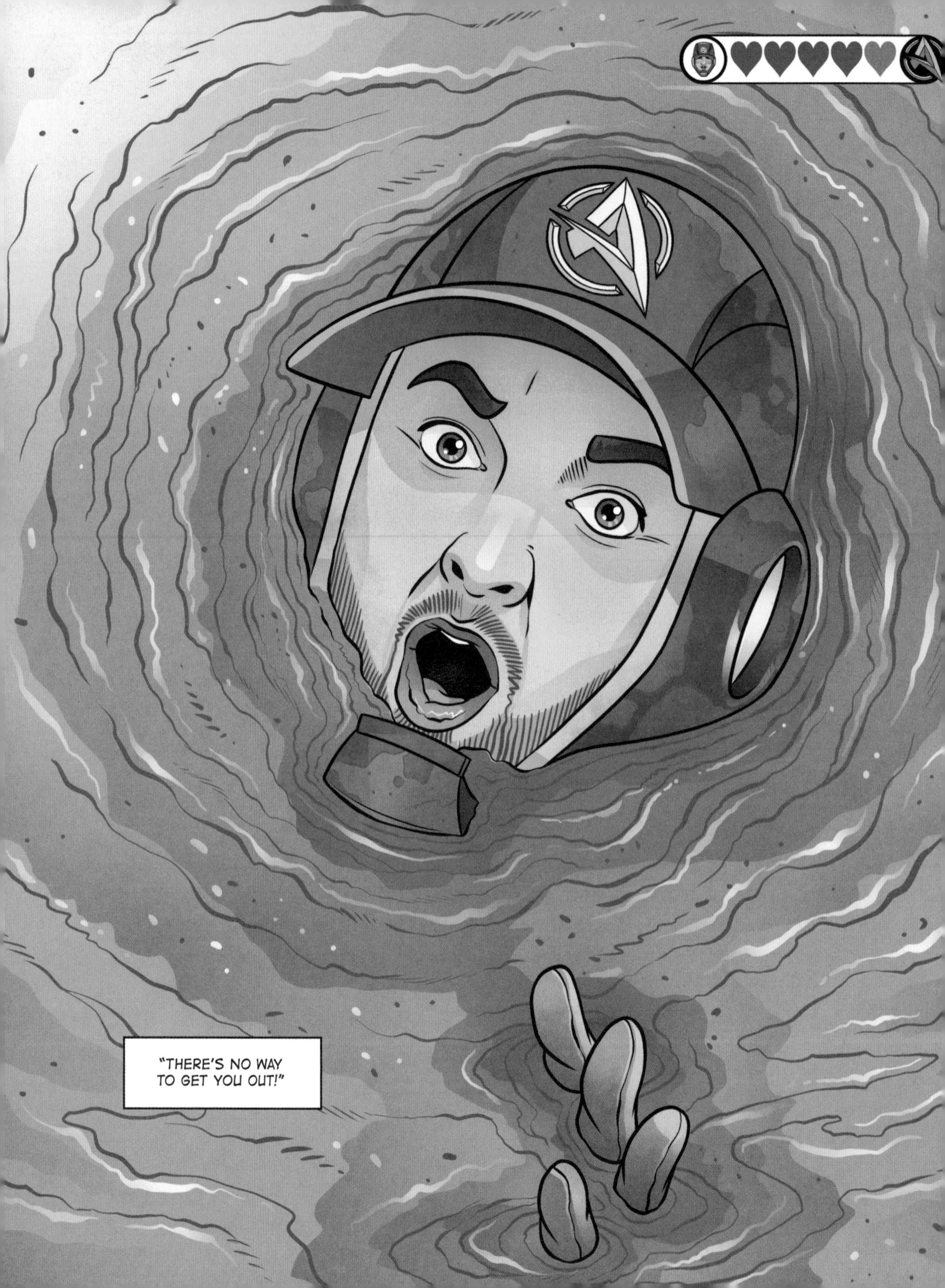
"THERE'S NO WAY TO GET YOU OUT!"

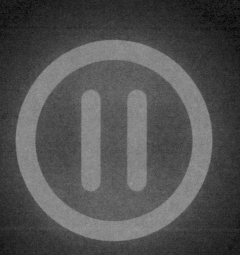

LEVEL FOUR

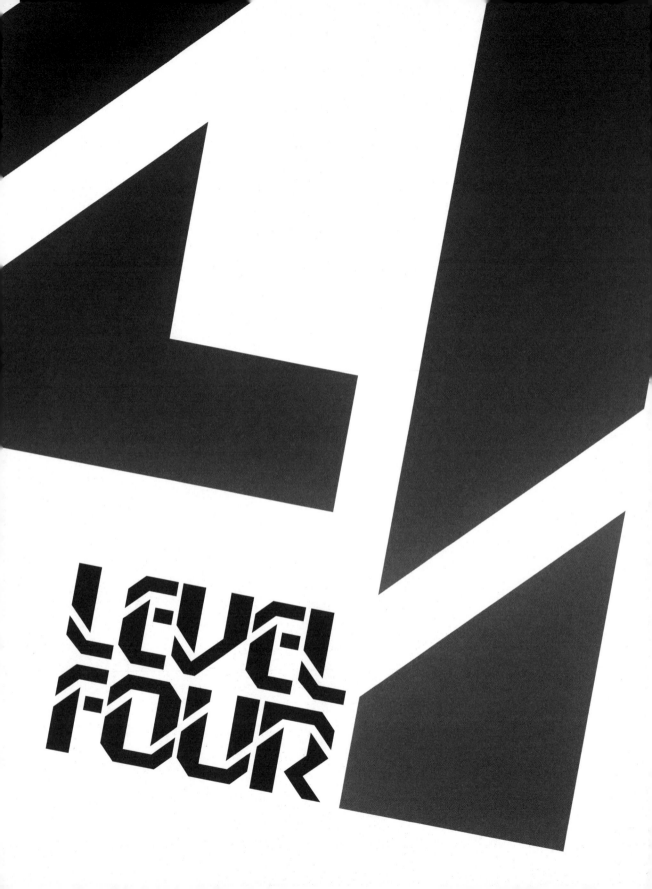

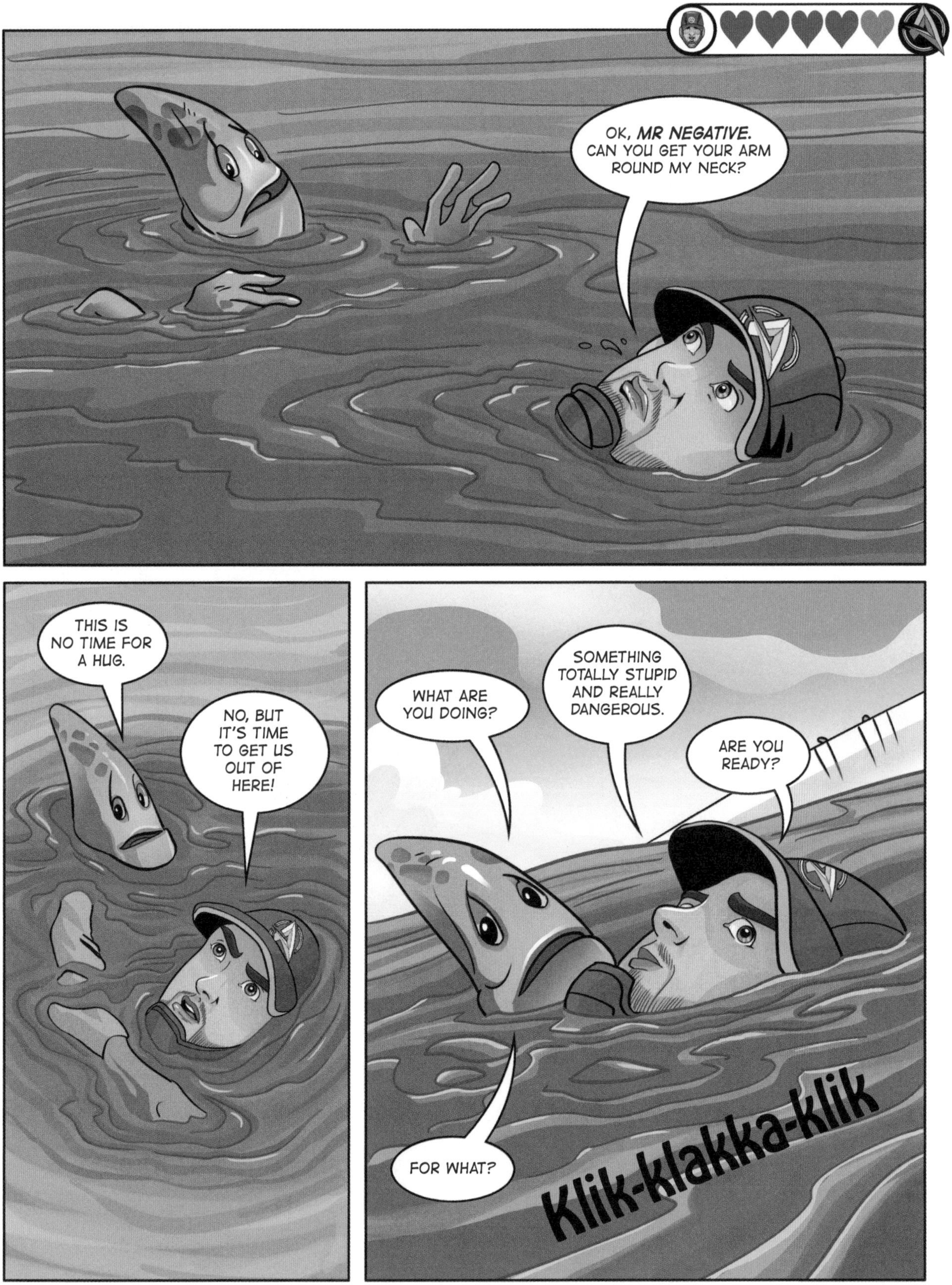
OK, MR NEGATIVE. CAN YOU GET YOUR ARM ROUND MY NECK?
THIS IS NO TIME FOR A HUG.
NO, BUT IT'S TIME TO GET US OUT OF HERE!
WHAT ARE YOU DOING?
SOMETHING TOTALLY STUPID AND REALLY DANGEROUS.
ARE YOU READY?
FOR WHAT?
Klik-klakka-klik

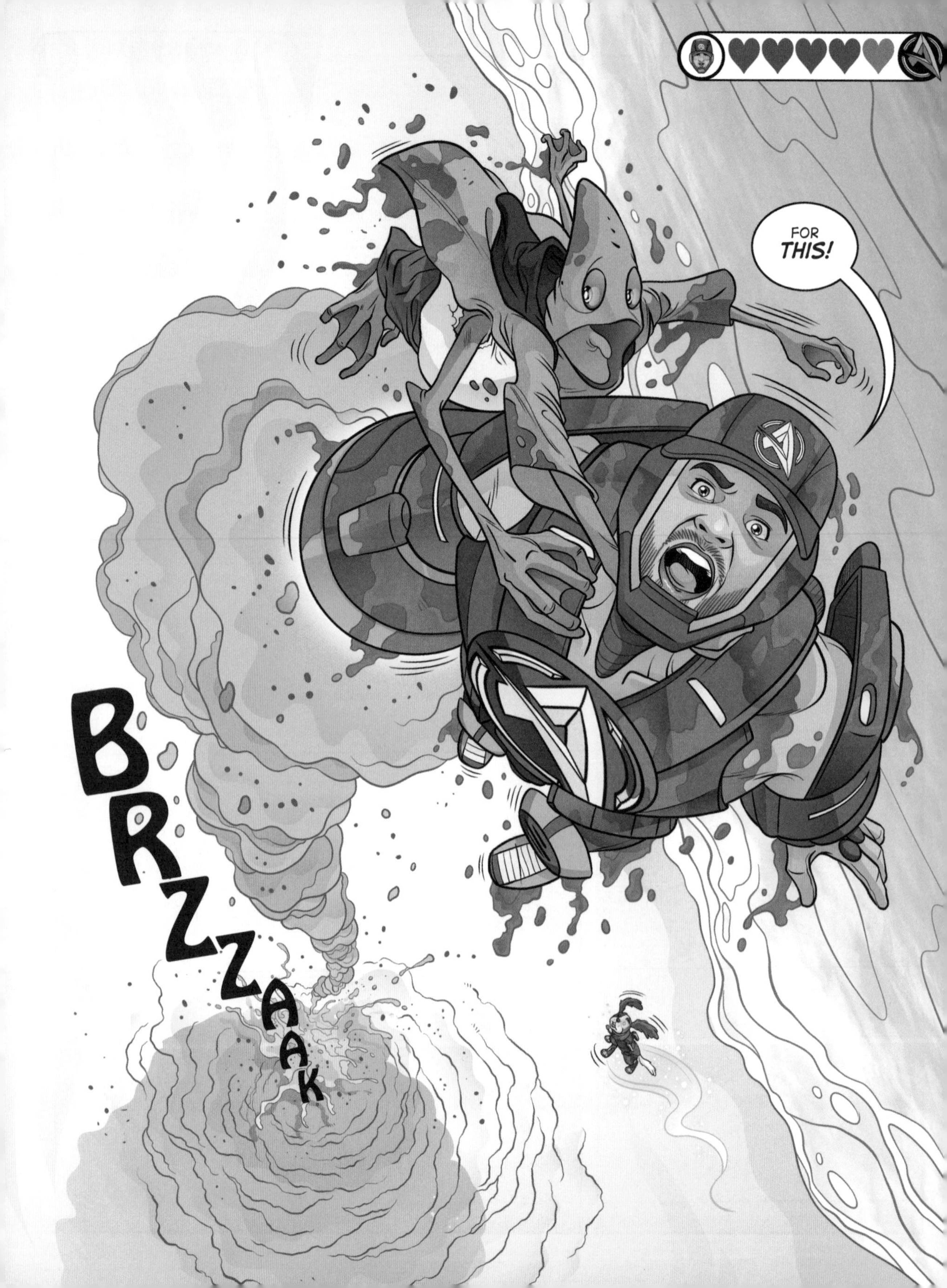
FOR THIS!
BRZZZAAK

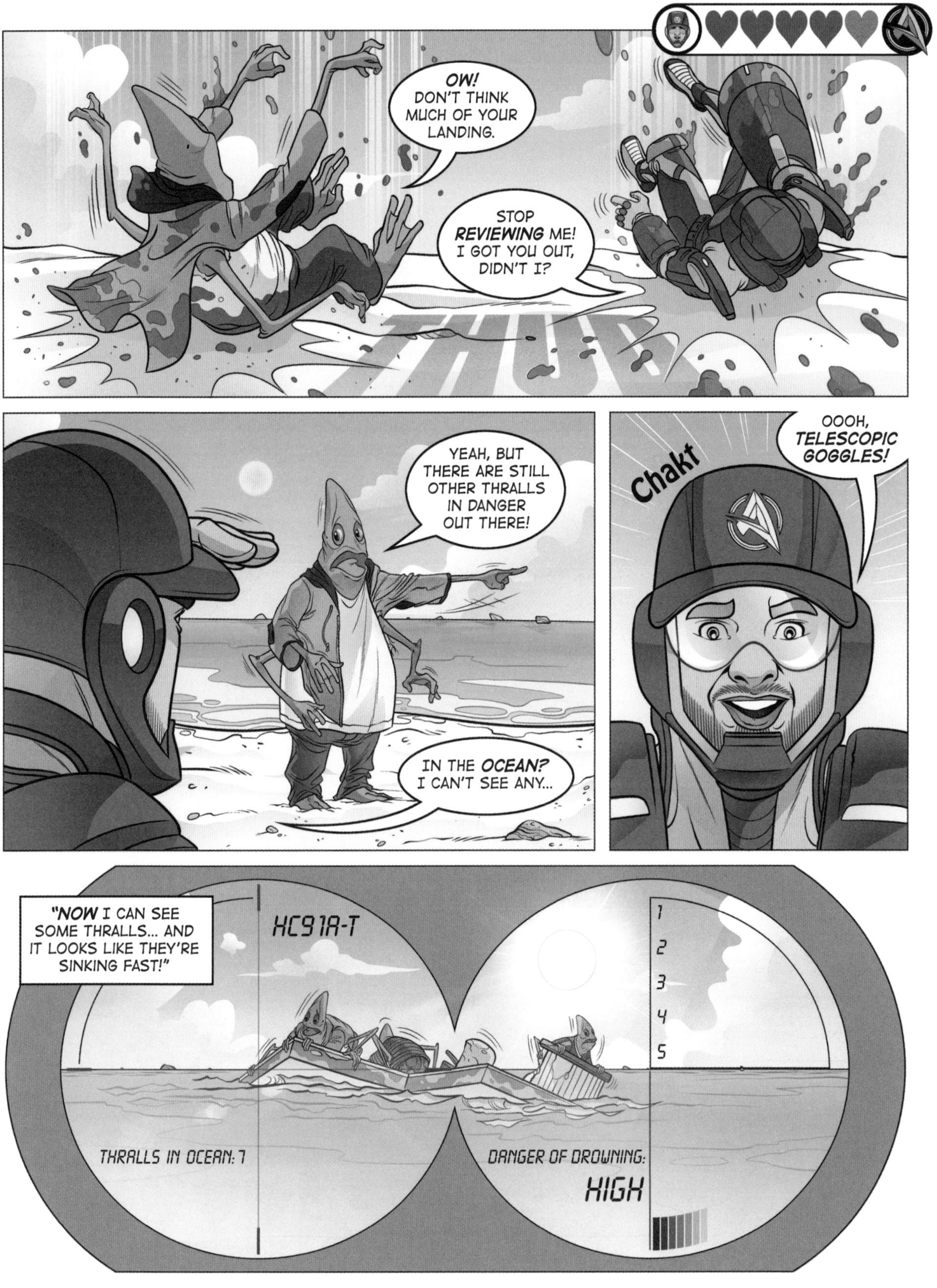
OW! DON'T THINK MUCH OF YOUR LANDING.
STOP REVIEWING ME! I GOT YOU OUT, DIDN'T I?
THUD
YEAH, BUT THERE ARE STILL OTHER THRALLS IN DANGER OUT THERE!
IN THE OCEAN? I CAN'T SEE ANY...
Chakt
OOOH, TELESCOPIC GOGGLES!
"NOW I CAN SEE SOME THRALLS... AND IT LOOKS LIKE THEY'RE SINKING FAST!"
HC91A-T
1
2
3
4
5
THRALLS IN OCEAN: 7
DANGER OF DROWNING:
HIGH

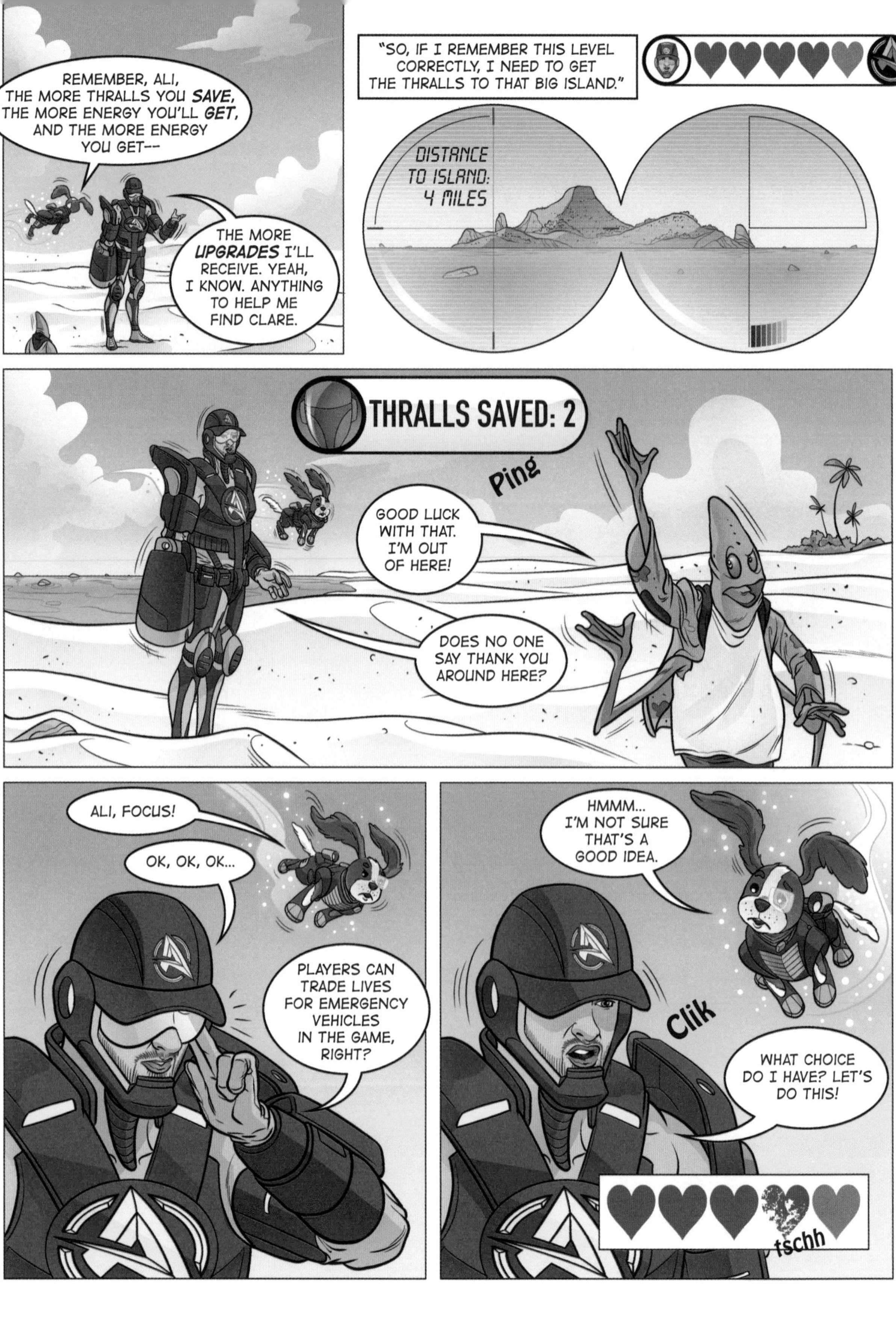
REMEMBER, ALI, THE MORE THRALLS YOU SAVE, THE MORE ENERGY YOU'LL GET, AND THE MORE ENERGY YOU GET--
THE MORE UPGRADES I'LL RECEIVE. YEAH, I KNOW. ANYTHING TO HELP ME FIND CLARE.
"SO, IF I REMEMBER THIS LEVEL CORRECTLY, I NEED TO GET THE THRALLS TO THAT BIG ISLAND."
DISTANCE TO ISLAND: 4 MILES
THRALLS SAVED: 2
Ping
GOOD LUCK WITH THAT. I'M OUT OF HERE!
DOES NO ONE SAY THANK YOU AROUND HERE?
ALI, FOCUS!
OK, OK, OK...
PLAYERS CAN TRADE LIVES FOR EMERGENCY VEHICLES IN THE GAME, RIGHT?
HMMM... I'M NOT SURE THAT'S A GOOD IDEA.
Clik
WHAT CHOICE DO I HAVE? LET'S DO THIS!
tschh

SELF-SACRIFICE TROPHY

Ping

UPGRADE UNLOCKED

Ping

THIS IS MORE LIKE IT! LET'S SEE WHAT WE'VE GOT.

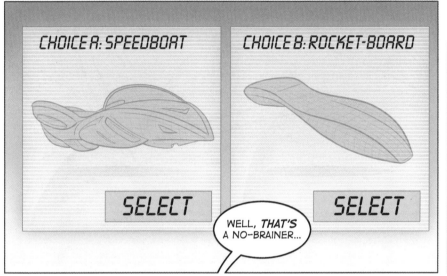

CHOICE A: SPEEDBOAT

SELECT

CHOICE B: ROCKET-BOARD

SELECT

WELL, **THAT'S** A NO-BRAINER...

RIGHT-- **THE ROCKET-BOARD.** YOU CAN FLY THE THRALLS TO SAFETY!

THE ROCKET-BOARD? NO WAY! NOT NOW. NOT EVER.

WHY?

YOU'RE NOT GETTING ME BACK IN THE SKY, NOT AFTER CLIMBING THAT TOWER.

NO. MORE. HEIGHTS. OK?

BESIDES...

SELECT

Beep

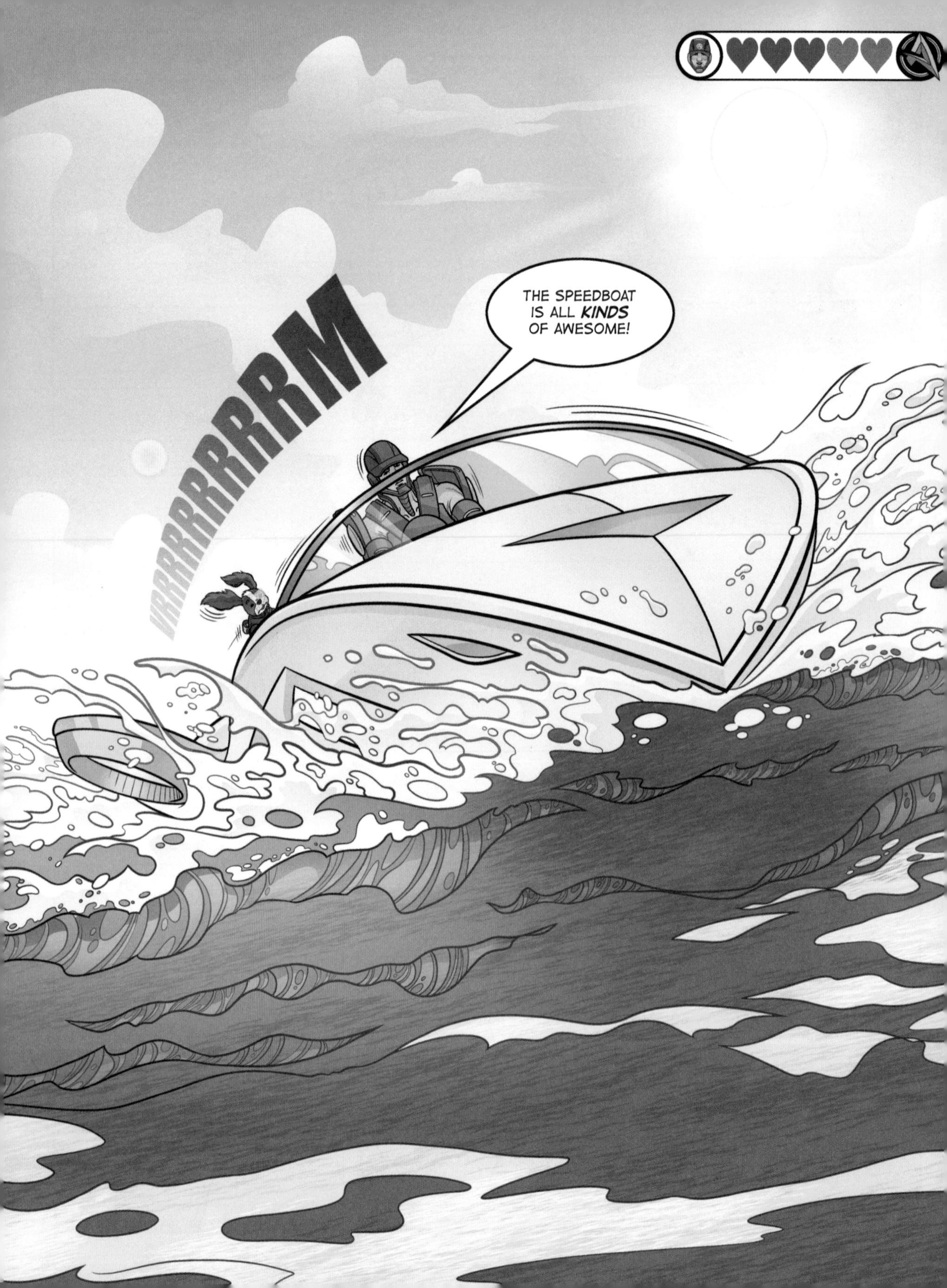
VRRRRRRRRRRRRRM
THE SPEEDBOAT IS ALL ***KINDS*** OF AWESOME!

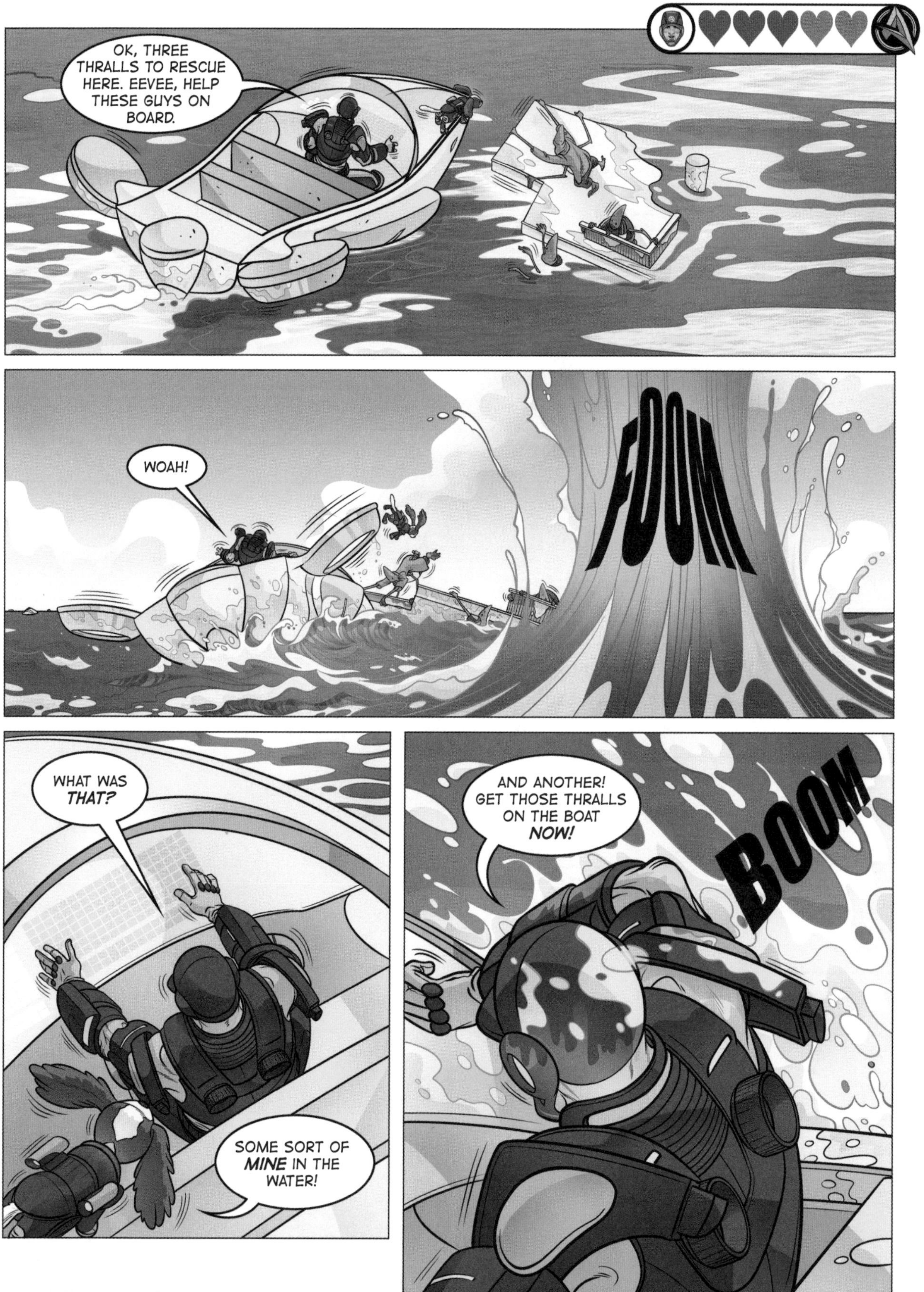
OK, THREE THRALLS TO RESCUE HERE. EEVEE, HELP THESE GUYS ON BOARD.
WOAH!
FOOM
WHAT WAS *THAT?*
SOME SORT OF *MINE* IN THE WATER!
AND ANOTHER! GET THOSE THRALLS ON THE BOAT *NOW!*
BOOM

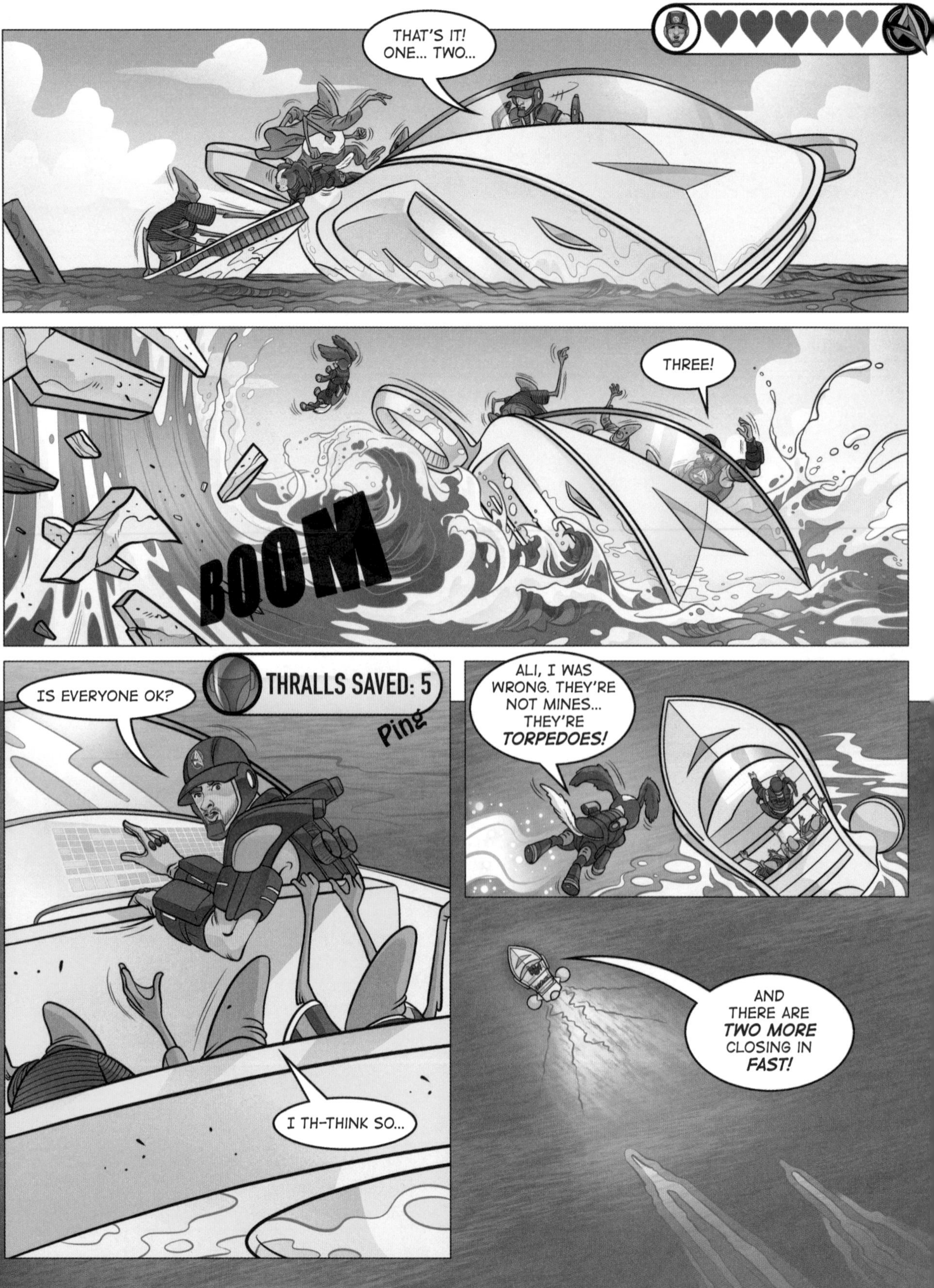
THAT'S IT! ONE... TWO...
THREE!
BOOM
THRALLS SAVED: 5
IS EVERYONE OK?
Ping
I TH-THINK SO...
ALI, I WAS WRONG. THEY'RE NOT MINES... THEY'RE *TORPEDOES!*
AND THERE ARE *TWO MORE* CLOSING IN *FAST!*

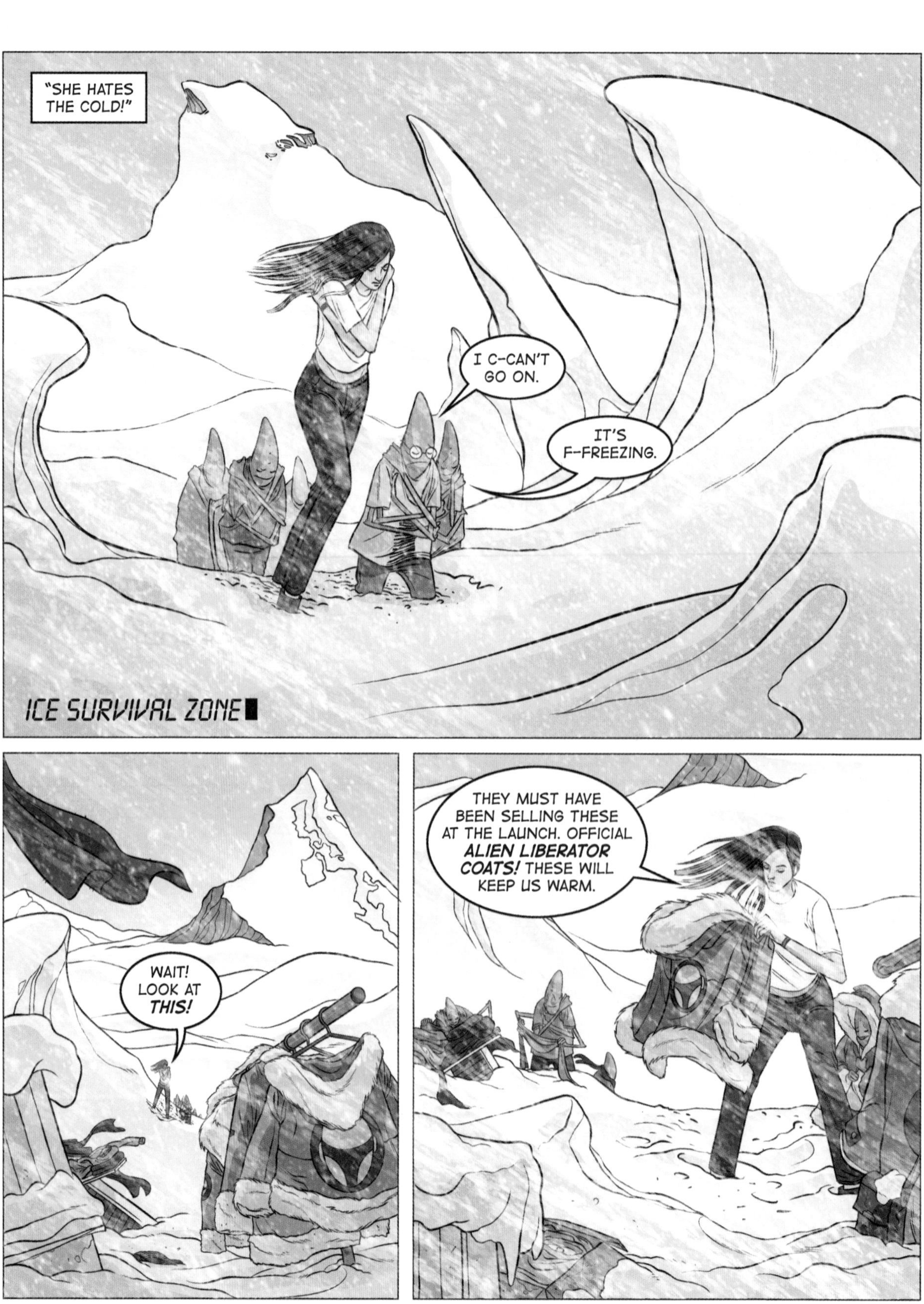
"SHE HATES THE COLD!"
I C-CAN'T GO ON.
IT'S F-FREEZING.
ICE SURVIVAL ZONE
WAIT! LOOK AT THIS!
THEY MUST HAVE BEEN SELLING THESE AT THE LAUNCH. OFFICIAL ALIEN LIBERATOR COATS! THESE WILL KEEP US WARM.

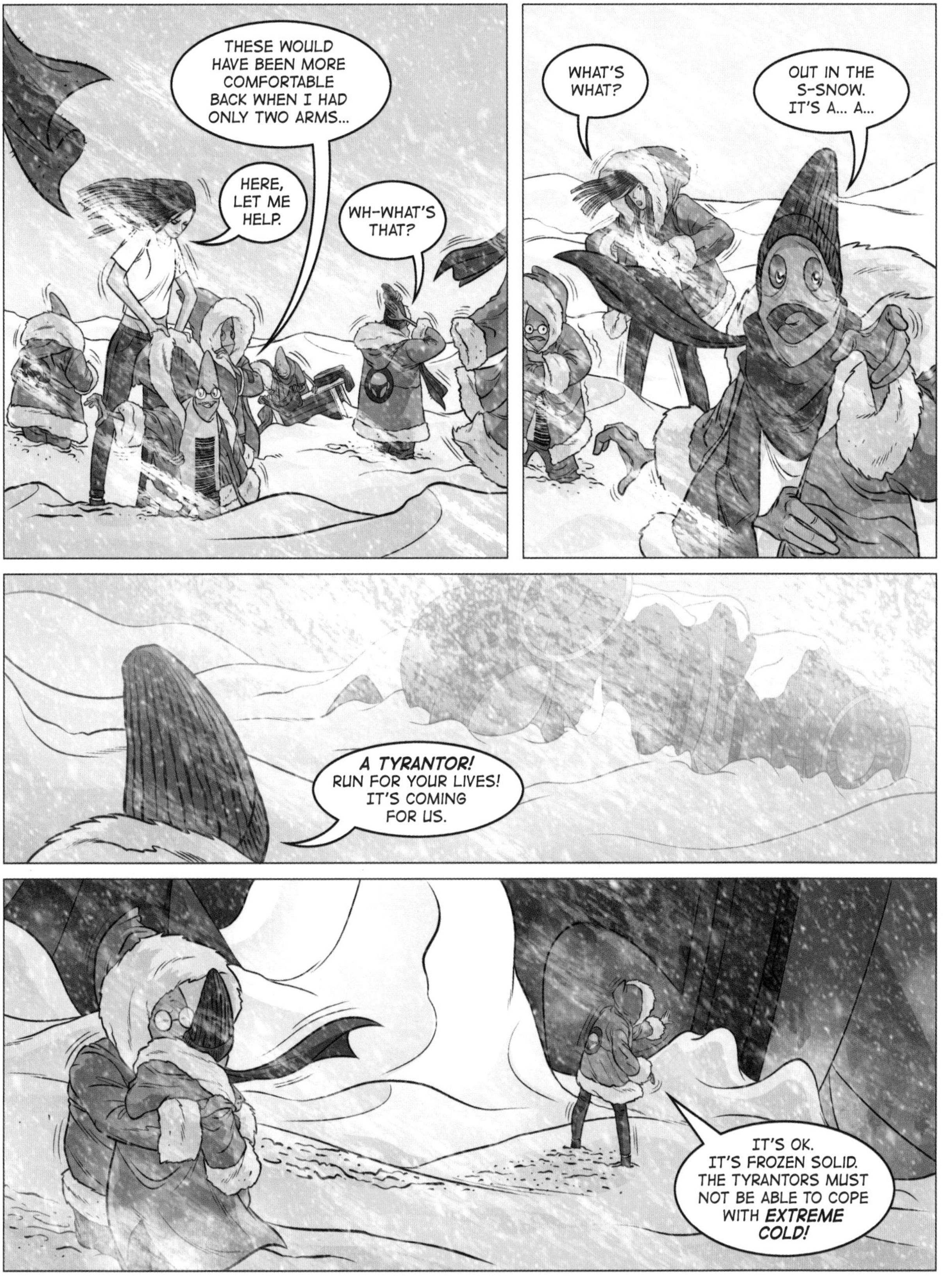

THESE WOULD HAVE BEEN MORE COMFORTABLE BACK WHEN I HAD ONLY TWO ARMS...
HERE, LET ME HELP.
WH-WHAT'S THAT?
WHAT'S WHAT?
OUT IN THE S-SNOW. IT'S A... A...
A TYRANTOR! RUN FOR YOUR LIVES! IT'S COMING FOR US.
IT'S OK. IT'S FROZEN SOLID. THE TYRANTORS MUST NOT BE ABLE TO COPE WITH EXTREME COLD!

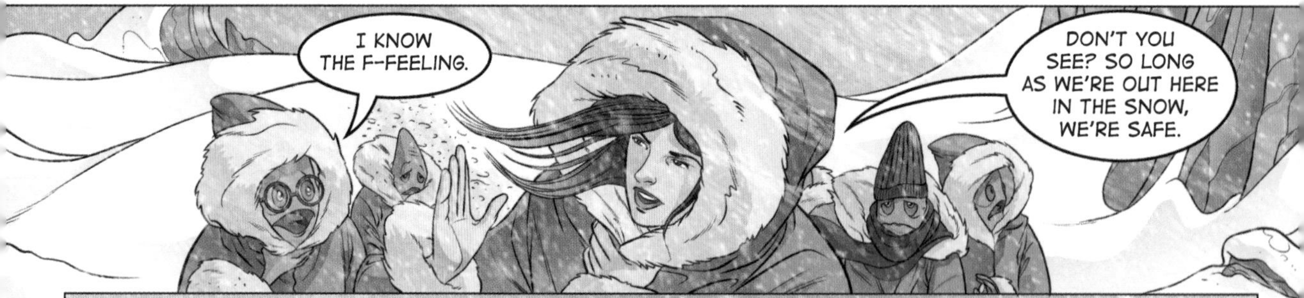
I KNOW THE F--FEELING.
DON'T YOU SEE? SO LONG AS WE'RE OUT HERE IN THE SNOW, WE'RE SAFE.

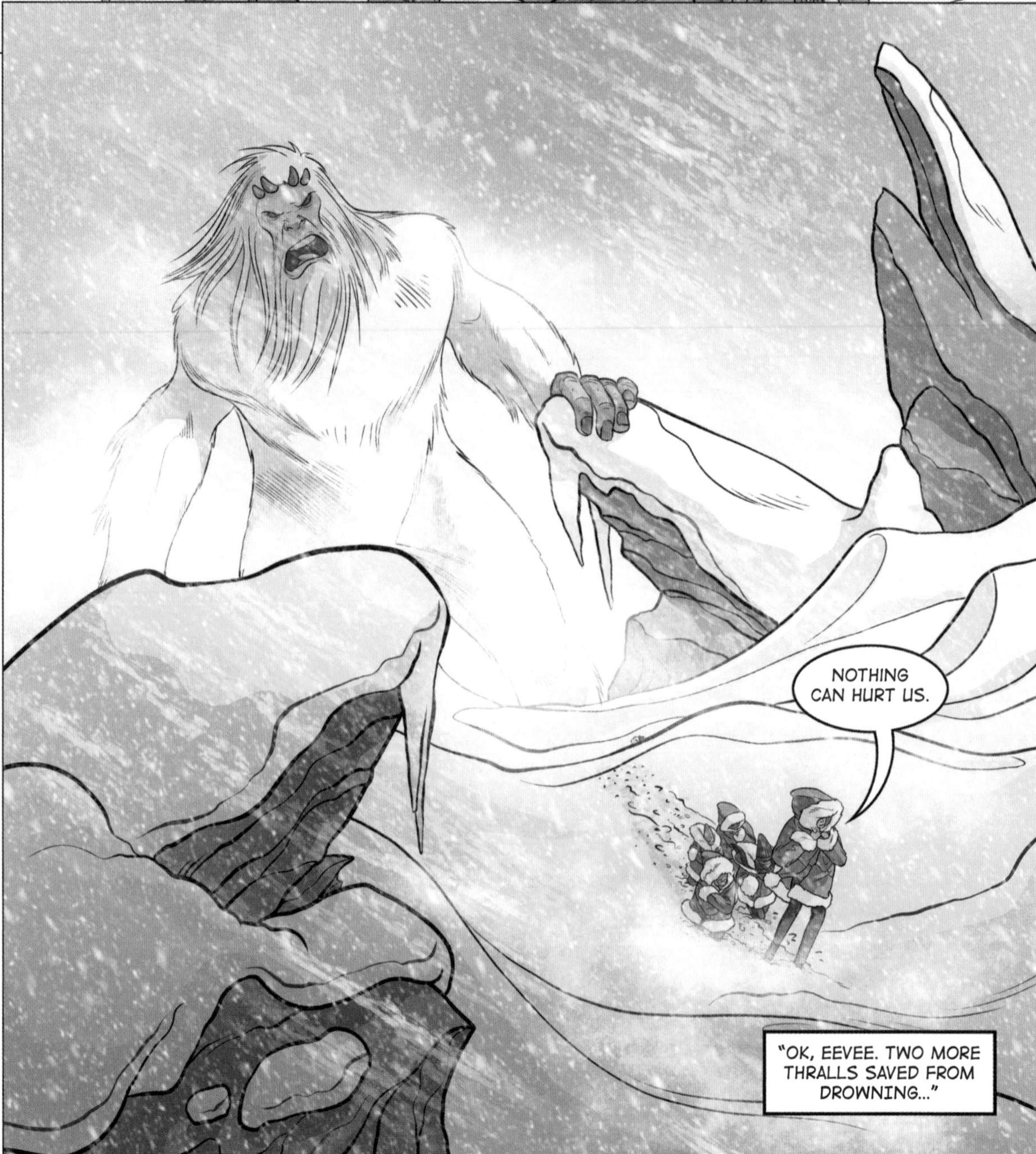
NOTHING CAN HURT US.
"OK, EEVEE. TWO MORE THRALLS SAVED FROM DROWNING..."

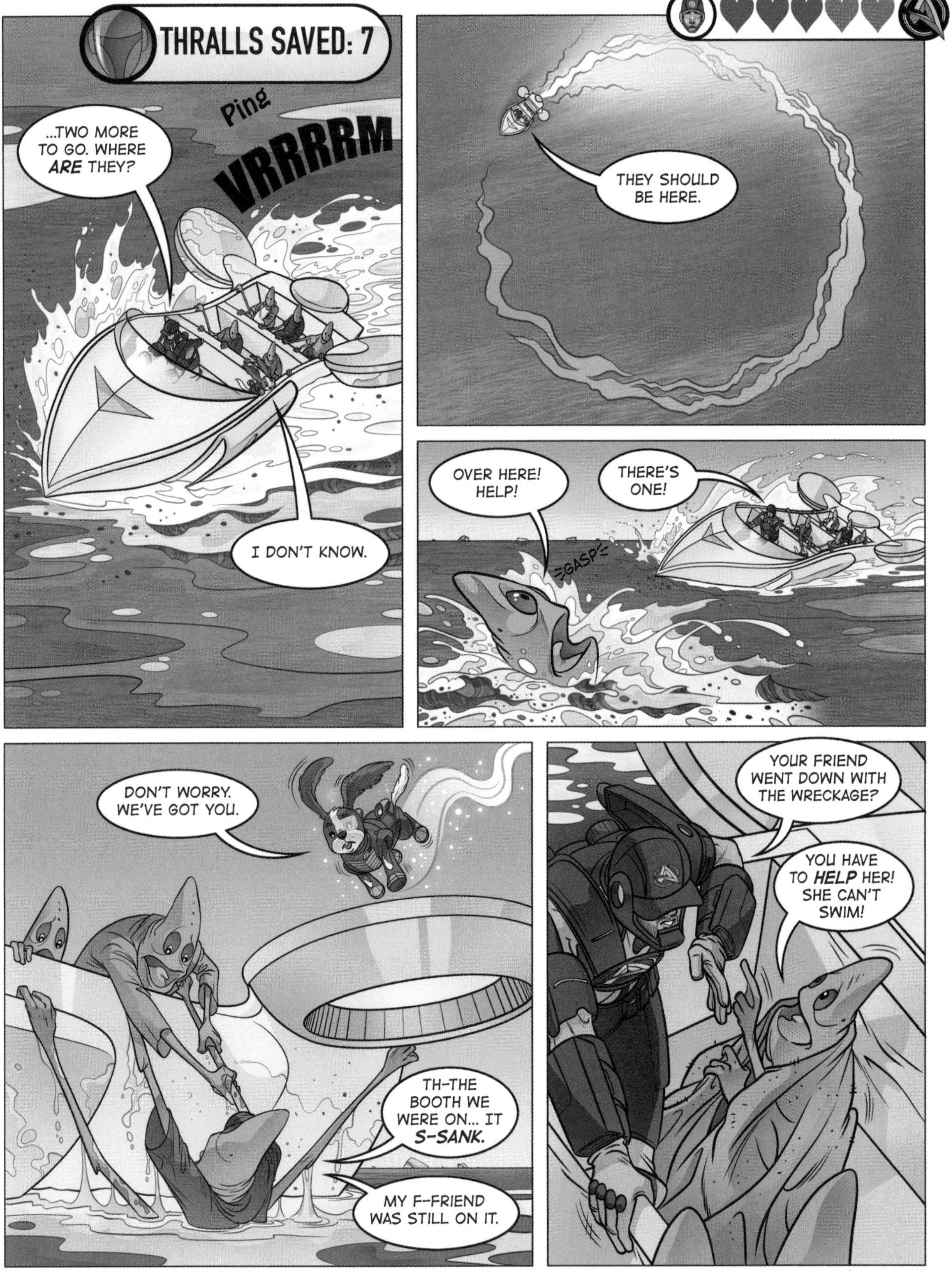
THRALLS SAVED: 7
Ping
VRRRRM
...TWO MORE TO GO. WHERE *ARE* THEY?
I DON'T KNOW.
THEY SHOULD BE HERE.
OVER HERE! HELP!
GASP
THERE'S ONE!
DON'T WORRY. WE'VE GOT YOU.
TH-THE BOOTH WE WERE ON... IT ***S-SANK.***
MY F-FRIEND WAS STILL ON IT.
YOUR FRIEND WENT DOWN WITH THE WRECKAGE?
YOU HAVE TO ***HELP*** HER! SHE CAN'T SWIM!

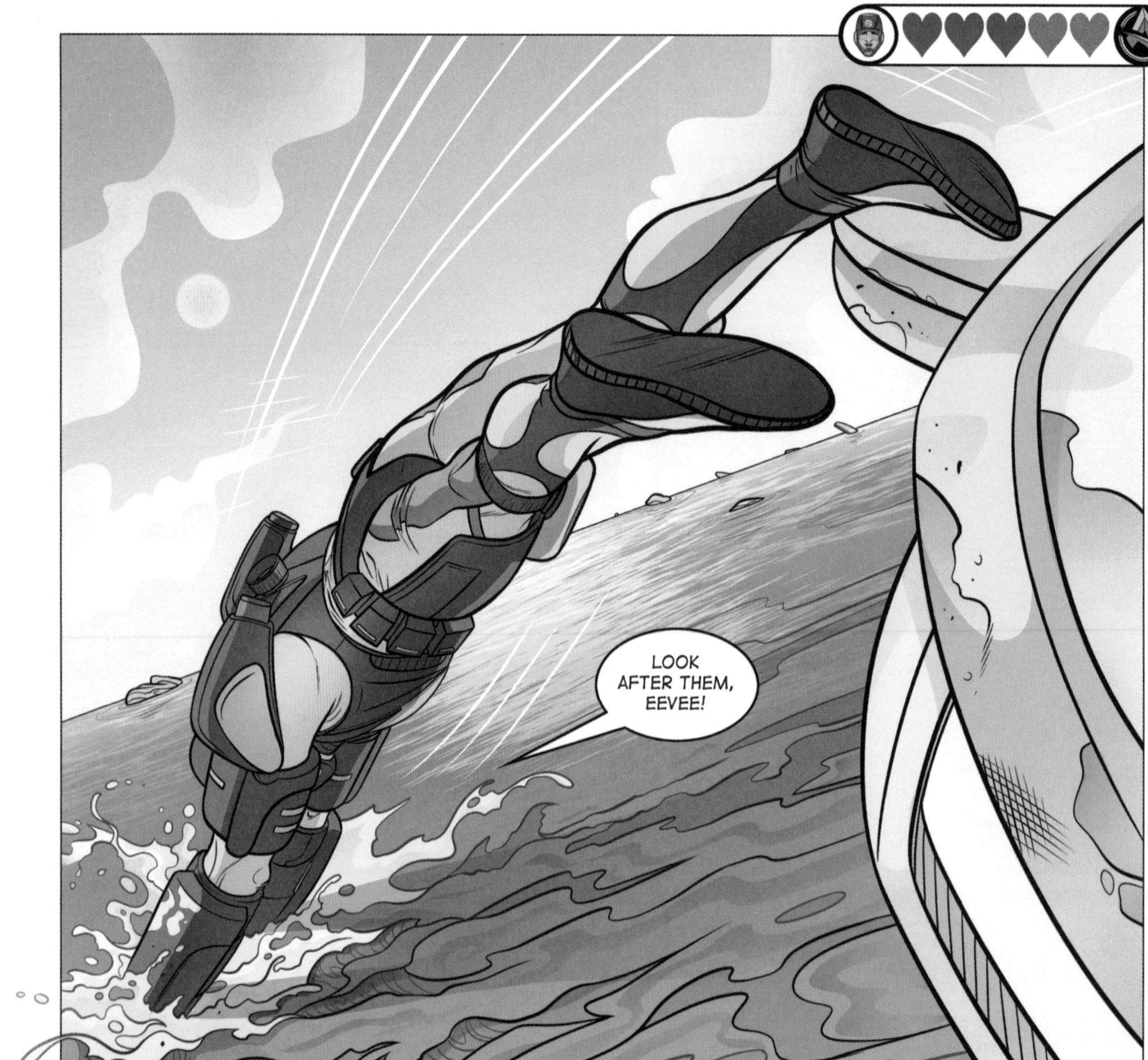
LOOK AFTER THEM, EEVEE!

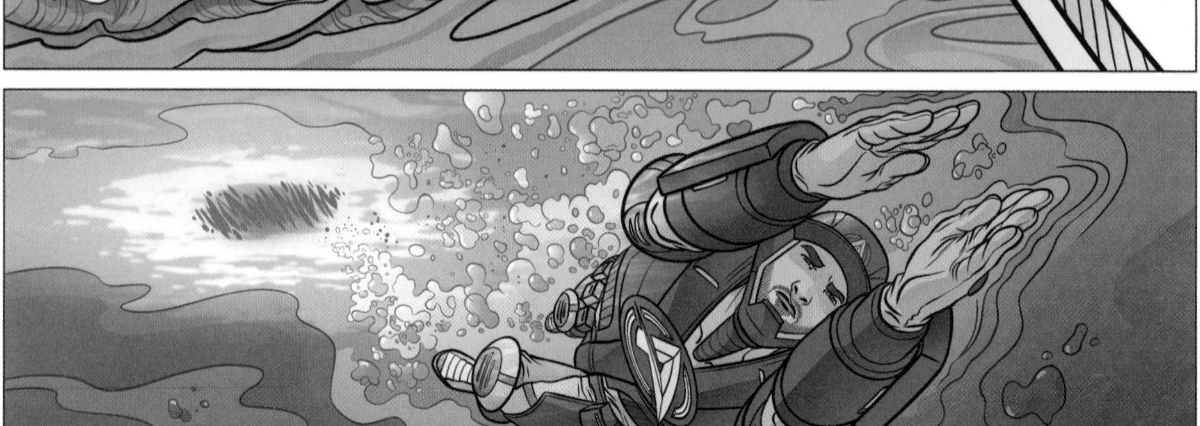

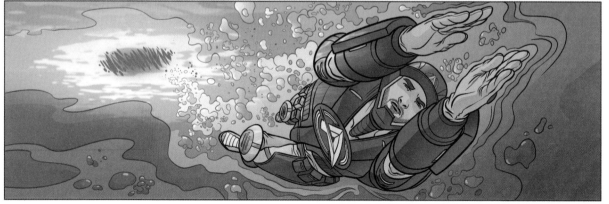

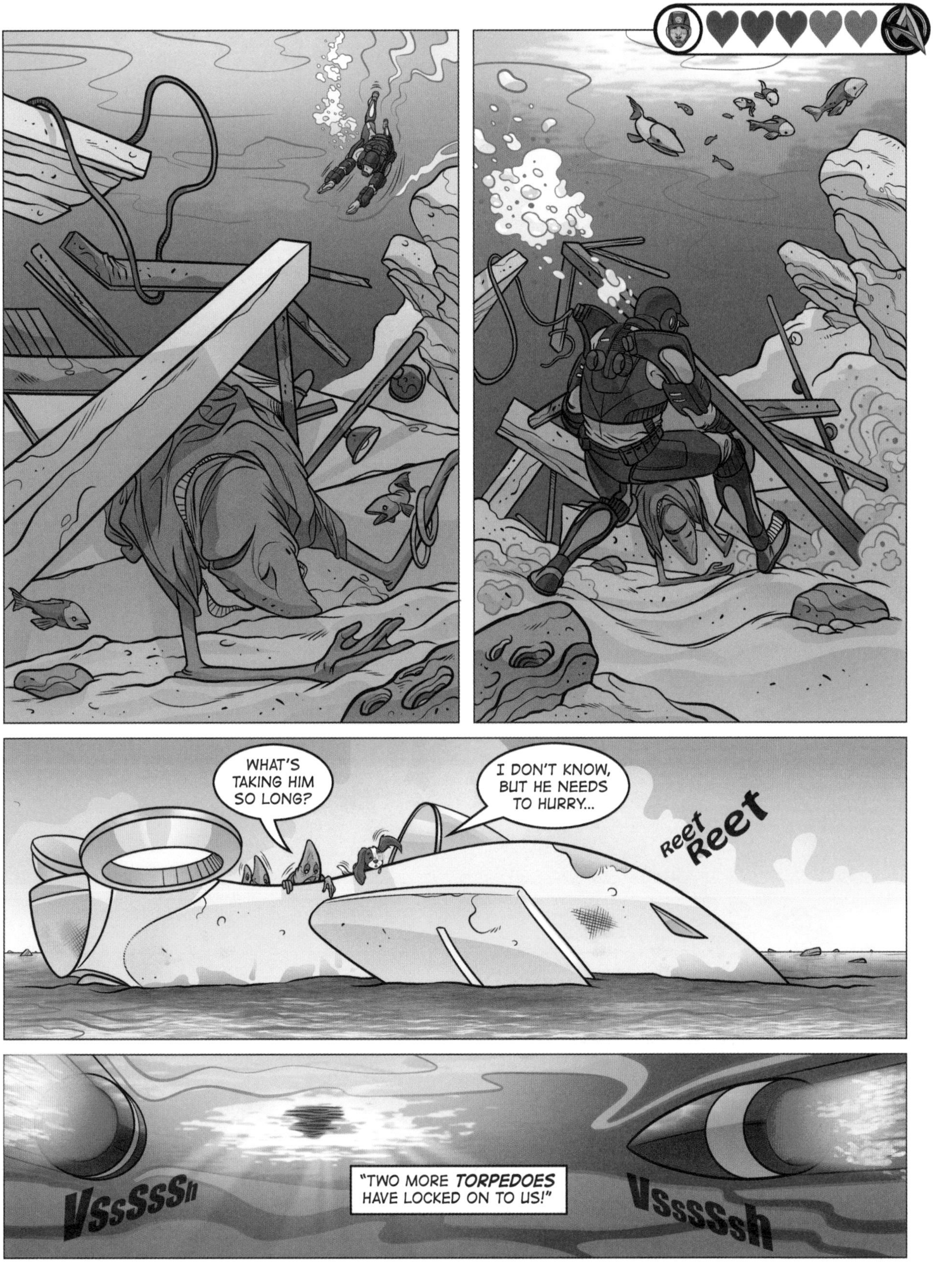
WHAT'S TAKING HIM SO LONG?
I DON'T KNOW, BUT HE NEEDS TO HURRY...
Reet Reet
"TWO MORE TORPEDOES HAVE LOCKED ON TO US!"
VsSsSSh
VsssSsh

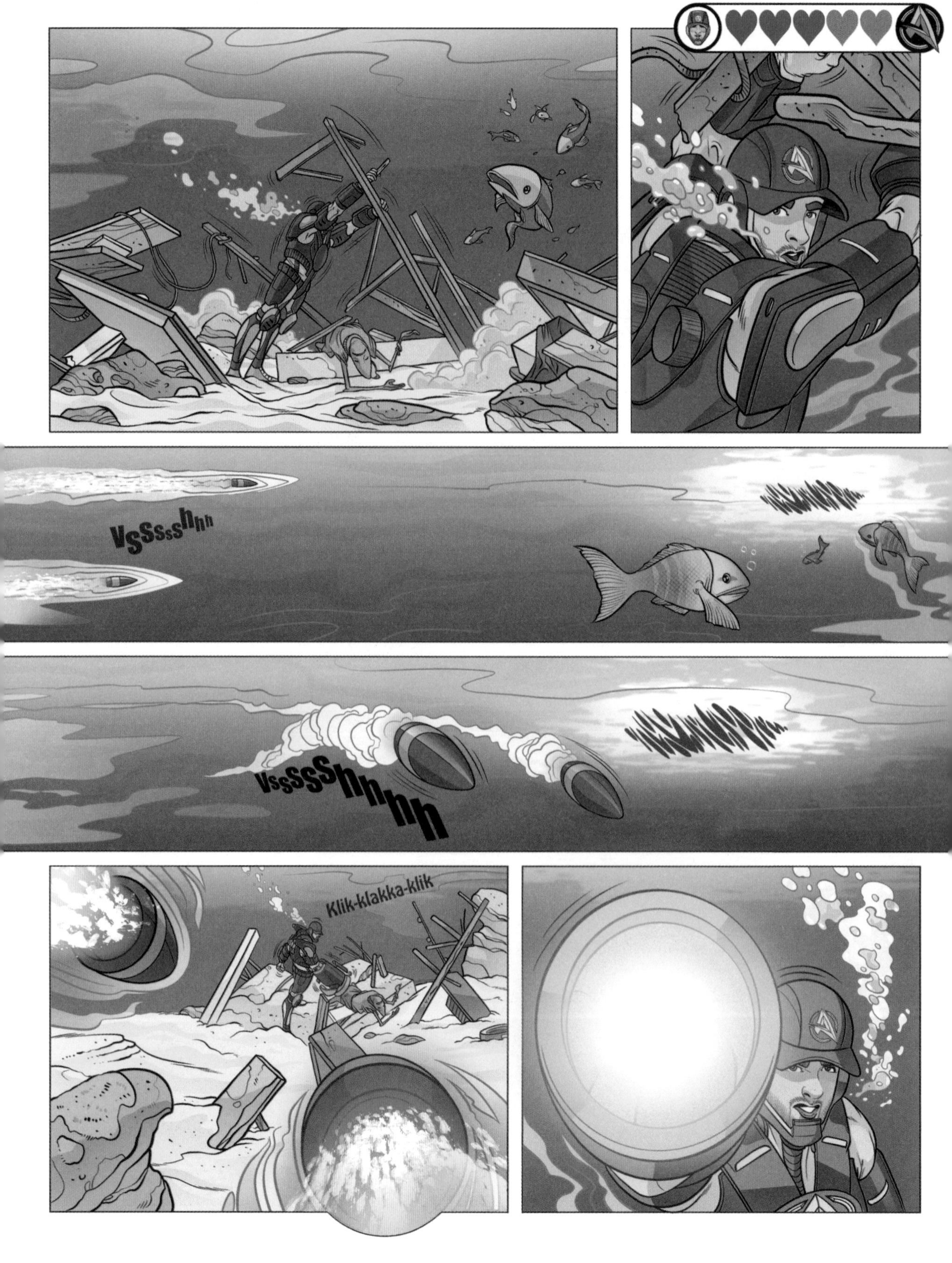

Vsssssshhh
Vssssshhhhh
Klik-klakka-klik

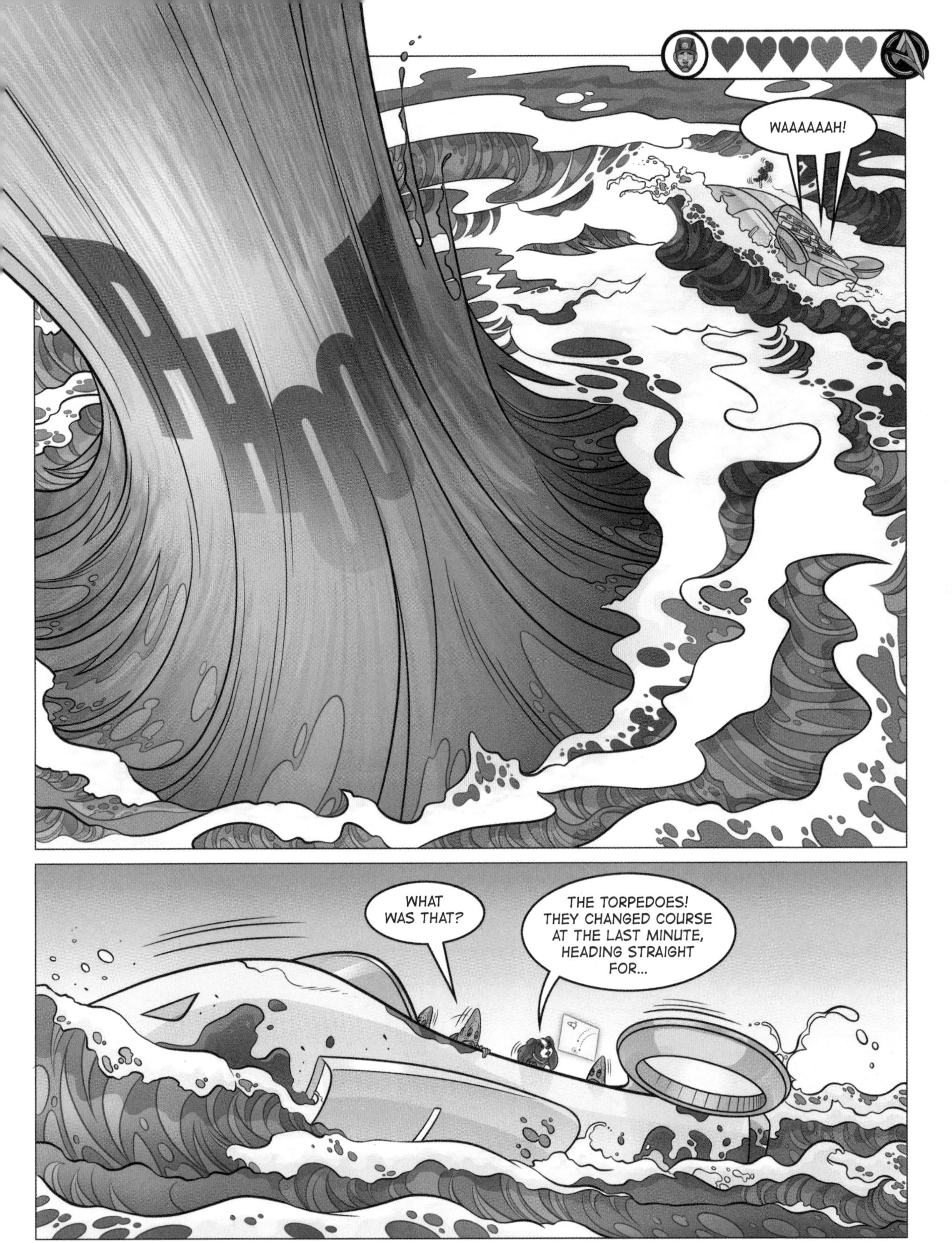
WAAAAAAH!
WHAT WAS THAT?
THE TORPEDOES! THEY CHANGED COURSE AT THE LAST MINUTE, HEADING STRAIGHT FOR...

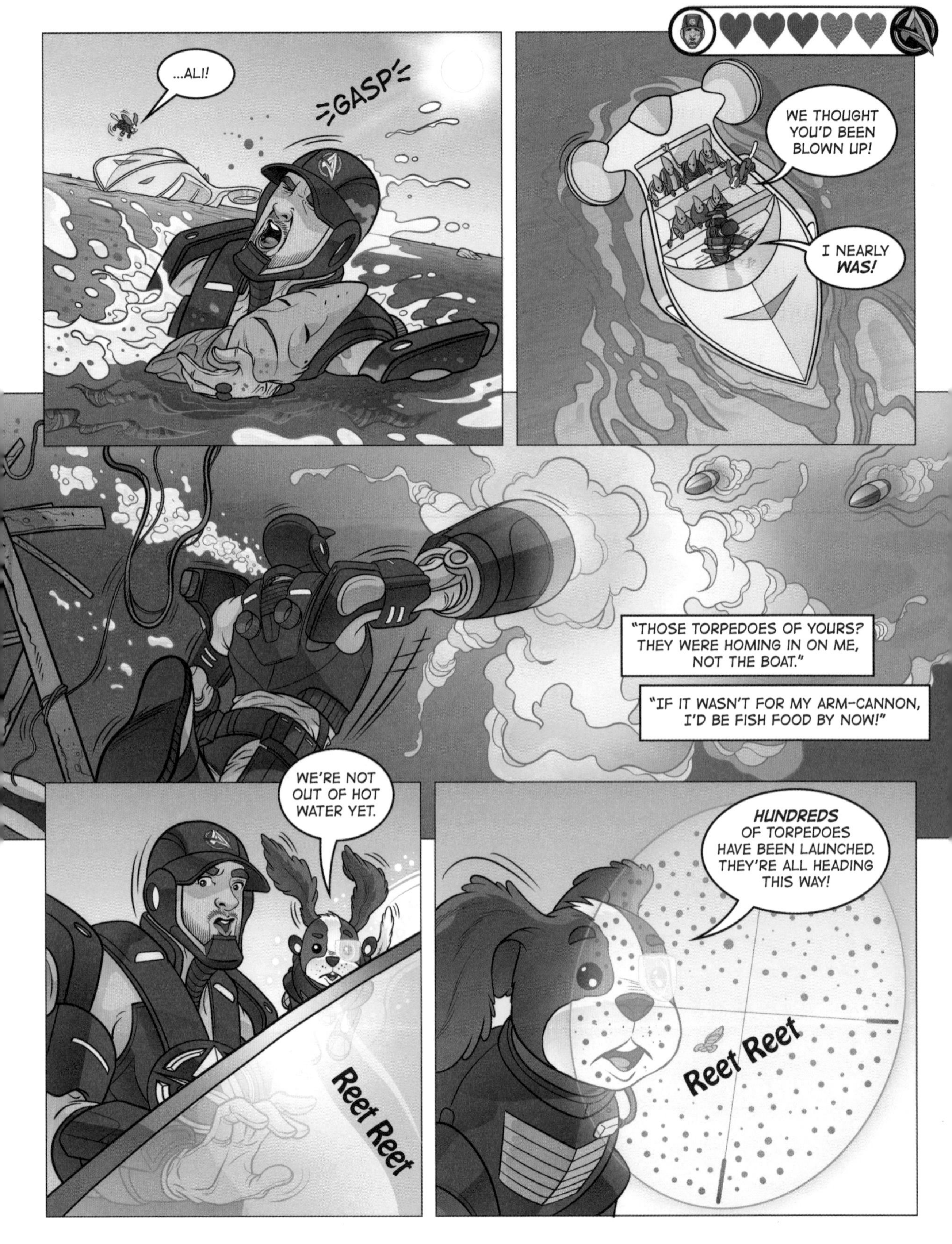
...ALI!
GASP
WE THOUGHT YOU'D BEEN BLOWN UP!
I NEARLY *WAS!*
"THOSE TORPEDOES OF YOURS? THEY WERE HOMING IN ON ME, NOT THE BOAT."
"IF IT WASN'T FOR MY ARM-CANNON, I'D BE FISH FOOD BY NOW!"
WE'RE NOT OUT OF HOT WATER YET.
Reet Reet
HUNDREDS OF TORPEDOES HAVE BEEN LAUNCHED. THEY'RE ALL HEADING THIS WAY!
Reet Reet

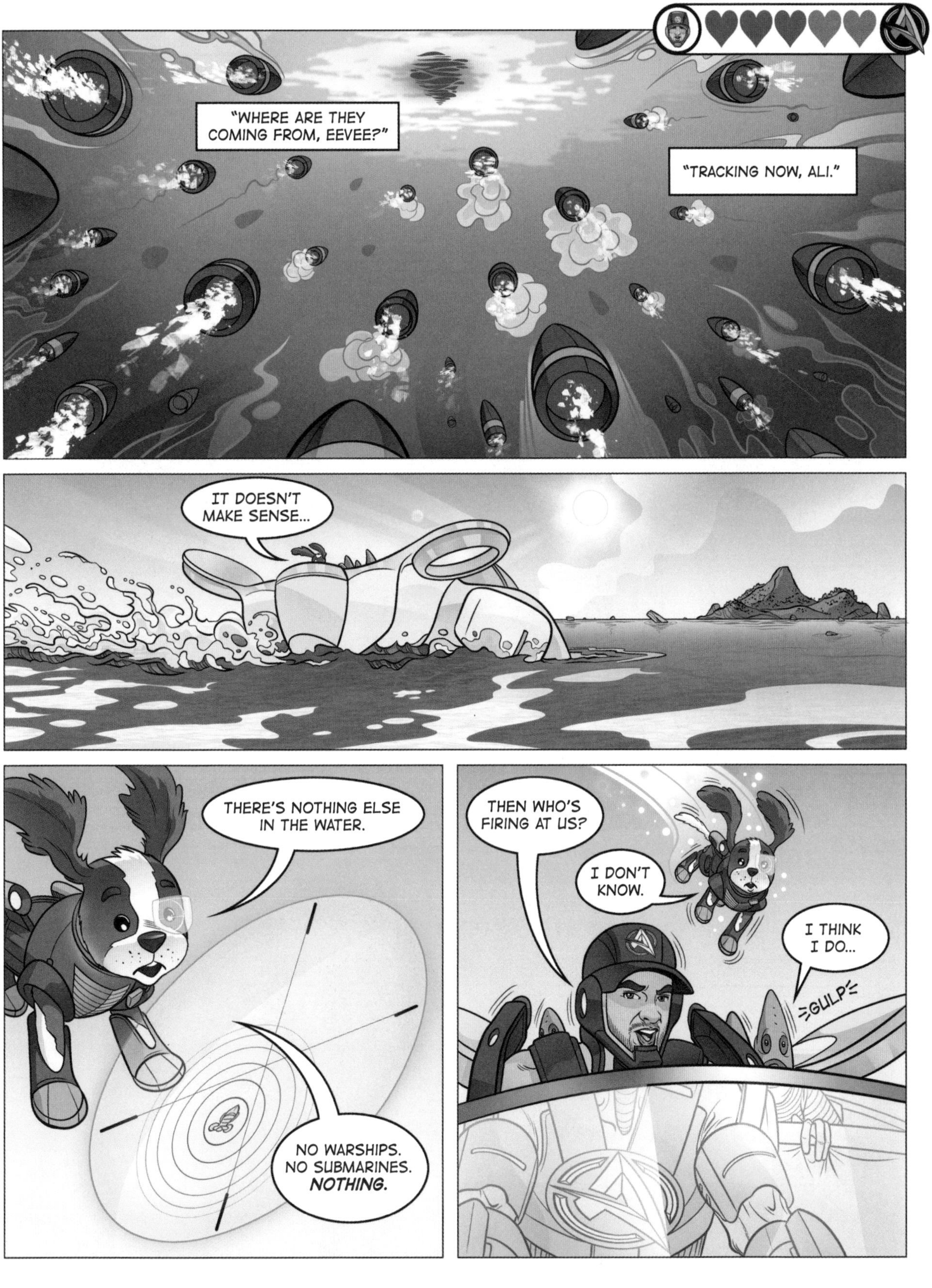
"WHERE ARE THEY COMING FROM, EEVEE?"
"TRACKING NOW, ALI."
IT DOESN'T MAKE SENSE...
THERE'S NOTHING ELSE IN THE WATER.
NO WARSHIPS. NO SUBMARINES. *NOTHING.*
THEN WHO'S FIRING AT US?
I DON'T KNOW.
I THINK I DO...
GULP

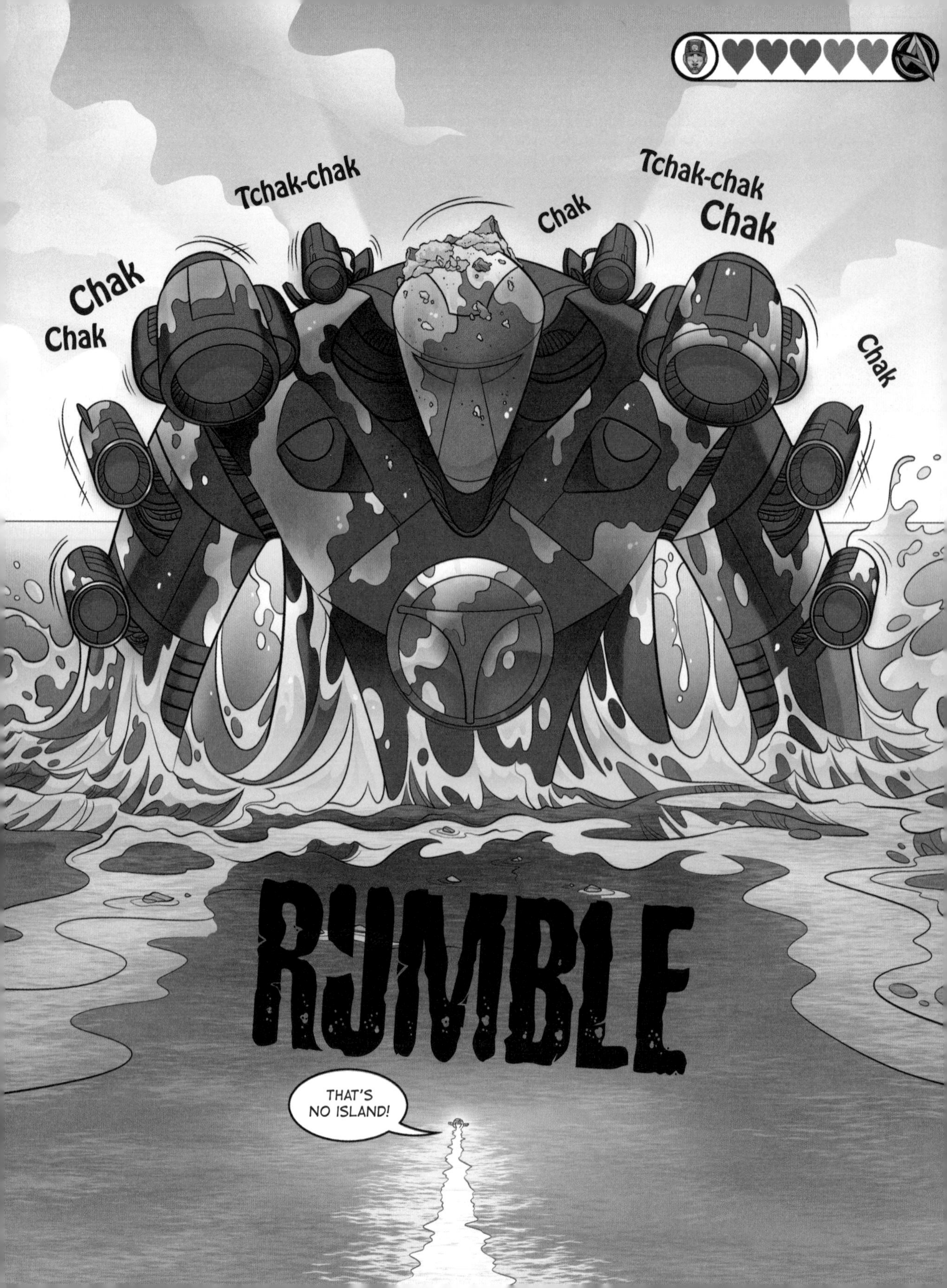

Chak
Chak
Tchak-chak
Chak
Tchak-chak
Chak
Chak
RUMBLE
THAT'S NO ISLAND!

LEVEL FIVE

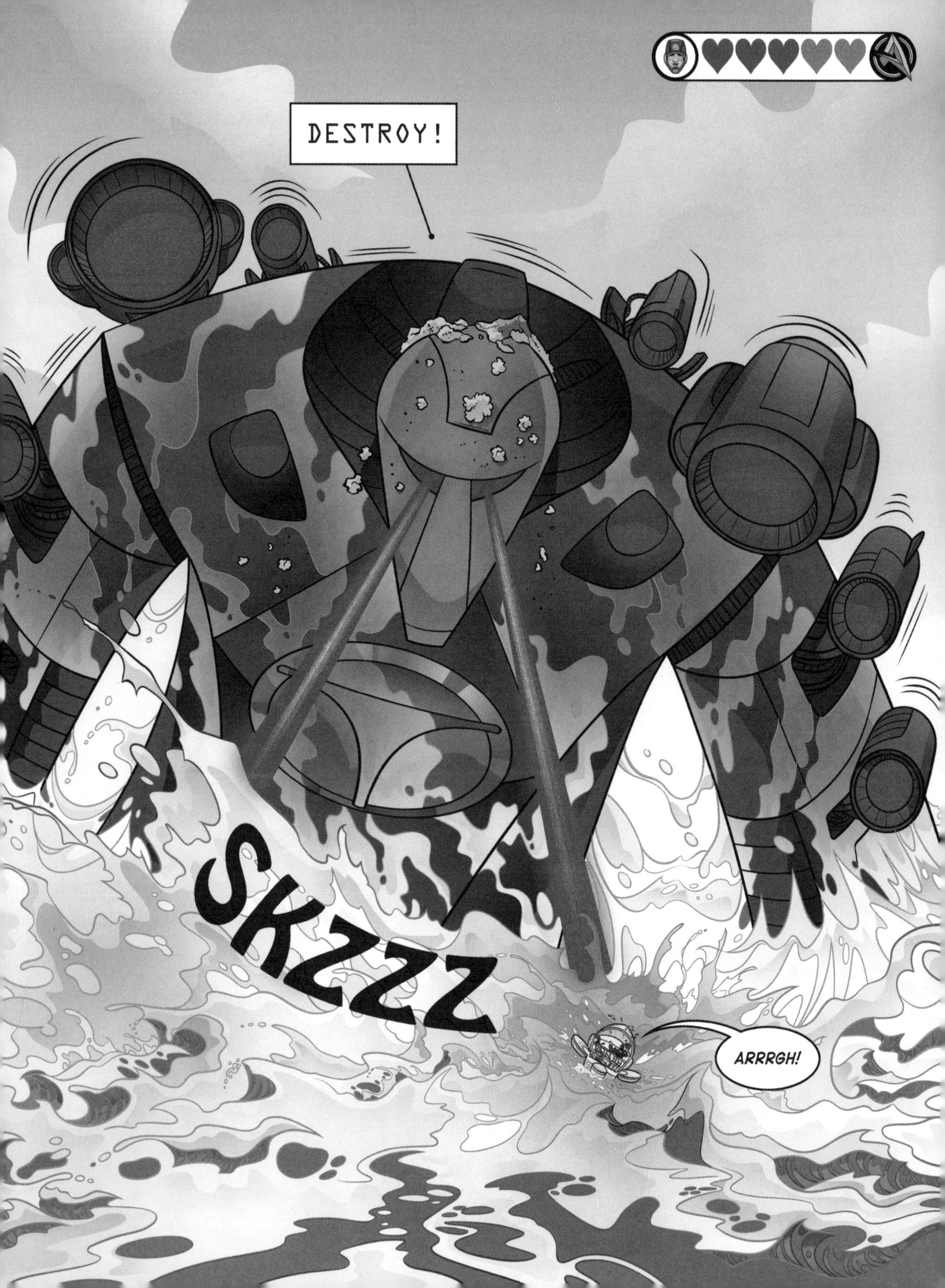
DESTROY!
SKZZZ
ARRRGH!

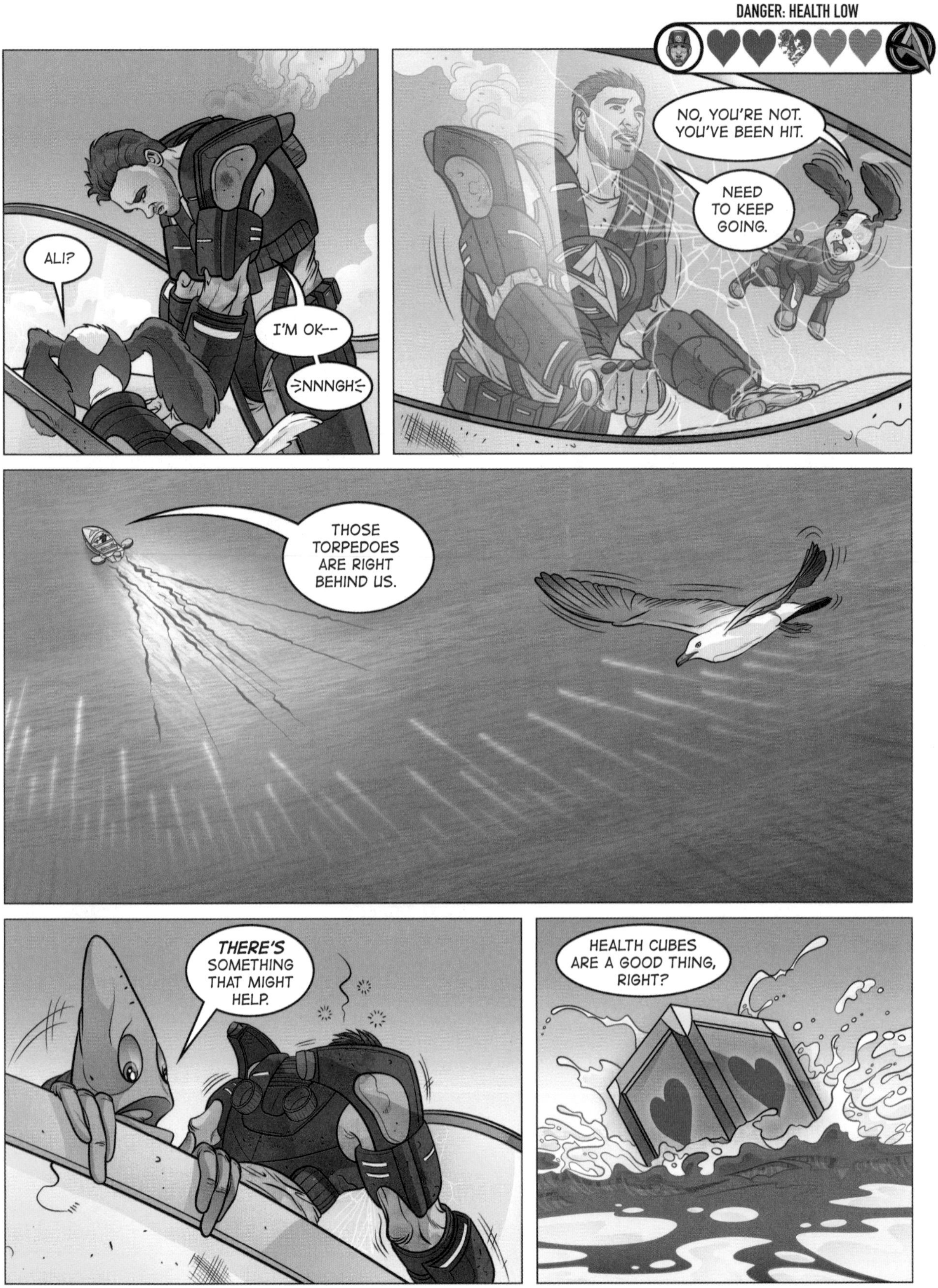
DANGER: HEALTH LOW
ALI?
I'M OK--
NNNGH
NO, YOU'RE NOT. YOU'VE BEEN HIT.
NEED TO KEEP GOING.
THOSE TORPEDOES ARE RIGHT BEHIND US.
THERE'S SOMETHING THAT MIGHT HELP.
HEALTH CUBES ARE A GOOD THING, RIGHT?

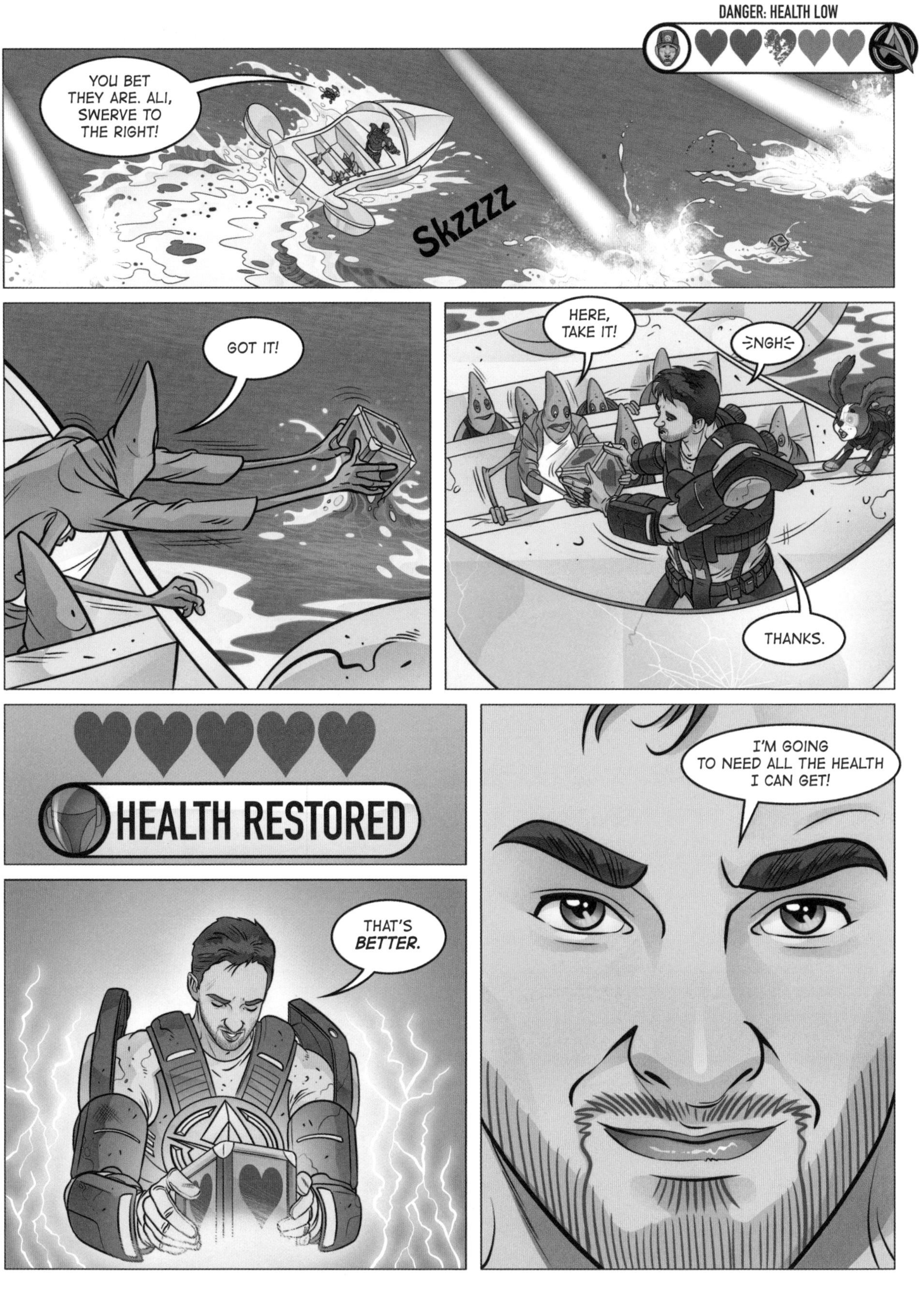
DANGER: HEALTH LOW
YOU BET THEY ARE. ALI, SWERVE TO THE RIGHT!
Skzzzz
GOT IT!
HERE, TAKE IT!
NGH
THANKS.
HEALTH RESTORED
THAT'S *BETTER.*
I'M GOING TO NEED ALL THE HEALTH I CAN GET!

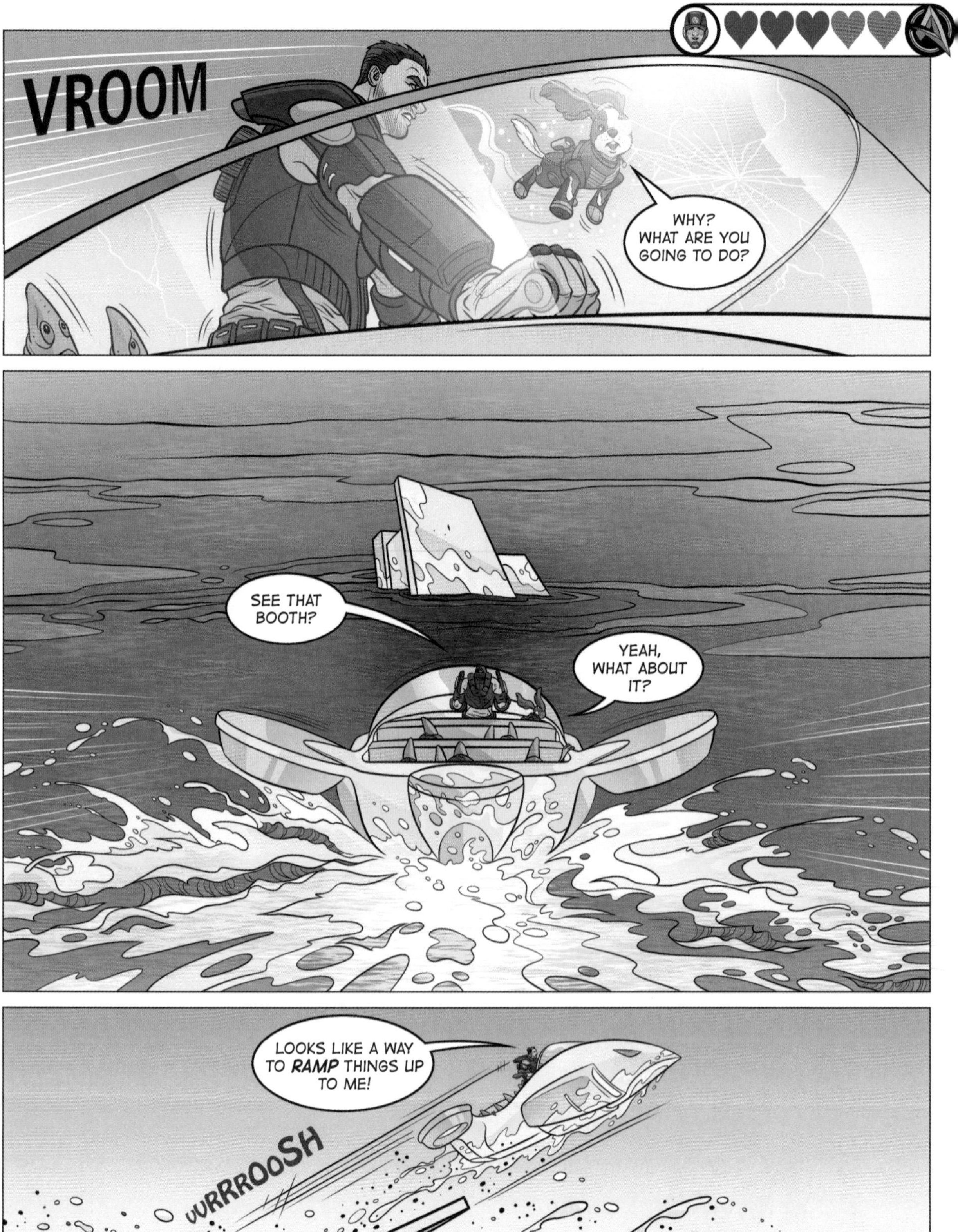
VROOM
WHY? WHAT ARE YOU GOING TO DO?
SEE THAT BOOTH?
YEAH, WHAT ABOUT IT?
LOOKS LIKE A WAY TO *RAMP* THINGS UP TO ME!
VURRROOSH

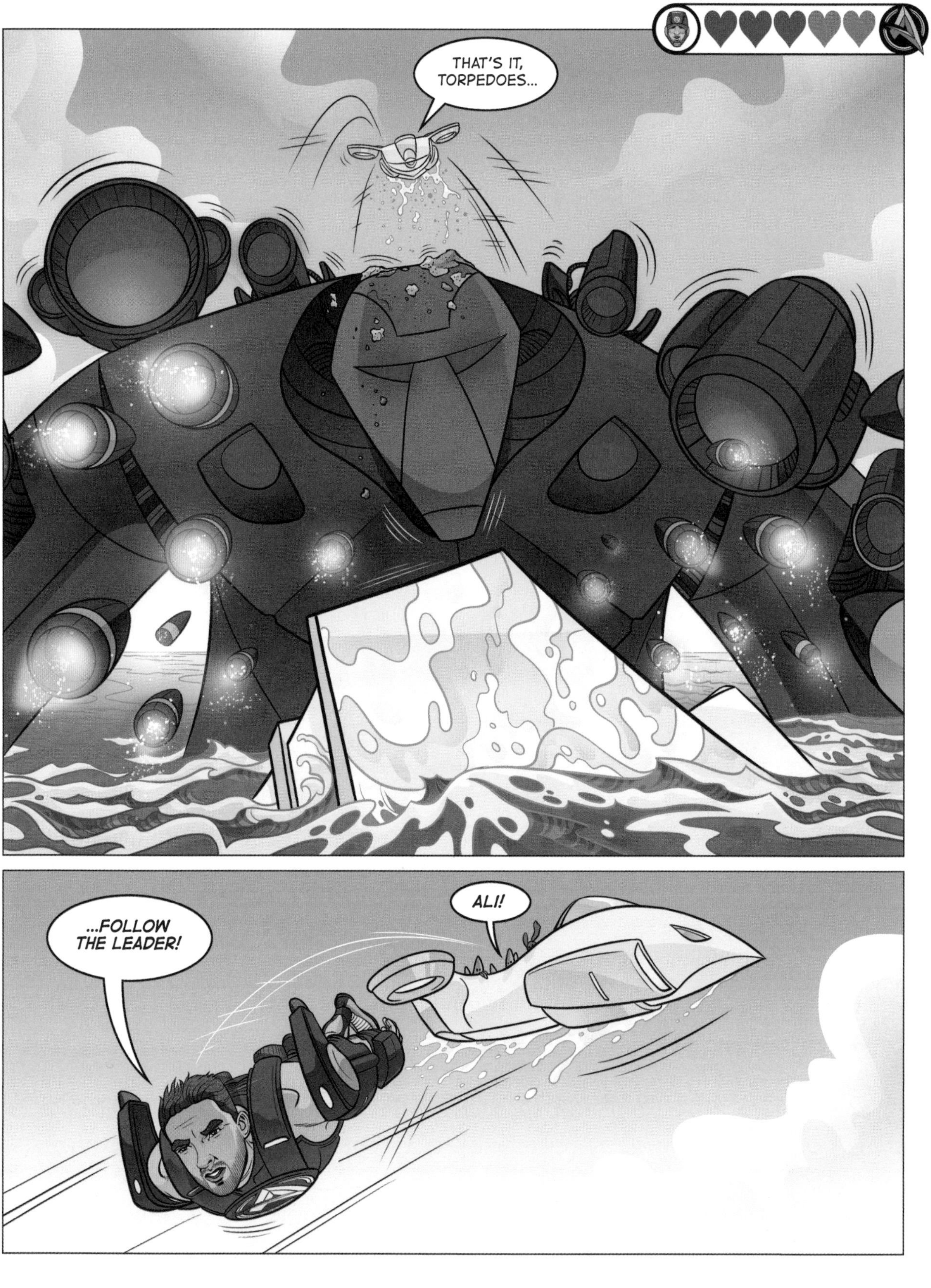
THAT'S IT, TORPEDOES...
...FOLLOW THE LEADER!
ALI!

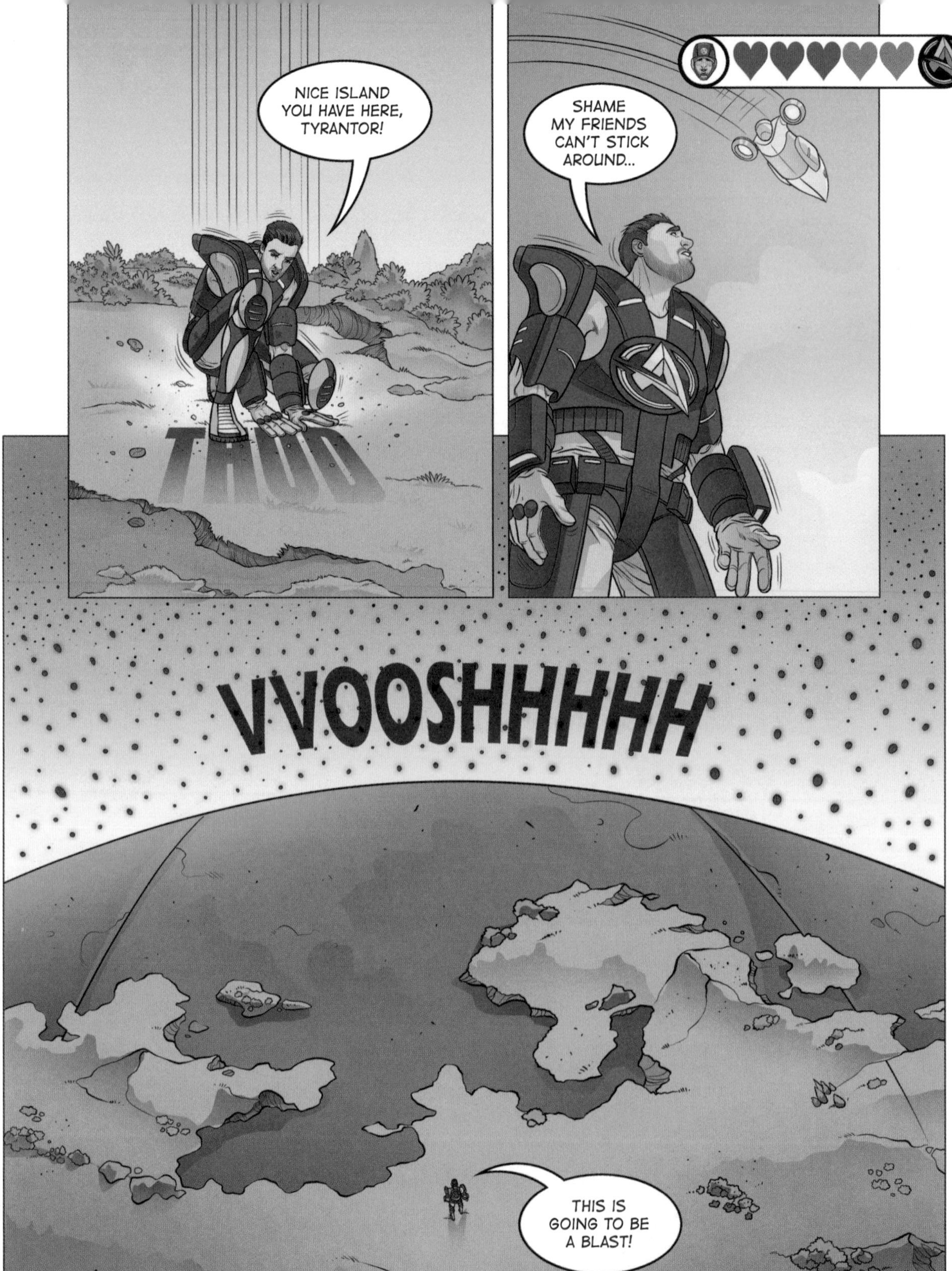
NICE ISLAND YOU HAVE HERE, TYRANTOR!
THUD
SHAME MY FRIENDS CAN'T STICK AROUND...
VVOOSHHHHH
THIS IS GOING TO BE A BLAST!

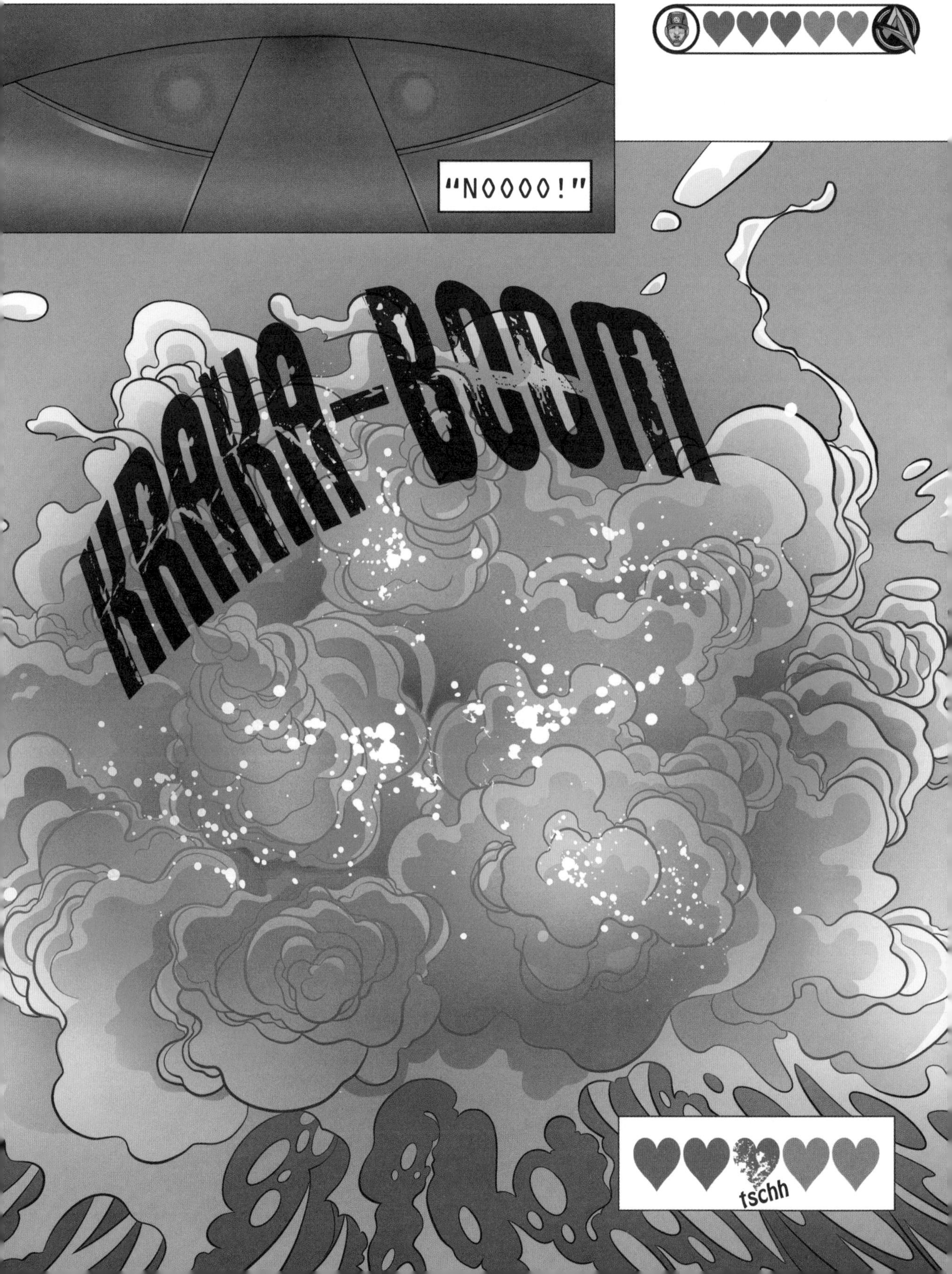
"NOOOO!"
KRAKKA-BOOM
tschh

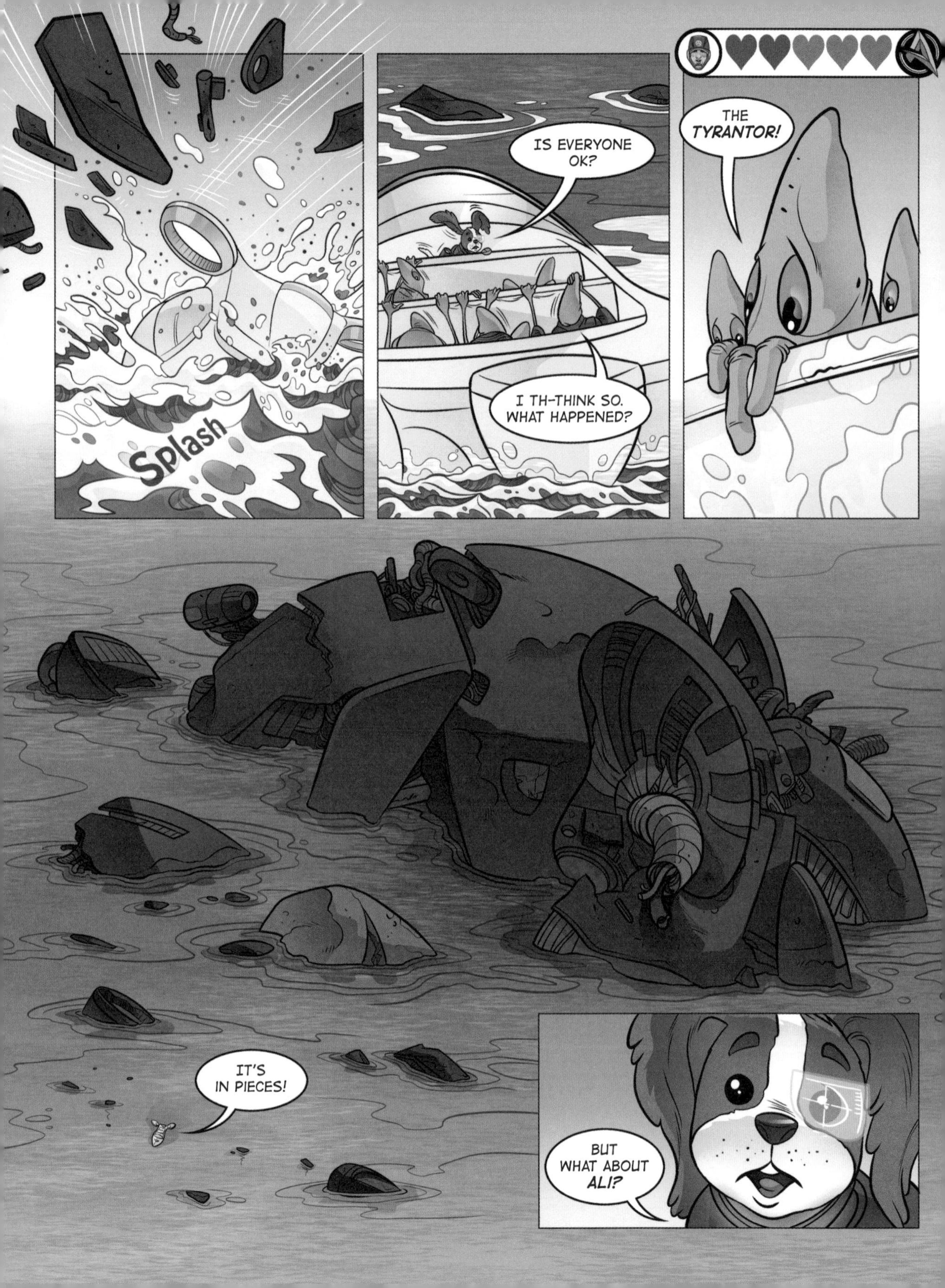
Splash
IS EVERYONE OK?
I TH-THINK SO. WHAT HAPPENED?
THE TYRANTOR!
IT'S IN PIECES!
BUT WHAT ABOUT ALI!?

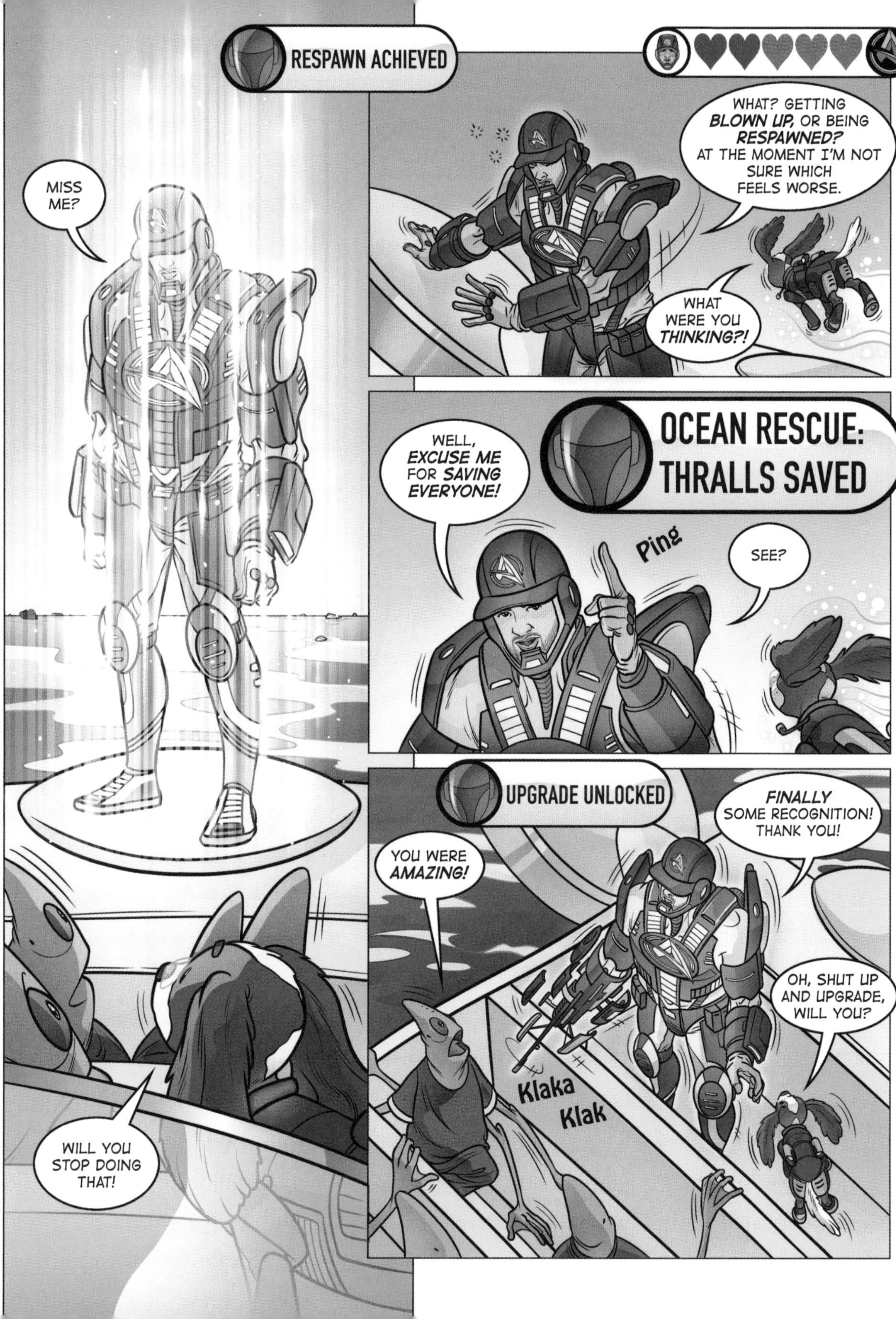
RESPAWN ACHIEVED
MISS ME?
WILL YOU STOP DOING THAT!
WHAT? GETTING BLOWN UP, OR BEING RESPAWNED? AT THE MOMENT I'M NOT SURE WHICH FEELS WORSE.
WHAT WERE YOU THINKING?!
OCEAN RESCUE: THRALLS SAVED
WELL, EXCUSE ME FOR SAVING EVERYONE!
Ping
SEE?
UPGRADE UNLOCKED
YOU WERE AMAZING!
FINALLY SOME RECOGNITION! THANK YOU!
OH, SHUT UP AND UPGRADE, WILL YOU?
Klaka Klak

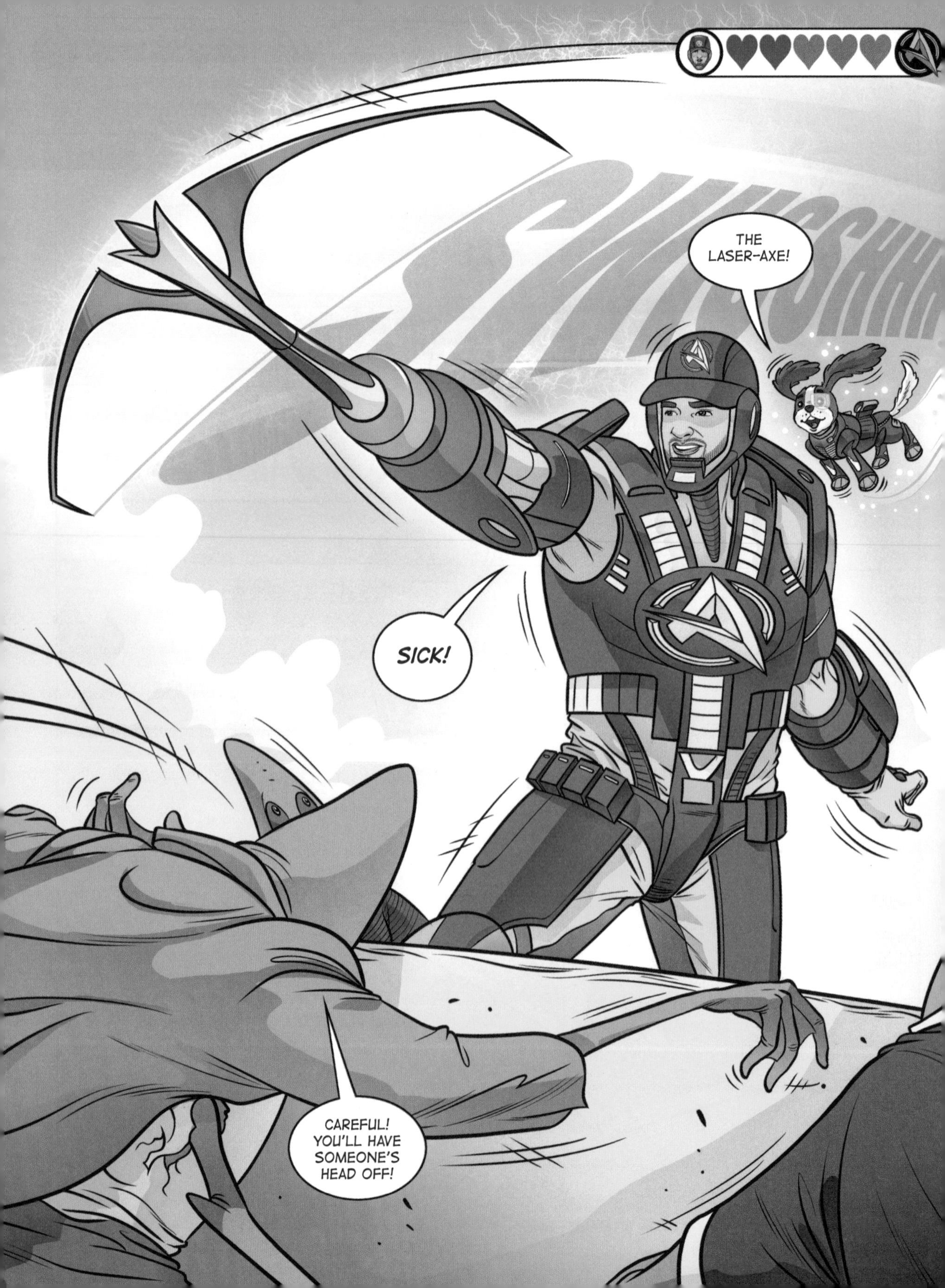
THE LASER-AXE!
SICK!
CAREFUL! YOU'LL HAVE SOMEONE'S HEAD OFF!

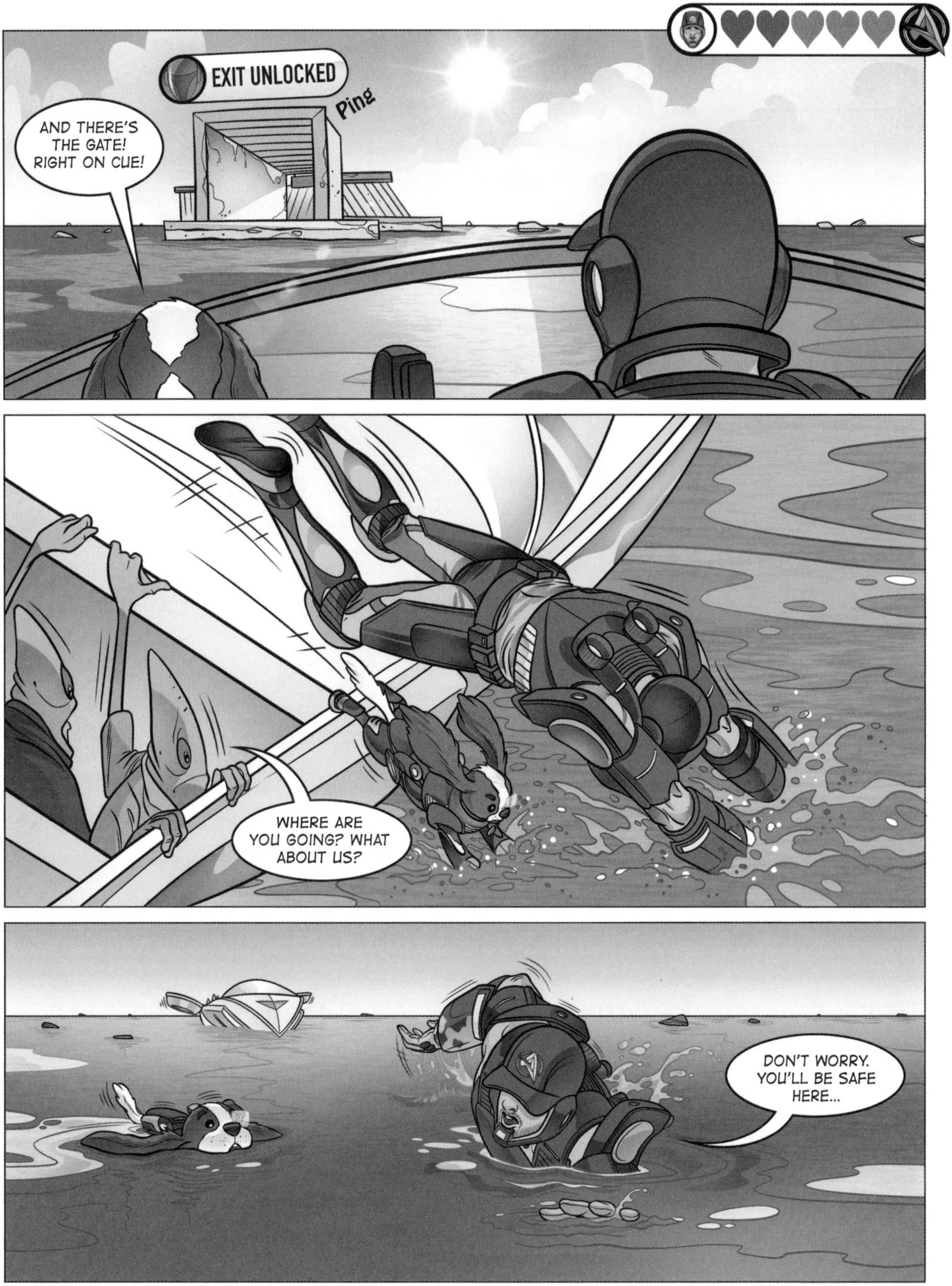
EXIT UNLOCKED
Ping
AND THERE'S THE GATE! RIGHT ON CUE!
WHERE ARE YOU GOING? WHAT ABOUT US?
DON'T WORRY. YOU'LL BE SAFE HERE...

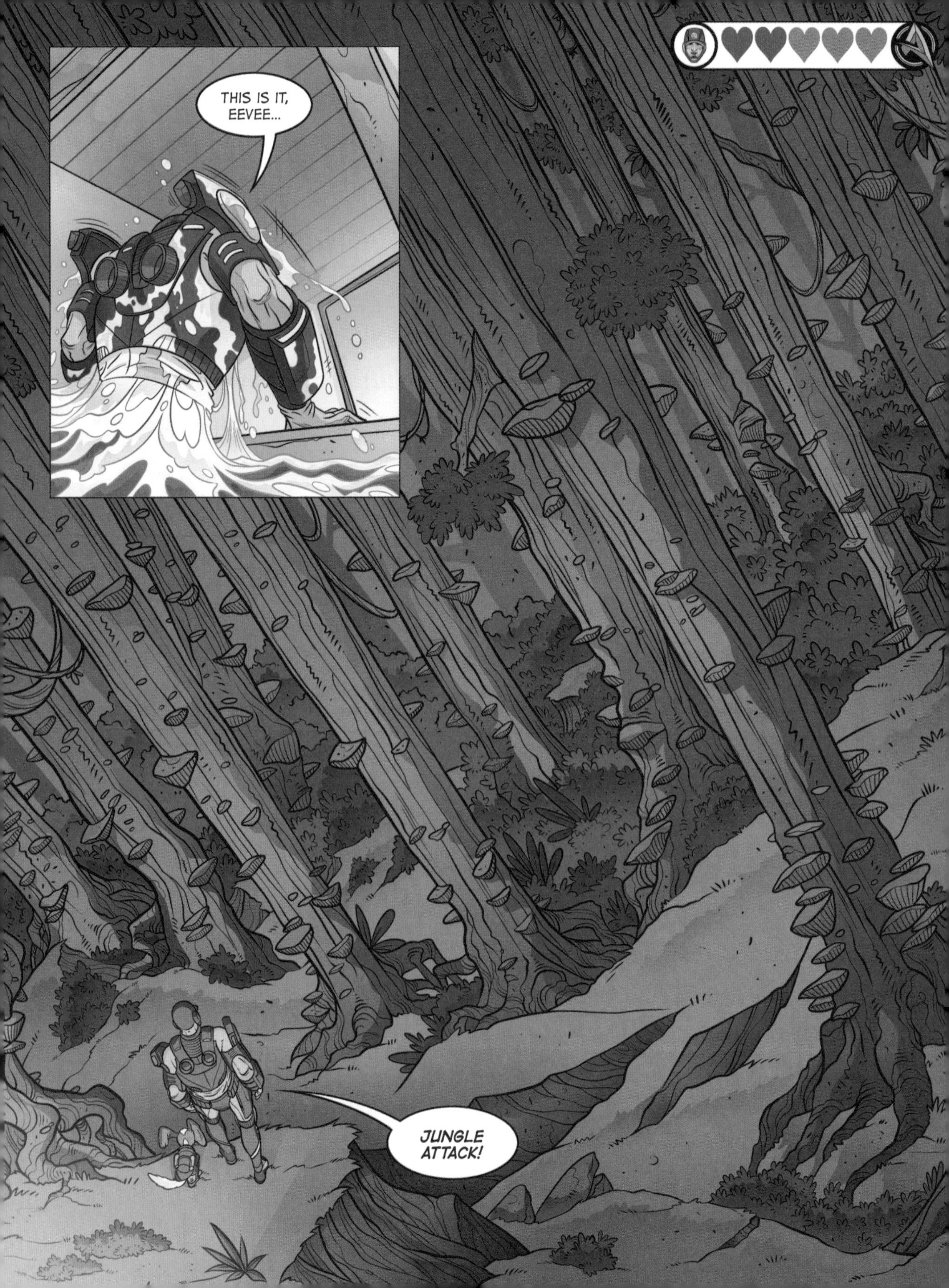
THIS IS IT, EEVEE...
JUNGLE ATTACK!

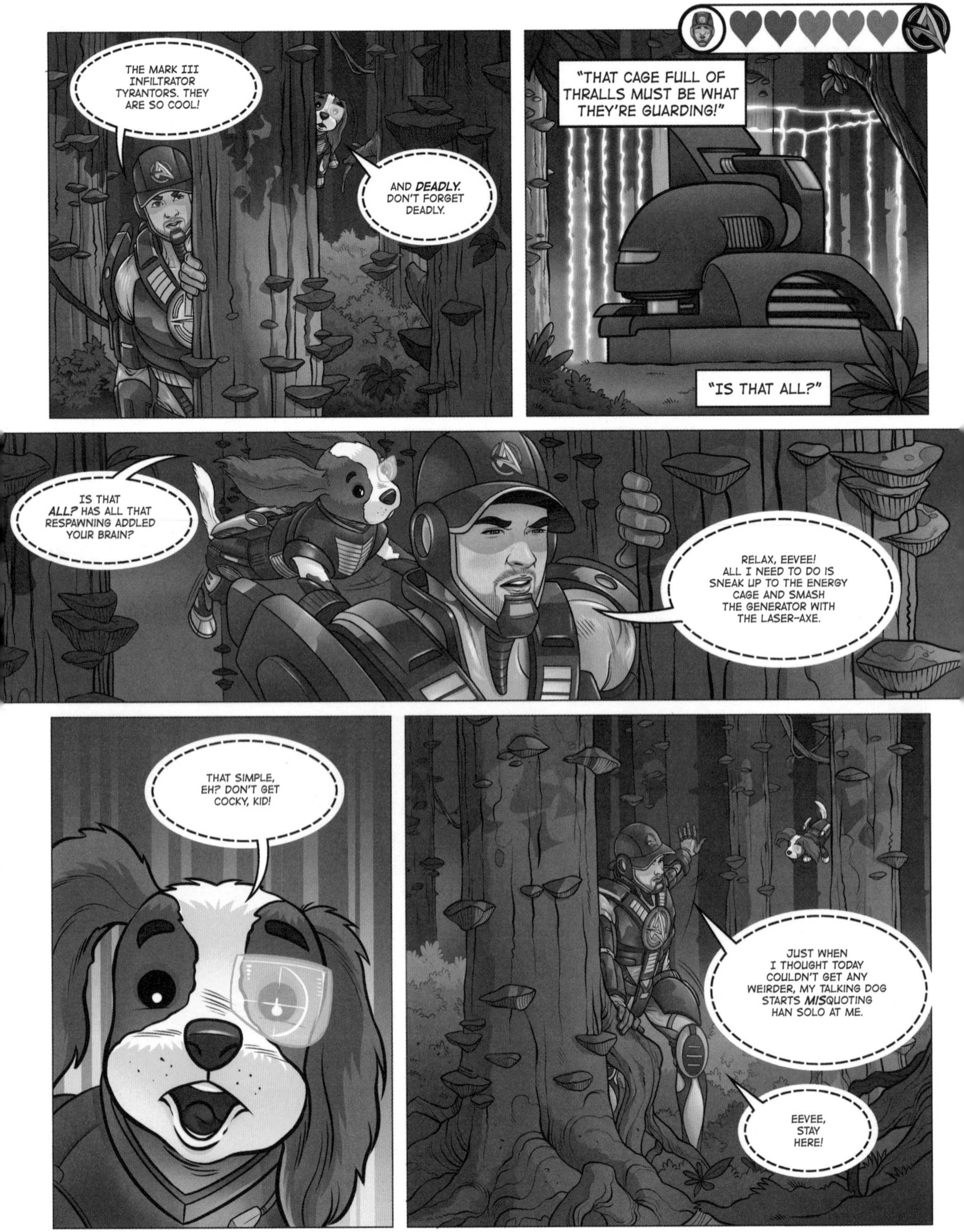

THE MARK III INFILTRATOR TYRANTORS. THEY ARE SO COOL!
AND *DEADLY.* DON'T FORGET DEADLY.
"THAT CAGE FULL OF THRALLS MUST BE WHAT THEY'RE GUARDING!"
"IS THAT ALL?"
IS THAT *ALL?* HAS ALL THAT RESPAWNING ADDLED YOUR BRAIN?
RELAX, EEVEE! ALL I NEED TO DO IS SNEAK UP TO THE ENERGY CAGE AND SMASH THE GENERATOR WITH THE LASER-AXE.
THAT SIMPLE, EH? DON'T GET COCKY, KID!
JUST WHEN I THOUGHT TODAY COULDN'T GET ANY WEIRDER, MY TALKING DOG STARTS *MIS*QUOTING HAN SOLO AT ME.
EEVEE, STAY HERE!

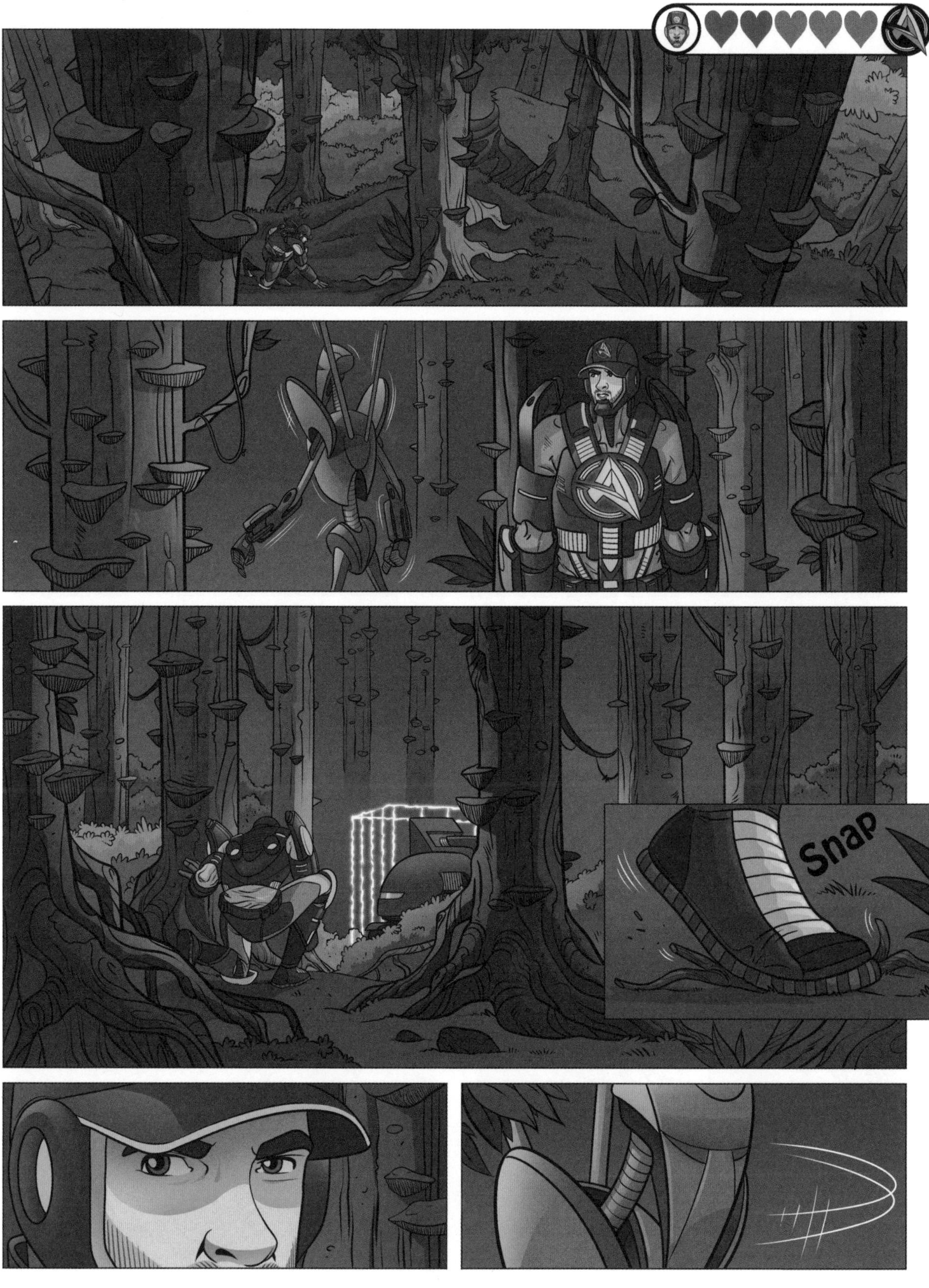
Snap

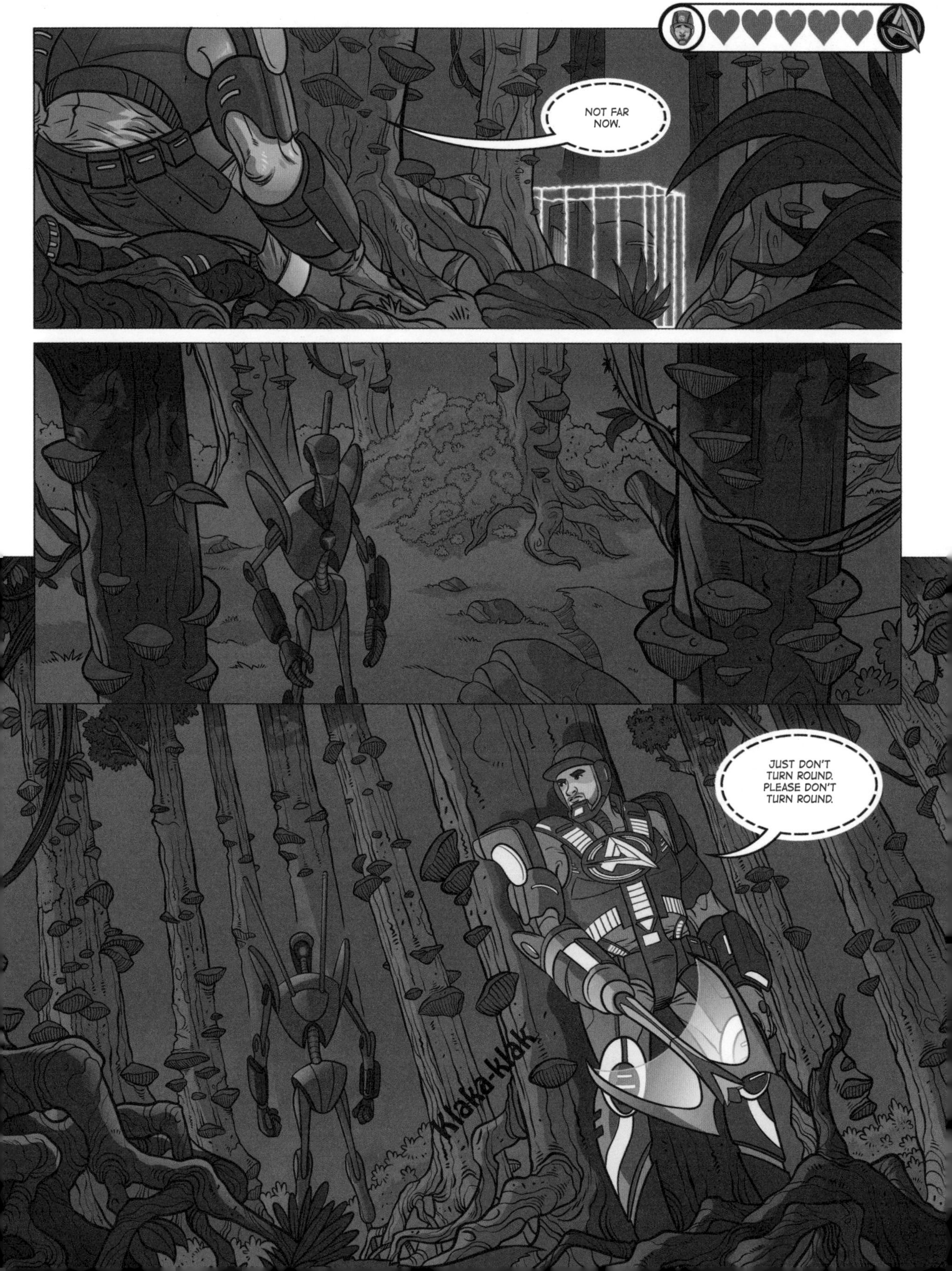
NOT FAR NOW.
JUST DON'T TURN ROUND. PLEASE DON'T TURN ROUND.
Klaka-klak

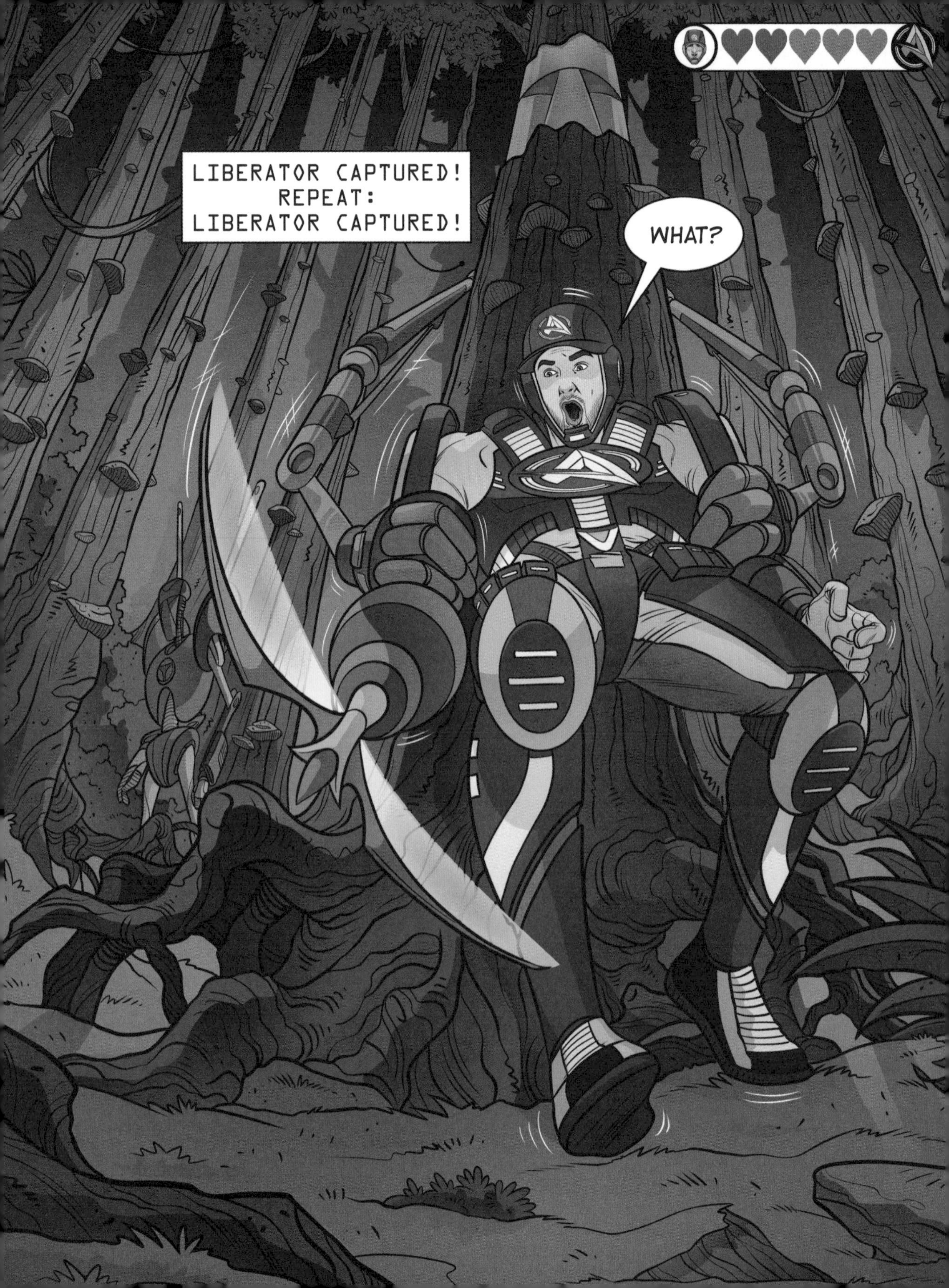
LIBERATOR CAPTURED!
REPEAT:
LIBERATOR CAPTURED!
WHAT?

LEVEL SIX

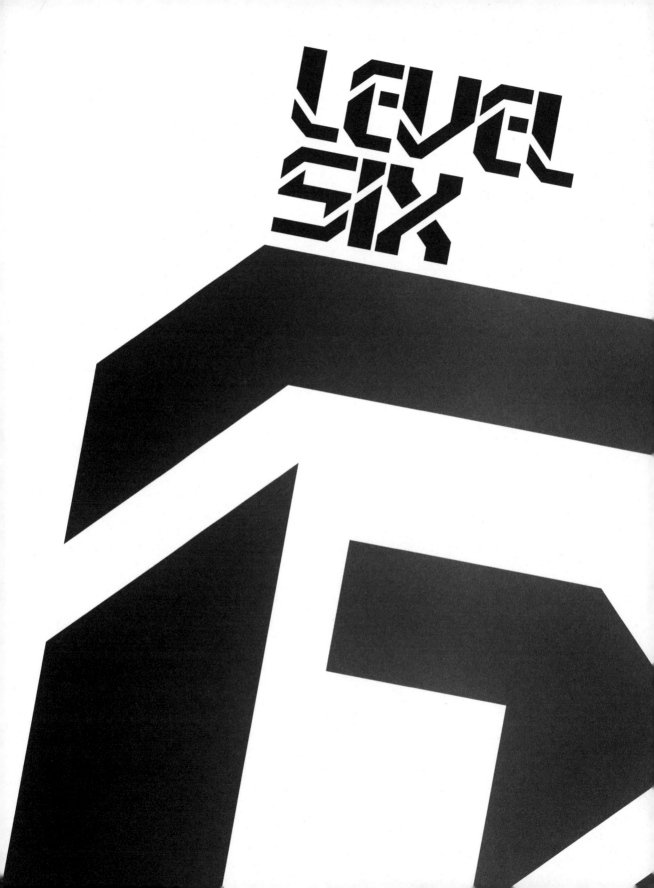

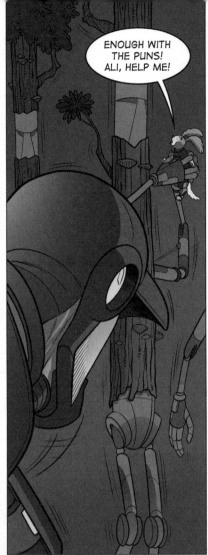

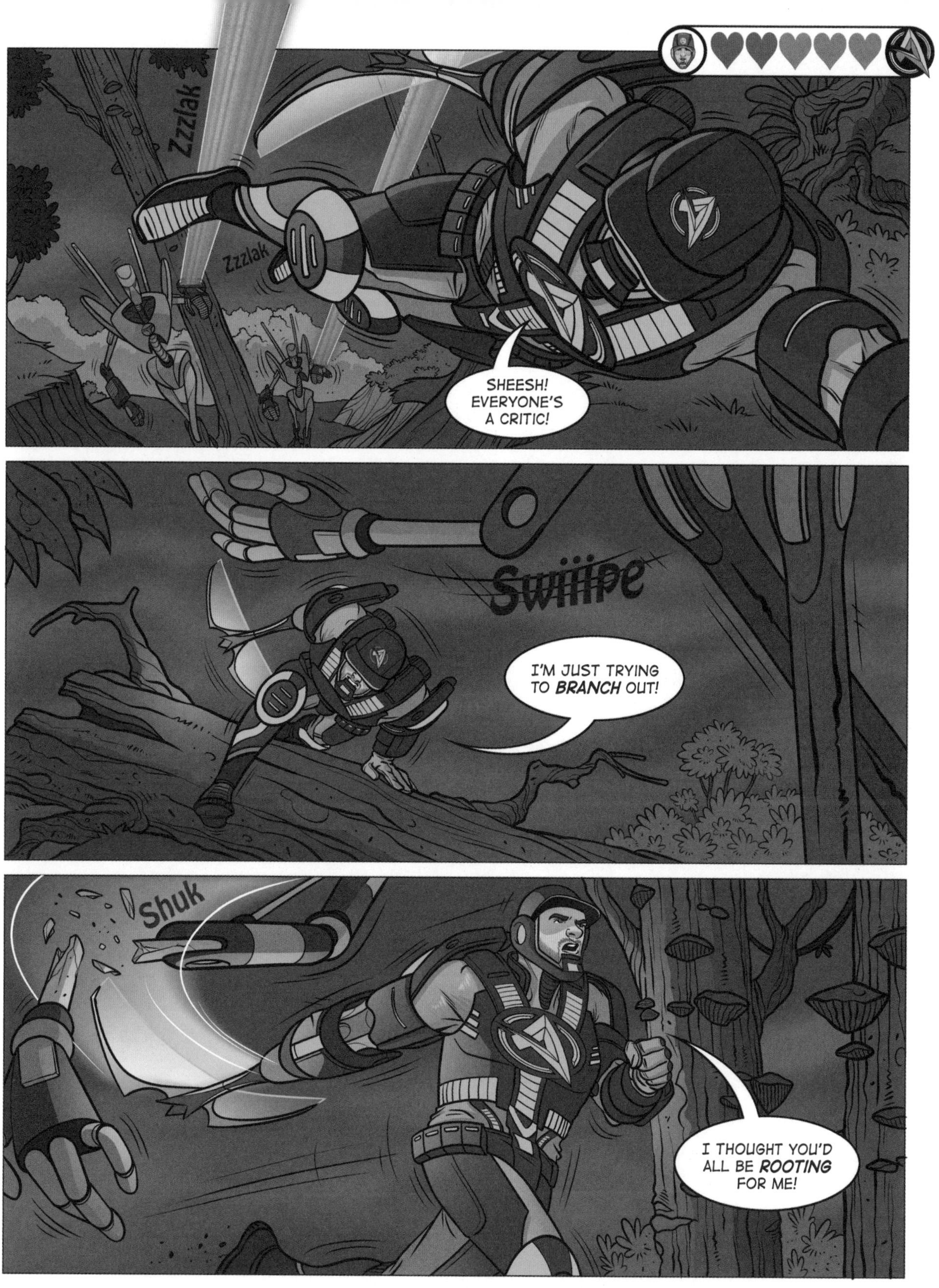
Zzzlak
Zzzlak
SHEESH! EVERYONE'S A CRITIC!
Swiiipe
I'M JUST TRYING TO *BRANCH* OUT!
Shuk
I THOUGHT YOU'D ALL BE *ROOTING* FOR ME!

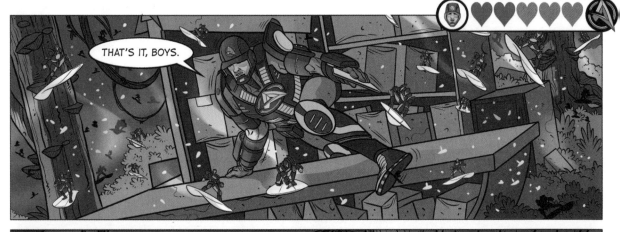

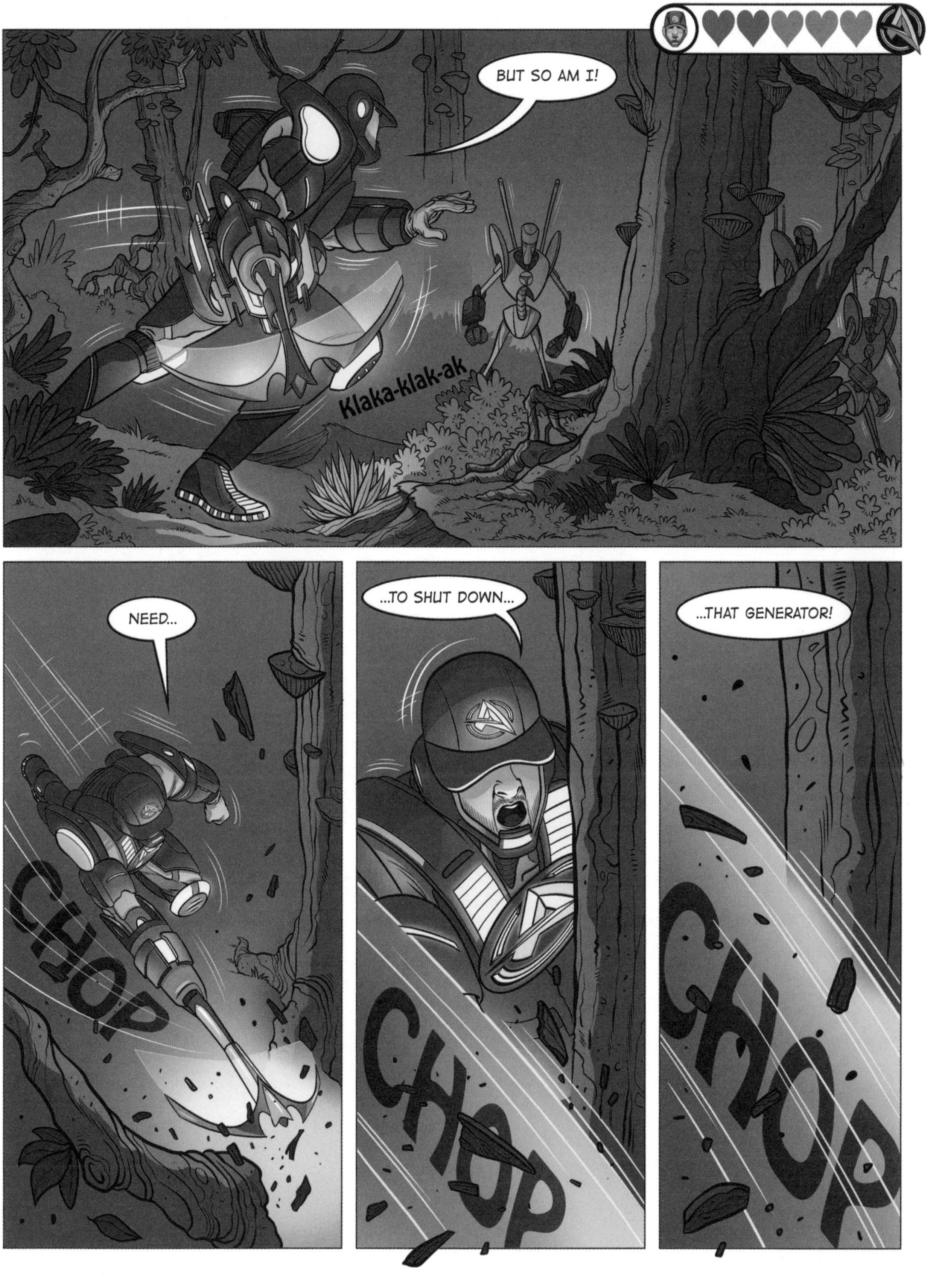
BUT SO AM I!
Klaka-klak-ak
NEED...
CHOP
...TO SHUT DOWN...
CHOP
...THAT GENERATOR!
CHOP

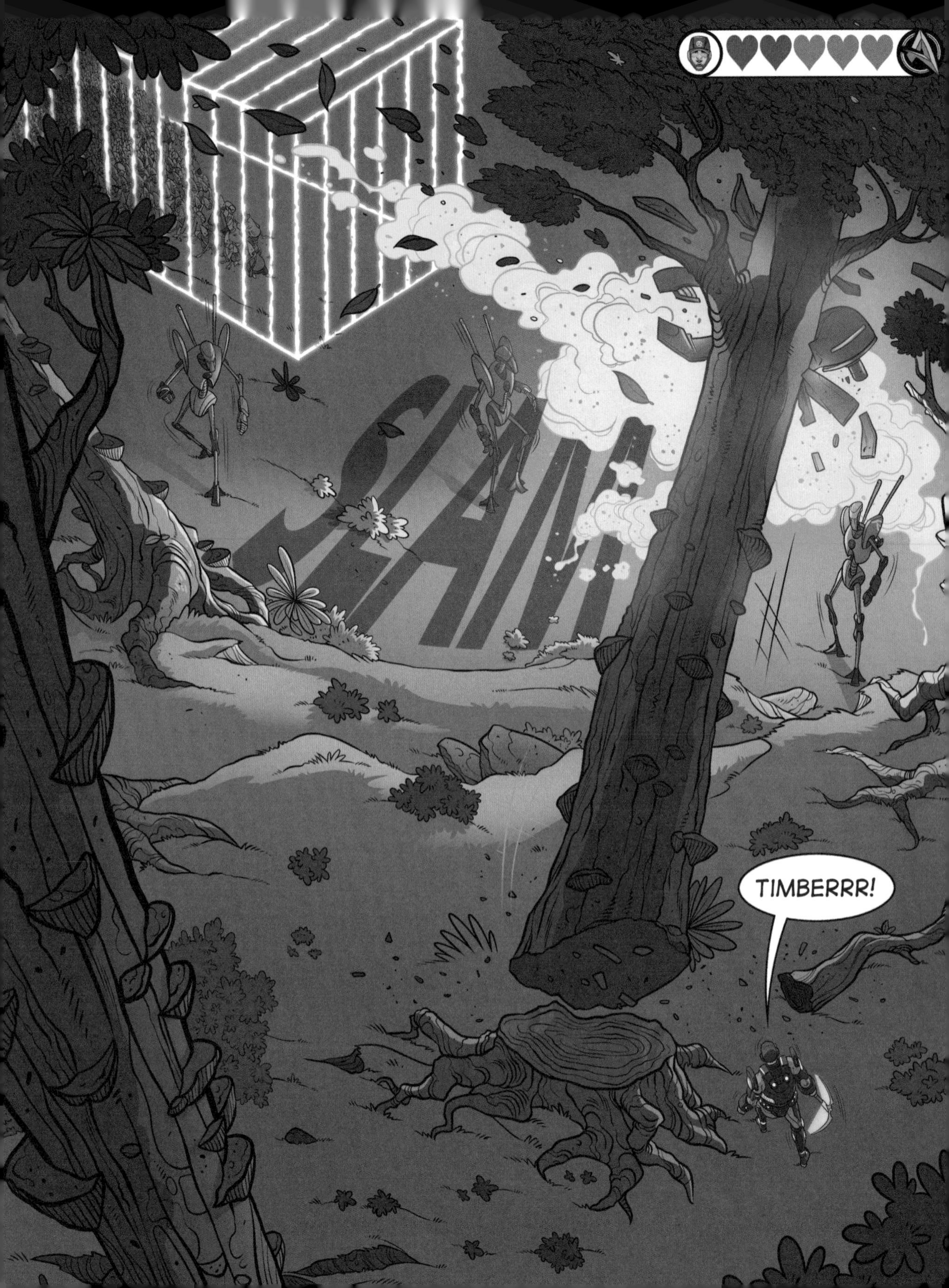
SNAP!
TIMBERRR!

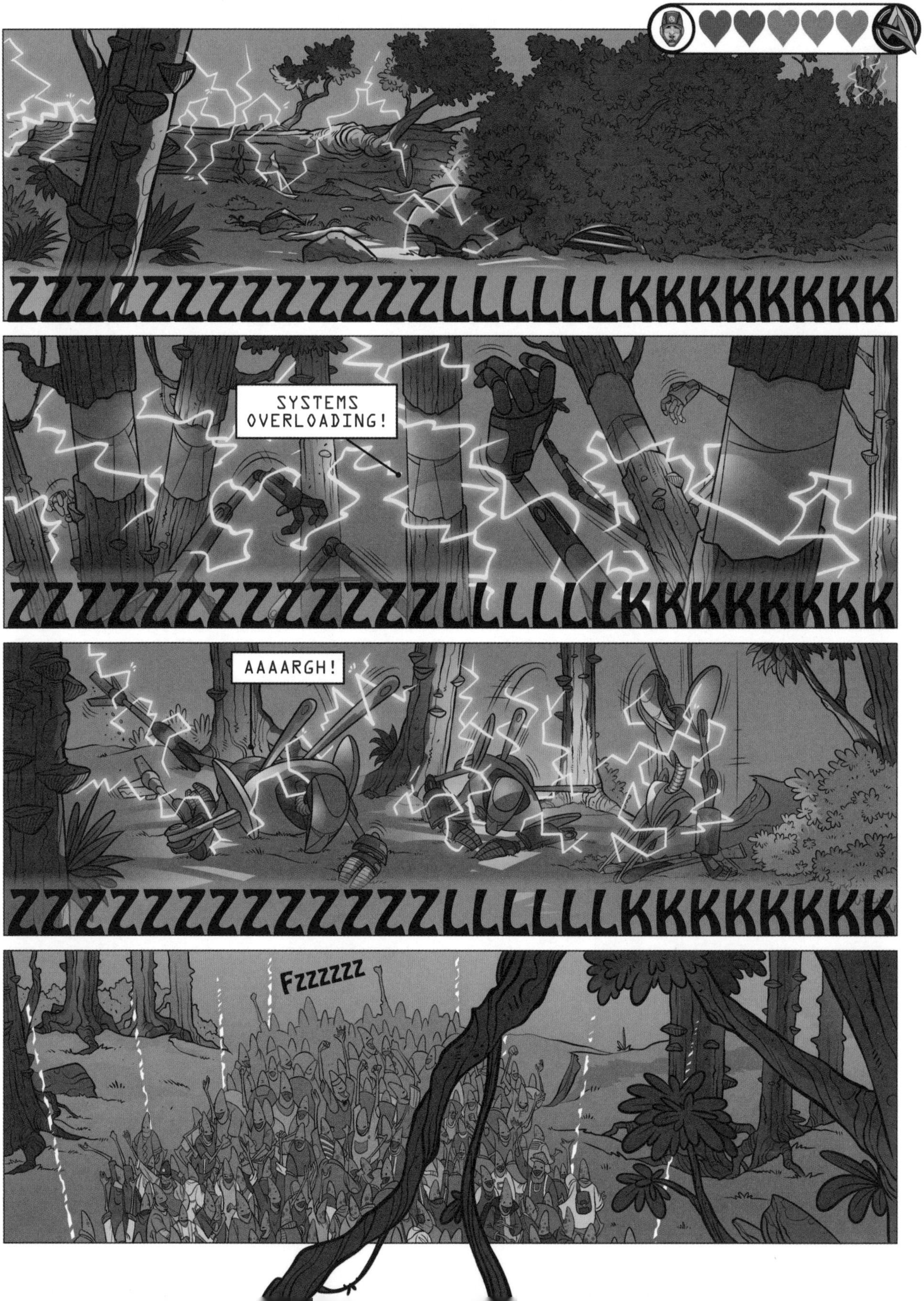
ZZZZZZZZZZZZZZZZZLLLLLLKKKKKKKK
SYSTEMS OVERLOADING!
ZZZZZZZZZZZZZZZZZLLLLLLKKKKKKKK
AAAARGH!
ZZZZZZZZZZZZZZZZZLLLLLLKKKKKKKK
Fzzzzzz

Thud

NOW THAT'S--

IF YOU'RE ABOUT TO SAY *TREE-MENDOUS,* I'LL SHOOT YOU MYSELF!

YOU SPOIL ALL MY FUN, EEVEE.

THAT'S IT. RUN! YOU'RE FREE!

THRALLS SAVED: 1

Ping

UPGRADE UNLOCKED

Ping

AND HERE WE GO AGAIN!

THE *FORCE-FIELD GENERATOR!* NICE!

SO NOW WHAT?

NOW WE TAKE A CLOSER LOOK AT THIS TABLET...

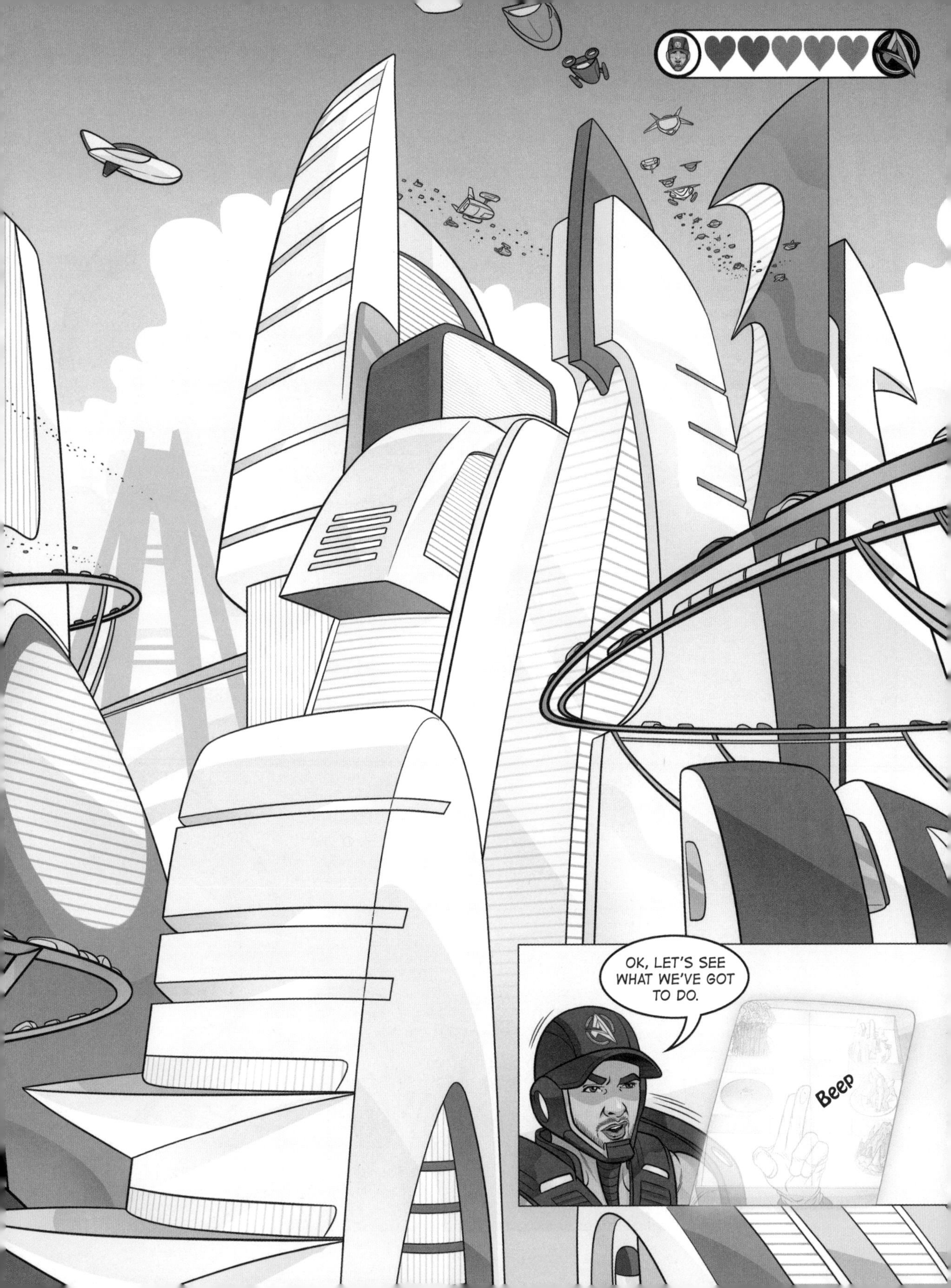
OK, LET'S SEE WHAT WE'VE GOT TO DO.
Beep

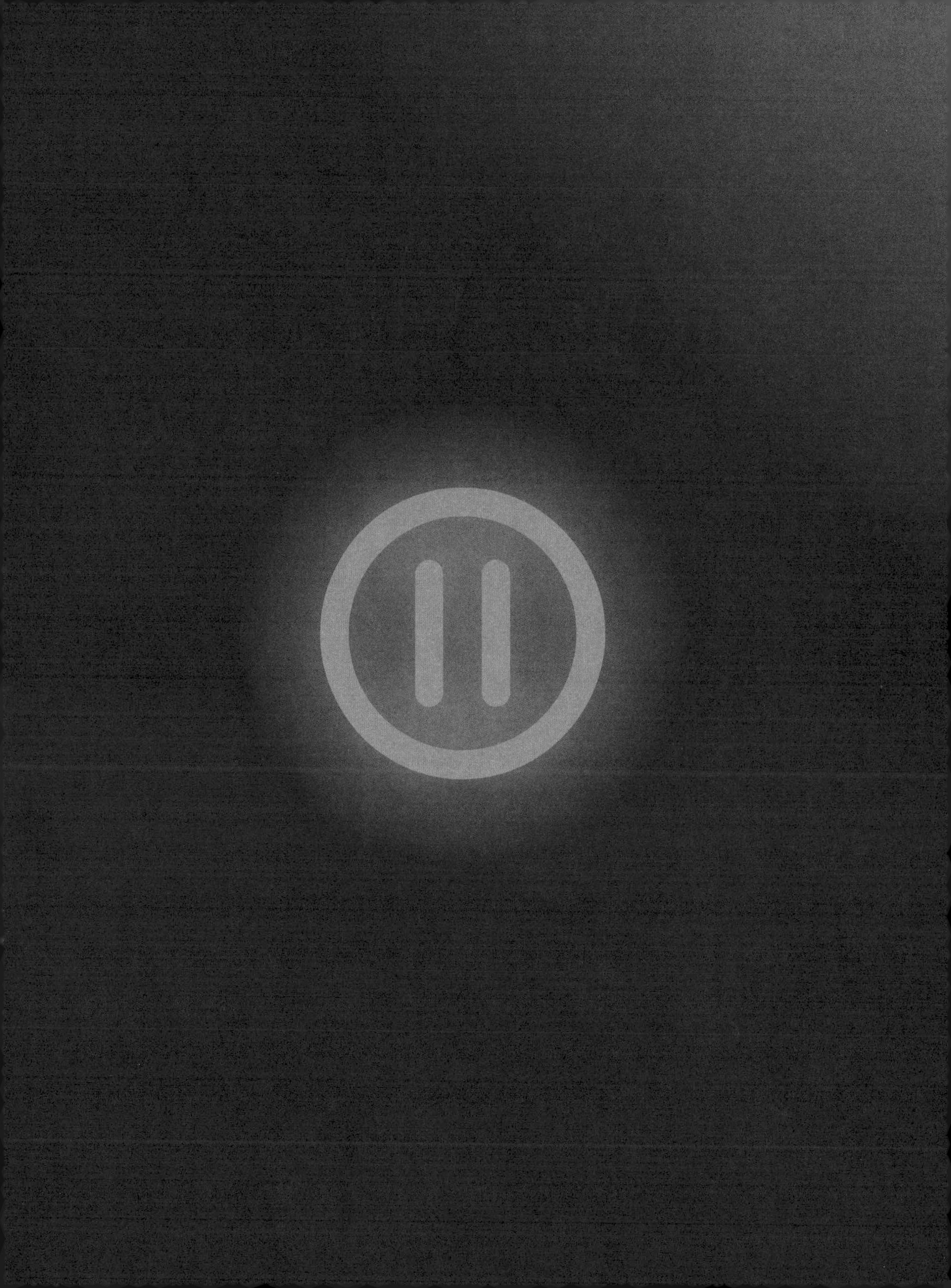

LEVEL SEVEN

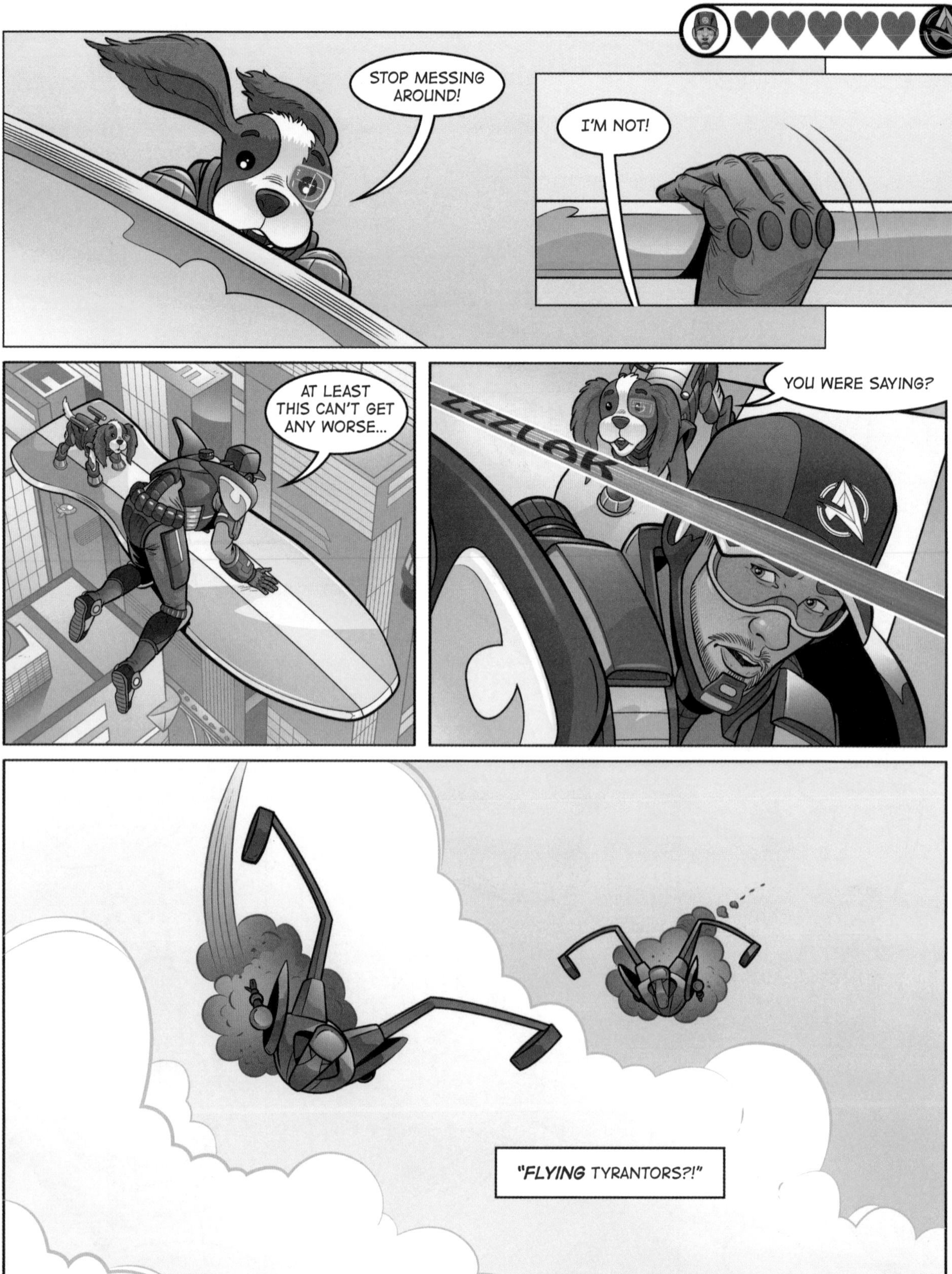
STOP MESSING AROUND!
I'M NOT!
AT LEAST THIS CAN'T GET ANY WORSE...
YOU WERE SAYING?
"FLYING TYRANTORS?!"

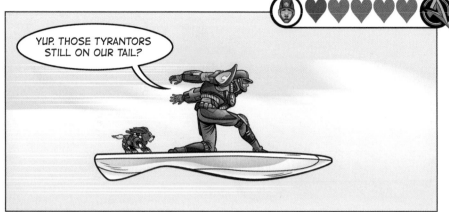

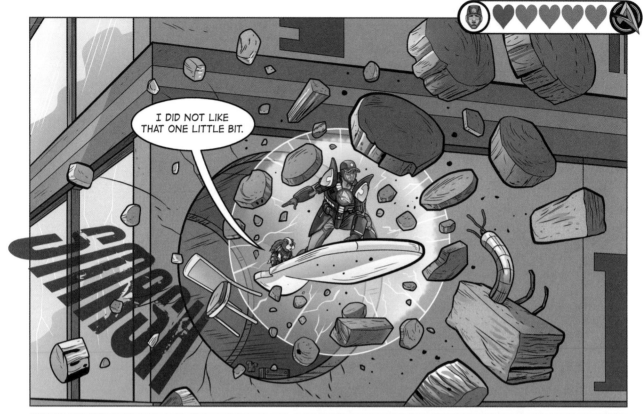

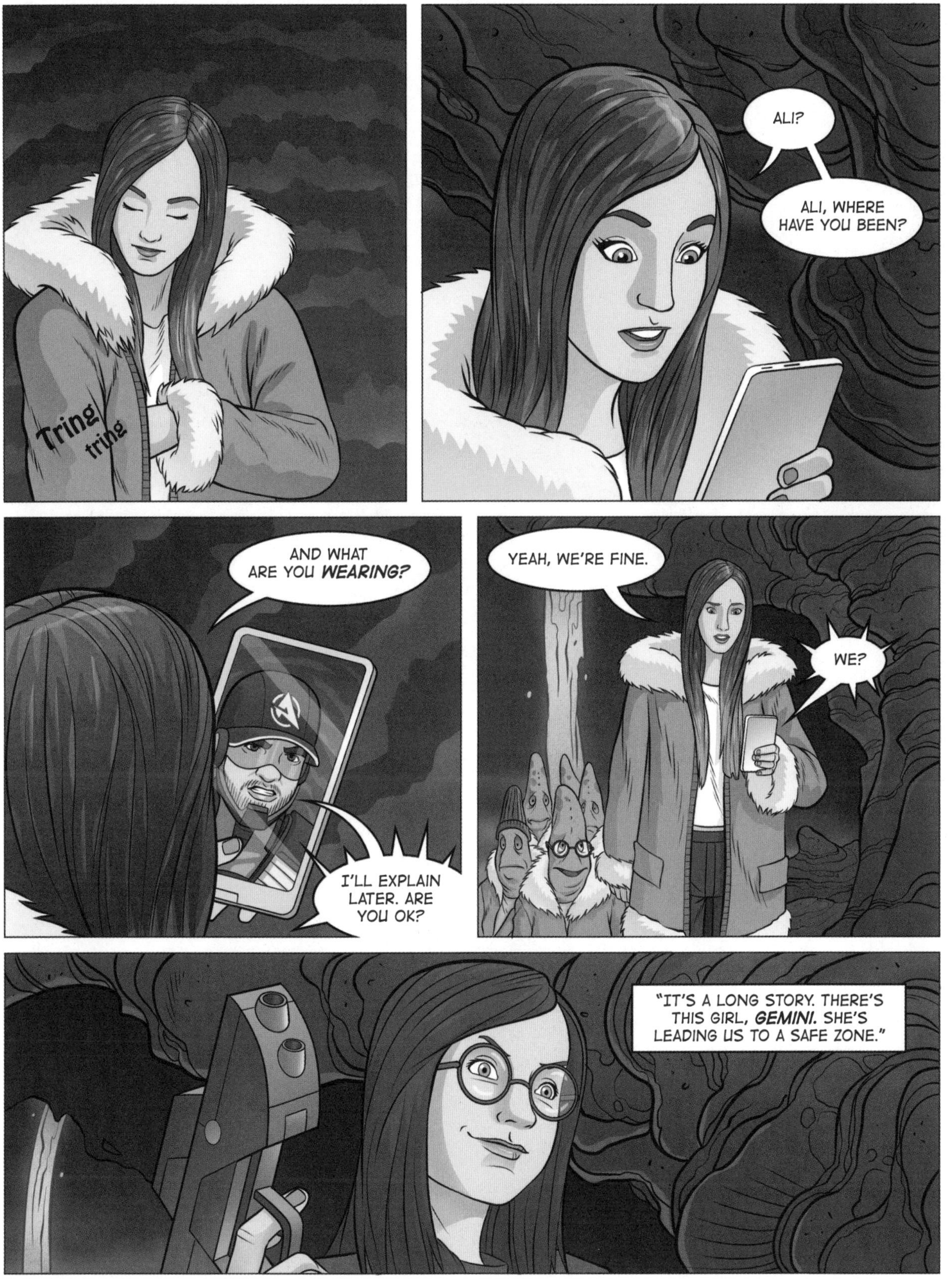
Tring tring
ALI?
ALI, WHERE HAVE YOU BEEN?
AND WHAT ARE YOU **WEARING?**
I'LL EXPLAIN LATER. ARE YOU OK?
YEAH, WE'RE FINE.
WE?
"IT'S A LONG STORY. THERE'S THIS GIRL, **GEMINI.** SHE'S LEADING US TO A SAFE ZONE."

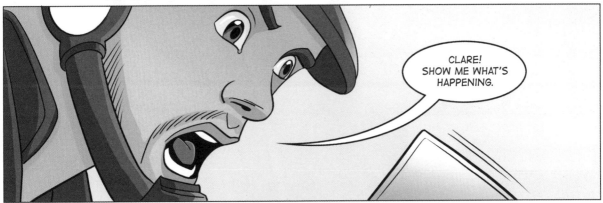

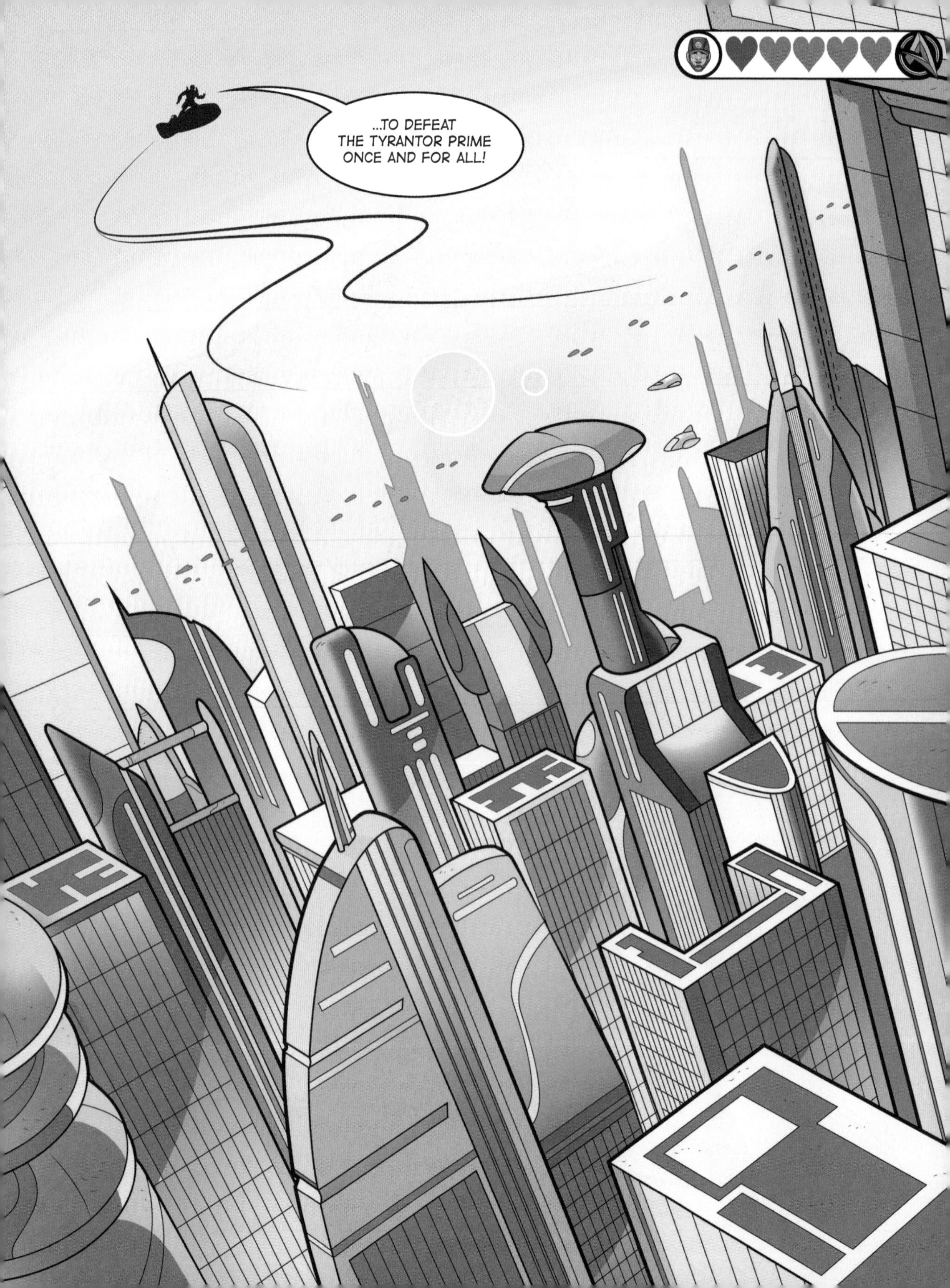
...TO DEFEAT THE TYRANTOR PRIME ONCE AND FOR ALL!

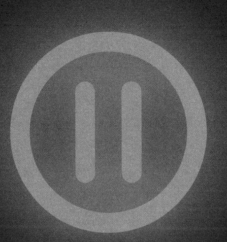

LEVEL EIGHT

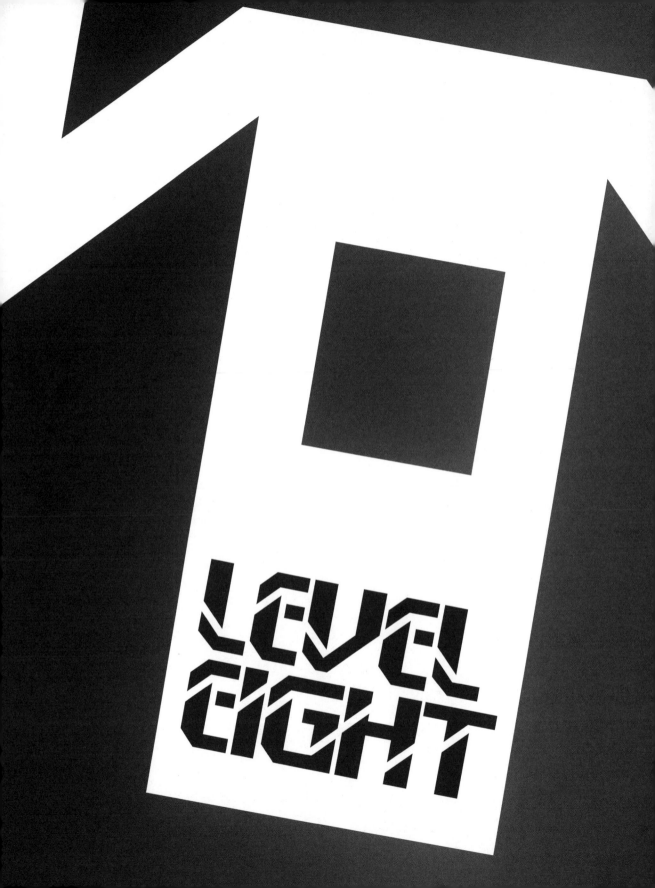

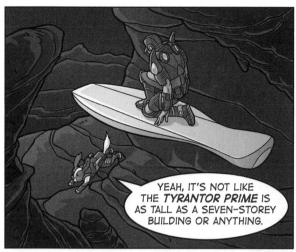

YEAH, IT'S NOT LIKE THE *TYRANTOR PRIME* IS AS TALL AS A SEVEN-STOREY BUILDING OR ANYTHING.

AT LEAST IT DIDN'T SEE US!

IT WAS TOO BUSY STARING AT THAT *BIG SCARY MACHINE.*

I'M GUESSING THAT'S THE SOURCE OF ALL THE ENERGY.

IT'S THE SOURCE OF ALL OUR PROBLEMS!

"ACCORDING TO MY SCANS, *THAT'S* WHAT TRANSFORMED THE EARTH AND EVERYONE ON IT."

BUT *HOW?* THE TYRANTORS AREN'T REAL--NOT REALLY. THEY'RE JUST VILLAINS FROM A VIDEO GAME.

"TRY TELLING CLARE THAT!"

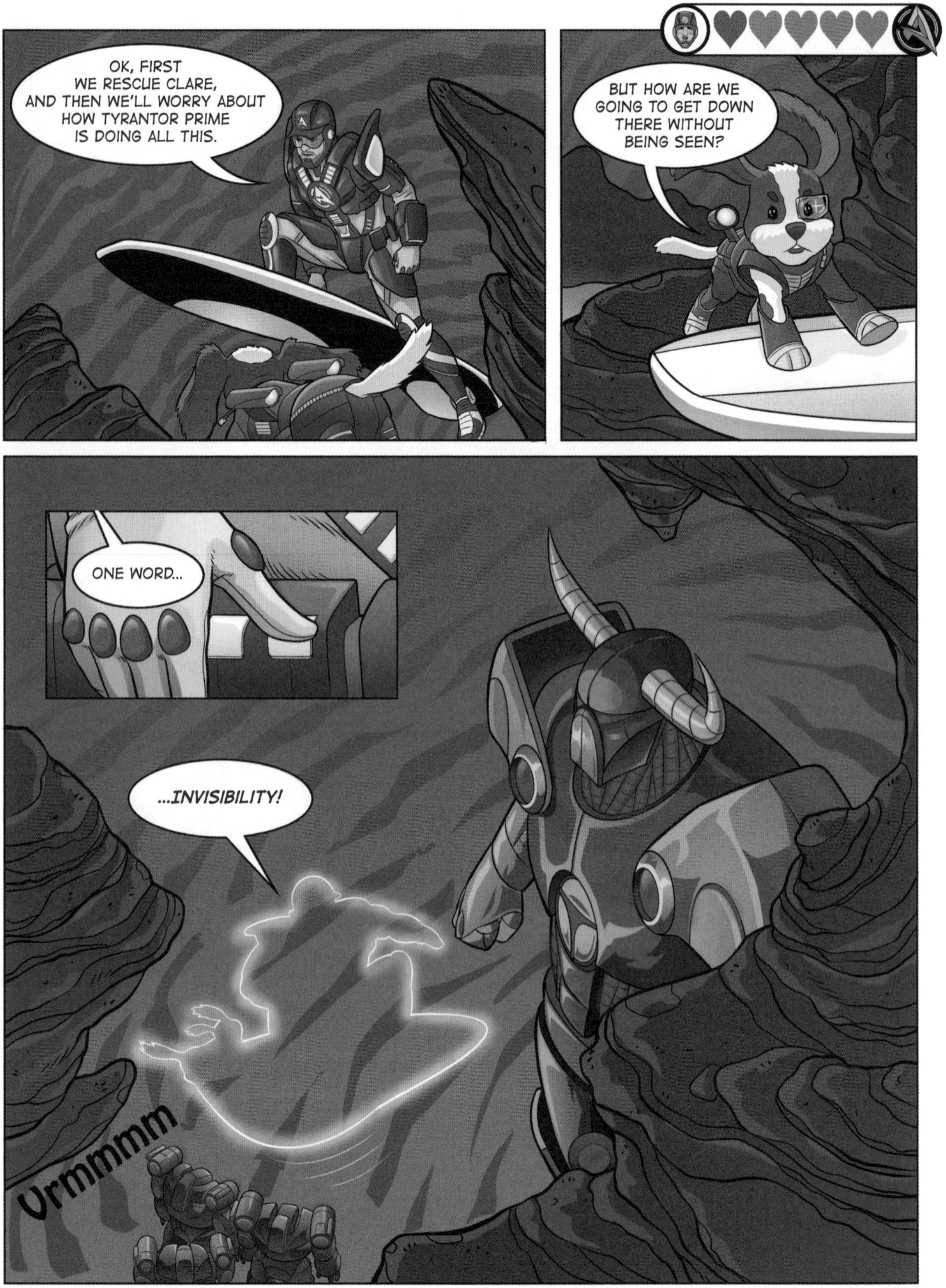
OK, FIRST WE RESCUE CLARE, AND THEN WE'LL WORRY ABOUT HOW TYRANTOR PRIME IS DOING ALL THIS.
BUT HOW ARE WE GOING TO GET DOWN THERE WITHOUT BEING SEEN?
ONE WORD...
...INVISIBILITY!
Vrmmmm

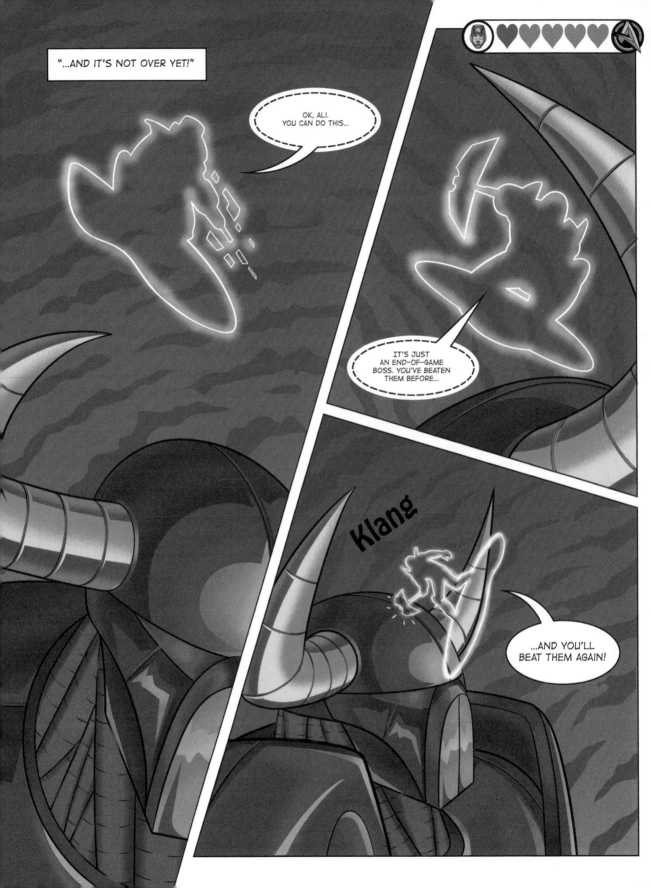

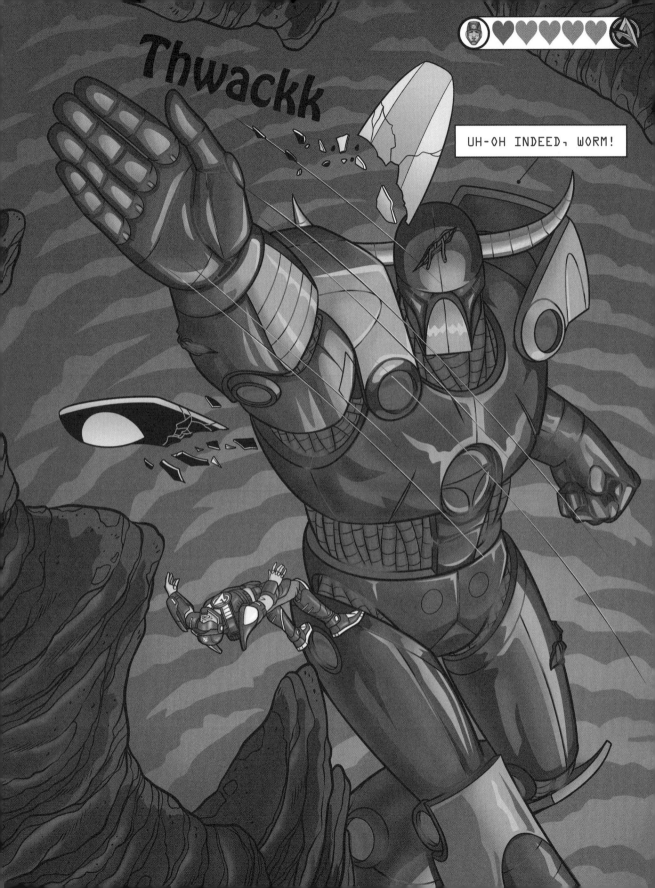

ALI!

ALI, ARE YOU OK? WHY DIDN'T YOU USE YOUR FORCE-FIELD?

I DON'T THINK IT'S WORKING ANY MORE.

CLARE, I THOUGHT I COULD BEAT THAT THING, BUT--

ALI! GET UP!

GNNNGH

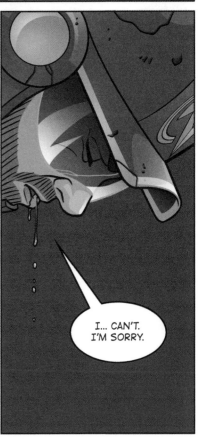

I... CAN'T. I'M SORRY.

DANGER: HEALTH LOW

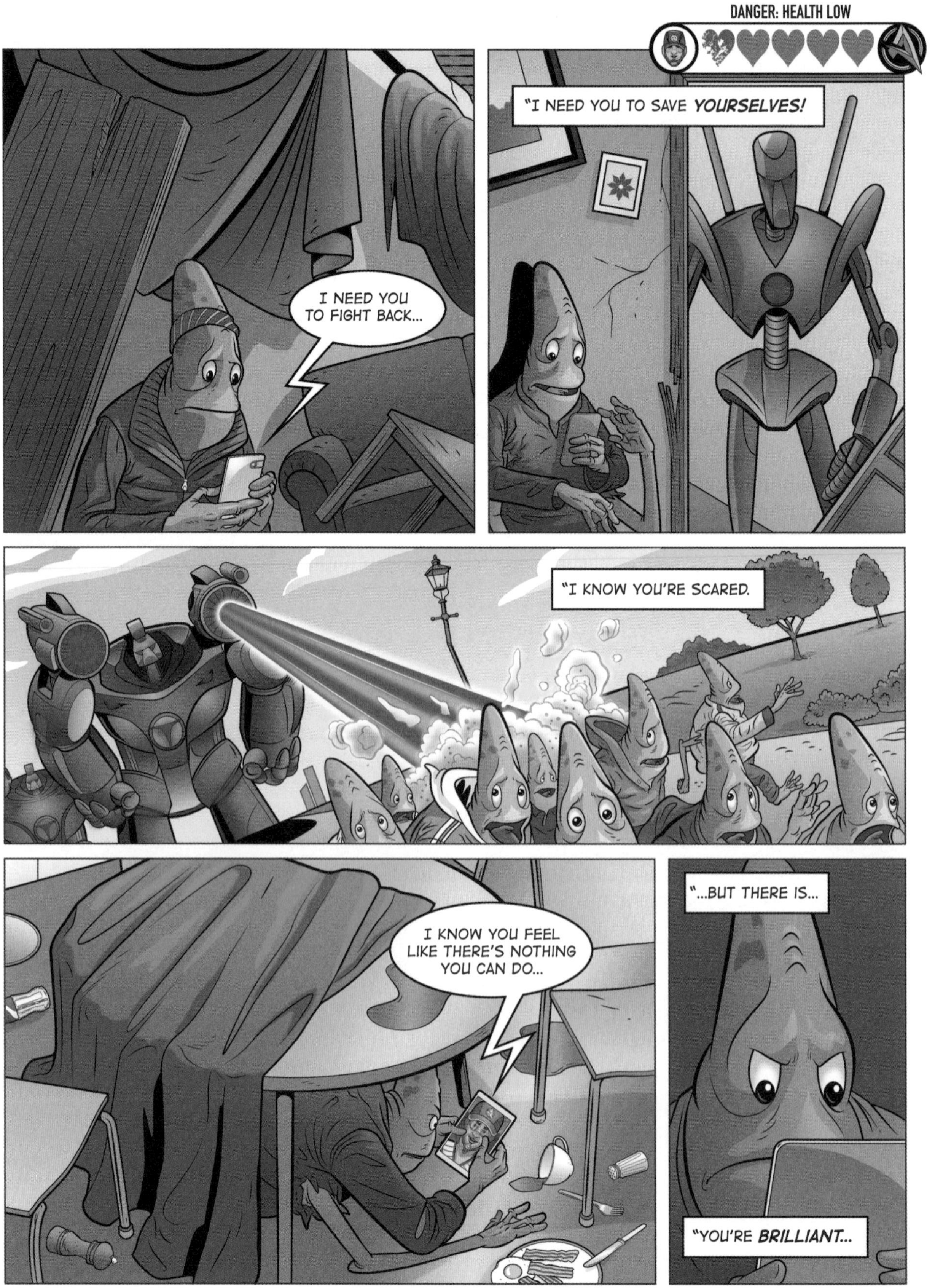
DANGER: HEALTH LOW
I NEED YOU TO FIGHT BACK...
"I NEED YOU TO SAVE YOURSELVES!
"I KNOW YOU'RE SCARED.
I KNOW YOU FEEL LIKE THERE'S NOTHING YOU CAN DO...
"...BUT THERE IS...
"YOU'RE BRILLIANT...

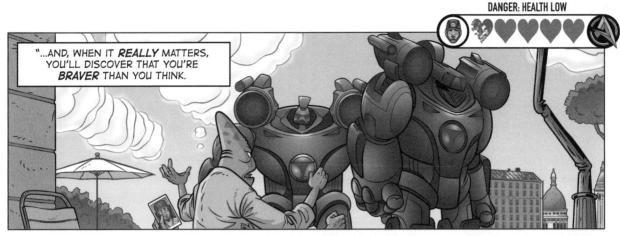

"...AND, WHEN IT **REALLY** MATTERS, YOU'LL DISCOVER THAT YOU'RE **BRAVER** THAN YOU THINK.

"TRUST ME--I KNOW!"

"JUST REMEMBER, YOU'RE **NOT** ALONE.

"THERE ARE **MILLIONS** OF YOU OUT THERE WHO ALL FEEL THE SAME WAY.

"**BILLIONS** OF YOU.

"AND, WHEN YOU WORK TOGETHER...

"...THERE'S **NOTHING** YOU CAN'T DO!"

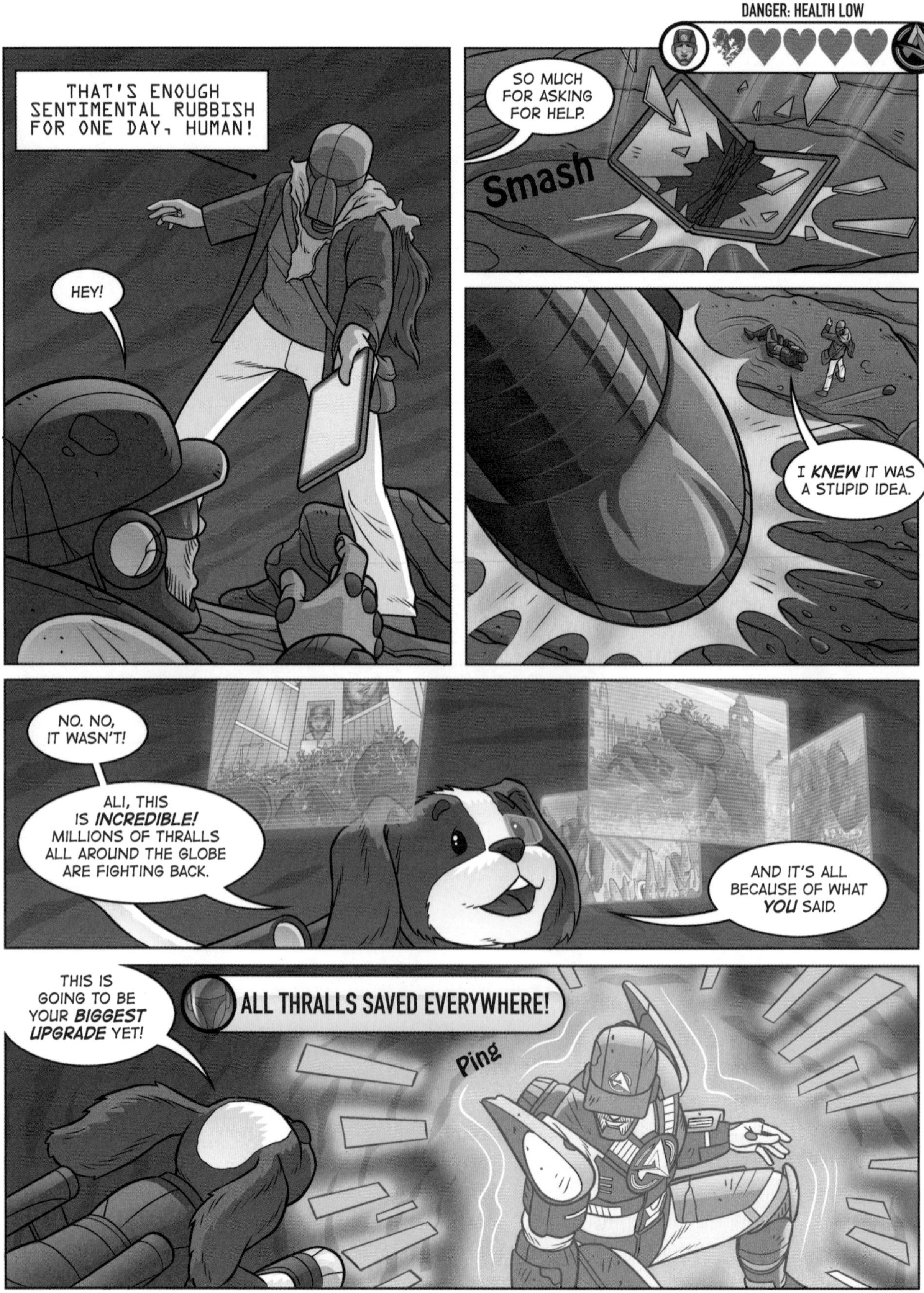

DANGER: HEALTH LOW
THAT'S ENOUGH SENTIMENTAL RUBBISH FOR ONE DAY, HUMAN!
HEY!
SO MUCH FOR ASKING FOR HELP.
Smash
I KNEW IT WAS A STUPID IDEA.
NO. NO, IT WASN'T!
ALI, THIS IS INCREDIBLE! MILLIONS OF THRALLS ALL AROUND THE GLOBE ARE FIGHTING BACK.
AND IT'S ALL BECAUSE OF WHAT YOU SAID.
THIS IS GOING TO BE YOUR BIGGEST UPGRADE YET!
ALL THRALLS SAVED EVERYWHERE!
Ping

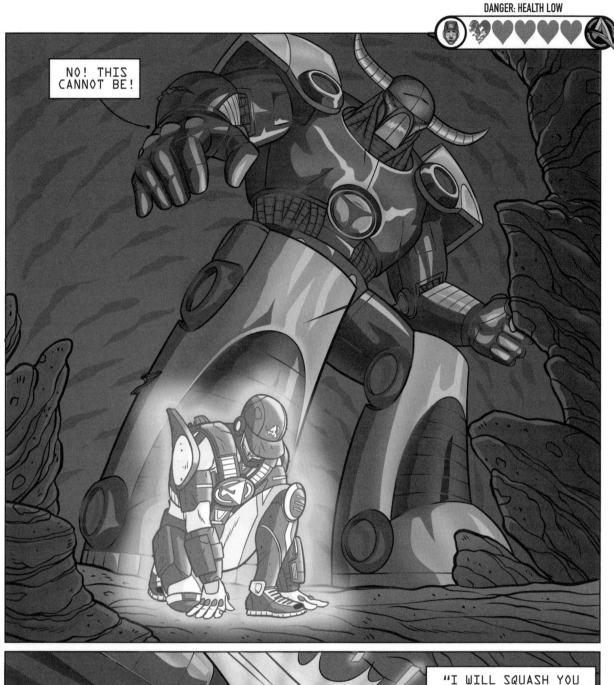

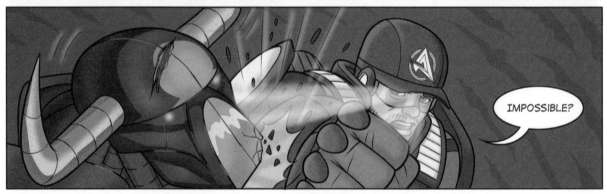

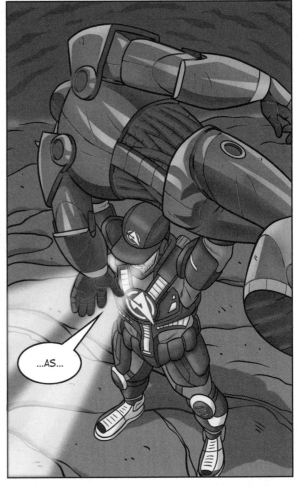

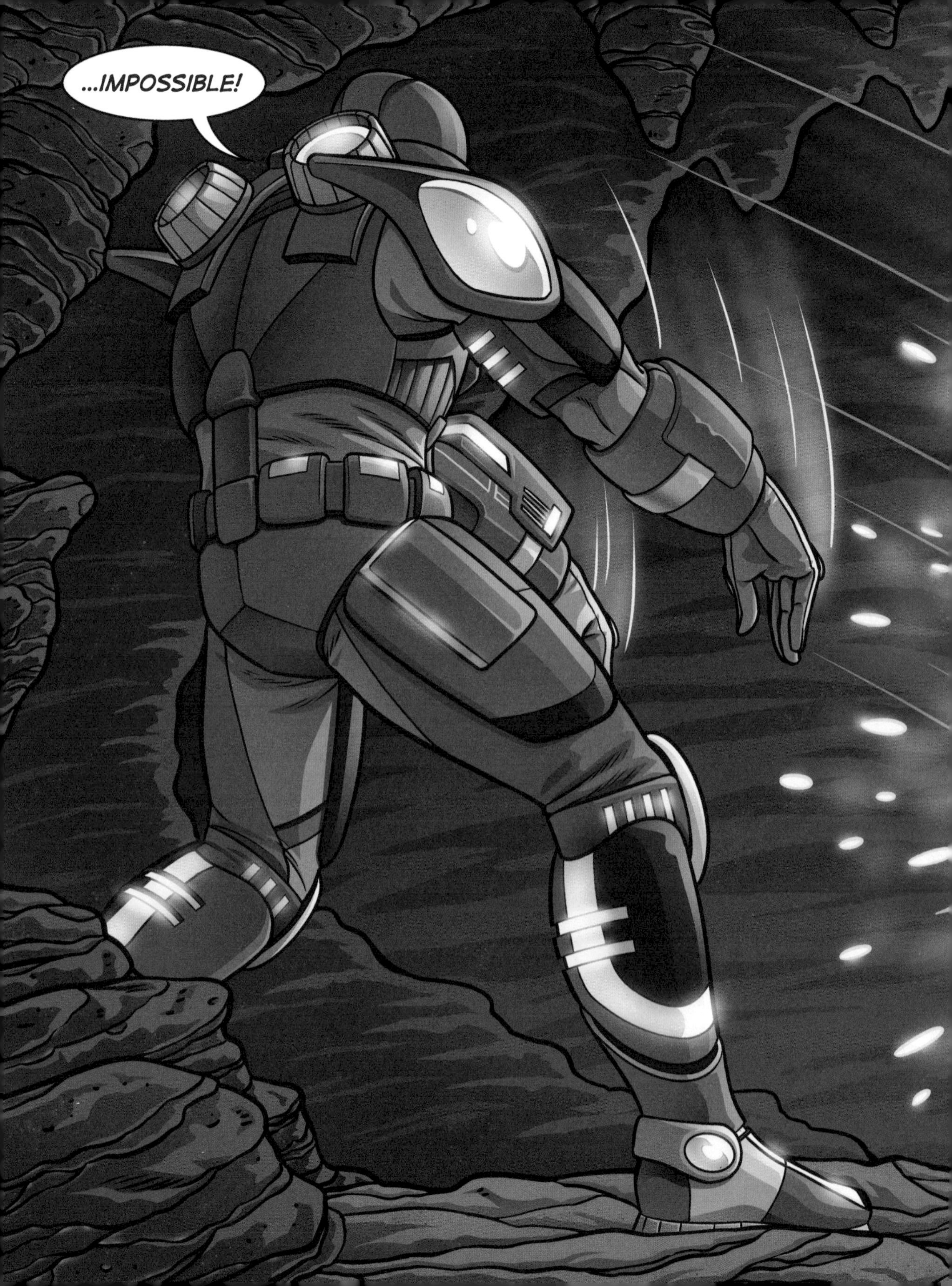
...IMPOSSIBLE!

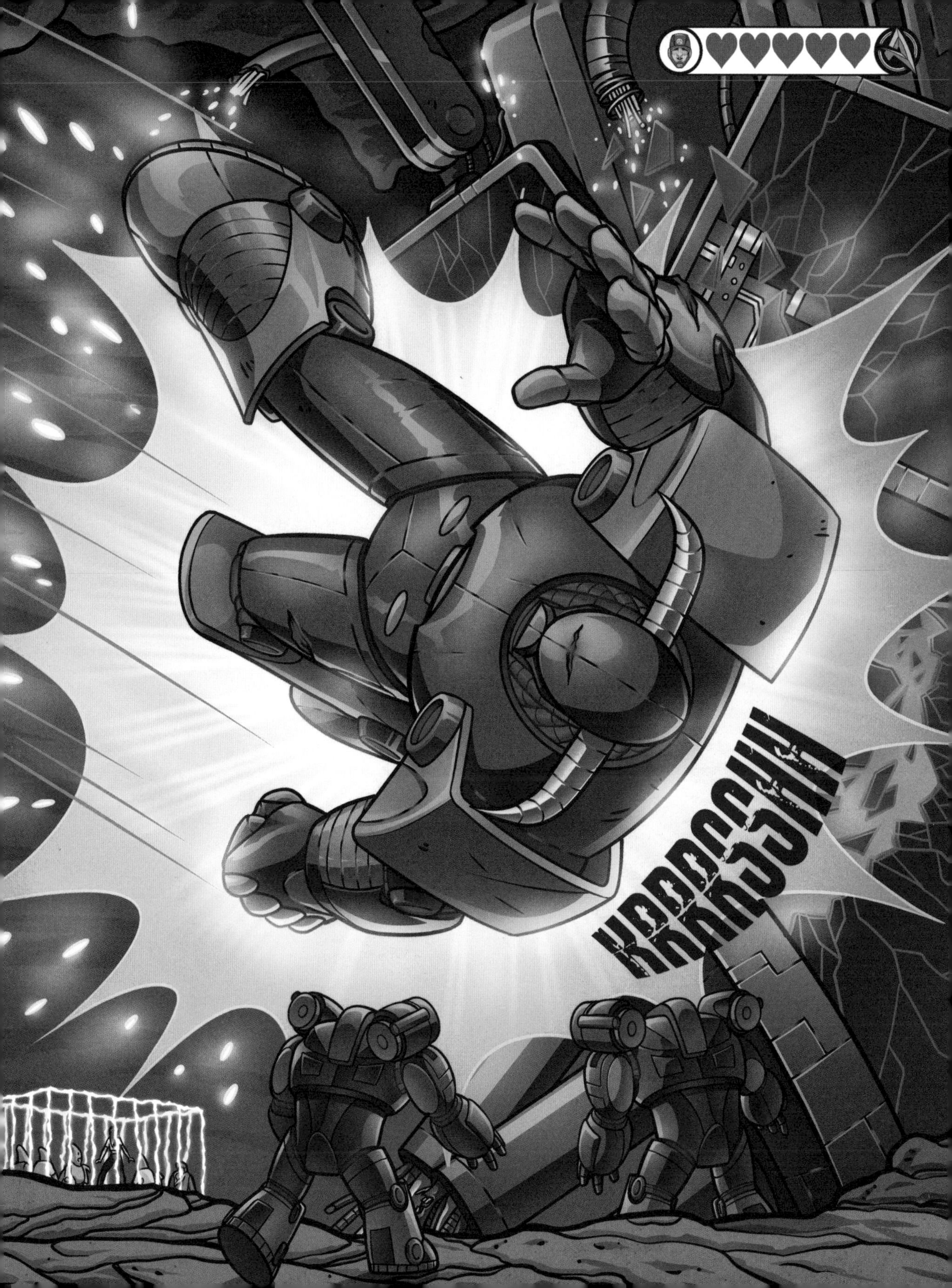
KRRRSSHH

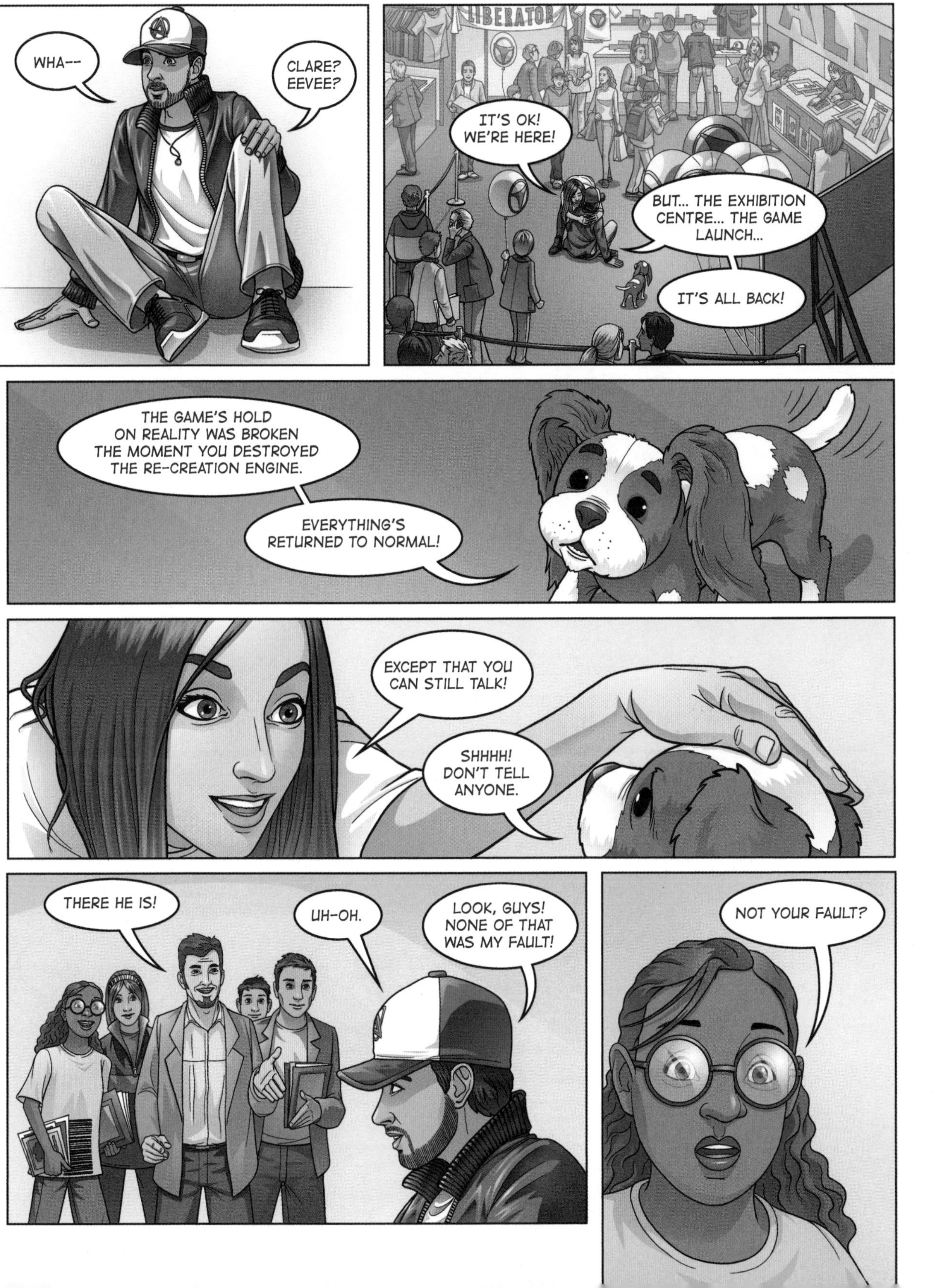
WHA--
CLARE? EEVEE?
IT'S OK! WE'RE HERE!
BUT... THE EXHIBITION CENTRE... THE GAME LAUNCH...
IT'S ALL BACK!
LIBERATOR
THE GAME'S HOLD ON REALITY WAS BROKEN THE MOMENT YOU DESTROYED THE RE-CREATION ENGINE.
EVERYTHING'S RETURNED TO NORMAL!
EXCEPT THAT YOU CAN STILL TALK!
SHHHH! DON'T TELL ANYONE.
THERE HE IS!
UH-OH.
LOOK, GUYS! NONE OF THAT WAS MY FAULT!
NOT YOUR FAULT?

STARRING	ALI-A
	CLARE SIOBHAN
	AND
	EEVEE
	AND INTRODUCING
	THOMAS CUSACK

STORY	ALI-A
	CAVAN SCOTT

ART	ALEK SOTIROVSKI
	MARTA MESAS
	DANIEL SANCHEZ LIMON
	PAUL MORAN
	GERGELY FÓRIZ
	JOHN BATTEN
	LEO CAMPOS
	MARTYN CAIN
	JANOS JANTNER
	KEVIN HOPGOOD

ALI, YOU SAVED THE DAY!

HEH! I COULD GET USED TO THIS...

YOU'RE OUR *HERO!*

I'M GLAD TO HEAR IT, ALI-A.

COMPUTER, INFORM THE GALACTIC COUNCIL. THE TEST WAS A SUCCESS.

WE'VE FOUND OUR *CHAMPION!*

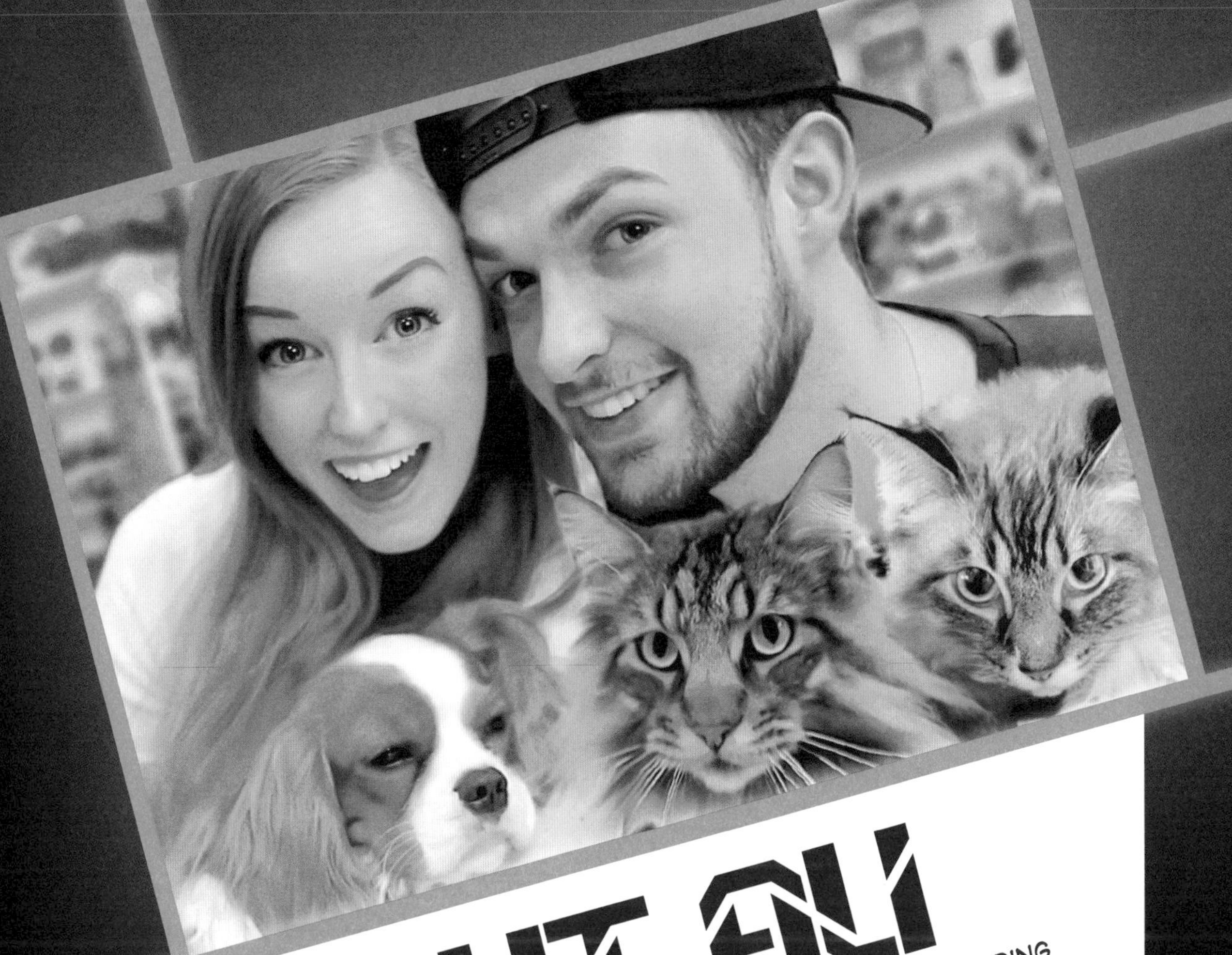

ABOUT ALI

ALI-A'S REAL ADVENTURE BEGAN IN 2009, WHEN HE STARTED UPLOADING SHORT GAMING CLIPS TO YOUTUBE. SINCE THEN, HE'S PICKED UP OVER 13 MILLION SUBSCRIBERS, ALL LOGGING IN REGULARLY TO CATCH HIS UNMISSABLE ***CALL OF DUTY*** AND ***POKEMON GO*** VIDEOS.

TODAY, HIS CONTENT ISN'T JUST ABOUT GAMING, WITH HIS SECOND CHANNEL ALLOWING FANS A GLIMPSE OF HIS LIFE WITH PARTNER, CLARE, AND HEROIC POOCH, EEVEE (WHO, AS FAR AS WE KNOW, CAN'T TALK IN REAL LIFE).

A FOR ACTION

ALI-A ON BECOMING AN ACTION HERO, FIGHTING GIANT ROBOTS ALONGSIDE CLARE AND EEVEE, AND THE FUTURE OF HIS GRAPHIC NOVEL ADVENTURES . . .

DID YOU EVER IMAGINE YOU'D BE INVOLVED IN CREATING A BOOK?

HONESTLY, IT WAS NEVER SOMETHING I EVEN CONSIDERED. I SAW A LOT OF YOUTUBERS DOING THEIR OWN BOOKS AND THOUGHT, *YOU KNOW WHAT, THAT'S PROBABLY SOMETHING I'LL LEAVE ALONE.* THEN, WHEN THE IDEA OF DOING AN ACTION-ADVENTURE WAS SUGGESTED, I REMEMBERED THE KIND OF STORIES I ENJOYED AS A KID, ABOUT HEROES GOING OFF ON ALL SORTS OF DANGEROUS MISSIONS. I THOUGHT DOING SOMETHING ON A SIMILAR SCALE WOULD BE REALLY EXCITING.

WAS IT ALWAYS GOING TO BE A GRAPHIC NOVEL?

NOT AT FIRST, BUT I WANTED THE STORY TO BE AS ACTION-PACKED AS POSSIBLE. PLUS, GAMES ARE OBVIOUSLY REALLY VISUAL, AND THE GUYS WHO WATCH MY VIDEOS ARE USED TO SEEING ME ON SCREEN, SO A GRAPHIC NOVEL MADE A LOT OF SENSE.

WHAT KIND OF COMICS DID YOU LIKE READING AS A KID?

I HAD A HUGE STACK OF COMICS LIKE THE *BEANO* THAT I'D PILE THROUGH, BUT THE ONE THAT REALLY STANDS OUT WAS *ASTERIX*. OH MAN, I USED TO GET REALLY SUCKED INTO THOSE STORIES. THEY WERE FILLED WITH ALL KINDS OF CRAZY ADVENTURES, AND THE CHARACTERS ALL HAD SUCH BIG PERSONALITIES. THEY REALLY INSPIRED *GAME ON!*

BUT THIS TIME THE MAIN CHARACTER IS YOU! WHAT WAS IT LIKE SEEING YOURSELF IN GRAPHIC-NOVEL FORM FOR THE FIRST TIME?

IT WAS SUPER COOL, ESPECIALLY AS I KNEW I WOULD BE GIVEN ALL THESE AMAZING ABILITIES AND ARMOUR UPGRADES. SEEING THE FIRST SKETCHES, IT REALLY HIT HOME HOW INCREDIBLE THIS WAS GOING TO BE. THE COMIC-BOOK ALI-A WOULD BE DOING THINGS THAT I'D NEVER BE ABLE TO DO IN REAL LIFE!

HOW DO YOU THINK THE REAL ALI WOULD COPE IF HE FOUND HIMSELF IN COMIC-BOOK ALI'S SHOES? COULD YOU SAVE THE EARTH FROM AN ALIEN INVASION?

I'D LIKE TO SAY THAT I'D STEP UP TO THE MARK, AND BE JUST AS EFFICIENT AT SAVING THE DAY. UNFORTUNATELY, I'M NOT SURE THAT WOULD ACTUALLY HAPPEN. I THINK THE COMIC-BOOK ALI IS WAY COOLER THAN THE REAL ME!

WHAT ABOUT EEVEE? SHE'D BE ABLE TO SAVE HELPLESS THRALLS FROM RAMPAGING ROBOTS, RIGHT?

OH, THOSE GUYS WOULD HAVE NOTHING TO WORRY ABOUT. EEVEE WOULD BREEZE THROUGH EVERYTHING! CLARE TOO.

WAS CLARE EXCITED THE FIRST TIME SHE SAW HER ILLUSTRATIONS?

SHE WAS SUPER EXCITED. IT MADE IT ALL SO REAL. SHE WAS GOING TO BE IN A BOOK! I KNEW FROM THE BEGINNING THAT I NEEDED BOTH CLARE AND EEVEE TO BE IN THE STORY. WE DO EVERYTHING TOGETHER, SO I COULDN'T GO ON AN ADVENTURE LIKE THIS AND NOT HAVE THEM ALONG. THE COMIC-BOOK ALI WOULD STRUGGLE IF CLARE AND EEVEE WEREN'T AROUND. HE NEEDS THEM BY HIS SIDE. THEY'RE A REAL TEAM.

WAS CREATING THE BOOK EVERYTHING YOU EXPECTED?

I'VE NEVER DONE ANYTHING LIKE THIS BEFORE. I THINK HAVING CAVAN FLESH OUT THE IDEA AND WRITE THE SCRIPT MADE IT EASIER TO VISUALIZE HOW EVERYTHING WOULD LOOK, MAKING SURE THAT THE ACTION WAS SPREAD THROUGHOUT THE BOOK TO KEEP PEOPLE TURNING THE PAGES. AND THEN SEEING THE SCRIPT COME TO LIFE WITH ALEKSANDAR AND THE TEAM'S INCREDIBLE ARTWORK HAS BEEN AN AMAZING EXPERIENCE. IT'S BEEN A LONG PROCESS, BUT EVERYONE HAS DONE SUCH A GREAT JOB. IT'S BEEN SO GOOD TO BE THERE FROM THE BEGINNING AND SEE IT ALL COME TOGETHER PIECE-BY-PIECE.

WERE YOU NERVOUS WHEN YOU FIRST ANNOUNCED THE BOOK?

DEFINITELY, BUT THE RESPONSE WAS GREAT. PEOPLE IMMEDIATELY STARTED TWEETING THAT THEY WERE LOOKING FORWARD TO READING IT. I WANT THEM TO HAVE THE SAME EXPERIENCE I HAD WHEN I WAS A KID; WANTING TO READ AS QUICKLY AS POSSIBLE TO FIND OUT WHAT HAPPENS NEXT, AND THEN GOING BACK TO READ IT ALL OVER AGAIN. I ALSO HOPE IT GETS PEOPLE READING WHO WOULDN'T NORMALLY PICK UP A BOOK. THAT WOULD BE AMAZING. AND, HEY, IF EVERYONE ENJOYS *GAME ON!* MAYBE WE CAN CREATE EVEN MORE ALI-A ADVENTURES DOWN THE LINE.

WHERE WOULD YOU LIKE TO SEE ALI-A GO NEXT?

THAT'S A TOUGH QUESTION. WE'VE SEEN HIM UP AGAINST ROBOTS, ALIENS AND EVEN KILLER TREES, BUT THERE ARE SUBTLE HINTS TOWARDS THE END THAT SOMETHING ELSE IS COMING--SOMETHING BIGGER! THERE ARE SO MANY PLACES THAT ALI-A COULD GO IN THESE STORIES, MAYBE EVEN OUTER SPACE! WHO KNOWS?

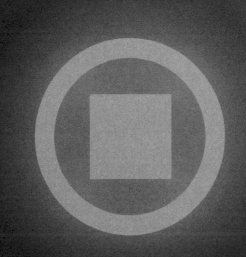

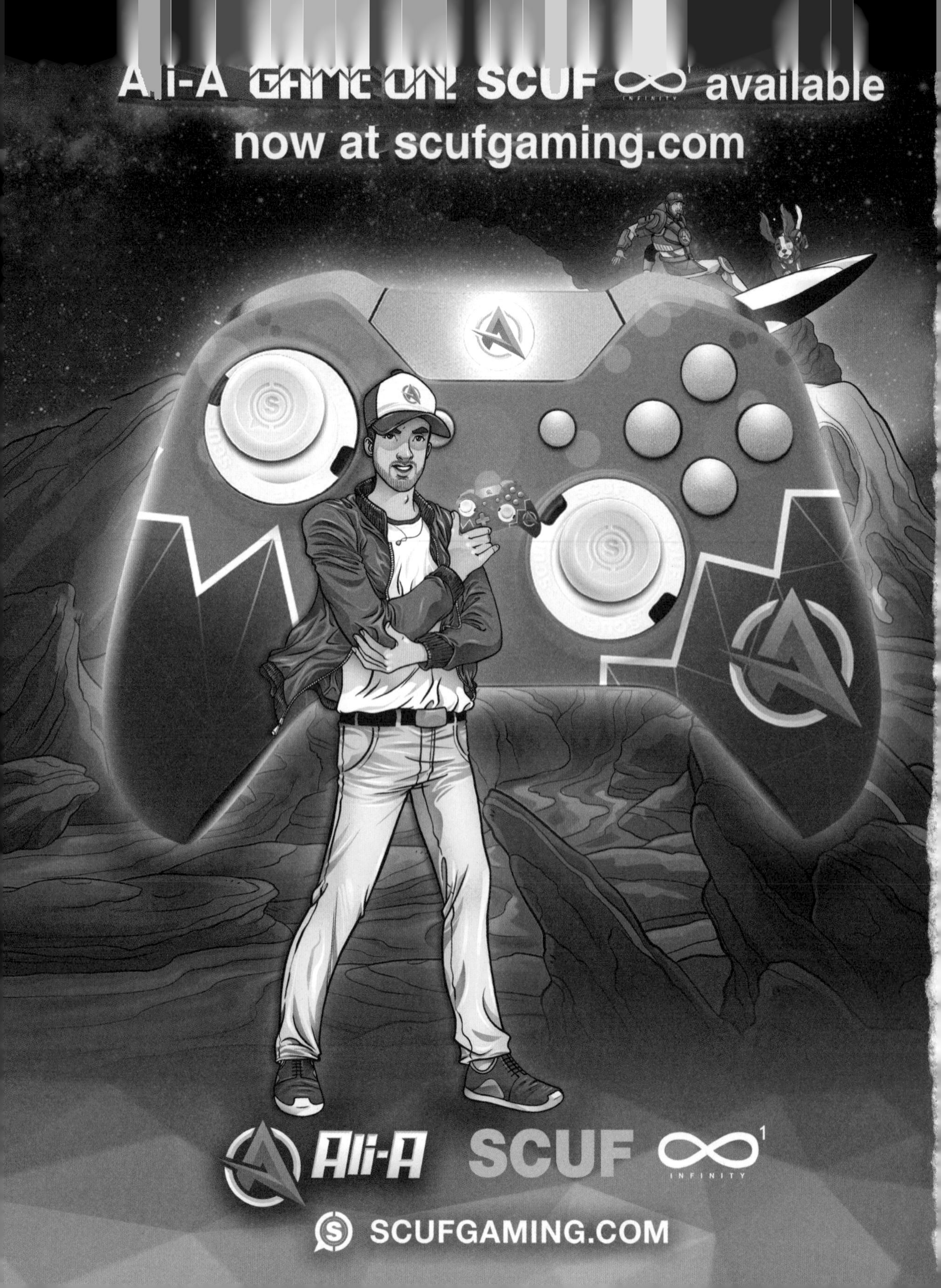
Ali-A GAME ON! SCUF ∞ available
now at scufgaming.com
Ali-A
SCUF
∞1
INFINITY
SCUFGAMING.COM